THE
DIVINERS

THE DIVINERS

Libba Bray

Ⓛ Ⓑ
LITTLE, BROWN AND COMPANY
NEW YORK   BOSTON

Copyright © 2012 by Martha E. Bray

Photograph on pages ii–iii and vi–vii courtesy of the Library of Congress

"Manhattan": written by Richard Rodgers, Lorenz Hart. Used by permission of Piedmont Music Company.

"Sitting on Top of the World": written by Ray Henderson, Sam M. Lewis, and Joe Young. Used by permission of Alfred Music Publishing Company.

Little, Brown and Company

Hachette Book Group
237 Park Avenue, New York, NY 10017
Visit our website at www.lb-teens.com

Little, Brown and Company is a division of Hachette Book Group, Inc.
The Little, Brown name and logo are trademarks of Hachette Book Group, Inc.

The publisher is not responsible for websites (or their content) that are not owned by the publisher.

First Edition: September 2012

ISBN 978-0-316-12611-3 (hc) / ISBN 978-0-316-23242-5 (International)

10 9 8 7 6 5 4 3 2 1

RRD-C

Printed in the United States of America

For my mom, Nancy Bray,
who taught me to love reading by example

And what rough beast, its hour come round at last,
Slouches towards Bethlehem to be born?

—"The Second Coming," William Butler Yeats

A LATE-SUMMER EVENING

In a town house at a fashionable address on Manhattan's Upper East Side, every lamp blazes. There's a party going on—the last of the summer. Out on the terrace overlooking Manhattan's incandescent skyline, the orchestra takes a much-needed break. It's ten thirty. The party has been on since eight o'clock, and already the guests are bored. Fashionable debutantes in pastel chiffon party dresses wilt into leather club chairs like frosted petits fours melting under the July sun. A cocky Princeton sophomore wants his friends to head down to Greenwich Village with him, to a speakeasy he heard about from a friend of a friend.

The hostess, a pretty and spoiled young thing, notes her guests' restlessness with a sense of alarm. It is her eighteenth birthday, and if she doesn't do something to raise this party from the dead, it will be the talk for days to come that her gathering was as dull as a church social.

Raising from the dead.

The weekend before, she'd been forced to go antiquing upstate with her mother—an absolutely hideous chore, until they came upon an old Ouija board. Ouija boards are all the rage; psychics have claimed to receive messages and warnings from the other side using Mr. Fuld's "talking board." The antiques dealer fed her mother a line about how it had come to him under mysterious circumstances.

"They say it's still haunted by restless spirits. But perhaps you and your sister could tame it?" he'd said with over-the-top flattery; naturally, her mother lapped it up, which resulted in her paying too much for the thing. Well, she'd make her mother's mistake pay off for her now.

The hostess races for the hall closet and signals to the maid. "Do be a darling and get that down for me."

The maid retrieves the board with a shake of her head. "You oughtn't to be messing with this board, Miss."

"Don't be silly. That's primitive."

With a zippy twirl worthy of Clara Bow, the hostess bursts into the formal living room holding the Ouija board. "Who wants to commune with the spirits?" She giggles to show that she doesn't take it seriously in the least. After all, she's a thoroughly modern girl—a flapper, through and through.

The wilted girls spring up from their club chairs. "What've you got there? Is that a wee-gee board?" one of them asks.

"Isn't it darling? Mother bought it for me. It's supposed to be haunted," the hostess says and laughs. "Well, I don't believe that, naturally." The hostess places the heart-shaped planchette in the middle of the board. "Let's conjure up some fun, shall we?"

Everyone gathers 'round. George angles himself into the spot beside her. He's a Yale man and a junior. Many nights, she's lain awake in her bedroom, imagining her future with him. "Who wants to start?" she asks, positioning her fingers close to his.

"I will," a boy in a ridiculous fez announces. She can't remember his name, but she's heard he has a habit of inviting girls into his rumble seat for a petting party. He closes his eyes and places his fingers on the scryer. "A question for the ages: Is the lady to my right madly in love with me?"

The girls squeal and the boys laugh as the planchette slowly spells out Y-E-S.

"Liar!" the lady in question scolds the heart-shaped scrying piece with its clear glass oracle.

"Don't fight it, darling. I could be yours on the cheap," the boy says.

Now spirits are high; the questions grow bolder. They're drunk on gin and good times and the silly distraction of the fortune-telling. *Every mornin', every evenin', ain't we got fun?*

"Say, let's summon a real spirit," George challenges.

A knot of excitement and unease twists in the hostess's gut. The antiques dealer had cautioned against doing just this. He warned that spirits called forth must also be put back to rest by breaking the connection, saying good-bye. But he was out to make a buck with a story, and besides, it's 1926—who believes in haunts and hobgoblins when there are motorcars and aeroplanes and the Cotton Club and men like Jake Marlowe making America first through industry?

"Don't tell me you're scared." George smirks. He has a cruel mouth. It makes him all the more desirable.

"Scared of what?"

"That we'll run out of gin!" the boy in the fez jokes, and everyone laughs.

George whispers low in her ear, "I'll keep you safe." His hand is on her back.

Oh, surely this is the most glorious night in existence!

"We summon now the spirit of this board to heed our call and tell us our fortunes true!" the hostess says with great intonation broken by giggles. "You must obey, spirit!"

There is a moment's pause, and then the planchette begins its slow migration across the scarred board's gothic black alphabet, spelling out a word.

H-E-L-L-O

"That's the spirit," someone quips.

"What is your name, o great spirit?" the hostess insists.

The planchette moves quickly.

N-A-U-G-H-T-Y-J-O-H-N

George raises an eyebrow mischievously. "Say, I like the sound of that. What makes you so naughty, old sport?"

Y-O-U-L-L-S-E-E

"See what? What are you up to, o naughty one?"

Stillness.

"I want to dance! Let's go uptown to the Moonglow," one of the girls, a pouty drunk, slurs. "When's the band comin' back, anyway?"

"In a minute. Don't have kittens," the hostess says with a smile and a laugh, but there's warning in both. "Let's try another question. Do you have any prophecy for us, Naughty John? Any fortune-telling?" She casts a sly glance at George.

The scryer remains still.

"Do tell us something else, won't you?"

Finally, there is movement on the board. "I . . . will . . . teach . . . you . . . fear," the hostess reads aloud.

"Sounds like the headmaster at Choate," the boy in the fez teases. "How will you do that, old sport?"

I-S-T-A-N-D-A-T-T-H-E-D-O-O-R-A-N-D-K-N-O-C-K

I-A-M-T-H-E-B-E-A-S-T

T-H-E-D-R-A-G-O-N-O-F-O-L-D

"What does that mean?" the drunken girl whispers. She backs away slightly.

"It doesn't mean anything. It's gibberish." The hostess scolds her guest, but she feels afraid. She turns on the boy with the reputation for trouble. "You're making it say that!"

"I didn't. I swear!" he says, crossing his heart with his index finger.

"Why are you here, old sport?" George asks the board.

The planchette moves so quickly they can barely keep up.

I-H-O-L-D-T-H-E-K-E-Y-S-O-F-H-E-L-L-A-N-D-D-E-A-T-H

W-R-A-T-H-I-S-C-O-M-E-A-R-M-A-G-E-D-D-O-N-B-A-B-Y-L-O-N-W-H-O-R-E

"Stop it this instant!" the hostess shouts.

W-H-O-R-E-W-H-O-R-E-W-H-O-R-E the piece repeats. The bright young things remove their fingers, but the piece continues to move.

"Make it stop, make it stop!" one girl screeches, and even the jaded boys pale and move back.

"Stop, spirit! I said stop!" the hostess shouts.

The planchette falls still. The party guests glance at one another with wild eyes. In the other room, the band members return to their instruments and strike up a hot dance number.

"Oh, hallelujah! Come on, baby. I'll teach you to dance the Black Bottom." The drunken girl struggles to her feet and pulls the boy in the fez after her.

"Wait! We have to spell out good-bye on the board! That's the proper ritual!" the hostess pleads as her guests desert her.

George slips his arm around her waist. "Don't tell me you're afraid of Naughty John."

"Well, I…"

"You know it was the old boy," he says, his breath tickling her ear sweetly. "He has his tricks. You know how that sort is."

She does know how that sort is. It was probably that wretched boy all along, playing them for fools. Well, she is nobody's fool. She is eighteen now. Life will be an endless swirl of parties and dances. *Night or daytime, it's all playtime. Ain't we got fun?* Her earlier fears have been put to bed. Her party looks like it will rage into the night. The carpets have been rolled up, and her guests dance full out. Long strands of pearls bounce against drop-waist dresses. Spats strike defiantly at the wood floors. Arms thrust out, pushing against the air—all of it like some feverish Dadaist painting come to life.

The hostess stashes the board in the cupboard, where it will soon be forgotten, and races toward the parlor with its bright electric lights—Mr. Edison's modern marvel—and joins the last party of the summer without a care.

Outside, the wind lingers for a moment at those lighted windows; then, with a gusty burst of energy, it takes its leave and scuttles down the sidewalks. It twines itself briefly around the cloche hats of two fashionable young ladies gossiping about the tragic death of Rudolph Valentino as they walk a poodle along the East River. It moves on, down neon-drenched canyons, over the elevated train as it rattles above Second Avenue, shaking the windows of the poor souls trying to sleep before morning comes— morning with its taxi horns, trolley cars, and trains; the bootblacks buffing the wingtips of businessmen in Union Square; the newsies hawking the day's headlines in Times Square; the telephone operators gazing longingly at the new shawl-collar coats tempting them from store windows; the majestic skyscrapers rising over it all like gleaming steel, brick, and glass gods.

The wind idles briefly before a jazz club, listening to this new music punctuating the night. It thrills to the bleat of horns, the percussive piano strides born of blues and ragtime, the syncopated rhythms that echo the jagged excitement of the city's skyline.

On the Bowery, in the ornate carcass of a formerly grand vaudeville theater, a dance marathon limps along. The contestants, young girls and their fellas, hold one another up, determined to make their mark, to bite back at the dreams sold to them in newspaper advertisements and on the radio. They have sores on their feet but stars in their eyes. Farther uptown, the Great White Way, named for the blinding incandescence of its theater lights, empties of its patrons. Some stage-door Johnnies wait in the alleys, hoping for a glimpse of the glamorous chorus girls or for a chance at an autograph from one of Broadway's many stars. It is a time of celebrity, of fame and fortune and grasping, and the young burn with secret ambition.

The wind takes it all in with indifference. It is only the wind. It will not become a radio star or a captain of industry. It will not run for office or fall in love with Douglas Fairbanks or sing the songs of Tin Pan Alley, songs of longing and regret and good times (*ain't we got fun?*). And so it travels on, past the slaughterhouses on Fourteenth Street, past the unfortunates selling themselves in darkened alleys. Nearby, Lady Liberty hoists her torch in the harbor, a beacon to all who come to these shores to escape persecution or famine or hopelessness. For this is the land of dreams.

The wind swoops over the tenements on Orchard Street, where some of those starry-eyed dreams have died and yet other dreams are being born into squalor and poverty, an uphill climb. It gives a slap to the laundry stretched on lines between tenements, over dirty, broken streets where, even at this hour, hungry children scour the bins for food. The wind has existed forever. It has seen much in this country of dreams and soap ads, old horrors and bloodshed. It has played mute witness to its burning witches, and has walked along a Trail of Tears; it has seen the slave ships release their human cargo, blinking and afraid, into the ports, their only possession a grief they can never lose. The wind was there when President Lincoln fell to an assassin's bullet. It smelled of gunpowder at Antietam. It ran with the buffalo and touched tentative fingers to the tall black hats of Puritans. It has carried shouts of love, and it has dried tears to salt tracks on more faces than it can number.

The wind skitters down the Bowery and swoops up the West Side, home of Irish gangs like the Dummy Boys, who ride horseback along Ninth Avenue to warn the bootleggers. It swoops along the mighty Hudson River, past the vibrant nightlife of Harlem with its great thinkers, writers, and musicians, until it comes to rest outside the ruin of an old mansion. Moldering boards cover the broken windows. Rubbish clogs the gutter out front. Once upon a time, the house was home to an unspeakable evil. Now it is a relic of a bygone era, forgotten in the shadow of the city's growth and prosperity.

The door creaks on its hinges. The wind enters cautiously. It creeps down narrow hallways that twist and turn in dizzying fashion. Diseased rooms, rotted with neglect, branch off left and right. Doors open onto brick walls. A trapdoor gives way to a chute that empties into a vast subterranean chamber of horrors and an even more terrifying room. It stinks still: of blood, urine, evil, and a fear so dark it has become as much a part of the house as the wood and nails and rot.

Something stirs in the deep shadows, something terrible, and the wind, which knows evil well, shrinks from this place. It flees toward the safety of those magnificent tall buildings that promise the blue skies, *nothing but blue skies*, of the future, of industry and prosperity; the future, which does not believe in the evil of the past. If the wind were a sentinel, it would send up the alarm. It would cry out a warning of terrors to come. But it is only the wind, and it knows well that no one listens to its cries.

Deep in the cellar of the dilapidated house, a furnace comes to life with a death rattle like the last bitter cough of a dying man laughing contemptuously at his fate. A faint glow emanates from that dark, foul-smelling earthen tomb. Yes, something moves again in the shadows. A harbinger of much greater evil to come. Naughty John has come home. And he has work to do.

EVIE O'NEILL, ZENITH, OHIO

Evie O'Neill pressed the sagging ice bag to her throbbing forehead and cursed the hour. It was noon, but it might as well be six in the morning for the pounding in her skull. For the past twenty minutes, her father had been beating his gums at her about last night's party at the Zenith Hotel. Her drinking had been mentioned several times, along with the unfortunate frolic in the town fountain. And the trouble that came between, of course. It was gonna be a real beast of a day, and how. Her head beat out requirements: *Water. Aspirin. Please stop talking.*

"Your mother and I do not approve of drinking. Have you not heard of the Eighteenth Amendment?"

"Prohibition? I drink to its health whenever I can."

"Evangeline Mary O'Neill!" her mother snapped.

"Your mother is secretary of the Zenith Women's Temperance Society. Did you think about that? Did you think about how it might look if her daughter were found carousing drunk in the streets?"

Evie slid her bruised eyeballs in her mother's direction. Her mother sat stiff-backed and thin-lipped, her long hair coiled at the nape of her neck. A pair of spectacles—"cheaters," the flappers called them—sat at the end of her nose. The Fitzgerald women were all petite, blue-eyed, blond, and hopelessly nearsighted.

"Well?" her father thundered. "Do you have something to say?"

"Gee, I hope I won't need cheaters someday," Evie muttered.

Evie's mother responded with a weary sigh. She'd grown smaller and more worn since James's death, as if that long-ago telegram from the war office had stolen her soul the moment she had opened it.

"You young people seem to treat everything like a joke, don't you?" Her father was off and running—*responsibility, civic duty, acting your age, thinking beyond tomorrow*. She knew the refrain well. What Evie needed was a little hair of the dog, but her parents had confiscated her hip flask. It was a swell flask, too—silver, with the initials of Charles Warren etched into it. Good old Charlie, the dear. She'd promised to be his girl. That lasted a week. Charlie was a darling, but also a thudding bore. His idea of petting was to place a hand stiffly on a girl's chest like a starched doily on some maiden aunt's side table while pecking, birdlike, at her mouth. *Quelle tragédie.*

"Evie, are you listening to me?" Her father's face was grim.

She managed a smile. "Always, Daddy."

"Why did you say those terrible things about Harold Brodie?"

For the first time, Evie frowned. "He had it coming."

"You accused him of...of..." Her father's face colored as he stammered.

"Of knocking up that poor girl?"

"Evangeline!" Her mother gasped.

"Pardon me. 'Of taking advantage of her and leaving her in the family way.'"

"Why couldn't you be more like..." Her mother trailed off, but Evie could finish the sentence: Why couldn't you be more like James?

"You mean, dead?" she shot back.

Her mother's face crumpled, and in that moment, Evie hated herself a little.

"That's enough, Evangeline," her father warned.

Evie bowed her throbbing head. "I'm sorry."

"I think you should know that unless you offer a public apology, the Brodies have threatened to sue for slander."

"What? I will not apologize!" She stood so quickly that her head doubled its pounding and she had to sit again. "I told the truth."

"You were playing a game—"

"It wasn't a game!"

"A game that has gotten you into trouble—"

"Harold Brodie is a louse and a lothario who cheats at cards and has a different girl in his rumble seat every week. That coupe of his is pos-i-tute-ly a petting palace. *And* he's a terrible kisser to boot."

Evie's parents stared in stunned silence.

"Or so I've heard."

"Can you prove your accusations?" her father pressed.

She couldn't. Not without telling them her secret, and she couldn't risk that. "I will not apologize."

Evie's mother cleared her throat. "There is another option."

Evie glanced from her mother to her father and back. "I won't breeze to military school, either."

"No military school would have you," her father muttered. "How would you like to go to New York for a bit, to stay with your Uncle Will?"

12

"I...ah...as in, Manhattan?"

"We assumed you'd say no to the apology," her mother said, getting in her last dig. "I spoke to my brother this morning. He would take you."

He would take you. A burden lifted. An act of charity. Uncle Will must have been defenseless against her mother's guilt-ladling.

"Just for a few months," her father continued. "Until this whole situation has sorted itself out."

New York City. Speakeasies and shopping. Broadway plays and movie palaces. At night, she'd dance at the Cotton Club. Days she'd spend with Mabel Rose, dear old Mabesie, who lived in her uncle Will's building. She and Evie had met when they were nine and Evie and her mother had gone to New York for a few days. Ever since, the girls had been pen pals. In the last year, Evie's correspondence had dwindled to a note here and there, though Mabel continued to send letters consistently, mostly about Uncle Will's handsome assistant, Jericho, who was alternately "painted by the brushstrokes of angels" and "a distant shore upon which I hope to land." Yes, Mabel needed her. And Evie needed New York. In New York, she could reinvent herself. She could be somebody.

She was tempted to blurt out a hasty yes, but she knew her mother well. If Evie didn't make it seem like a punishment to be endured, like she had "learned her lesson well," she'd be stuck in Zenith, apologizing to Harold Brodie after all.

She sighed and worked up just the right amount of tears—too much and they might relent. "I suppose that *would* be a sensible course. Though I don't know *what* I'll do in Manhattan with an old bachelor uncle as chaperone and all my dear friends back here in Zenith."

"You should have thought of that before," her mother said, her mouth set in a gloating smile of moral triumph.

Evie suppressed a grin. *Like shooting fish in a barrel*, she thought.

Her father checked his watch. "There's a train at five o'clock. I expect you'd better start packing."

Evie and her father rode to the station in silence. Normally, riding in her father's Lincoln Boattail Roadster was a point of pride. It was the only convertible in Zenith, the pick of the lot at her father's motorcar dealership. But today she didn't want to be seen. She wished she were as inconsequential as the ghosts in her dreams. Sometimes, after drinking, she felt this way—the shame over her latest stunt twining with the clamped-down anger at the way these petty, small-town people always made her feel: "Oh, Evie, you're just too much," they'd say with a polite smile. It was not a compliment.

She *was* too much—for Zenith, Ohio. She'd tried at times to make herself smaller, to fit neatly into the ordered lines of expectation. But somehow, she always managed to say or do something outrageous—she'd accept a dare to climb a flagpole, or make a slightly risqué joke, or go riding in cars with boys—and suddenly she was "that awful O'Neill girl" all over again.

Instinctively, her fingers wandered to the coin around her neck. It was a half-dollar her brother had sent from "over there" during the war, a gift for her ninth birthday, the day he'd died. She remembered the telegram from the war department, delivered by poor Mr. Smith from the telegram office, who mumbled an apology as he handed it over. She remembered her mother uttering the smallest strangled cry as she sank to the floor, still clutching the yellowed paper with the heartless black type. She remembered her father sitting in his study in the dark long after he should have been in bed, a forbidden bottle of Scotch open on his desk. Evie

14

had read the telegram later: REGRET TO INFORM YOU ... PRIVATE
JAMES XAVIER O'NEILL ... KILLED IN ACTION IN GERMANY ... SUDDEN
ATTACK AT DAWN ... GAVE HIS LIFE IN SERVICE TO OUR COUNTRY ...
SECRETARY OF WAR ASKS THAT I CONVEY HIS DEEPEST SYMPATHIES
ON THE LOSS OF YOUR SON. ...

They passed a horse and buggy on its way to one of the farms
just outside town. It seemed quaint and out of place. Or maybe she
was the thing that was out of place here.

"Evie," her father said in his soft voice. "What happened at
the party, pet?"

The party. It had been swell at first. She and Louise and Dottie in their finery. Dottie had lent Evie her rhinestone headache
band, and it looked so spiffy resting across Evie's soft curls. They'd
enjoyed a spirited but meaningless debate about the trial of Mr.
Scopes in Tennessee the year before and the whole idea that the
lot of humanity was descended from apes. "I don't find it hard to
believe in the slightest," Evie had said, cutting her eyes flirtatiously
at the college boys who'd just sung a rousing twelfth round of "The
Sweetheart of Sigma Chi." Everyone was drunk and happy. And
Harold came around with his flattery.

"*Hello, ma baby; hello, ma honey; hello ma Evie gal,*" he sang
and bowed at her feet.

Harry was handsome and terribly charming and, despite what
she'd said earlier, a swell kisser. If Harry liked a girl, that girl got
noticed. Evie liked being noticed, especially when she was drinking. Harry was engaged-to-be-engaged to Norma Wallingford. He
wasn't in love with Norma—Evie knew that—but he was in love
with her bank account, and everyone knew they'd marry when he
graduated from college. Still, he wasn't married yet.

"Did I tell you that I have special powers?" Evie had asked
after her third drink.

Harry smiled. "I can see that."

"I am quite serious," she slurred, too tipsy not to take his dare. "I can tell your secrets simply by holding an object dear to you and concentrating on it." There were polite chuckles among the party-goers. Evie fixed them with a defiant stare, her blue eyes glittering under heavily kohled lashes. "I am pos-i-*tute*-ly serious."

"You're pos-i-tute-ly lit, is what you are, Evie O'Neill," Dottie shouted.

"I'll prove it. Norma, give me something—scarf, hat pin, glove."

"I'm not giving you anything. I might not get it back." Norma laughed.

Evie narrowed her eyes. "Yes, how smart you are, Norma. I am starting a collection of only right-hand gloves. It's ever so bour-geois to have two."

"Well, you certainly wouldn't want to do anything *ordinary*, would you, Evie?" Norma said, showing her teeth. Everyone laughed, and Evie's cheeks went hot.

"No, I leave that to you, Norma." Evie brushed her hair away from her face, but it sprang back into her eyes. "Come to think of it, your secrets would probably put us to sleep."

"Fine," Harold had said before things could get really heated. "Here's my class ring. Tell me my deep, dark secrets, Madame O'Neill."

"Brave man, giving a girl like Evie your ring-ski," someone shouted.

"Quiet, *s'il vous plaît*-ski!" Evie commanded with a dramatic flair to her voice. She concentrated, waiting for the object to warm in her hands. Sometimes it happened and sometimes it did not, and she hoped on the soul of Rudolph Valentino that this would be one of those times it took. Later, she'd have a headache from the effort—that was the downside to her little gift—but that's what gin was for. She'd numbed herself a bit already, anyway. Evie opened one eye a slit. They were all watching her. They were watching, and nothing was happening.

Chuckling, Harry reached for his ring. "All right, old girl. You've had your fun. Time for a little sobering up."

She wrenched her hands away. "I *will* uncover your secrets— just you wait and see!" There were few things worse than being ordinary, in Evie's opinion. Ordinary was for suckers. Evie wanted to be special. A bright star. She didn't care if she got the most awful headache in the history of skull-bangers. Shutting her eyes tightly, she pressed the ring against her palms. It grew much warmer, unlocking its secrets for her. Her smile spread. She opened her eyes.

"Harry, you naughty boy..."

Everyone pressed closer, interested.

Harold laughed uncomfortably. "What do you mean?"

"Room twenty-two at the hotel. That pretty chambermaid... L...El...Ella! Ella! You gave her a big wad of kale and told her to take care of it."

Norma moved closer. "What's this about, Harry?"

Harry's mouth was tight. "I'm sure I don't know what you're talking about, Evangeline. Show's over. I'll have my ring back now."

If Evie had been sober, she might have stopped. But the gin made her foolishly brave. She tsk-tsked him with her fingers. "You knocked her up, you bad boy."

"Harold, is that true?"

Harold Brodie's face was red. "That's enough, Evie! This isn't funny any longer."

"Harold?" Norma Wallingford.

"She's lying, sweetheart." Harold, reassuring.

Evie stood and did a little Charleston on the table. "That's not what your ring says, pal."

Harold grabbed for Evie and she squeaked out of reach, grabbing a tumbler from someone's hand. "Holy moly! It's a raid! A Harold Brodie raid! Run for your lives!"

Dottie had grabbed the ring and given it back to Harry. Then she and Louise had practically dragged Evie outside. "Sister, you are blotto. Let's go."

"I remain unflapper-able in the face of advuss...advarse... trouble. Oh, we're moving. Wheee! Where are we going?"

"To sober you up," Dottie said, tossing Evie into the freezing fountain.

Later, after several cups of coffee, Evie lay shivering in her wet party dress under a blanket in a darkened corner of the ladies' lounge. Dottie and Louise had gone to find her some aspirin, and, alone and hidden, she eavesdropped as two girls stood before the gilt-framed mirrors gossiping about the row Harold and Norma had gotten into.

"It's all that awful Evie O'Neill's fault. You know how she is."

"She never knows when to let well enough alone."

"Well, she's really done it this time. She's finished in this town. Norma will see to that."

Evie waited till she heard them leave, then moved to the mirror. Her mascara had left big black splotches under her eyes, and her damp curls drooped. Her wretched headache was really kicking up its heels in earnest. She looked as messy as she felt. She wished she could cry, but crying wouldn't help anything.

Harold burst in, closing the door behind him and holding it shut. "How did you find out?" he growled, grabbing her arm.

"I t-told you. I g-got it from your—"

His hand tightened around her arm. "Stop fooling around and tell me how you know! Norma's threatening to leave me thanks to your little party trick. I demand a public apology to clear my name."

She felt woozy and sick, the aftereffects of her object reading. It was like a mean drunk followed by the worst hangover you could imagine. Harold Brodie wasn't a charming, good-time playboy, she now realized. He was a cad and a coward. The last thing she was going to do was apologize to somebody like that.

"G-go chase yourself, Harry."

Dottie and Louise pounded on the door from the other side. "Evie? Evie! Open up!"

Harold let go of her arm. Evie could feel a bruise starting. "This isn't over, Evangeline. Your father owes his business to my father. You might want to reconsider that apology."

Evie threw up all over Harold Brodie.

☀

"Evie?" her father prompted now, bringing her back to the moment.

She rubbed her aching head. "It was nothing, Pop. I'm sorry you caught hell for it."

He didn't take her to task for saying *hell*.

At the station, her father left the engine idling long enough to see her to the platform. He tipped the porter to take her trunks, and made sure they would be delivered to her uncle's apartment in New York. Evie carried only her small plaid valise and a beaded handbag.

"Well," her father said, glancing down at the idling convertible. He passed her a ten-spot, which Evie tucked into the ribbon of her gray felt cloche. "Just a little pin money."

"Thanks, Pop."

"I'm no good with good-byes. You know that."

Evie forced a devil-may-care smile. "Sure. It's jake, Pop. I'm seventeen, not seven. I'll be just fine."

"Well."

They stood awkwardly on the wooden platform.

"Better not let the breezer leave without you," she said, nodding toward the convertible.

Her father kissed her lightly on the forehead and, with a final admonishment to the porter, drove away. As the Lincoln shrank to a point down the road, Evie felt a pang of sadness, and something else. Dread. That was the word. Some unknowable, unnameable fear. She'd been feeling it for months, ever since the dreams began.

"Man, I got those heebie jeebie blues," Evie said softly and shivered.

A pair of Blue Noses on the next bench glared their disapproval at Evie's knee-length dress. Evie decided to give them a real show. She hiked her skirt and, humming jauntily, rolled down her stockings, exposing her legs. It had the desired effect on the Blue Noses, who moved down the platform, clucking about the "disgrace of the young." She would not miss this place.

A cream coupe swerved dangerously up the road and came to a stop below, just narrowly missing the platform. Two smartly dressed girls stepped out. Evie grinned and waved wildly. "Dottie! Louise!"

"We heard you were leaving and wanted to come see you off," Louise said, climbing over the railing.

"Good news travels fast."

"In this town? Like lightning."

"It's swell. I'm too big for Zenith, Ohio, anyway. In New York, they'll understand me. I'm going to be written up in all the papers and get invited to the Fitzgeralds' flat for cocktails. After all, my mother's a Fitzgerald. We must be related *somewhere*."

"Speaking of cocktails..." Grinning, Dottie retrieved what looked like an innocent aspirin bottle from her pocketbook. It was half-filled with clear liquid. "Here. Just a little giggle water to see you through. Sorry it couldn't be more, but my father marks the bottles now."

"Oh, and a copy of *Photoplay* from the beauty parlor. Aunt Mildred won't miss it," Louise added.

Evie's eyes pricked with tears. "You don't mind being seen with the town pariah?"

Louise and Dottie managed weak smiles—confirmation that Evie *was* the town pariah, but still, they'd come.

"You are absolute angels of the first order. If I were Pope, I'd canonize you."

"The Pope would probably love to turn a cannon on you!"

"New York City!" Louise twirled her long rope of beads. "Norma Wallingford will eat herself to bits with envy. She's sore as hell about your little stunt." Dottie giggled. "Spill: How'd you really find out about Harold and the chambermaid?"

Evie's smile faltered for a moment. "Just a lucky guess."

"But—"

"Oh, look! Here comes the train," Evie said, cutting off any further inquiry. She hugged them tightly, grateful for this last kindness. "Next time you see me, I'll be famous! And I'll drive you all over Zenith in my chauffeured sedan."

"Next time we see you, you'll be on trial for some ingenious crime!" Dottie said with a laugh.

Evie grinned. "Just as long as they know my name."

A blue-uniformed porter hurried people aboard. Evie settled into her compartment. It was stuffy, and she stood on the seat in her green silk-satin Mary Janes to open the window.

"Help you with that, Miss?" another porter, a younger man, offered.

Evie looked up at him through lashes she had tinted with cake mascara that morning and offered him the full power of her Coty-red smile. "Oh, would you, honey? That'd be swell."

"You heading to New York, Miss?"

"Mm-hmm, that's right. I won a Miss Bathing Beauty contest, and now I'm going to New York to be photographed for *Vanity Fair*."

"Isn't that something?"

"Isn't it, just?" Evie fluttered her eyelashes. "The window?"

The young man released the latches and slid the window down easily. "There you are!"

"Why, thank you," Evie purred. She was on her way. In New York, she could be anyone she chose to be. It was a big city—just the place for big dreamers who needed to shine brightly.

Evie angled her head out the train window and waved to Louise and Dottie. Her bobbed curls blew about her face as the sleepy town slowly moved behind her. For a second, she wished she could run back to the safety of her parents' house. But that was like the fog of her dreams. It was a dead house—had been for years. No. She wouldn't be sad. She would be grand and glittering. A real star. A bright light of New York. "See you soon-ski!" she yelled.

"You bet-ski!"

Her friends were shrinking to small dots of color in the smoke-hazed distance. Evie blew kisses and tried not to cry. She waved slowly to the passing rooftops of Zenith, Ohio, where people liked to feel safe and snug and smug, where they handled objects every day in the most ordinary of ways and never once caught glimpses into other people's secrets that should not be known or had terrible nightmares of dead brothers. She envied them just a bit.

"You gonna stay up there the whole ride, Miss?" the porter asked.

"Just wanna say a proper good-bye," Evie answered. She turned her hand in a last benediction, waving to the houses like a queen. "So long, suckers! You're all wet!"

MEMPHIS CAMPBELL, HARLEM, NEW YORK CITY

It was morning in Harlem, and mornings belonged to the numbers runners. From 130th Street north to 160th Street, from Amsterdam Avenue on the West Side clear over to Park Avenue on the east, scores of runners staked out their turf, ready to write out slips for their customers and race those hopeful number combinations back to their bankers, operating from the back rooms of cigar stores and barbershops, speakeasies and brownstone basements. It all had to happen before ten AM, when the clearinghouse down on Wall Street published the daily financial number, and somebody beat the thousand-to-one odds and struck it big or, more likely, struck out. It rarely worked out in Harlem's favor, but they played the game anyway, on the chance that someday their luck would change.

Memphis Campbell, seventeen, perched beneath the street lamp in his spot on the corner of Lenox Avenue and 135th Street, near the subway entrance, catching his customers as they headed off to work. He kept an eye out for cops as he wrote out slip after slip: "Yes, Miss Jackson, fifteen cents on the washerwoman's gig." "Forty-four, eleven, twenty-two. Got it." "A dollar on the death gig, though I'm sorry to hear that your aunt's cousin passed." "Well, if you saw it in a dream, you'd be a fool not to play that number, sir."

The numbers were all around them, patterns waiting to be discovered and turned into riches, luck pulled from thin air—from hymnals, billboards, weddings, funerals, births, boxing matches, horse races, trains, professions, fraternal orders, and dreams. Especially dreams.

Memphis didn't like thinking about his dreams. Not lately.

When the work rush cleared, he took orders in apartment-building lobbies, stuffing the slips into a leather pouch he kept in his sock in case he got shaken down. He stopped in at the DeLuxe Beauty Shop, which was doing a brisk business in hair and gossip.

"So I told her, I may be a scalp specialist, but I am no miracle worker!" the owner, Mrs. Jordan, regaled the chuckling women in the shop. "Hey there, Memphis. How you?"

The ladies sat up straighter.

"Lord, that boy is handsome as Pharaoh," one of the young women clucked, fanning herself with a magazine. "Honey, you got yourself a girl?"

"On every block!" Mrs. Jordan laughed.

Memphis knew he was handsome. He was six feet tall and broad-shouldered, with high cheekbones thanks to some Taino blood down the line. Floyd at Floyd's Barbershop kept Memphis's hair close-cropped and oiled sweet, and Mr. Levine, the tailor, made sure his suits were sharp. But it was Memphis's smile everyone noticed first. When Memphis Campbell decided to turn on the full power of his charm, it always started with the smile: shy at first, then wide and blindingly bright, accompanied by a puppy-dog look that got even his aunt Octavia to relent sometimes.

Memphis employed the smile now. "Getting late, ladies."

"So it is." Mrs. Jordan kept her hot comb working, straightening the hair of the woman in her chair. "Put me down for my usual gig. Got those numbers from *Aunt Sally's Policy Players Dream Book.* Gonna make me rich someday."

"Gonna make you broke someday," a large woman reading a copy of the *New Amsterdam News* announced with a snort.

Mrs. Jordan pointed the hot comb at her. "It's going to pay off. You'll see. Right, Memphis?"

Memphis nodded. "Just last week, I heard of a man playing the same gig for a year. Won big," he said. Memphis thought again of his disquieting dream. Maybe it meant something after all. Maybe it was a portent of good luck, not bad. "Say, Mrs. Jordan, does Aunt Sally's book say anything about a crossroads or a storm?"

"Oh, a storm means money coming in, I think. Storm is fifty-four."

"Is not, either! A storm means a death coming. And it's eleven you play for that."

The ladies set to squabbling about the various interpretations of dreams and possible number combinations. No one could ever agree on any one right answer. That's part of what made the game so exciting—all those possibilities.

"What about an eye with a lightning bolt underneath?" Memphis asked.

Mrs. Jordan paused, the hot comb still in her customer's hair. "I don't rightly know. But somebody else might could tell you. Why you ask, honey?"

Memphis realized he was frowning. He relaxed again into that charming smile people had come to expect from him. "Oh, just something I saw in a dream is all."

The customer in the chair bristled. "Ow! Fifi, you about to burn my scalp off with that hot comb!"

"I am not! You're just too tender-headed is your trouble."

"Good day to you, ladies. I hope your number comes in," Memphis said and beat a hasty retreat.

Above Harlem, the morning's gray clouds frayed into thin wisps, revealing a perfect blue sky as Memphis passed the Lenox Drugstore, where he and his little brother, Isaiah, liked to stop in for hamburgers and talk with the owner, Mr. Reggie. He crossed the street to avoid the Merrick Funeral Home, but he could not sweep away the memory. It crept up from deep inside, still with the power to squeeze the breath out of him:

His mother lying up front in the open casket covered with lily of the valley, her hands crossed over her chest. Isaiah asking, "When Mama's gonna wake up, Memphis? She's missing the party, and all these people here to see her, too." His father sitting on the cane-back chair, staring down into his big, trumpet-playing hands while mourners cried and hollered and somebody sang, "Swing Low, Sweet Chariot." The feel of the dirt in Memphis's fingers as he dropped clods of it onto the grave. The soft *thud* as it hit the top of the coffin, the finality of the sound. He remembered his father packing up their apartment off 145th Street and sending Memphis and Isaiah to share the cramped back room of Aunt Octavia's place a few blocks farther uptown while he went off to Chicago to look for work. He'd promised to send for them when he was settled. That had been two years, ten months, and fifteen days ago, and they were still sharing the back room at Octavia's.

Memphis swiped a milk bottle from a stoop and took a big swig, as if he could chase away the past. His skin itched with restlessness, a feeling that the world was about to be ripped wide open. And he was sure it had to do with the dream.

For two weeks running, it had been the same: The crossroads. The crow flying to him from the field. The darkening sky, and the dust clouds rising on the road just ahead of whatever was coming.

And the symbol—always the symbol. It was getting to where he was afraid to sleep.

A phrase came to him quickly. Memphis knew that if he didn't write it down, it would be gone later, when he was ready to write. So he stopped and jotted this new bit of poetry in his head onto two blank numbers slips, then shoved them into a different pocket. Later, when he could head up to the graveyard, where he liked to write, he'd copy them into the brown leather notebook that held his poems and stories.

Memphis turned the corner. Blind Bill Johnson sat on a stoop with his guitar. His upturned hat lay at his feet, a collection of small change scattered across the hat's worn lining. "*Met a man on a dark road, he had a mark upon his hand,*" the bluesman sang in his gravelly whisper of a voice. "*Met a man on a dark road, he had a mark upon his hand. Said the storm's a-comin', rain down hard upon the land.*" As Memphis passed, Blind Bill called, "Mr. Campbell! Mr. Campbell! 'Zat you?"

"Yes, sir. How'd you know?"

The old man wrinkled up his nose. "Floyd's good with the scissors, but that oil he use could wake a dead man." He broke into a hard, raspy laugh. His fingers sought the collection of change in the hat, touching each coin until he had two dimes. "Put twenty cents on my number, Mr. Campbell. One, seven, nine. Go on now, and put that in. Put it in for old Blind Bill," he said with urgency.

Memphis wanted to tell him he should save his money for other things. Everybody knew Bill lived over in the Salvation Army mission, and sometimes on the streets, when the weather was decent. But it wasn't his place to say anything, so he pocketed the coins and wrote out a slip. "Yes, sir. I'll put it in."

"I just need a change of luck is all."

"Don't we all," Memphis said and moved on.

Behind him, the bluesman took up his guitar again, singing about shadowy men on dark roads and bargains struck under moonless skies, and though they were in the heart of the city with its rumbling trains and bustling sidewalks, Memphis felt a strange twisting in his gut.

"Memphis!" another runner called from down the street. "You better get to it! It's almost ten o'clock!"

Memphis forgot about his bad dreams. He tossed the empty milk bottle into a rubbish bin, shouldered his knapsack, and ran down the street toward the Hotsy Totsy to wait for the day's number to come in.

On a street lamp, a crow cawed. Blind Bill stopped his song and tensed, listening. The bird cawed once more. Then it flapped its shiny wings and shadowed Memphis Campbell's steps.

THE MUSEUM OF THE
CREEPY CRAWLIES

Evie disembarked from the train with a wave to the porters and conductors with whom she had played poker from Pittsburgh to Pennsylvania Station. She was now in possession of twenty dollars, three new addresses in her brown leather journal, and a porter's hat, which she wore upon her golden head at a rakish angle.

"So long, fellas! It's been swell."

The conductor, a young man of twenty-two, leaned out from the train's stairwell. "You'll be sure to write me, won't ya, sweetheart?"

"And how. Just as soon as I practice my penmanship," Evie lied. "My aunt will be waiting. She's legally blind, so I'd better fly to her side. Poor dear Aunt Martha."

"I thought her name was Gertrude."

"Gertrude and Martha. They're twins, and both blind, the poor, poor dears. Farewell!" Her heart thumping, Evie rushed up the stairs from the platform. New York City—at last!

Uncle Will's telegram had been quite specific: She was to hail a taxi outside Pennsylvania Station on Eighth Avenue and tell the driver to take her to the Museum of American Folklore, Superstition, and the Occult on Sixty-eighth Street, off Central Park West. She had been sure it would be no trouble at all. Now, in the hubbub of Pennsylvania Station, she felt more than a little lost. She went the wrong way twice and finally found herself in the enormous main room, with its floor-to-ceiling arched windows and the giant, center-placed clock whose filigreed arms reminded passengers that time was fleeting—as were trains.

Nearby, a very glamorous woman wearing a full-length Russian sable despite the heat was drawing an ever-thickening crowd of followers and shutterbugs. "Who is that?" Evie whispered urgently to one of the admirers.

He shrugged. "Don't know. But her press agent paid me a dollar to stand around and gape like she was Gloria Swanson. Easiest buck I ever made."

Evie scurried to keep up with the hustle and bustle of the crowd and nearly wiped out a newsboy hawking the *Daily News*. "Valentino poisoned? Read all about it! Anarchists' bomb plot goes bust! Teacher goes ape for evolution! All the news right here, right here! Only two cents! Paper, Miss?"

"No, thank you."

"Nice topper." He winked and Evie remembered the porter's hat.

A mirror hung in the window of a druggist's shop, and Evie stopped to fix her hair and replace the porter's hat with her own brimless gray cloche, turning her head left and right to make sure she was at her best. She took the twenty-dollar bill she'd won playing poker and, after a moment of deliberation, stuffed it into the pocket of her red, summer-weight traveling coat.

"I can't say I blame you for taking in the view. I've been looking for a while."

The voice was male, and a little gravelly. Evie caught his reflection in the mirror. Thick, dark hair with a longer piece in front that refused to stay swept back. Amber eyes and dark brows. His smile could only be described as wolfish.

Evie turned slowly. "Do I know you?"

"Not yet. But I hope to remedy that." He stuck out a hand. "Sam Lloyd."

Evie curtsied. "Miss Evangeline O'Neill of the Zenith O'Neills."

"The Zenith O'Neills? Now I feel underdressed. Let me just get my dinner jacket." He grinned again, and Evie felt a little off balance. He was of medium height and compact build. His shirt-sleeves had been rolled to his elbows; his trousers were worn at the knees. Faint black smudges stained the tips of his fingers, as if he'd been shining shoes. A pair of aviator's goggles hung around his neck. Her first New York admirer was a bit rough around the edges.

"Well, it was nice to meet you, Mr. Lloyd, but I'd better—"

"Sam." He picked up her case so quickly she didn't even see his hand move. "Let me carry that for you."

"Really. I can—" She made a swipe for her case but he held it up.

"I insist. My mother would skin me for being so unchivalrous."

"Well"—Evie looked around nervously—"just as far as the door, then."

"Where ya headed?"

"My, you ask a lot of questions."

"Let me guess: You're a Ziegfeld girl?"

Evie shook her head.

"Model? Actress? Princess? You're too pretty to be just anybody."

"Are you on the level?"

"Me? I'm so on the level I can't get off it."

He was flattering her, but she was enjoying it. She loved

attention. It was like a glass of the best champagne—bubbly and intoxicating—and as with champagne, she always wanted more of it. Still, she didn't want to seem like an easy mark.

"If you must know, I've come to join a convent," Evie said, testing him.

Sam Lloyd looked her over and shook his head. "Seems a waste to me. Pretty girl like you."

"Serving our lord is never a waste."

"Oh, sure. Of course, they say now that we've got Freud and the motorcar, God is dead."

"He's not dead; just very tired."

The corners of his mouth twitched in amusement, and Evie felt the warmth bubble up again. He thought her clever, this Sam Lloyd with his knowing grin.

"Well, it's a big job," he shot back. "All that smiting and begetting. Say, which convent you heading to?"

"The one with all the ladies in black and white."

"What's the name? Maybe I know it." Sam bowed his head. "I'm very devout."

Evie held back a small *ha!* "It's ... St. Mary's."

"Of course. Which St. Mary's?"

"The absolute most St. Mary's you can think of."

"Listen, before you commit your life to Christ, maybe you'd let me show you around the city? I know all the hot spots. I'm a swell tour guide." He took her hand in his, and Evie felt both excited and unnerved. She hadn't been in the city for even five minutes, and already some young man—some admittedly quite attractive young man—was trying to get her to go off alone with him. It was thrilling. And a little terrifying.

"Listen, I have to tell you a secret"—he looked around—"I am a scout for some of the biggest names in this town. Ziegfeld. The

Shuberts. Mr. White. I know 'em all. They would string me up if I didn't introduce a talent like you."

"You think I'm talented?"

"I know you are. I can tell. I have a sense about these things."

Evie raised one eyebrow. "I can't sing. I can't dance. I can't act."

"See? A real triple threat." He grinned. "Well, there goes the St. Mary's talent show."

Evie laughed in spite of herself. "All right, then. You with your keen observations—what, exactly, do you find special about me?" she asked coyly, glancing up at him through her lashes the way she'd seen Colleen Moore do in *We Moderns*.

"There's just something about you," he said without really saying anything at all, which disappointed her. Sam rested his hand on the wall above her head, leaning closer. Evie's stomach fluttered. It wasn't that she didn't know her way around the fellas, but this was a New York City fella. She didn't want to make a scene and come off as a complete rube. She was a girl who could take care of herself. Besides, if her parents heard about this, they'd yank her straight back to Ohio.

Instead, Evie looped under the handsome Sam Lloyd's arm and snatched her valise back. "I'm afraid I have to go now. I believe I see the, um, top nun going into the ladies' lounge."

"Top nun? Do you mean the Mother Superior?"

"And how! Sister...Sister, um..."

"Sister Benito Mussolini Fascisti?"

"Exactly!"

Sam Lloyd smirked. "Benito Mussolini is prime minister of Italy. And a fascist."

"I knew that," Evie said, her cheeks flushing.

"Of course you did."

"Well..." Evie stood uncertainly for a few seconds. She stuck out her hand for a shake. With a smirk, Sam Lloyd drew her to him and kissed her hard on the mouth. She heard the shoe-shine men chuckling as she pulled away, red-faced and disoriented. Should she slap him? He deserved a slap. But was that what sophisticated Manhattan moderns did? Or did they shrug it off like an old joke they were too tired to laugh at?

"You can't blame a fella for kissing the prettiest girl in New York, can you, sister?" Sam's grin was anything but apologetic.

Evie brought up her knee quickly and decisively, and he dropped to the floor like a grain sack. "You can't blame a girl for her quick reflexes now, can you, pal?"

She turned and hurried toward the exit. In a pained voice, Sam Lloyd called after her: "Best of luck to the nuns. The good sisters of St. Mary's don't know what they're in for!"

Evie wiped the kiss from her mouth with the back of her hand and pushed her way out onto Eighth Avenue, but when she saw the majesty of the city, all thoughts of Sam Lloyd were forgotten. A trolley jostled down the center of the avenue on steel tracks. Motorcars swerved around the throngs of people and one another with the furious grace of a corps de ballet. She craned her neck to take in the full view. Far above the busy streets, men balanced daringly on beams of steel, erecting new buildings like the ones whose tops already pierced the clouds, as if even the sky couldn't hold back the ambition of their spires. A sleek dirigible sailed past, a smear of silver in the blue. It was like a dreamscape that could change in the blink of an eye. A taxi careened to the corner and Evie got inside.

"Where to, Miss?" the cabbie asked, flipping his meter on.

"The Museum of American Folklore, Superstition, and the Occult, please."

"Oh. The Museum of the Creepy Crawlies." The cabbie chuckled. "Good thing you're goin' to see it while you can."

"What do you mean?"

"They say the place is in arrears on its taxes. The city's had its sights set on that spot for years. They want to put some apartment buildings there."

"Oh, dear." Evie examined the photograph her mother had given her. It was a picture of Uncle Will—tall, lanky, fair-haired—standing in front of the museum, a grand Victorian mansion complete with turrets and stained-glass windows and bordered by a wrought-iron fence.

"Can't happen soon enough, if you ask me. That place makes people uncomfortable—all those crazy objects s'posed to be fulla hocus-pocus."

Objects. Magic. Evie drummed her fingers against the door.

"You know about the fella that runs the place, don't ya?"

Evie stopped drumming. "What do you mean?"

"Odd fella. He was a conscie."

"A what?"

"Conscientious objector," the cabbie said, spitting the words out like poison. "During the war. Refused to fight." He shook his head. "I hear he might be one of them Bolsheviks, too."

"Well, if so, he never mentioned it to me," Evie said, pulling the wrinkles from her glove.

The cabbie caught her eye in the mirror. "You know him? What's a nice girl like you doing with a fella like that?"

"He's my uncle."

At that, the cabbie fell blessedly quiet.

At last the taxi turned onto a side street near Central Park and pulled up to the museum. Tucked away among the grit and steel of Manhattan, the museum itself seemed a relic, a building out of time and place, its limestone facade long since grimed by age, soot, and vines. Evie glanced from the sad, dingy shadow before her to the beautiful house in her photograph. "You sure this is the joint?"

"This is the place. Museum of the Creepy Crawlies. That'll be one dollar and ten cents."

Evie reached into her pocket and pulled out nothing but the lining. With mounting alarm, she searched all her pockets.

"Whatsa matter?" The cabbie eyed her suspiciously.

"My money! It's gone! I had twenty dollars right in this pocket and . . . and it's gone!"

He shook his head. "Mighta known. Probably a Bolshevik, like your uncle. Well, little lady, I've had three fare jumpers in the past week. Not this time. You owe me one dollar and ten cents, or you can tell your story to a cop." The cabbie signaled to a policeman on horseback down the block.

Evie closed her eyes and retraced her steps: The tracks. The druggist's window. Sam Lloyd. Sam . . . Lloyd. Evie's eyes snapped open as she recalled his sudden passionate kiss. *There's just something about you. . . .* There sure was—twenty dollars. Not an hour in the city and already she'd been taken for a ride.

"That son of a . . ." Evie swore hard and fast, stunning the cabbie into silence. Furious, she pulled her emergency ten-dollar bill from her cloche, waited for the change, and then slammed the taxi door behind her.

"Hey," the cabbie yelled. "How's about a tip?"

"You bet-ski," Evie said, heading toward the old Victorian mansion, her long silk scarf trailing behind her. "Don't kiss strange men in Penn Station."

Evie rapped the brass eagle's-head door knocker and waited. A plaque beside the museum's massive oak doors read HERE BE THE HOPES AND DREAMS OF A NATION, BUILT UPON THE BACKS OF MEN AND LIFTED BY THE WINGS OF ANGELS. But neither men nor angels answered her knock, so she let herself in. The entry was ornate: black-and-white marble floors, wood-paneled walls dimly lit by gilded sconces. High above, the pale blue ceiling boasted a mural of angels watching over a field of Revolutionary soldiers. The building smelled of dust and age. Evie's heels echoed on the marble as she made her way down the long hall. "Hello?" she called. "Uncle Will?"

A wide, elaborately carved staircase wound up to a second-floor landing lit by a large stained-glass window, and then curved out of sight. To Evie's left was a gloomy sitting room with its drapes drawn. To her right, pocket doors opened onto a musty dining hall whose long wooden table and thirteen damask-covered chairs looked as if they hadn't been used in years.

"Holy smokes. Who died?" Evie muttered. She wandered till she came to a long room that housed a collection of objects displayed behind glass.

"'The Museum of the Creepy Crawlies,' I presume."

Evie passed from display to display, reading the typewritten cards placed beneath:

GRIS GRIS BAG AND VOUDON DOLL,
NEW ORLEANS, LOUISIANA

BONE FRAGMENT FROM CHINESE RAILROAD
WORKER AND REPUTED CONJURER,
NORTHERN CALIFORNIA, GOLD RUSH PERIOD

CRYSTAL BALL USED IN SÉANCES OF
MRS. BERNICE FOXWORTHY DURING
AMERICAN SPIRITUALISM PERIOD, C. 1848,
TROY, NEW YORK

OJIBWAY TALISMAN OF PROTECTION,
GREAT LAKES REGION

ROOT WORKER'S CUTTINGS,
BATON ROUGE, LOUISIANA

FREEMASON'S TOOLS AND BOOKS, C. 1776,
PHILADELPHIA, PENNSYLVANIA

There was a series of spirit photographs populated with faint figures, gauzy as lace curtains in a wind. Poppet dolls. A ventriloquist's dummy. A leather-bound grimoire. Books on alchemy, astrology, numerology, root workers, voudon, spirit mediums, and healers, and several volumes of accounts of ghostly sightings in the Americas starting in the 1600s.

The Diary of a Mercy Proud lay open on a table. Evie turned her head sideways, trying to make sense of the seventeenth-century handwriting. "*I see spirits of the dead. For this they hath branded me a witch. . . .*"

"They hanged her. She was only seventeen."

Evie turned, startled. The speaker stepped from the shadows. He was tall and broad-shouldered and had ash-blond hair. For a moment, with the light from the old chandelier shining down on him, he seemed like some severe angel from a Renaissance painting, come to life.

"What crime did she commit?" Evie said, finding her voice again. "Did she turn the gin to water?"

"She was different. That was her sin." He offered his hand for a quick shake. "I'm Jericho Jones. I work for your uncle. He asked me if I could keep you company while he teaches his class."

So this was the famous Jericho with whom Mabel was so besotted. "Why, I've heard so much about you!" Evie blurted out. Mabel would kill her for being so indiscreet. "That is, I hear Uncle Will would be lost without...whatever it is that you do."

Jericho looked away. "I highly doubt that. Would you like to see the museum?"

"That'd be swell," Evie lied.

Jericho led her up and down staircases and into preserved, musty rooms holding more collections of dull, dusty relics, while Evie fought to keep a polite smile.

"Last but not least, here is the place where we spend most of our time: the library." Jericho opened a set of mahogany pocket doors, and Evie let out a whistle. She'd never seen such a room. It was as if it had been transported here from some spooky fairy-tale castle. An enormous limestone fireplace took up the whole of the far wall. The furnishings weren't much—brown leather club chairs worn to stuffing in places, a dotting of old wooden tables, bankers' lamps dimmed to a faint green glow at each. A second-floor gallery crammed with bookcases circled the entire room. Evie craned her head to take in the full view. The ceiling had to be twenty feet high, and what a ceiling it was! Spread across its expanse was a panorama of American history: Black-hatted Puritans condemning a cluster of women. An Indian shaman staring into a fire. A healer grasping snakes in one hand while placing the other on the forehead of a sick man. Gray-wigged founding fathers signing the

Declaration of Independence. A slave woman holding a mandrake root aloft. Painted angels and demons hovered above the historical scene, watching. Waiting.

"What do you think?" Jericho asked.

"I think he should have fired his decorator." Evie plopped into one of the chairs and adjusted a seam on her stockings. She was itching to get out and see Mabel and explore the city. "Will Unc be long?"

Jericho shrugged. He sat at the long table and retrieved a book from a tall stack. "This is an excellent history of eighteenth-century mysticism in the colonies if you'd care to pass the time with a book."

"No, thanks," Evie said, suppressing the urge to roll her eyes. She didn't know what Mabel saw in this fella. He was going to take work; that was for sure. "Say"—Evie lowered her voice—"I don't suppose you have any giggle water on you?"

"Giggle water?" Jericho repeated.

"You know, coffin varnish? Panther sweat? Hooch?" Evie tried. "Gin?"

"No."

"I'm not particular. Bourbon'll do just as well."

"I don't drink."

"You must get awfully thirsty then." Evie laughed. Jericho did not.

"Well, I should get back to the museum," he said, walking quickly toward the doors. "Make yourself comfortable. Your uncle should be with you shortly."

Evie turned to the stuffed grizzly looming beside the fireplace. "I don't suppose *you've* got any hooch? No? Maybe later."

Other than Jericho, she hadn't seen a single soul in the museum. She was hungry and thirsty and a little put out that she'd been left all on her own without so much as a hello from her uncle.

If she was going to live in New York, she'd have to start fending for herself.

Evie patted the bear's matted fur. "Sorry, old sport, you're on your own," she said, and left the library in search of food. She heard male voices and followed the sound to a large room in the back of the museum where Uncle Will, in gray trousers, waistcoat, and blue tie, his shirtsleeves rolled to his elbows, stood lecturing. His hair had darkened to a dirty blond over the years, and he sported a trim mustache.

"The presence of evil is a conundrum that has taxed the minds of philosophers and theologians alike...." he was saying.

Evie peeked around the corner to take in the whole of the room. A class of college boys sat taking notes on Will's lecture.

"Now we're cookin'," Evie whispered. "Sorry I'm late!" she called as she breezed into the room. The college boys' heads swiveled in Evie's direction as she scraped a chair across the floor to join them. Uncle Will regarded her over the tops of his round tortoiseshell glasses.

"Go on, Uncle Will. Don't mind me." Evie perched on the edge of the chair beside one of the College Joes and did her best to look interested.

"Yes..." For a moment, Uncle Will's bewildered expression threatened to become permanent. But then he found his stride again and began pacing the room with his hands behind his back. "As I said, how does one explain the presence of evil?"

The boys all looked to one another to see who would answer.

"Man makes evil through his choices," someone said.

"It's God and the Devil, fighting it out. That's what the Bible says, at least," another boy argued.

"How can there be a Devil if there is a God?" a boy in golf knickers asked. "I've always wondered that."

Uncle Will waved a finger, making a point. "Ah. Theodicy."

"Is that a cross between theology and idiocy?"

Will allowed a small smile. "Not exactly. Theodicy is a branch of theology concerned with the defense of God in the face of the existence of evil. It brings about a conundrum: If God is an all-knowing, all-powerful deity, how can he allow evil to exist? Either he is not the omnipotent god we've been told, or he *is* all-powerful and all-knowing, and also cruel, because he allows evil to exist and does nothing to stop it."

"Well, that certainly explains Prohibition," Evie quipped.

The college boys laughed appreciatively. Again Uncle Will looked at Evie as if she were a subject he had yet to classify.

"Any good world would allow for us to have free will, yes?" he continued. "Can we agree to this point? But once human beings have free will, they also have the ability to make choices—and commit evil. Thus, this very good thing, free will, allows the possibility of evil into our fine world." The room was silent. "One to ponder. But, if I may continue with our earlier discussion…"

The boys sat up straight, ready to take notes as Will paced and talked. "America has a rich history of beliefs, a tapestry woven together by threads from different cultures. Our history is rife with the supernatural, the unexplained, the mystical. The earliest settlers came here for religious freedom. The immigrants who followed introduced their hopes and haunts, from the vampire legend of Eastern Europe to the 'hungry ghosts' of China. The original Americans believed in shamans and spirits. The slaves of West Africa and the Caribbean, stripped of all they had, still carried with them their customs and beliefs. We are not only a melting pot of cultures, but also of spirits and superstitions. Yes?"

A boy in a navy blazer raised his hand. "Do *you* believe in the supernatural, Dr. Fitzgerald?"

"Ah. It would seem illogical, wouldn't it? After all, we live in the modern age. It's difficult enough to get people even to believe in Methodism." Will smiled as the boys chuckled. "And yet, there are mysteries. How does one explain the stories of people who exhibit unusual powers?"

Evie felt a tingle down her spine.

"Powers?" a boy repeated in a skeptical tone bordering on contempt.

"People who claim to be able to speak to the dead, such as psychics or spiritual mediums. People who say they have been healed by the laying on of hands. Who can see glimpses of the future or know a card before it is played. The early records of the Americas talk of Indian spirit walkers. The Puritans knew of cunning folk. And during the American Revolution, Benjamin Franklin wrote of prophetic dreams that influenced the course of the war and shaped the nation. What do you say to that?"

"Those people need the services of a psychiatrist—though I'll make an exception for Mr. Franklin."

Another round of chuckles followed, and Evie joined in, though she was still discomfited. Uncle Will waited for the laughing to subside.

"This very museum, as you may know, was constructed by Cornelius Rathbone, who amassed his fortune building railroads. How did he know that the age of steel was coming?" Will paused at the lectern and waited. When no one answered, he continued pacing, his hands behind his back. "He claimed he knew because of the prophetic visions of his sister, Liberty Anne. When Cornelius and Liberty were young, they spent hours in the woods playing at all sorts of games. One day, Liberty went into the forest and was lost for two full days. The men of the town searched but could find no trace of her. When she emerged at last, her hair had gone completely white. She was only eleven. Liberty Anne claimed she had met a man there, 'a strange, tall man, skinny as a scarecrow, in a stovepipe hat and whose coat opened to show the wonders and frights of the world.' She fell ill with a fever. The doctor was sent for, but there was nothing he could do. For the next month, she lay in a dream trance, spouting prophecy, which her worried brother transcribed in his diary. These prophecies were astonishing in their accuracy. She claimed to see 'the great man from Illinois taken from us while visiting our American cousin'—a reference to the assassination of President Lincoln in the balcony of Ford's Theatre while he watched a production of the play *Our American Cousin*. She spoke of 'a great steel dragon criss-crossing the land, belching black smoke,' which most interpret to mean the Transcontinental Railroad. She predicted the Emancipation Proclamation, the Great War, the Bolshevik revolution, and the invention of the motorcar and the aeroplane. She even spoke of the fall of our banks and the subsequent collapse of our economy."

"Clearly, she couldn't see everything," the boy in the golf trousers said. "That will never happen."

Will rapped his knuckles on the desk. "Knock wood, as they say." Will grinned and the College Joes laughed at his superstitious joke. He fidgeted with a silver lighter, turning it end over end, occasionally flicking his thumb across the flint wheel so that it sparked. "Liberty Anne died a month to the day after she emerged from the woods. Toward the end, her prophecies became quite dark. She talked of 'a coming storm,' a treacherous time when the Diviners would be needed."

"Diviners?" Evie repeated.

"That was her name for people with powers like her own."

"And what would these Diviners do?" the boy in the golf pants asked.

Will shrugged. "If she knew, she didn't say. She died shortly after making the prophecy, leaving her brother, Cornelius, bereft. He became obsessed with good and evil, and with the idea that this was a country haunted by ghosts. That there was something beyond what we see. He spent his life—and his fortune—trying to prove it."

The boys fell into heated discussion until one of them shouted over the others. "Yes, but Professor, do *you* yourself actually believe that there is another world beyond this one, and that the entities from that world can act to help or hurt us? Do you believe that our actions here—good or bad—can create an external evil? Do you believe there are ghosts and demons and Diviners among us?"

Uncle Will took a cloth from his pocket and wiped the lenses of his spectacles. "'There are more things between heaven and earth, Horatio, than are dreamt of in your philosophy,'" Will said, hooking the spectacles over his ears again. "That quote is from William Shakespeare, who seemed to know a thing or two about both humanity and the supernatural. But for your *examinations*, you will need to know the following concrete information...."

The boys groaned as Will fired off a dizzying plethora of information and their pencils struggled to keep up.

Evie slipped out and went to wait for Will in his office. The steady click of the mantel clock kept her company as she took a look around. His desktop was awash in newspaper clippings and perilous-looking stacks of books. Bored, Evie leafed through the newspaper clippings. They were reports from towns across the country of ghost sightings, hauntings, and such strange goings-on as dead relatives appearing for seconds in a favorite chair and red-eyed "demon" dogs who frightened the caretaker of a junkyard in upstate New York. Some of the clippings were two or three years old, but most were recent—from the past year. Evie started reading an article about a girl who claimed to be able to speak to the dead and who had been warned by "kind spirits" of trouble to come. She'd just gotten to the part about the girl's sudden disappearance when Uncle Will announced his presence with a soft clearing of his throat.

Evie shuffled the clippings to one side. "Hello, Unc."

"That's my desk."

"So it is," Evie said brightly. "And a tidy one it is, too."

"Yes. Well. I suppose it's fine this time," Uncle Will murmured. He took a cigarette from a small silver case in his breast pocket. "You're looking well." Will lit his cigarette and inhaled deeply. "Did Jericho show you the museum?"

"Yes, he did. It's very . . . interesting."

"Was your trip comfortable?"

"Swell, although I was pickpocketed at Penn Station," Evie said, and then wished she hadn't. What if Will decided she couldn't look after herself and sent her back to Ohio?

Uncle Will raised an eyebrow. "Really?"

"A hideous young man named Sam Lloyd. Well, that was the name he gave me before he kissed me and stole my twenty dollars."

Will squinted. "He what?"

"But don't worry. I can take care of myself. If I ever see that fella again, he'll wish he'd never tangled with me," Evie said.

Will blew out a plume of smoke. It hung thickly in the air. "Your mother has told me that you were in a spot of trouble back home. A prank of some sort."

"A prank," Evie muttered.

"And you're to stay until October?"

"December, if possible. Until the coast is clear back home."

"Hmm." Will's expression darkened. "Your mother has petitioned for you to attend the Sarah Snidewell School for Girls. They are overburdened at present, so your schooling, it would appear, falls to me. I'll provide you with books, and, of course, you are free to attend my lectures. I suggest you make use of our many fine museums and lectures through the Society for Ethical Culture and whatnot."

It dawned on Evie that she was free from the tedium of school. The day just kept getting better.

Uncle Will thumbed absently through a book. "You're seventeen, is it?"

"According to my last birthday."

"Well. Seventeen's certainly old enough to do mostly as you please. I won't keep you on a leash as long as you keep out of trouble. Do we have a deal?"

"Deal," Evie said, astonished. "Are you sure you're related to my mother? There wasn't a mix-up in the nursery?"

Will's smile flickered for a second and disappeared. "Your mother has never quite recovered from your brother's death."

"She's not the only one who misses James."

"It's different for her."

"So they say." Evie swallowed down her anger. "That bit you were talking about back there—people who could see the future or…" She took a breath. "Read objects. Diviners. Do you know anyone like that?"

"Not personally, no. Why do you ask?"

"Oh, no reason," Evie said quickly. "I suppose if there were Diviners, they'd be all over the papers and radio, wouldn't they?"

"Or, if history is any indication, they'd be burned at the stake." Will gestured to the many bookcases surrounding them. "We've an entire library devoted to such stories if you'd like to read more about America's supernatural beliefs." He stubbed out his cigarette in an overflowing ashtray. "I'm afraid I'm running a bit behind, and I'm sure you'd like to unpack and freshen up. The Bennington isn't far from here—ten blocks. Shall I have Jericho walk you over?"

"No," Evie said. Even a ten-block walk with stoic Jericho would probably be painfully dull. "I'll be jake on my own."

"Pardon?"

"Jake. Swell. Um, fine. I'll be fine. I'll go find Mabel. You remember Mabel Rose? My pen pal?"

"Mmm," Will said, distracted by another book. "Very well. Here is your key. There's a dining room just off the Bennington's lobby. Help yourself to something to eat, and ask them to put it on my bill. Jericho and I should be home by half past six at the latest."

Evie slipped the key into her handbag. She hadn't had a key back in Zenith; her every move had been monitored by her parents. Things would be different here. Things would be perfect. She went to hug Uncle Will, who stuck out his hand for a shake.

"Welcome to New York, Evie."

IT'S JUST THE BENNINGTON, DEAR

"Mabel!" Evie embraced her friend and waltzed her around the lobby of the Bennington, drawing stares from the denizens of the apartment building. "Oh, I'm so happy to see you!"

"Golly, you've changed," Mabel said, taking in Evie's stylishly curled short hairdo and her flapper fashion—the drop-waisted nautical dress and red coat with its poppy-embroidered capelet at the back.

"You haven't. Still the same old Mabel. Let me look at you!" With a dramatic flair, Evie stepped back to take in the sight of Mabel's drab, ill-fitting dress with a hemline that landed well below her knees. It was funereal. Actually, it was a dress that needed a good burial. "Mabel, you still haven't bobbed your hair?"

Mabel ran a hand over her long, thick, auburn curls, which were softly coiled and pinned at the back of her neck. "I am exercising my individualism."

"You certainly are. And so is the good old Bennington." Evie let out a low whistle, startling a man retrieving his mail from the brass mailboxes set into the wall. The Bennington had the shabby beauty of a formerly fashionable address. The marble floors had chipped corners, the furniture was worn, and the paint was dingy, but to Evie, these quirks only made it all the more charming.

"Be it ever so humble," Mabel said.

"Can you believe it? You and me and Manhattan? We'll be the queens of the city!"

As Evie began to lay out their plans, starting with a shopping trip to Bergdorf's, an absolutely stunning girl strode into the lobby. She wore men's pajamas under a man's blue silk bathrobe, and her jet-black hair had been cut into a Louise Brooks shingle bob with bangs. Her dark eyes were smeared with traces of the previous night's mascara and kohl. A silk sleep mask had been pushed down around her neck.

"Who is *that*?" Evie whispered.

"*That* is Theta Knight. She's a Ziegfeld girl."

"Holy smokes. A friend of yours?"

Mabel shook her head. "She terrifies me. I've never worked up the nerve to say more than hello and 'Isn't it a nice day?' She lives here with her brother." Mabel pursed her lips knowingly. "Well, she *says* he's her brother. They don't look a thing alike."

"Her lover?" Evie whispered, excited.

Mabel shrugged. "How should I know?"

"These came for you, Miss Knight." The doorman handed over a dozen long-stemmed red roses. Theta stifled a yawn as she ripped open the envelope on the card.

"'A rose for a rose. With my dearest affections, Clarence M. Potts.' Oh, brother!" Theta shoved the flowers back at him. "Give these to your girl, Eddie. Just toss the card first, or you'll be in hot water."

"Oh, you can't throw those roses away. They're the bee's knees!" Evie blurted.

Theta squinted at her. "These stems? They're from creepy Mr. Potts. He's forty-eight, and he's had four wives. I'm only seventeen, and I'm not looking to walk the middle aisle and be wife number five. I know plenty of chorus girls who're regular gold diggers, but not me, sister. I got plans." She nodded to Mabel. "Heya. Madge, right?"

"Mabel. Mabel Rose."

"Nice to meet ya, Mabel." Theta fixed her liquid gaze on Evie. "And you are?"

"Evangeline O'Neill. But everyone calls me Evie."

"Theta Knight. You can call me anything—just not before noon." She produced a cigarette from her pajama pocket and waited for the doorman to light it, which he did. "Thanks, Eddie."

"Evie's staying with her uncle, Mr. Fitzgerald," Mabel explained. "She's from Ohio."

"Sorry," Theta deadpanned.

"You said it—and how! Are you from New York?"

Theta arched a thread-thin eyebrow. "Everybody in New York's from someplace else."

Evie decided she liked Theta. It was hard not to be taken by her glamour. She'd never known anyone in Ohio who lived on her own terms, wore silk men's pajamas into a public lobby, and could toss a dozen roses like they were a cup of Automat coffee. "Are you really a Ziegfeld girl?"

"Guilty."

"That must be terribly exciting!"

"It's a living," Theta said on a stream of smoke. "You should come to the show some night."

Evie thrilled at the thought. A Ziegfeld show! "I'd love to."

"Swell. Name your night and I'll leave a coupla tickets for you both. Well, I'd love to stay and beat my gums, but if I'm gonna hit on all sixes later, I gotta grab my beauty sleep. Swell to meet ya, Evil."

"It's Evie."

"Not anymore," Theta called over her shoulder as she disappeared into the elevator.

✳

"I can't believe you're really here," Mabel said. She and Evie were seated in the Bennington's down-at-heel dining room having a couple of club sandwiches and Coca-Colas. "What did you do to get drummed out of Ohio so quickly?"

Evie toyed with the ice in her glass. "Remember that little trick I told you about a few months ago? Well . . ." Evie told Mabel the story of Harold Brodie's ring. "And the terrible thing is that I'm right, and he comes off looking like the wronged party, the hypocrite!"

"Gee whiz," Mabel said.

Evie studied Mabel's face carefully. "Oh, Mabesie. You believe me, don't you?"

"Of course I do."

"And you don't think I'm some sort of sideshow act?"

"Never." Mabel swirled the ice in her glass, thinking. "But I wonder why you're suddenly able to do it. You didn't fall and hit your head or something, did you?"

Evie arched a brow. "Thank you."

"I didn't mean anything by it! I just thought there might be a medical reason. A scientific reason," Mabel said hastily. "Did you tell your uncle about it?"

Evie shook her head emphatically. "I'm not rocking the boat.

Everything's copacetic with Unc right now, and I want it to stay that way."

Mabel bit her lip. "And did you meet Jericho?"

"I did indeed," Evie said, finishing her Coca-Cola.

"What did you think?" Mabel asked, leaning in.

"Very...solid."

Mabel let out a small squeak. "Isn't he beautiful?"

Evie thought about the Jericho she'd just met—quiet, serious, sober Jericho. There was nothing remotely seductive about him. "He is to you, and that's what matters. So what have you done about this situation?"

"Well...last Friday, when we were both standing at the mailboxes?"

"*Yes?*" Evie wiggled her eyebrows suggestively.

"I stood very close to him...."

"Uh-huh."

"And I said, just like this, 'Nice day, isn't it?'"

"And?"

"And that was it. Well, he said yes. So we were both in agreement about the weather."

Evie collapsed against the banquette. "Holy smokes. It's like a party without any confetti. What we need is a plan, old girl. A romantic assault of epic proportions. We will shake the walls of Jericho! That boy won't know what hit him."

Mabel perked up. "Swell! What's the plan?"

Evie shrugged. "Beats me. I just know we need one."

"Oh," Mabel said.

"Oh, Mabesie, sugar. Don't worry about that. I'll think of something. In the meantime, we'll visit the shops, go see Theta in 'No Foolin'' at the Follies—I'll bet she knows all the hot spots—Charleston till we drop. We are going to live, kiddo! I intend to make this the most exciting four months of our lives. And, if I play my cards right, I'll stay on." Evie danced in her seat. "So where are your folks tonight?"

Mabel flushed. "Oh. There's a rally for the appeal of Sacco and Vanzetti downtown. My mother and father are representing *The Proletariat*," she said, reminding Evie of the name of the socialist newspaper Mabel's parents operated and distributed. "I'd be there but, well, I couldn't not see you on your first night in town!"

"Well, I suppose I'll see them tomorrow."

Mabel's face clouded. She shook her head. "My mother will be speaking to the women's garment workers union. And Papa's got the newspaper to see to. They do so much for so many."

Mabel's letters were filled with stories of her parents' crusading efforts in the city. It was clear that she was very proud of them. It was also clear that their causes left them with little time or energy for their daughter.

Evie patted Mabel's hand. "It's just as well. Parents get in the way. My mother is impossible since she caught the disease."

Mabel looked stricken. "Oh, dear. What's she got?"

A slow smile stretched the corners of Evie's lips. "Temperance. In the extreme."

Their laughter was interrupted by the approach of two elderly ladies. "That is not how young ladies behave in the social sphere, Miss Rose. This carrying-on is most unseemly."

"Yes, Miss Proctor," Mabel said, chastened. Evie made a face that only Mabel could see, and Mabel had to bite her lip to keep from laughing again. "Miss Lillian, Miss Adelaide, may I present Miss Evie O'Neill. Miss O'Neill is staying with her uncle, Mr. Fitzgerald, for a time." Under the table, Mabel's foot pressed Evie's in warning.

Miss Lillian smiled. "Oh, how lovely. And what a sweet face. Doesn't she have a sweet face, Addie?"

"Very sweet, indeed."

The Misses Proctor wore their long gray hair curled like turn-of-the-century schoolgirls. The effect was odd and disconcerting, like porcelain dolls who had aged and wrinkled.

"Welcome to the Bennington. It's a grand old place. Once upon a time, it was considered one of the very best addresses in the city," Miss Lillian continued.

"It's swell. Um, lovely. A lovely place."

"Yes. Sometimes you might hear odd sounds in the night. But you mustn't be frightened. This city has its ghosts, you see."

"All the best places do," Evie said with mock-seriousness.

Mabel choked on her Coca-Cola, but Miss Lillian did not take note. "In the seventeen hundreds, this patch of land was home to those suffering from the fever. Those poor, tragic souls moaning in their tents, jaundiced and bleeding, their vomitus the color of black night!"

Evie pushed her sandwich away. "How hideously fascinating. I was just saying to Mabel—Miss Rose—that we don't talk enough about black vomit." Under the table, Mabel's foot threatened to push Evie's through the floor.

"After the time of the fever, they buried paupers and the mentally insane here," Miss Lillian continued as if she hadn't heard. "They were exhumed before the Bennington was built, of course— or so they said. Though if you ask me, I don't see how they could possibly have found all those bodies."

"Dead bodies *are* such trouble," Evie said with a little sigh, and Mabel had to turn her head away so as not to laugh.

"Indeed," Miss Lillian clucked. "When the Bennington was built, in 1872, it was said that the architect, who had descended from a long line of witches, fashioned the building on ancient occult principles so that it would always be a sort of magnet for the otherworldly. So as I said, don't pay any mind to the odd sounds or sights you might experience. It's just the Bennington, dear."

Miss Lillian attempted a smile. A blot of red lipstick marked her teeth like a bloodstain. At her side, Miss Addie smiled into the distance and nodded as if greeting unseen guests.

"Please do excuse us, but we must retire," Miss Lillian said. "We're expecting company soon, and we must prepare. You will do us the honor of calling one evening, won't you?"

"How could I not?" Evie answered.

Miss Addie turned suddenly to Evie, as if truly seeing her for the first time. Her expression was grim. "You're one of them, aren't you, dear?"

"Miss O'Neill is Mr. Fitzgerald's niece," Mabel supplied.

"No. One of *them*," Miss Addie said in an urgent whisper that sent a shiver up Evie's spine.

"Now, now, Addie, let's leave these girls to their dinner. We've work to do. Adieu!"

The Proctor sisters were barely out of the dining room when Mabel convulsed in a fit of giggling. "'After the fever, there were the paupers,'" she mimicked, still laughing.

"What do you suppose she meant, 'You're one of them'? Does she say that to everyone she meets?" Evie asked, hoping she didn't sound as unsettled as she felt.

Mabel shrugged. "Sometimes Miss Addie wanders the floors in her nightgown. My father's had to return her to her flat a few times." Mabel tapped her index finger against the side of her head. "Not all there. She probably meant you're one of those flappers, and she does not approve," she teased, wagging her finger like a schoolmarm. "Oh, this really is going to be the best time of our lives, isn't it?" she said with such enthusiasm that Evie put Miss Addie's upsetting comment out of her mind.

"Pos-i-tute-ly!" Evie said, raising her glass. "To the Bennington and its ghosts!"

"To us!" Mabel added. They clinked their glasses to the future.

Evie and Mabel spent the afternoon catching up, and by the time Evie returned to Uncle Will's apartment it was nearly seven, and Will and Jericho had returned. The apartment was larger than she remembered, and surprisingly homey for a bachelor flat. A grand bay window looked out onto the leafy glory of Central Park. A settee and two chairs flanked a large radio cabinet, and Evie breathed a sigh of relief. There was a tidy kitchenette, which looked as if it rarely saw use. The bathroom boasted a tub perfect for soaking, but devoid of even the simplest luxuries. She'd soon fix that. Three bedrooms and a small office completed the suite. Jericho showed her to a narrow room with a bed, a desk, and a chifforobe. The bed squeaked, but it was comfortable.

"That goes to the roof," Jericho said, pointing to a fire escape outside her window. "You can see most of the city from up there."

"Oh," Evie managed to reply. "Swell." She intended to do more than watch the city from the roof. She would be in the thick of it. Her trunk had arrived, and she unpacked, filling the empty drawers and wardrobe with her painted stockings, hats, gloves, dresses, and coats. Her long strands of pearls she draped from the posts of her bed. The one item she did not put away was her coin pendant from James. When she'd finished, Evie sat with Jericho and Uncle Will in the parlor as the men finished a supper of cold sandwiches in wax paper bought from the delicatessen on the corner.

"How did you come to be in the employ of my uncle?" Evie asked Jericho with theatrical seriousness. Jericho looked to Uncle Will, whose mouth was full. Neither said a word. "Well. It's a regular mystery, I guess," Evie went on. "Where's Agatha Christie when you need her? I'll just have to make up stories about you. Let's see...you, Jericho, are a duke who has forfeited his duchy—funny word, *duchy*—and Unc is hiding you from hostile forces in your native country who would have your head."

"Your uncle was my legal guardian until I turned eighteen this year. Now I'm working for him, as his assistant curator."

The men continued eating their sandwiches, leaving Evie's curiosity unsatisfied. "Okay. I'll bite. How did Unc—"

"Must you call me that?"

Evie considered it. "Yes. I believe I must. How did Unc become your guardian?"

"Jericho was an orphan in the Children's Hospital."

"Gee, I'm sorry. But how—"

"I believe the question has been answered," Uncle Will said. "If Jericho wishes to tell you more, he will on his own terms and in his own time."

Evie wanted to say something snappy back, but she was a guest here, so she changed the subject. "Is the museum always that empty?"

"What do you mean?" Uncle Will asked.

"Empty, as in devoid of human beings."

"It's a little slow just now."

"Slow? It's a morgue! You need bodies in there, or you're going to go under. What we need is some advertising."

Will looked at Evie funny. "Advertising?"

"Yes. You've heard of it, haven't you? Swell modern invention. It lets people know about something they need. Soap, lipstick, radios—or your museum, for instance. We could start with a catchy slogan, like, 'The Museum of American Folklore, Superstition, and the Occult—we've got the spirit!'"

"Things are fine as they are," Will said, as if that settled the matter.

Evie whistled low. "Not from what I saw. Is it true the city's trying to take it for back taxes?"

Will squinted over the top of his slipping spectacles. "Who told you that?"

"The cabbie. He also said you were a conscie, and probably a Bolshevik. Not that it matters to me. It's just that I was thinking I could help you spruce the place up. Get some bodies in there. Make a mint."

Jericho glanced from Will to Evie and back again. He cleared his throat. "Mind if I turn on the radio?"

"Please," Will answered.

The announcer's voice burbled over the wires: "And now, the Paul Whiteman Orchestra, playing 'Wang Wang Blues.'" The orchestra launched into a swinging tune, and Evie hummed along.

CITY OF DREAMS

The girl was exhausted and angry. For seventy-eight straight hours, she and her beau, Jacek, had loped through the dance marathon with hopes of winning the big prize, but Jacek had fallen asleep at last, nearly toppling her. The emcee had tapped them on the shoulder, signaling the end of the contest, and with it their dreams.

"Why'd ya have to go and fall asleep, you big potato!" She punched him in the arm as they left the contest and he staggered, barely able to stay awake.

"Me? I held you up four different times. And you kept stepping on my feet with those boats o' yours."

"Boats!" Tears stung at her eyes. She swung at him and stumbled, exhausted by the effort.

"Come on, Ruta. Don't be that way. Let's go home."

"I ain't going nowhere with you. You're a bum."

"You don't mean that. Here. Sit with me on this step. We can catch the train in the morning."

The exhaustion she'd fought for so long finally caught up with her. "I ain't goin' back like this, with everybody laughing at us like

I ain't nothin' special and never will be!" she half sobbed. But Jacek didn't hear. He'd already fallen asleep on the stoop of a flophouse. "You can live there for all I care!" she shouted.

The tracks of the Third Avenue El formed a cage over Ruta's head as she walked south on the Bowery looking for an El entrance where there weren't bums lying on the rickety stairs, just waiting. With each exhausted step, she felt the bitter disappointment of returning empty-handed to Greenpoint, Brooklyn, where her family lived in a two-room apartment in a crumbling building on a street where nearly everyone spoke Polish and the old men smoked cigarettes in front of store windows draped with fat strands of kielbasa. It was a world away from the bright lights of Manhattan. She looked uptown, toward the distant, hazy glow of Park Avenue, where the rich people lived. She just wanted her piece of it. None of this answering the telephone switchboard at a second-rate law office every day, making barely enough to go to the pictures. Ruta was only nineteen years old, and what she knew most was want—a constant longing for the good life she saw all around her.

Ruta Badowski. Ruta. She hated that name. It was so Polish, brought over by her parents, but she'd been born here, in Brooklyn, New York, U.S.A. She'd change her name to something more American, like Ruthie or Ruby. Ruby was good. Ruby...Bates. Tomorrow, Ruta Badowski would quit her job at the switchboard and Ruby Bates would take the bus to Mr. Ziegfeld's theater and audition to be a chorus girl. One day, her name would be in lights, and Jacek and the rest could watch her from the cheap seats and go chase themselves.

"Good evening."

Ruta gasped; the voice startled her. She squinted in the gloom. "Who's there? You better get lost. My brother's a cop."

"I've always had a great appreciation for the law." The stranger stepped from the shadows.

Her eyes must've been playing tricks on her, because the man seemed almost like a ghost in the light. His clothes were funny—hopelessly out of date: a tweed suit even though it was warm, a vest and suit jacket, and a bowler hat. He carried a walking stick with the silver head of a wolf at the top. The wolf's face was set in a snarl and its eyes were red like rubies. Ruby—ha! That gave her a small shudder, though she couldn't say why. It occurred to her that she wasn't in a safe place. These dance marathons were usually held in bad neighborhoods, where they wouldn't draw too much attention from the city.

"This is a dreadful place for a young lady to be walking alone," the stranger said, as if he'd read her thoughts. He offered his arm. "Might I be of assistance?"

Ruby Bates might be on her way to being a glamorous star, but Ruta Badowski had grown up on the streets. "Thanks all the same, mister, but I don't need help," she said crisply. When she turned to go, her ankle gave way, and she winced in pain.

The stranger's voice was deep and soothing. "My sister and I run an establishment nearby, a grand boardinghouse with a kitchen. Perhaps you'd care to wait there? We've a telephone if you wish to call your family. My sister, Bryda, has likely made paczki and coffee."

"Paczki?" Ruta repeated. "You're Polish?"

The stranger smiled. "I guess we're all just dreamers trying to find our way in this extraordinary country, aren't we, Miss...?"

"Ruta—Ruby. Ruby Bates."

"Pleased to make your acquaintance, Miss Bates. My name is Mr. Hobbes." He tipped his hat. "But my friends call me John."

"Thanks, Mr. Hobbes," Ruta answered. She swooned slightly from exhaustion.

"I have smelling salts, which might aid you now." The man doused his handkerchief and held it out for her. Ruta inhaled. The scent was pungent and made her nose burn a little. But she did feel peppier. The stranger offered his arm again, and this time she took it. From the outside, he seemed a big man, but his arm was thin as a matchstick beneath his heavy coat. Something about that arm made Ruta cold inside, and she withdrew her own quickly.

"I'm good now. Them salts helped. I'll take you up on that cuppa Joe, though."

He gave her a courtly little bow. "As you wish."

They walked, the stranger's silver-tipped stick thudding a hollow rhythm against the cobblestones. He hummed a tune she didn't recognize.

"What's that song? I ain't heard it on the radio before."

"No. I expect you haven't," the stranger answered.

With his left arm, he gestured to the broken-down Bowery, with its Christian missions and flophouses, fleabag hotels and tattoo parlors, restaurant-supply stores and rinky-dink manufacturers.

"'Babylon is fallen, is fallen, that great city.'"

He pointed to where a couple of drunks slept on the stoop of a flophouse. "Terrible. Someone should clean up this sort of riffraff, turn them back at the borders. They're not like you and me, Miss Bates. Clean. Good citizens. People with ambitions. Contributors to this shining city on the hill."

Ruta hadn't ever thought about it before, but she found herself nodding. She looked at those men with a new disgust. They *were* different from her family. *Foreign.*

"Not our kind." The stranger shook his head. "Once upon a

time, the Bowery was home to the most stupendous restaurants and theaters. The Bowery Theatre—that great American theater, which was a sock in the eye to the elitist European theaters. The great thespian J. B. Booth, father of John Wilkes Booth, trod its boards. Are you a patron of the arts, Miss Bates?"

"Yeah. I mean, yes. I am. I'm an actress." For some reason, Ruta felt a little giddy. The streets had a pretty glow to them.

"But of course! Pretty girl such as you. There's something quite special about you, isn't there, Miss Bates? I can tell that you have a very important destiny to fulfill, indeed. 'And the woman was arrayed in purple and scarlet and decked with gold and precious stones. . . .'"

The stranger smiled. In spite of the late hour, the strangeness of the circumstances, and the aching in her legs, Ruta smiled, too. The stranger—no, he wasn't a stranger at all, was he? He was Mr. Hobbes. Such a nice man. Such a smart man—classy, too. Mr. Hobbes thought she was special. He could see what no one else could. It was what her grandmother would call a *wróżba*, an omen. She wanted to cry with gratitude.

"Thank you," she said softly.

"'And upon her forehead was written a name of mystery,'" the stranger said, and his face was alight with a strange fire.

"You a preacher or something?"

"I'm sure you must be eager to call your family," Mr. Hobbes said in answer. "No doubt they'll be worried?"

Ruta thought of her family's cramped apartment in Greenpoint and tried not to laugh. Her father would be awake next to her mother, coughing off the damp and the cigarettes and the factory dust in his lungs. Her four brothers and sisters would be crammed together in the next room, snoring. She wouldn't be missed. And she wasn't in a hurry to return.

"I don't wanna wake 'em," she said, and Mr. Hobbes smiled.

They walked a dizzying number of side streets, until Ruta felt quite lost. The Manhattan Bridge loomed in the distance like the gate to an underworld. A light drizzle fell. "Hey—hey, Mr. Hobbes, is it gonna be much farther?"

"Here we are. Your chariot awaits," he said, and Ruta saw a broken-down wagon, the old-fashioned kind, drawn by an old nag.

"I thought you said it was nearby."

"But you're tired. I'll drive us the rest of the way."

Ruta climbed into the buggy, and its gentle swaying rhythm and the clopping of the horse rocked her to sleep. When the old buggy stopped, all she saw was a hulking ruin of an old mansion on a hill surrounded by weedy vacant lots.

Ruta shrank back. "I thought you said you had a boarding-house. Ain't nothing here but a wreck."

"My dear, your eyes play tricks on you. *Look again*," Mr. Hobbes whispered low.

He waved his arm, and this time she saw a charming block of attached row houses, warm and homey, and at the end, a fancy mansion like the kind millionaires lived in, people with names like Carnegie and Rockefeller. Why, this Mr. Hobbes fella might even be a millionaire himself! The light drizzle turned to rain. Her velvet beaded shoes with the rhinestone buckles—her prized possession, worth a week's pay—would be ruined, so she followed the man across the street toward shelter. A black cat crossed her path, startling her, and she laughed nervously. She was getting as bad as her superstitious aunt Pela, who saw evil omens everywhere. The door screamed shut on its hinges behind her and Ruta jumped. The man smiled beneath his heavy mustache, but the smile brought little warmth to his piercing blue eyes. This thought occurred to her fleetingly, but she dismissed it as silly. She was out of the rain, and in a minute she could sit and rest her bone-weary legs.

The place smelled wrong, though. Like damp and rot and something else she couldn't put her finger on, but it unsettled her stomach. She put a hand to her nose.

"Alas, a poor unfortunate cat was lost in the walls. His *aroma*, I'm afraid, lingers," Mr. Hobbes said. "But you're cold and tired. Come sit. I'll make a fire."

Ruta followed the man into another room. Squinting against the dark, she could see the outline of a fireplace. She stumbled and put out a hand to steady herself. The wall felt wet and sticky against her flesh. She yanked her hand away quickly and wiped it on her dress, shuddering.

Mr. Hobbes stepped in front of the cold, blackened fireplace, and in the next moment a roaring fire appeared. Ruta tried to make sense of the sudden flames licking inside the chimney. *No*, she told herself. He had put in wood and struck a match. Of course he had. She couldn't remember it, but that's what must have happened. Boy, that marathon had done a number on her head.

"I-I think I oughta ring my folks after all. They'll be pretty sore if I don't."

"Of course, my dear. I'll wake my sister. But first, I promised coffee."

Suddenly, the cup was in her hand.

"Drink. I won't be a moment."

With a bow and a tip of his funny hat, the big man disappeared from view. She could hear him humming, though, and she decided she didn't like that song. It made her skin crawl for some reason. The coffee was strong and hot. It had a bitter aftertaste, but it filled her empty stomach, and Ruta drank it down. Still, it was no match for her exhaustion. Her eyelids fluttered as she watched the fire. Heavier and heavier...

Ruta woke with a snap of her head and a chalky taste on her tongue. The fire was out. How long had she slept? Had she called her family? No. She hadn't. Where was Mr. Hobbes? What about his sister? A rat skittered across her shoe. Ruta screamed and leaped up, noticing that she felt oddly watched, as if the room itself were alive. She could swear the walls were breathing. But that was impossible!

"Mr. Hobbes?" she called. "Mr. Hobbes!"

He didn't answer. Where was he? Where was *she*? Why had she gone with him? She was smarter than that—running off with a complete stranger. No, he wasn't a stranger, she reminded herself. He was Mr. Hobbes, kindly Mr. Hobbes who thought she was pretty and special. Mr. Hobbes who might be related to millionaires. Who might be her ticket to the big time.

So why did her breath catch so?

Around her, the house seemed alive with some evil. There. She'd said it. *Evil.* This word occurred to her just as she passed the lone gas lamp. Its sputtering flame cast doubt on the true nature of the walls. One minute, they were a rich golden hue. The next, Ruta stared at filthy paper peeling away from the plaster in ragged strips. Long streaks smudged across a spot illuminated beneath the lamp. She looked closer and saw dirty fingerprints. No. Not dirt. Blood. A bloody handprint. Four. Only four fingerprints. One was missing.

Ruta's heart fluttered wildly and her legs jellied. This had been a terrible mistake. She would leave at once. Ruta turned and watched in horror as the last of the illusion crumbled and the house transformed before her eyes into a dark, rotting hole, the rot crawling up the walls to meet her. The smell hit her like a punch, making her gag. And there were rats. Oh, god, how she hated rats. With a little cry, Ruta stumbled forward, as if she could outrun the dark coming to get her. Where was the door? It was nowhere to be found! Almost as if the house were keeping it from her. As if it wanted to keep her here.

"'And upon her forehead was a name written in Mystery: Babylon the Great, the Harlot...'"

She couldn't see the stranger but she could hear him, now whistling that god-awful song of his. There had to be another way out of here! A window off to her right looked promising, and she raced to it. Through the wooden slats nailed there, she could see a bum stumbling into the vacant lot across the street to take a piss.

"Hey! Hey, mister, help me! Please help me!" she shouted. When he didn't hear her, she beat her palms against the wood. She tore at the immovable planks until her nails were bloodied, her palms crosshatched with splinters. Outside, the oblivious drunk finished his business and wandered off into the night, and Ruta sank to the filthy floor, sobbing.

When Ruta was three, her mother had locked her in a trunk so the landlord wouldn't find out they'd had another baby and kick them out on the street. She'd sat there alone, cramped, quiet in the dark, and utterly terrified. It seemed like hours before they let her out, and ever since, any feeling of being trapped made her feel like a scared child again. Panic emptied her mind of logic. She wandered the sprawling house in desperation. Mazelike hallways funneled her into squalid rooms; doors opened onto brick walls. All around her, she heard the man's terrible whistling. At last she spied a door she hadn't tried. She put her hand on the knob. The floor gave way beneath her, and she plummeted down a long chute into a foul, forgotten hole of a basement. Her ankle throbbed where it had bent beneath her weight and she cried out with the pain. She tried to take a step but it was agony, and she crashed back to the hard, cold dirt floor.

The floors above her creaked. She could hear the stranger's distant whistling. Her mind emptied of everything but thoughts of survival. She blinked in the darkness, forcing her eyes to adjust. She had fallen quite a ways; the cellar was very deep, probably twenty feet below street level. She was sure she could scream all day and not be heard. What she needed was a weapon. She dragged herself by inches, feeling with her hand for something, anything she could use. Finally, her hand came to rest on a smooth stick. It was lightweight, but applied with enough force against an eye or a throat, it could wound. She held the stick tightly to her chest and waited. Far above her, a door clanged open, allowing the thinnest shaft of light to penetrate. She could see a staircase behind a wall, but there was no way she could manage it in her current state. The stick was her best shot. She might have to do more than wound.

Mr. Hobbes closed the door and the light vanished. She was plunged into total darkness again, just like in the trunk. Ruta struggled to keep her breathing quiet when she wanted to scream with all her might. The stranger's footsteps drummed dully but evenly toward her, and she realized he no longer had his cane. His song echoed in the cellar. This time, he added words: "Naughty John, Naughty John, does his work with his apron on. Cuts your throat and takes your bones, sells 'em off for a coupla stones."

The saliva caught in the back of Ruta's throat; she was too frightened to swallow. The old furnace flared suddenly to life, filling the room with an orange light that cast macabre shadows.

Ruta scuttled behind the gauzy ruin of a curtain hanging on a forgotten clothesline and watched through the grainy fabric. She couldn't see Mr. Hobbes, but she could still hear him.

"'...Babylon the Great, the Harlot Adorned and Cast upon the Sea, the Abomination of the Earth. And this was the fifth offering as commanded by the Lord God.'"

Ruta's tongue was heavy in her mouth. Disquieting things skittered at the edges of her vision, but when she turned her head, they had vanished. Her left leg had gone numb.

"'And I saw a new heaven and a new earth: for the first heaven and the first earth were passed away; and there was no more sea. And I John saw the holy city, new Jerusalem, coming down from God out of heaven, prepared as a bride adorned for her husband. And I heard a great voice out of heaven saying, Behold, the tabernacle of God is with men, and he will dwell with them, and they shall be his people, and God himself shall be with them, and be their God.' Are you listening, Ruby?"

Ruta held fast to her stick and was silent.

The man fed something into the furnace and it flared. "'And he that sat upon the throne said, Behold, I make all things new. I am Alpha and Omega, the beginning and the end. I will give unto him that is athirst of the fountain of the water of life freely. He that overcometh shall inherit all things; and I will be his God, and he shall be my son.'"

The man walked the perimeter of the room as he spoke. "'But the unbelieving, and the abominable, the whoremongers and idolaters shall have their part in the lake which burneth with fire and brimstone. For only the chosen shall rise with the Beast. And the world fall to ash.'"

He was on the far side of the room; she could tell by his voice. Ruta's vision blurred and her stomach roiled. With horror, she realized she could not move her legs at all. What was happening to her? She thought back to the doused handkerchief and the coffee she'd drunk, and her heart beat wildly. What had been in them?

She looked again at the stick in her hand and saw that it was a bone. Ruta cried out and dropped it in revulsion. The curtain shot back. Mr. Hobbes loomed over her like a fiery god.

"Don't be put off by my appearance, my dear. I am only beginning to manifest."

His arms and neck had been branded with strange tattoos, symbols she didn't understand. The symbols rippled and bulged. His flesh moved as if something slithered just underneath. The fear could only find voice in her first language, and so she whispered the prayers in Polish.

The man frowned. "Prayers? I thought you were a modern girl for a modern age."

Backlit by the furnace, the stranger was a dark demon. The numbness had reached her arms now. Ruta's teeth chattered. "P-please. Please. I w-won't tell nobody."

"But you will." The stranger dragged Ruta by her useless arm. "I told you that you had an important destiny to fulfill, and so you shall: You, Ruby Bates, are the beginning of the end. *Naughty John, Naughty John, does his work with his apron on. . . .*"

When he reached the wall just behind the furnace, he felt along it with his bone-pale fingers. A hidden door opened, revealing another, secret room inside.

"*Nie, nie, nie,*" Ruta whispered, as if she could will the door to stay closed.

"'I am he that liveth, and was dead; and, behold, I am alive for evermore, amen; and have the keys of hell and of death.'"

He smiled at her, and in his eyes she saw the fire and the endless swirling black, and her bladder let go.

"The ritual begins again," the stranger said. He pulled Ruta into the hidden room, and all she could do was scream.

PASSING STRANGER

"New York City's famous Hotsy Totsy Club presents the Count Carruthers Orchestra and the beautiful Hotsy Totsy Girls!"

In the wings, Memphis Campbell watched as the scantily clad chorines launched into a high-energy dance number. The club was on fire tonight. Gabe's trumpet wailed, and the Count's fingers tore up all eighty-eight keys on the piano. Gabe played a bit from "America the Beautiful," turning it briefly into a dirge and letting his trumpet slide into despair before picking up the beat again. The white folks in the audience didn't get it, but smiles broke out on the faces of the black folks.

Gabe hit his last piercing note. The audience applauded as the chorines bowed and sashayed offstage laughing and talking. A curvaceous girl named Jo stroked Memphis's cheek as she walked past. "Hey, Memphis."

"Hey, yourself."

Memphis's pal Alma rolled her eyes as she adjusted the front of her costume. "You making money or making time tonight, Memphis?"

"Both, I hope."

Jo giggled and tickled her fingers up his arm. Memphis employed the smile with Jo. "'PASSING stranger!'" he said, putting his hand to his heart. "'You do not know how longingly I look upon you/You must be he I was seeking, or she I was seeking (it comes to me as of a dream)/I have somewhere surely lived a life of joy with you...'"

"You write that, baby?" Jo purred.

Memphis shook his head. "That's Walt Whitman. 'To a Stranger.' You ever read his poems?"

"She doesn't read anything other than the gossip columns," Alma said. Jo gave her a murderous glance.

"You're missing out," Memphis said, aiming his full-wattage smile at Jo.

"This boy lives at the library over on 135th Street. Wants to be the next Langston Hughes," Alma informed everyone.

"That so?" Jo asked.

"I could read some poems to you sometime."

"How 'bout Sunday?" Jo said. She licked her lips.

"Sundays always were my lucky days."

Alma rolled her eyes again and pulled Jo back into line. "Come on, girls. We don't have time for foolishness. We need to get changed for the moon number."

"Bye, baby." Jo blew Memphis a kiss and he pretended to catch it.

"Memphis!" the stage manager bellowed around the cigar clenched between his teeth. "I'm not paying you to play with the girls. Papa Charles wants you. Hop to."

In the narrow hallway, Memphis passed Gabe and the Count, who were on their way out back.

"Hey, boss," Gabe said, gripping Memphis's hand. "We going to that rent party on Saturday? Plenty of flossy chicks and whiskey."

"Whose whiskey? Don't get some coffin varnish off someone you don't know and put us both in the morgue." It was a fact that disreputable bootleggers sometimes mixed the booze with kerosene or gasoline.

Gabe spread his hands wide and grinned. "Leave it to Gabe, brother."

Memphis laughed. Other than Isaiah, Gabe had been the one constant in his life. They'd met in the fourth grade, when Gabe had gotten into trouble with the principal for selling cigarettes behind the school and Memphis had been assigned to be his buddy and set him straight. It set the tone of their friendship: Memphis was still there to get Gabe out of trouble, and Gabe was there to help Memphis get into it. The one thing Gabe was serious about was music. He was one of the hottest trumpet players in town. Word was definitely spreading about the skinny kid with the big sound. Even Duke Ellington had come to hear Gabe play. It was one of the reasons Papa Charles kept him on. Gabe was a prankster and a troublemaker, but once he started playing that horn, it was all worth it.

"Going out for a smoke. You want some mezz?" Gabe asked. His eyes were already a little red.

Memphis shook his head. "Gotta keep a clear head, Gabe."

"Suit yourself, Grandma."

"I usually do," Memphis said. He swiped a hand across the overhead light, feeling the warmth of the bulb, and then passed through a tunnel into the building next door where all the offices were. Several secretaries sat at long tables, counting money from the morning's numbers racket. Memphis tipped his cap to them and slipped into Papa Charles's office. From his seat behind a mahogany desk, Papa Charles waved Memphis toward a waiting chair while he finished his telephone call.

Papa Charles was the undisputed king of Harlem. He controlled the numbers racket, the horse races and boxing matches. He ran the bootlegging and fixed things with the cops. If you needed a loan, you went to Papa Charles. When a church needed a new building, Papa Charles gave them the money. Schools, fraternal organizations, and even Harlem's professional basketball team, the New York Renaissance, or Rens, were financed in part by Papa Charles, the Dapper Gentleman. And at several clubs and speakeasies, like the Hotsy Totsy, he showcased some of the best musicians and dancers in town.

"Well, as long as I'm running the numbers in Harlem, it'll stay black," Papa Charles said firmly into the telephone, "and you can tell Dutch Schultz and his associates that I say so." He hung up forcefully and opened the lid on a silver box, selecting a cigar. He bit off the end and spat it into his wastebasket. Memphis lit the cigar's tip, trying not to cough as the first puffs of smoke billowed out.

"Trouble?"

Papa Charles waved the thought and the smoke away. "White bootleggers want to run the Harlem rackets now. I don't intend to let them. But they're working hard at it. Heard the police raided one of Queenie's joints last night."

"I thought she paid off the police."

"She does." He let that land while he drew on the cigar, turning the air thick and spicy. "The white folks'll lose interest in our games. They've got bootlegging to keep them busy. Still, might want to be extra careful out there. I'm telling all my runners. How's your aunt Octavia doing?"

"Fine, sir."

"And Isaiah? He getting along all right?"

"Yes, sir."

"Good, good. And on the streets?"

"Smooth as Gabe's licks."

Papa Charles smiled. "Best way to learn the business is from the streets up. Someday, you can be working right here next to me."

Memphis didn't want to work for Papa Charles. He wanted to read his poetry at one of Miss A'Lelia Walker's salons, alongside Countee Cullen, Zora Neale Hurston, and Jean Toomer—maybe even beside Mr. Hughes himself.

"You all right, son? Something the matter?"

Memphis found his smile. "You know me, sir. I don't wear worry."

Papa Charles smiled around his cigar. "That's the Memphis I know."

Good old Memphis. Reliable Memphis. Charming, easygoing Memphis. Look-after-your-brother Memphis. Memphis had been the star once. The miracle man. And it had ended in sorrow. He wouldn't ever risk that again. These days, he kept his feelings confined to the pages of his notebook.

"It's time to collect the gratuities from our grateful friends," Papa Charles said—code for the protection money every business paid to the Dapper Gentleman if they wanted to *stay* in business and have his protection. The city ran on corruption as much as on electricity.

"Yes, sir."

"Memphis, you sure you all right?"

Memphis offered up the smile again. "Never better, sir."

On the way out of the club, Memphis nodded at Papa Charles's chauffeur, who stood guard beside a brand-new Chrysler Imperial before blending into the crowds out for a good time on Lenox Avenue. He hit up the various nightclubs Papa Charles ran—the Yeah

Man, the Tomb of the Fallen Angels, and the Whoopee—along with smaller speakeasies hidden in brownstone basements on tree-lined side streets. Memphis followed big men through back rooms gray with cigarette smoke where people sat at green felt tables playing cards, hustling pool, or rolling craps. The women would cup his chin, call him handsome, ask him to dance. He'd beg off, using the smile to smooth the rejection. Sometimes the club owners offered him a drink or let him listen in on the jazz or watch the revue girls dance. Other times, they made him wait upstairs in a dimly lit office, where Memphis was never sure if they'd be coming back with money or a Tommy gun. In the neat columns of the ledger, he wrote down the amount paid, dodging questions about whether Papa Charles knew if the fix was in for this fight or that game.

"I'm just a runner," he'd say and use the smile.

On the streets, he kept an eye out for plainclothes cops. If he got arrested, Papa Charles would have him out in a few hours, but he still didn't want to take the chance.

It was well after eleven when Memphis returned to the Hotsy Totsy. Gabe came running up to him. "Where you been, boss man?"

"Out on business. Why?"

"Come quick! It's Jo. She fell and hurt herself."

"Then call a doctor."

"She's asking for *you*, Memphis."

Jo sat at the bottom of the stage stairs, crying, surrounded by concerned chorines. Through the crack in the curtain, Memphis could see the audience getting restless. It was time for the next number to start, and already Jo's ankle was swelling up. "Caught my heel on the second step and turned it," she burbled through her tears. "Oh, please, Lord, don't let it be broken."

"You'd better tell Francine she's on," one of the chorines said.

Jo shook her head. "I gotta go on tonight. I need the money!" She looked up at Memphis, her eyes hopeful. "I remembered about you. What you could do. Please, can you help me, Memphis?"

Memphis's jaw tightened. "I can't do that anymore."

Jo sobbed and Gabe put a hand on Memphis's arm. "Come on, brother. Just try...."

"I told you, I can't!" Memphis shook off Gabe's hand and stormed down the stairs as the stage manager cradled Jo in his arms and carried the miserable girl away. Onstage, the emcee announced the next number, the Black Bottom, and the other girls plus Francine scampered out wearing smiles and very little else. Memphis deposited the money he'd collected on his rounds with the secretaries. He pushed out into the night again, his mind troubled by memories of a time when he was someone else, a golden boy with healing hands: Miracle Memphis, the Harlem Healer.

The healing power had come on Memphis suddenly after an illness when he was fourteen. For days, he'd lain in a state of semi-consciousness, seeing the strangest sights as the fever burned through his body. His mother never left his side. When he recovered, they went straight to church to give thanks. On that Sunday morning at the old Mother AME Zion Church, Memphis healed for the first time. His seven-year-old brother, Isaiah, had fallen out of a tree and broken his arm. The bone stuck up under the skin at a terrible angle. Memphis was only trying to quiet his screaming brother when he put his hands on him. He never expected the intense warmth that built suddenly between Isaiah's skin and his own hands. The trance came on him hard and fast. His eyes rolled back and he felt as if he had left his body and was trapped inside a waking dream. He saw things in that strange empty space he inhabited for those long seconds, things that he didn't understand:

faces in the mist, spectral shadows, and a funny man in a tall hat whose coat seemed to be made of the land itself. There was a bright light and a fluttering of wings, and when Memphis came to, shaking, a crowd had gathered around him in the churchyard. Isaiah had weaseled out from under his brother's touch and was swinging his arm around in perfect circles. "You fixed it, Memphis. How'd you do that?"

"I-I don't know." Despite the New York summer heat soaking the collar on his Sunday best, Memphis shivered.

"It's a miracle," someone said. "Praise Jesus!"

Memphis saw his mother standing at the edge of the awestruck congregation, one hand pressed to her mouth, and was afraid she might slap him for what he'd done. Instead, she hugged him close. When she stepped back, there were tears in her eyes. "My son is a healer," she whispered, cupping his face.

"You hear that? This boy's a healer," someone shouted. "Let us pray."

They bowed their heads and reached out for him, and as Memphis felt their hands blessing his head and shoulders, his mother's fingers clasped in his, his fear turned to exultation. *I did that*, he thought in wonder. *How did I do that?*

Only Aunt Octavia was skeptical. "Why would the good Lord give that gift to a boy?" she'd asked his mother later, in the house on 145th Street. They were in the front parlor sitting beside the radio and snapping beans for the next day's supper. It had been too hot to sleep well, and Memphis had gotten up for a cup of water. When he heard them talking, he hid in the darkened hallway, listening. "Sometimes a gift is really a curse in disguise, Viola. A test from the Good Lord. Might be the Devil himself in that boy."

"Hush up, Octavia," his mother had said. She rarely stood up to her older sister, and Memphis felt proud of her even as Octavia's words sowed doubt under his skin. "My boy is something special. You'll see."

"Well, I hope you're right, Vi," Octavia had said after a pause, and then there was nothing but the sharp *snip, snip, snip* of string beans being broken into halves and dropped into a bowl.

News of Memphis's powers quickly spread through the Harlem churches. When Pastor Brown balked at using Memphis's gift during services at Mother AME Zion—"We're not that sort of religion, Viola"—Memphis's mother had taken him to the various Pentecostal and Spiritualist storefront churches, over Octavia's objections: "Low-class holy rollers—and some of 'em talk to the *dead*, Vi. Nothing good's gonna come of this, mark me."

There, on the fourth Sunday of every month, for eight months running, Memphis stood beside the pulpit looking out at faces both hopeful and skeptical. While the choir sang "Wade in the Water," and people prayed and sometimes shouted out to God, congregants would come forward with their ailments and Memphis would lay hands on them, feeling the warmth build under his palms, seeing into that other place in his mind, the place of vague faces in the mist. Miracle Memphis. And then, when it had mattered most, the miracle had failed him. No, not just failed—turned on him.

From time to time, he'd catch Octavia eyeing him from the doorway, wearing an expression somewhere between contempt and fear. "Doesn't take much for the Devil to get inside, Memphis John. You remember that."

Memphis usually thought his aunt's obsessive thoughts about the Devil were crazy. But what if she was right? What if there was something terribly wrong, a shadow side to him that was biding its time, waiting? The thought was like his dream—unsettling and unreadable.

The trouble with Jo back at the club had left Memphis rattled, and so, his business taken care of for the evening, he hopped the double-decker Fifth Avenue Coach Company bus going uptown and got off around 155th Street. He walked several blocks north, then west toward the river, where the houses thinned out, until he came to a small African graveyard on a bluff, the final resting spot of freed slaves and black soldiers. There, in the peace and quiet of possible ancestors, Memphis liked to sit and write. Memphis found the lantern he kept secreted inside the knothole of a sheltering oak. He struck a match from the book he'd pocketed at the Yeah Man club. The flame inside the lantern gave off a comforting glow. Memphis perched on the cool ground and opened his notebook. In its way, writing was like healing: a cure for the loneliness he felt. Sometimes the cure took; other times, it didn't. But he kept trying. He bent his head over his notebook, writing by lantern light, chasing after words like trying to grab the tails of comets. All around him, Harlem was alive with writers, musicians, poets, and thinkers. They were changing the world. Memphis wanted to be part of that change.

He was startled from his concentration by the cawing of a crow perched on a headstone nearby. Memphis's mother had told him that birds were heralds. Warnings. It was silly, of course—nothing more than some leftover African superstition. Birds were just birds. He was reminded for just a moment of the crows in his dream, but the thought was fleeting. The hour was late and Memphis's eyes burned with exhaustion. There would be no more words tonight. He blew out the lantern, bundled everything into his knapsack, and headed down the empty street with its lonely gas lamp. The moon sat full and gold above the ruin of the old house on the hill, the former Knowles mansion, now dwarfed by the rows of apartment buildings in the distance. No one had lived there in all the time Memphis had been going to the graveyard. The house gave Memphis the creeps, and he usually walked down the center of the street, far from it.

Cold light washed over the boarded-up windows and refuse-strewn lawn. It pooled on the marble limbs of a broken angel statue and made the dead trees seem alive. Memphis glanced quickly at the house and stopped. From the corner of his eye, he thought he saw movement. Something about the house was different, though he couldn't say what.

The bothersome crow flitted past, making Memphis jump, and he hurried on his way. Once back on the crowded streets of Harlem, Memphis shook his head and laughed softly at his skittishness. He took comfort in the neon signs, the wild strands of jazz creeping out of clubs whenever happy swells of people pushed through the doors in their finery. Blind Bill Johnson shuffled up the street, his cane testing the path ahead of him. Memphis didn't feel like talking to the old man, so he dodged down a side street and raced on. It felt good to run in the warm September night. He had his notebook of poems, his books, and a pocket full of money. What was there to be worried about? It was time to stop worrying and get on with living. With his world slung on his back, Memphis walked the rest of the way back to Harlem. He passed the brownstones of Sugar Hill, peering from afar into the warm amber light of windows and lives he hoped would someday be his, and headed for home.

His brother, Isaiah, was asleep in the narrow bed by the window in the back room. Memphis took off his shoes, undressed, and slipped into his own bed as quietly as possible. Isaiah sat up and Memphis held his breath, hoping his brother would roll over and fall back to sleep. He hoped he hadn't woken him.

Isaiah sat very still, staring into the dark. "I am the dragon. The beast of old," he said.

Memphis raised himself onto his elbows. "Ice Man? You all right?"

Isaiah didn't move. "I stand at the door and knock."

A few seconds later, he fell back on the pillow, fast asleep. Memphis felt his brother's forehead, but it was cool. Nightmare, he guessed. Memphis sure knew about those. He rolled onto his side and let his body go limp. His eyelids grew heavy and sleep overtook him.

In the dream, Memphis stood on a dusty road bordered by cornfields. Overhead, the clouds tangled into dark, angry clumps. In the distance sat a farmhouse, a red barn, and a gnarled tree stripped of leaves. A crow cawed from a mailbox on a wooden post. The crow flew to the fields and perched on the shoulder of a tall man in a funny hat. His skin was as gray as the sky, his eyes black and shining. The half moons of his nails were caked with dirt, and every finger wore a ring. "The time is now," the man said, though Memphis did not see his lips move.

The dream shifted. Memphis stood in a long corridor. At the end was a metal door, and on the door was the symbol: the eye surrounded by the sun's rays, a lightning bolt directly beneath it like a long zigzag of a tear. He heard the soft flutter of wings, and then he was lost in heavy fog, and his mother's voice called to him: "*Oh, my son, my son . . .*"

Memphis was not aware of the tears damp on his own cheeks. He moaned softly in his sleep, rolled over, and was lost to a different dream, of pretty chorus girls waving fans of feathers who blew sweet kisses and promised him the world.

EVIE'S DREAM

Evie's dream began as it often did, with fog and the snow and the forest. James stood on the edge of the wood in his crisp khaki uniform, pale and grim. Evie's lips formed his name in her sleep, but inside the dream, there was no sound. With one arm, James motioned to her to follow.

The trees grew sparser as they came to a small clearing filled with soldiers. A boy in sergeant's stripes began shouting orders, and the camp blurred with sudden movement—cigarettes tamped under boots, tin coffee mugs abandoned, gas masks donned, positions taken, every man alert and waiting. Dark clouds swirled overhead. Flashes of lightning broke the gloom like a charge—one, two, three! Someone was pulling her down into a deep trench, and Evie slid along the earthen, tomblike walls, hiding from an enemy she could not see. There was a haunting silence, like the world holding its breath, and then Evie watched in awe as a fierce wave of bruising light spread across the sky, followed seconds later by a violent force that knocked her to the ground like the punch of an invisible giant.

The air swirled with smoke and ash. Evie climbed out of the trench and fell onto a soldier whose bones shattered into dust. It was as if he'd been hollowed out completely. His eyes were gone, his mouth stretched into a hideous grin. Bloody tears scarred his shriveled, sunken cheeks. Evie screamed and scrambled forward across the scorched ground, where soldiers' strewn bodies lay like trampled wildflowers. The beautiful trees were no more than blackened wisps now. Here and there, she caught glimpses of ghostly soldiers on the field's misty edges, but when she turned her head, they were gone. Evie called for James, and there he was on the path up ahead, safe! She ran to him, but his expression was one of warning. He was saying something, but she couldn't hear it. His eyes. Something was happening to his eyes. James stretched out his arms and threw back his head. There was another blinding flash.

Evie woke, biting off the start of a scream. The little fan beside her bed whirred, but she was drenched with sweat. With trembling fingers, she felt for the lamp switch, then blinked against the sudden light. The unfamiliarity of the new room made her jittery. She needed to breathe. She climbed onto the rickety fire escape and up to the roof, where it was cool and open. Jericho was right—the view was great from up there. Manhattan unfurled before her like a jeweler's velvet adorned with diamonds. The trains still rattled over the tracks, even at this hour. The city was as restless as she was. On the ledge, a pigeon cooed and pecked at scraps of bread.

"You and me, kiddo, we're gonna take this town by storm," Evie joked even as she wiped away the tears that blurred the skyline into fractured light. "Don't be a sap, old girl," she scolded. "Buck up."

Evie let the wind kiss her cheeks. She opened her arms as if to embrace Manhattan. Starting tomorrow, she told herself, things would be different. There would be shopping, a picture show with Mabel. On Saturday, they could take the subway out to Coney Island, dip their toes in the Atlantic, and ride the Thunderbolt roller coaster. In the evening, she'd find a party and dance as if there were no dead brothers or terrible dreams. It was all going to be the berries.

Evie brought her arms back to hug herself. She rubbed her nose on her sleeve and crooned in a soft voice, *"The city's bustle cannot destroy the dreams of a girl and boy. I'll turn Manhattan into an isle of joy."*

The train rattled past, startling the pigeon into flight.

☀

In the blazing canyons of brick and neon, the city carried on. People met and parted, hurried and idled. Subways rumbled. Car horns bleated. Traffic lights cycled from green to yellow to red and back again.

In Harlem, Blind Bill Johnson lay on his cot in the long room of other cots inside the YMCA and waited on sleep. It was warm in the room, like the press of sun on the back of his neck when he used to work the cotton fields back in Mississippi. He could see that butter-thin sun of memory now, the way it had broken through rain clouds and glinted off the dark car that carried the shadow men.

Mabel Rose read Tolstoy by lamplight and tried to block out the sound of her parents' arguing in the other room. At last, she rolled onto her back, staring up at the ceiling and imagining that a few floors above, Jericho lay in his bed, also awake, thinking only of her.

In the African graveyard, leaves scuttled across long-quiet

86

graves and onto the lawn of the house on the hill. The broken angel statue did not feel the cool of the long shadow passing over the yard. Its sightless eyes took no notice of the stranger wiping the blood from his hands as he took in the majesty of the starry sky. And its deaf ears did not hear the chilling whistle of the tune from long ago as it idled briefly on the wind before being lost to the frantic, yearning jazz of the city.

Miss Addie stood at her large bay window looking out at the Central Park Reservoir and Belvedere Castle, bathed in the slightly orange glow of the moon. She rocked gently on her heels and sang a song she had known since childhood.

"Tea's almost ready," Miss Lillian said, joining her at the window. "Ah. Look how the moon hits the Belvedere. Beautiful."

"Indeed." Miss Addie put a hand to the glass, as if she could hold the castle in her palm. "Do you feel the change, sister?"

Miss Lillian nodded solemnly. "Yes, sister."

"They're coming." Miss Addie turned her eyes back to the park, keeping watch over the night until the moon paled against the early dawn sky and the untouched tea had gone ice-cold in its cup.

THE FOUR HORSEMEN OF THE APOCALYPSE

Evie's first week in New York City had proved to be every bit as exciting as she'd hoped. In the afternoons, she and Mabel took the El to the movie palace to watch Douglas Fairbanks, Buster Keaton, and Charlie Chaplin, and one particularly warm day they'd ridden the Culver Avenue Line out to Coney Island. There, they dipped their toes in the cold surf of the Atlantic and strolled past the penny arcades and carnival-like amusements, pretending not to notice the calls of the Boardwalk Romeos who begged for their attention. When Mabel had finished with her schoolwork and Evie with her recommended reading from Will, they window-shopped at Gimbels, trying on shawl-collar coats trimmed in fur and brimless cloche hats that made them feel like movie stars. After, they'd buy freshly roasted peanuts at Chock Full O'Nuts or stop for a sandwich at the Horn & Hardart Automat, where Evie thrilled at retrieving her food from the little glass compartment after she'd deposited her coin and pushed the button.

Evenings, Evie and Mabel went downstairs to the Bennington's shabby dining room and sat beneath its sputtering lights to drink egg creams and plot their great Manhattan adventures. When Mabel had to help her parents at a workers' rally one evening, Evie took the liberty of calling on Theta and Henry in their flat. Henry had met her at the door wearing a smoking jacket over a pair of baggy Moroccan pants worn with an unbuttoned tuxedo shirt. It was clear at a glance that he and Theta couldn't be related—his freckled fairness was a stark contrast to her dark, smoky looks—but it was also clear by the way they were with each other that they were not lovers, only dear friends. Henry had raised an eyebrow at Evie as he leaned against the door frame and said, in his long, slow drawl, "I don't suppose you've come about the leak under the sink?" Evie had laughed and promised to chew enough Doublemint gum to fix it and Henry had swung the door open wide with a grand "Entrez, mademoiselle!" Theta lay on a velvet fainting couch wearing her silk men's pajamas, a peacock-patterned scarf tied dramatically around her head. "Oh. Hiya, Evil. What's doing?" The three of them had knocked back shots of gin stolen from a party Theta had been to at the Waldorf-Astoria Hotel and made up silly songs that Henry picked out on the ukulele, and no one complained that Evie was completely tone-deaf. Then they played cards until the wee hours, and Evie crawled home to Will's apartment just ahead of the morning sun with the feeling that everything was possible in Manhattan and that a great adventure lay ahead of her—just as soon as she slept off the night.

Now the first hints of red and gold limned the treetops in Central Park and an Indian-summer sun shone over Manhattan. Evie, Mabel, and Theta, outfitted in their fashionable best, boarded the crowded trolley for an afternoon jaunt to the movies. The three of them raced to the back and squeezed into a double seat, talking excitedly.

"Evie, how is Jericho these days?" Mabel asked and bit her lip. She tried to seem casual about it, but she had absolutely no poker face, and Evie knew she must be dying inside.

"Who's Jericho?" Theta asked.

"My uncle's assistant," Evie explained. "The big blond fellow."

"He's absolute perfection," Mabel said, and both of Theta's pencil-thin eyebrows shot up.

"You goofy for him?"

"And how," Evie confirmed. "It is my solemn mission to join together these two lovebirds. We're off to a slow start, but I'm sure we'll pick up steam for Operation Jericho now."

"Yeah?" Theta appraised Mabel coolly. "What you need is a visit to the barber, kiddo."

Mabel clamped a hand protectively over the braid coiled at the back of her neck. "Oh. Oh, I don't think I could."

"Well, of course, if you're scared..." Theta winked at Evie.

"Yes, of course. Not all of us can be brave," Evie tutted, patting Mabel's hand.

"I could bob my hair anytime I wanted to," Mabel protested.

"You don't have to, Pie Face," Evie said, batting her lashes.

"Not if you're scared," Theta teased.

"I'll have you know I've faced down angry mobs at my mother's political rallies and walked on picket lines. I'm certainly not afraid of the barber!" Mabel sniffed.

"Fine. Let's put some dough on it. I'll pony up a buck if you bob your hair today."

"Two dollars," Evie chimed.

Mabel paled. But then she tilted her chin just like her society-born mother. "Fine!" she said and signaled the trolley driver to stop.

Mabel glanced nervously at the Esquire Barbershop window,

with its ad proclaiming WE BOB HAIR! LOOK LIKE THE STARS OF STAGE AND SCREEN! along with a drawing of a beautiful flapper in a feathered headdress.

"Mabesie, that style would be swell on you," Evie said. "Jericho would adore it."

"Jericho is a deep thinker and a scholar. He doesn't pay attention to hairstyles," Mabel said, but she sounded terrified.

Theta touched up her lipstick in a store window. "Even a scholar's got eyes, kid."

Evie brushed her hand across an imaginary screen. "Just picture it: You breeze into the museum as a whole new Mabel—Mabel the Enchantress! Mabel the Flapper! Mabel the Hot Jazz Baby!"

"Mabel Who Better Make Up Her Mind or We'll Miss the Picture," Theta added.

"I'll do it."

"Attagirl!" Evie said. She pushed Mabel toward the barbershop. Evie and Theta hurried to the windows and pressed their faces to the glass to watch. Mabel spoke to the barber, who ushered her into a chair. She looked nervously in the girls' direction. Evie waved and gave her a winning smile.

"She won't do it," Theta said.

"I say she will."

"Fine. Let's up the ante on it. Ten dollars."

Ten dollars was a princely sum, but Evie wasn't about to back down.

"Done!"

They shook on it and put their faces back to the window. Inside, Mabel sat in the barber's chair and let him wrap an apron around her neck.

"I'm going to buy the swankiest stockings with your ten dollars, Theta."

Theta smirked. "Ain't over yet, kiddo."

Mabel gripped the padded armrests of the barber's chair as he pumped the foot pedal, lifting her higher. He brought his scissors toward Mabel's hair. Her eyes widened and she jumped from the chair, threw down the apron, and bolted for the door, setting the bell over it tinkling like Santa's sleigh.

"Ah, applesauce!" Evie hissed.

Theta held out her palm. "I'm gonna enjoy those stockings, Evil."

"I'm sorry, I-I just couldn't," Mabel stammered as the girls made their way toward Times Square. "I saw those scissors and I thought I'd faint!"

"It's all right, Mabesie. Not everybody can be a Zelda," Evie said, linking arms with her pal.

"If I'm going to win Jericho, I have to win him as I am."

"And you shall!" Evie reassured her. "Somehow."

At Forty-second Street and Fifth Avenue, they waved to the policeman perched in the glass enclosure atop the traffic tower with its red, green, and yellow signals. He tipped his hat and the girls laughed, buoyed by the crowds crossing amid the motorcars and double-decker buses. Steam pulsed up through sewer grates, as if the city and its bustling people were but part of a great mechanism powered by unseen machinery. As they waited to cross the street, a ragged man in a rickety wheelchair rattled his tin cup at them. He was dressed in a filthy army uniform; his legs were missing below the knees. "A bit of charity for one who served," he rasped.

Evie reached into her coin purse and retrieved a dollar, which she stuffed into his cup. "There you are."

"Thank you," he said. He looked at Evie and muttered softly,

"The time is now; the time is now; the time is now. Careful... careful..."

"If you fall for every sob story on the street, you'll be broke by next week, Evil," Theta cautioned as they crossed to the other side of the street.

"My brother served. He didn't come back."

"Oh, gee, kiddo. I'm sorry," Theta said.

"It was a long time ago," Evie said. She didn't want to start their friendship on such a sour note. "Oh, look at that woman's dress, will you? It's the cat's particulars!"

When they reached the Strand movie palace, the girls bought twenty-five-cent tickets and a white-gloved, red-suited usher showed them to their seats in the balcony overlooking the enormous gilded stage with its gold curtain. Evie had never seen anything so grand. The seats were plush velvet. Friezes and murals decorated the walls. Marble columns reached up to ornately decorated boxes and balconies. In the corner, a man played a Wurlitzer organ, and down below sat a pit for a full orchestra.

The house lights dimmed. The light from the projectionist's booth played across the slowly opening curtain. Evie could hear the clack of the film as it moved through its paces. Flickering words filled the screen: PATHE NEWS. GENEVA, SWITZERLAND. THE 7TH GENERAL ASSEMBLY OF THE LEAGUE OF NATIONS MEETS. Official-looking men in suits and hats stood before a beautiful building. THE ASSEMBLY WELCOMES GERMANY TO THE LEAGUE OF NATIONS.

"We want Rudy!" Evie shouted at the screen. Mabel's eyes widened in alarm, but Theta smirked, and Evie felt a small thrill that her rebelliousness had hit the mark. A man four seats down shushed her. "Get a job, Father Time," she muttered, and the girls tried to stifle their giggles.

On-screen, a movie-star-handsome man inspected a factory and shook the hands of workers. The screen cut to white words on a black background: AMERICAN BUSINESSMAN AND INVENTOR JAKE MARLOWE SETS NEW RECORD IN INDUSTRIAL PRODUCTION.

"That Jake Marlowe sure is a Sheik," Evie murmured appreciatively.

"My parents don't like him," Mabel whispered from beside her.

"Your parents don't like anybody who's rich," Evie said.

"They say he won't let his workers unionize."

"It's his company. Why shouldn't he do as he sees fit?" Evie said.

The disgruntled man waved for an usher. The girls immediately quieted and tried to look innocent. The newsreel ended and the picture began. *Metro presents Rex Ingram's production of Vincent Blasco Ibañez's literary masterpiece THE FOUR HORSEMEN OF THE APOCALYPSE* flashed upon the screen and they fell silent, held rapt by the screen's glow and Rudolph Valentino's beauty. Evie imagined herself on the silver screen kissing someone like Valentino, her picture in *Photoplay* magazine. Maybe she'd live in a Moorish-style mansion in the Hollywood Hills, complete with tiger-skin rugs. That was what Evie loved best about going to the pictures: the chance to dream herself into a different, more glamorous life. But then the film came to the scenes of war. Evie stared at the soldiers in the trenches, the young men crawling across the rain-soaked no-man's-land of the battlefield, falling to explosions. She felt dizzy, thinking of James and her terrible dreams. Why did they haunt her? When would they stop? Why did James never speak to her in them? She'd give anything just to hear his voice.

By the end of the picture, they were all misty-eyed—Mabel and Theta cried for the dead movie star; Evie for her brother.

"There'll never be another like Rudy," Mabel said, blowing her nose.

"You said it, sister," Theta purred as they stepped out into the late-afternoon sun. She stopped when she saw Evie's angry face. "Whatsa matter, Evil?"

"Sam. Lloyd," Evie growled. She took off at a clip toward a cluster of people who were watching a three-card monte game.

"Who's Sam Lloyd?" Mabel asked Theta.

"Don't know," Theta said. "But I'm pretty sure he's a dead man."

"Watch the Queen of Hearts, folks. She's the money card." Sam arranged three cards on top of a cardboard box, moving them around so quickly they were a blur. "Now, sir, sir—yes, you. Would you care to wager a guess? There's no charge for this first round. Just to show you it's an honest game I'm running."

Evie turned the box over, upsetting the cards and the money. "Remember me, Casanova?"

It took Sam a minute, but then he smiled. "Well, if it isn't my favorite nun. How's the Mother Superior, sister?"

"Don't you 'sister' me. You stole my money."

"Who, me? Do I look like a thief?"

"And how!"

The crowd watched the argument with interest, and Sam looked around nervously. He snugged his Greek fisherman's cap low over his brow. "Doll, I'm sorry you got fleeced, but it wasn't me."

"If you don't want me to call a cop over here right this second and tell him you just tried to take advantage of me, you will give me my twenty dollars."

"Now, sister, you wouldn't—"

"I pos-i-tute-ly would! Do you know the Museum of American Folklore, Superstition, and the Occult?"

"Yeah, I know it, but—"

"You can find me there. You'd better bring me my twenty bucks if you know what's good for you."

"Or what?" Sam taunted.

Evie spied Sam's jacket draped across a fire hydrant. She swiped it and slipped her arms through the sleeves.

"Give that back!" Sam growled.

"Twenty bucks and it's all yours. The museum. See you soon-ski!" Laughing, Evie ran down the block.

"Who *is* that?" Mabel asked once she'd caught up and they'd ducked into a cafeteria.

"Sam Lloyd." Evie nearly spat the name. She told them about her encounter with him at Pennsylvania Station, about how he'd kissed her and picked her pocket.

Theta sipped her coffee, leaving a perfect red Cupid's bow mark on the white ceramic cup. "He looks like he could make off with more than just your twenty dollars, if you catch my drift. You better keep an eye on that one, Evil."

"I don't have enough eyes to keep on that one," Evie grumbled.

"Go through his pockets. See if you can find your money," Mabel suggested.

"Why, Mabel. What a spiffing idea! Is that what the progressive education of Little Red Schoolhouse has taught you?" Evie rifled through the jacket's many pockets, but she found nothing except a collection of lint, half a roll of Lifesavers, and a colored-pencil postcard of mountains and tall trees. Something had been scrawled in Russian on the back of it. She knew she could try to read any of the objects to find out more about Sam Lloyd, but it wasn't worth the headache. She'd trust that he'd come looking for the coat. It was September, and the weather would turn soon enough.

When Evie returned to the museum, Uncle Will and Jericho sat at the table talking to a barrel-chested gentleman with the sort of sad brown eyes one saw on pet-store puppies not chosen for Christmas and a nose that looked to have been on the wrong end of a few fights. A detective's badge was pinned to his suit.

"Unc! What'd they get you for? You need bail?"

"Terrence, this is my niece, Evie O'Neill. Evie, this is Detective Malloy."

Despite the sad eyes, Detective Malloy had a warm smile. He offered his hand. "I'm an old friend from the days when your uncle worked for the government."

"Oh? When was that, Unc?" Evie asked.

Will ignored her. "I know I said we'd go to Chinatown for dinner, but I'm afraid I have to go downtown with Detective Malloy for a bit."

"So you *do* need bail," Evie said to Will.

"No, I do *not*. The police have asked for my help. There's been a murder."

"A murder! Oh, my. Let me just change my shoes," Evie said excitedly. "I won't be a minute."

"You're not coming," Uncle Will said.

Evie hopped on one foot while removing her shoes and putting on her new oxfords. "Miss a real-life murder scene? Not on your life."

"It's ugly, Miss. Not meant for a lady," Detective Malloy said.

"I don't scare so easily. I promise I'll be as tough as Al Capone." Evie laced up the first shoe.

"You're staying here." Will turned his back, dismissing her.

"Unc, you promised to take Jericho and me to Chinatown for dinner. No sense coming back uptown for me."

"Evangeline . . ."

"I promise I'll be no trouble at all. I'll sit in the back of the car and wait until you've finished," Evie promised.

Will sighed. "All right by you, Terrence?"

"Okay by me." The detective held the door for her. "But don't complain to me if you have nightmares after, Miss O'Neill."

Evie stifled a gallows laugh at that.

THE HARLOT ADORNED ON THE SEA

The Manhattan Bridge grew bigger as they pulled onto Pike Street. In front of the tenements, a swarm of kids played stickball. As the car moved through, they watched it with narrow-eyed suspicion.

"Future hooligans," Detective Malloy said as he parked the police car at the end of the street. "Any of you little sh—" He glanced at Evie. "Little *brats* touch this car, I promise you they'll be dragging the river for your teeth."

The men stepped out of the car, and Evie followed.

"You were to wait in the car," Will reminded her.

Evie had finagled her way down here. She wasn't about to get this far and not see the actual murder scene. A murder in Manhattan! Already she imagined writing to Dottie and Louise about her adventures: "Dearest darlings, you won't believe what I saw today.... Naturally, like any modern girl, I wasn't afraid...." It would be just like the Agatha Christie novels she adored. But only if she could get closer.

"Oh, Uncle Will, but anything could happen to a girl waiting in the car." Evie glanced meaningfully at the kids playing stick-ball. "What would my mother say?"

She mustered up a face of pure innocence.

"Then Jericho can wait with you."

Evie glanced quickly at Jericho. "I'd feel better staying with you, Uncle Will. I promise I'll stay out of the way. And you don't need to worry that I'm one of those Fainting Frannys who goes goofy at the sight of blood. Why, last year, when Betty Hornsby nearly cut her finger clean off trying to juggle steak knives at a party, I was the only one who didn't wilt on the spot seeing all that blood everywhere. It was a real mess but I was ab-so-lute-ly like a stone. Promise."

She did her best to look completely nonplussed, as if she saw dead bodies all the time. Uncle Will started to object, but Detective Malloy shrugged. "As long as she promises not to faint, it's fine by me. But this is no mystery novel, Miss O'Neill. I'm giving you fair warning."

At the pier, a crowd of onlookers had gathered. Cops in blue uniforms with brass buttons shooed them back. Three oyster houseboats bobbed at the end of the pier where they were tied with hawsers.

"Body's over here," Malloy said. "Was some fishermen that found her. The body was dumped here sometime in the past day or so, near as we can tell. It was hidden by a heap of oyster shells, which is why nobody saw it earlier. You okay, Fitz?"

Uncle Will had paled. "I hate the smell of fish."

"Cheer up. What you're gonna see will make you forget about the smell. Body's a real mess." Malloy glanced at Evie. She refused to give him the satisfaction of a reaction. "Got some kind of weird mumbo-jumbo with it, too, which is why I came for you. I'm telling you, Fitz, I've never seen anything like it."

Malloy led them to a spot piled high with shucked oyster shells, pink-white in the evening sun. A police photographer had set up his tripod. The flash lamp in his hand went off, blinding Evie with its brightness. The lamp's magnesium powder scorched the air, leaving a sharp tang on Evie's tongue. As they drew closer, the smells of fish, urine, and rotting flesh overpowered Evie. A violent heaving washed up inside her, which she willed back down. She breathed surreptitiously through her mouth. Black flies swarmed the spot, and Evie waved them away from her face.

"This is as far as you go, Miss," Detective Malloy said, and it was clear it was an order. He nodded at Jericho in some unspoken male code that indicated Jericho should stay with Evie, which only irritated her further.

Detective Malloy led Will around the wall of oyster shells and she watched her uncle's face go even paler, saw him put a hand to his mouth to hold back a shout or vomit. He turned away for a minute and bent over to breathe, and Evie saw her chance.

"Unc, are you all right?" she said, rushing at him.

"Evie…" he started, but it was too late. Evie had turned around.

The only time she could recall ever feeling so punched clean of breath was the day the telegram from the war department arrived. It took a moment for her mind to register that what lay sprawled on the old wooden pier had been a human being. She took it in by degrees: A shoe half-off. The filthy, shredded stockings pooling around swollen, blackened ankles. The torn dress and bruised limbs. The skin of her eyelids slack and sunken around empty sockets.

Her eyes. The killer had taken her eyes.

Dizziness whooshed up and over Evie as if someone had swung a hammer hard against a carnival bell. She dug her fingernails into her palms to keep herself alert.

The girl's battered body had been arranged on the pier with her arms and legs stretched out. Her head was shorn of all hair except for a few tufts the scissors had missed. Cheap five-and-dime-store pearls ringed her neck, and toy rings encircled her fingers. Her blood-drained face was made up in garish fashion—heavy powder and rouge. A red slash of lipstick barely disguised the blue of her dead lips. HARLOT had been scrawled across her forehead.

A policeman had offered Will smelling salts and he stood, a little woozy. Evie hadn't moved an inch. Back at the apartment, it had seemed very exciting—a real murder scene, something to tell new friends about. But now, looking at the violated corpse, Evie doubted she'd ever want to discuss this. She wished she could unsee it. A single tear trickled down her cheek. She wiped it quickly away and stared down at her shoes.

"She's been dead about a week, give or take," Detective Malloy said. His voice seemed to come to Evie through a tunnel. "Pocketbook has a tag inside with a name and address. Ruta Badowski of Brooklyn. Nineteen years old. Family's been contacted. A little over a week ago, Ruta went to one of those crazy dance marathons with her steady fella, Jacek Kowalski. We pulled him in for questioning, got nothing. He claims he slept on a stoop and went to work at the brick factory the next morning. Boss confirms it."

Evie chanced another peek at the girl's disfigured face. Nineteen. Only two years older than Evie. She'd been out dancing. Now she was dead.

"This is what I wanted you to see." Malloy opened the girl's dress. On her chest, above her dingy brassiere, was a large brand of a five-pointed star encircled by a snake eating its tail.

"What is that, Fitz, some kind of voodoo charm?" Malloy asked.

"It has nothing to do with voodoo. And *voudon* is simply West

African and Caribbean spiritualism, which is nature based," Uncle Will said with impatience.

Malloy made a gesture of apology. "Okay, okay. Don't get sore, Fitz. What is it, then?"

Will crouched low to get a better look. Evie didn't know how he could do it without screaming. "It's a pentacle, a symbol of the universe," Will explained. "Many religions and orders use them— pagans, Gnostics, Eastern religions, ancient Christians, Freemasons. The Seal of Solomon is the most famous such symbol. It's often used as a form of protection."

"Didn't help *her* much," Malloy said.

Uncle Will walked around the body. "This one is inverted." Will gestured to the two points up and the one down. "I've heard it said that the inverted pentagram suggests a lack of balance, the triumph of the material over the spiritual. Some claim that such a pentagram can be used for darker purposes, for sorcery or forbidden magic—to call forth demons or angels." Will stood up and faced away for a minute, taking three big gulps of air and blowing them out again. "Fish. Hate the smell of fish."

"Here, Unc," Evie said, passing him a tiny compact of solid perfume from her purse. Will gave it a sniff and passed it back. Evie held it up to her nose as well. She felt faint again, and she forced herself to look up at the magnificent span of steel arching across the river to Brooklyn.

"Could the murderer work in a factory, or with cattle?" Jericho said, breaking his silence. She hadn't even noticed that he'd come to stand beside her.

"We've already checked around the city to see if the brand looks familiar. Nothing so far," Malloy said. "There's something else."

Malloy signaled for one of the flat foots, who brought him a yellowed scrap of paper, which he handed to Will. Evie inched next to her uncle, reading from just behind.

"'The Harlot, the Whore of Babylon, was adorned in gold and jewels and worldly treasures, and she did look upon the glory of the Beast in all his raiment and cried out, for now her eyes were opened and she knew the wickedness of the world which must be redeemed through blood and sacrifice. And the Beast took her eyes and cast the Harlot Adorned upon the eternal sea within the Mark. This was the fifth offering.'"

"That from the Bible?"

"Not any Bible I've read." Will drew in his notebook and jotted down notes.

Evie pointed to a series of symbols drawn along the bottom of the paper. "What are those?" Her voice sounded foreign to her ears.

Will turned the paper sideways and back. "Not sure yet. Sigils of some sort, I would guess. Terrence, I'd like to ask you some questions. Privately, if you please."

The men moved away to a windy spot down the pier to talk. Evie looked again at the girl's body, focusing on her shoes. They were water-damaged and worn, but Evie could tell they were special, probably the girl's best pair. One rhinestone buckle remained, hanging loose from the strap. It was a final indignity and Evie wanted to right it. She tried to clip it back on, but it wouldn't stick.

"Oh, please," she whispered, near tears.

With renewed determination, she gripped it tightly. The object opened its secrets so quickly that Evie had no time to react. The images were fleeting, like a film sped up: A strip of peeling yellow wallpaper. Furnace. Butcher's apron. A lock turning. The brand. Blue eyes rimmed in red. Terrible eyes, windows into hell.

Whistling—a jaunty little tune horribly out of place, like a lullaby on a battlefield. And then her head was filled with screams.

Gasping, Evie dropped the buckle. She staggered to the edge of the pier and vomited up her pie from the Automat. Behind her, the policemen laughed. "No place for a girl," one said. Someone was handing her a handkerchief.

"Thank you," she said, mortified.

"You're welcome," Jericho said and let her clean up in peace.

On the river, a ferry cut the gray water into undulating peaks that rippled out into smoothness again. Evie watched the ferry chug along and tried to make sense of what she'd just seen. Those horrible pictures in her head were probably clues. But how could she possibly tell anyone how she'd come to know them? What if they didn't believe her? What if they *did* believe her and made her hold that buckle and look again into that nightmare? She couldn't face that. No one had to know about what she'd seen. Uncle Will would sort this out. There was no need for her to say anything.

"Evie. Time to go," Uncle Will called.

"Coming," Evie said, forcing strength into her voice.

A strong wind blew off the East River. It caught the edge of the dead girl's beige scarf, pulling it up like a hand reaching for help. Evie turned and went around the long way, avoiding the sight of her altogether.

KEEPING AWAY THE GHOSTS

"I told you it wasn't a good idea," Uncle Will said. They were sitting in a restaurant in Chinatown. Evie's headache had begun in earnest. All she could do was chase the glistening dumplings in her soup bowl with her spoon.

"Who would do something like that?" Evie asked finally.

"Given the course of human history, the more accurate question is, why don't more people do things of that nature?" Will said. He expertly navigated a piece of beef to his mouth with his chopsticks.

"It could be a gang killing. Maybe her family owed money to someone," Jericho suggested.

"But why go to all that trouble, then?" Will mused. "Why make it seem occult in nature—and oddly occult at that?"

Will and Jericho considered various ideas, rejecting most of them. Evie remained silent. She was desperate for a drink.

"Is it taken from the Book of Revelation?" Jericho asked. "The harlot. The Whore of Babylon."

"Yes, I thought that, too. Revelation does mention the Whore of Babylon. But *the harlot adorned*...It's a very specific phrase. I'm not sure I've heard that before." He shook his head and took another bite of his food. "At least it's not coming to mind."

Evie stared into her bowl and thought of the terrible things she'd seen while holding Ruta Badowski's shoe buckle. What if they were important? "Have...have you ever heard this tune?" Evie asked, then whistled the song she'd heard while under.

Will pursed his lips, thinking it over. "What is it, something from a radio program? If you guess it you win a prize from Pears soap or some such?"

Evie shook her head. It hurt to do so. "Just a silly song I heard the other day. I wondered if it might mean something and..." What? What could she say that made any sort of sense? "It's nothing."

"As you say. Would you like to try the duck?"

Evie fought a wave of nausea as she waved the chopsticks and offending food away. But she felt a sense of relief, too. Perhaps the disconcerting images she'd seen and the song she'd heard had nothing to do with the girl's murder. They could have been anything, really. Anything at all.

A quiet commotion up front drew Evie's attention. The hostess, a girl in a red dress, about Evie's age, shoved a bundle at a young man, speaking to him in Chinese. Her voice carried the tone of an order not to be contradicted. Under the girl's penetrating gaze, the young man slunk away, letting the door to the kitchen bang behind him. The girl in the red dress appeared at their table with a silver tray of small fortune tea cakes. Evie noted her pale green eyes. "Will there be anything else?" she asked with a hint of polite annoyance.

"No, thank you." Uncle Will paid the check while Evie extracted the slip of paper from a tea cake.

"What does it say?" Jericho asked.

"'Your life will soon change.'" Evie tossed it aside. "I was hoping for 'You will meet a tall, dark stranger.' What does yours say, Jericho?"

"'To gain trust you must risk secrets.'"

"Intriguing. Unc?"

Will left his untouched on the tray. "I never read fortunes if I can help it."

They exited onto the narrow, winding cobblestones of Doyers Street, known as "the bloody angle" for its bend and the large number of gangland murders committed there. But that night, the street was peaceful. Across the narrow crooked strip of cobblestone, a crowd of men were lighting candles inside small white lanterns and watching them float up into the dusky sky. The smell of incense wafted into the street.

"Mid-Autumn Festival," Uncle Will explained. "It is an important cultural tradition, a celebration of harvest."

Farther down, paper lanterns adorned the front of a shop: Mee Tung Co., Importers. They fluttered in the evening breeze. Pieces of paper with Chinese lettering had been pasted on a brick wall beside the shop. Men on the street gave the postings a surreptitious glance as they passed by.

"What's that?" Evie whispered.

"Listings of which businesses are not aligned with the Tongs."

"Those silver things for putting ice in gin?" Evie mimed with her fingers. "Adore them!"

"Tongs are brotherhoods or governing associations, and there are two in Chinatown—Hip Sing Tong and On Leong Tong. They've run Chinatown for decades and, from time to time, they've also engaged in bloody warfare. The businessmen put up these postings as a plea of neutrality, so that they will be left out of the violence."

"What's going on there?" Evie asked. A light shone in the window of a shop where a line of men had gathered.

"Sending letters home to their wives, most likely."

"Their wives don't live here with them?"

"The Chinese Exclusion Act of 1882." Uncle Will stared at her, waiting for a response. "What do they teach in schools these days? We're going to have a nation of creationists with no grasp of history."

"Then I suppose it's lucky you're tutoring me."

"Yes. Well," Will said uncertainly before settling into lecturing mode. "The Chinese Exclusion Act was a law designed to keep more Chinese from coming here once they'd finished building our railroads. They couldn't bring their families over. They weren't protected by our laws. They were on their own."

"Doesn't sound terribly American."

"On the contrary, it's very American," Will said bitterly.

They'd passed around the back of the Tea House and saw the boy who'd been browbeaten by the hostess in the restaurant. He was kneeling before a small bowl of fire, feeding thin sheets of colored paper into it.

"What is he doing?" Evie said.

"Keeping the ghosts away," Uncle Will said. He did not offer further explanation.

A PLACE IN THE WORLD

In the back parlor of Sister Walker's brownstone, Memphis waited on the pristine blue sofa while his brother, Isaiah, sat at the dining room table concentrating on a spread of downturned cards. Sister Walker held one in her hand so that only she could see the face of it. "What card am I holding, Isaiah?"

"The Ace of Clubs," Isaiah said.

Sister Walker smiled. "Very good. You got nineteen out of twenty. Very good, indeed, Isaiah. You may help yourself to the candy dish."

"Next time, I'ma get all twenty, Sister." Isaiah reached into the candy dish sitting on the lace doily in the center of Sister Walker's freshly waxed dining room table, fished out two Bit-O-Honeys, and tore off the candy's blue and red waxed paper.

"Well, we'll see, but you did a fine job today. And you feel fine, Isaiah?"

"Yessh, ma'am," Isaiah slurred around the candy.

"Don't talk with food in your mouth," Memphis chided.

"Well, how'm I 'posed to answer? Only got one mouth," Isaiah said, glowering. It didn't take much to make him hot under the collar, Memphis knew.

"Thank you, Sister," Memphis said pointedly, looking at Isaiah, who was ignoring him.

"Of course. Now, Isaiah, you remember what to tell your aunt Octavia, don't you?"

"You were helping me with my 'rithmetic."

"Which I did, so it's not lying. You remember that it's best you not tell your auntie about the other work we do with the cards."

"Don't worry," Memphis said. "We won't, will we, little man?"

"I wish I could tell ever'body, so they'd know I'm something," Isaiah crowed.

"You *are* something, Isaiah," Sister Walker said and handed him another Bit-O-Honey.

"Something else," Memphis teased. He put his hand on Isaiah's head and moved it around. "Got a head like a football. Bumpy, too."

"That's my brains!" Isaiah twisted under Memphis's head-vise grip.

"Is that what it is? Thought you'd been hiding candy up there all this time."

Isaiah took a swipe at Memphis. Laughing, Memphis dodged it and Isaiah charged again, nearly toppling a lamp.

Sister Walker shooed them both toward the door. "All right now, gentlemen, please take your foolishness outside and leave my house in one piece."

"Sorry, Sister," Memphis said. Isaiah was already pulling him out onto the stoop. "See you next week."

Aunt Octavia was waiting for them in the dusky parlor when

they returned. She had on her apron, and she did not look happy. "Where you two been? You know supper's at six fifteen, and if you're late, you don't eat."

"Sorry, Auntie. Sister Walker wanted to be sure that Isaiah understood his arithmetic," Memphis said, shooting Isaiah a warning look.

"Margaret Walker," Octavia harrumphed. She pointed a serving spoon at them. "I don't know if I want you to keep associating with that woman. I've been hearing some things lately about her that don't set well with me."

"Like what?" Isaiah pressed.

"She doesn't go to church, for one."

"She does, too! She's a member at Abyssinian Baptist."

"Ha!" Octavia snorted. "Selma Johnson goes to Abyssinian and says Margaret Walker hardly ever crosses that threshold. The Lord wouldn't know her if you showed him a picture. You're more likely to find that crazy old Blind Bill Johnson in church than you are Miss Margaret Walker."

Memphis hoped he could divert his aunt from what sounded like the beginnings of a tear. She went on tirades sometimes about people for perceived slights and imagined injuries—"*The Lord wouldn't know Miss So-and-So if you showed Him a picture.*" "*Barnabas Damson hasn't got the sense God gave an animal cracker, if you ask me.*" "*Corinne Collins doesn't have any business teaching Sunday school. Why, she can't even keep up with her own children, who run around like a bunch of fools in a foolyard.*" "*Do you know I saw Swoosie Terell at the grocer's, and she acted high-hat, and after I made her a plum pie when her mother was sick.*" He wondered what trivial sin Sister Walker had committed that had set Octavia off.

"They say Margaret Walker got up to some trouble years back," Octavia continued. "She was in prison and moved here to start a new life. If she weren't an old friend of your mama's, I wouldn't give her the time of day."

"Sister Walker was a jailbird?" Isaiah's eyes were huge.

"You don't know that's true, so don't go repeating it, Ice Man," Memphis warned.

"You don't know everything, Memphis John!" Aunt Octavia was in his face. "Ida Hampton told me, and I expect she knows a lot more about what's what than you do."

Memphis wondered if Ida Hampton bothered to tell anyone what was what about her little gambling habit.

"I hear she gets up to all manner of things that ain't right."

Aren't, Memphis silently corrected.

"She might even be into voodoo."

"Sister Walker is not practicing voodoo. She's helping Isaiah with his counting and computing."

"Well, I don't know if it's right for you to be associating with her." Aunt Octavia turned to Isaiah with her hands on her hips, like she meant business. "She do anything like that with you, Isaiah? Make you do magic with cards or put your hands on a crystal ball and talk to spirits? Anything like that?"

Memphis tried to give his little brother a warning with his eyes: *Don't say anything. . . .*

"No, ma'am."

"You look me in my face when you say that. Look me right in my eyes and tell me again." Isaiah's head moved just slightly as he tried to peek around Octavia and keep Memphis in sight, but his aunt got wise and moved over, blocking his view. "Don't you look at your brother. *I'm* the one asking. You look at *me*."

Memphis held his breath. He could hear his blood pounding against his skull.

"She helps me with my 'rithmetic," Isaiah said.

Aunt Octavia stood for a minute. "Well. You be careful around her, you hear me?"

Memphis let out his breath in a small whoosh. "Yes, ma'am," he and Isaiah said as one.

"Memphis, I know you wouldn't get your brother mixed up in the Devil's business," Octavia said, fixing him with a stare. "Not after all this family's been through."

Memphis's jaw tightened. "No, Auntie. I wouldn't."

Octavia held his gaze for a few seconds longer, then poured iced tea into their glasses. "I promised your mama I'd look after you. I couldn't live with myself if something happened to either one of you." Octavia cupped Isaiah's cheeks in her palms and kissed the top of his head. "Go wash yourself up for supper. Memphis, you say grace tonight. And after dinner, you can get the Bible from the china cabinet for Bible study." When Memphis didn't answer, Octavia called loudly from the kitchen, "Did you hear me, Memphis John Campbell?"

"Yes, ma'am," Memphis grumbled. One day, he'd get the two of them out of his aunt's house.

When they were washed to Octavia's satisfaction, they sat around the old wooden table that their grandfather, a carpenter, had made as a wedding present to his young wife, their heads bowed.

"Dear Lord, we thank you for this bounty which we are about to receive...." Memphis said the words without feeling. He wasn't thinking of being grateful for supper, but of the bounty he hoped to receive for himself. He prayed for his place in the world: his own words in a book and a reading at a salon on Striver's Row, a place at the table with Whitman and Cullen and Mr. Hughes.

"...In Jesus's name we pray. Amen."

Octavia passed a casserole dish of baked sweet potatoes.

"I want you two to be very careful out there. You hear about that business down under the bridge?"

The boys shook their heads.

"I expect not. I heard it from Bessie Watkins, who got it from Delilah Robinson, whose husband works down at the docks. He called her just a little while ago. Woman got herself carved up by a madman."

"That's inappropriate dinner talk!" Isaiah said through a mouthful of potatoes.

"Take your elbows off the table. And don't talk with food in your mouth. That's what's inappropriate." Octavia shook her head as she buttered a piece of bread. "Don't know what this world's coming to. Feels like it's all spinning too fast toward Judgment Day."

Memphis hated it when his aunt talked this way. She never missed a chance to worry that the end was nigh—and she never missed a chance to worry everybody else with her thoughts.

"Well, all the same, I want you to be careful. Isaiah, I don't want you going anywhere after dark by yourself. Memphis, you see to it, now."

Memphis swallowed down his mouthful of potatoes. "Me? Marvin left you in charge, didn't he?"

"Don't use that tone with me. And don't call your father Marvin."

"That's his name, isn't it?"

"As a matter of fact, I got a letter from your father today."

"Is he coming back?" Isaiah said.

Octavia put her let-'em-down-easy smile on, and Memphis knew what was in the letter without even reading it.

"Not yet, baby. He's still getting settled."

"He's been getting settled for nearly three years," Memphis said, dropping an unwieldy spoonful of beans onto his plate.

"The man's working hard and sending back money for the two of you. You don't know everything, Memphis John."

"What happened to the lady under the bridge?" Isaiah asked, and Memphis shot his aunt a dirty look.

"Never mind about that, now. Eat your beans. And drink your milk or you won't grow."

"And then we'll have to call you Shrimpy. Old Shrimpy Campbell," Memphis teased, trying to distract his brother. "So puny, folks had to carry him around on a piece of toast. So small he wore a hat made from a tooth. So incredibly stunted that even the tadpoles felt sorry for him."

Isaiah blurbled up some milk, laughing. Octavia started to reprimand them both, but even she couldn't keep from giggling. So Memphis kept the story going, spinning it out wildly, as if it could weave them all together and keep them there in that moment with strings of words.

In the quiet of her kitchen, Sister Walker turned on the radio. It hummed and hissed, then came to life with a man's voice promising the benefits of the Parker Dental System. She left it on. That nagging cough was back, and she fished a lozenge from a tin near the sugar canister, then lit a match under the kettle for tea. The work with Isaiah was promising. Very promising. It had been a long time since she'd seen anybody like him. But she cautioned herself against too much excitement. She knew well that such a promise could flare, then dim and fall away entirely, like she'd heard it had with Memphis.

Sister Walker stepped back into the parlor and turned on a lamp. The bulb chased the evening shadows from the room. She lifted a painting of Paris from its hook and rested it against the wall by her feet. Behind the painting, a small, faint square had been cut into the plaster. She lifted the square and from the space inside the wall retrieved a thick portfolio. Sitting on the pristine sofa, she flipped through the files, reading over the material, looking for anything she might have missed. In the kitchen, the teakettle screamed. Sister Walker startled, then laughed at her own skittishness. She secured the files and sealed the wall, centering the picture again. The tea was hot; it soothed the rattle in her chest as she riffled through the newspaper clippings she'd been accumulating.

If she was right about Isaiah Campbell, the power was coming back. What did that mean? How many others like him were there? What were they capable of?

And how long before they were found?

THE HEARTS OF MEN

It was late when Evie, Will, and Jericho returned to the museum. Up in the tall stacks of the library, Uncle Will pushed from shelf to shelf on the rolling ladder, running a finger along weathered spines, handing things to Jericho. He shouted down to Evie, "See if you can locate a Bible. You should find one in the collections room."

Evie didn't relish going into that room, especially at night. "Can't Jericho do it? He knows the museum better than I do."

"Jericho is assisting me, and as far as I can tell, you're capable of walking. You did insist on coming today, did you not?"

"Yes, but—"

"Then make yourself useful."

Evie stepped quickly through the rooms of the museum, switching on lamps as she went. She didn't care if the electric bill was enormous; she wanted it as bright as the Great White Way. At the doorway of the collections room, Evie paused, searching with her eyes only, in the hope that she'd locate what she needed without having to actually walk around in that cavernous space filled with mysterious objects. When it was clear she'd have to go in, she cranked up the old Victrola to keep her company and chase away the shivers. It was a tinny recording of someone playing ragtime piano. The jaunty tune helped ease her jitters as she got on with her search of the room. In the corner by the fireplace, she tripped over something under the Persian rug. Lifting a corner, she saw an iron ring in the floor for a small door, like a storm cellar. It was too heavy to lift and looked as though it hadn't been touched in years. She patted the rug back down. On a side table, Evie spied a Bible holding up a potted fern. "And Mother says *I'm* a heathen."

The music had stopped. The record hissed with a few seconds of silence, and then a man on the record began talking. "Been able to see the dead all my life," he drawled. "Some of 'em just wants peace and rest. Not all of 'em, though. Not by a long shot. There's evil in this world, evil in the hearts of men, evil that live on—" Evie scraped the needle across the record and ran from the room without turning out the lights.

"What took you so long?" Will asked when Evie came panting into the room. He and Jericho had assembled a stack of books, which they were tucking into Will's attaché case.

"I walked to Jerusalem for the Bible. I knew you'd want an original," Evie snapped. "Did you know there's a door in the floor?"

"Yes," Will answered.

"Well, where does it *go*?" Evie asked with irritation.

"There are stairs to a secret cellar and a tunnel. This was a stop on the Underground Railroad. Sojourner Truth herself hid former slaves below," Will explained. He took the Bible and put it in his case. "It's probably only home to rats and dust now. Shall we?"

Evie and Jericho waited on the long, wide front steps as Uncle Will locked the museum. The lamps had come on, giving Central

Park an eerie glow. Out of the corner of her eye, Evie caught sight of something that drew her gaze back.

"What is it?" Jericho asked. He followed Evie's gaze into the park.

"I thought I saw someone watching us," Evie said, scanning the park. She saw nothing there now. "I must've been mistaken."

"It's been a very long day," Jericho said gently. "I wouldn't be surprised if your eyes played tricks on you."

"I suppose you're right," Evie said, but she had the nagging feeling she'd seen Sam Lloyd, of all people. She had a vague impression of him leaning against a tree in that overconfident posture that annoyed her so. But Jericho was right—there was no one there now, only the lamppost and the park.

☼

Sam stayed hidden behind a jagged slope of rock until they were gone. She'd seen him. Just for a second, but it was enough. What was it about that girl that made him lose his street smarts? He'd come to the museum hoping to sweet-talk her into giving him back his jacket, but then he'd seen the detective and decided to return when the museum was empty to steal the jacket—and anything else he might need.

Sam had bided his time in the hustle and bustle of Times Square. He'd spotted his mark in a sailor idling uncertainly on the corner of Broadway and Forty-third Street. The streets had been crowded with people heading home from work. Most pickpockets considered this a good time to ply their trade, when folks were distracted. But Sam had a little something extra on his side: an eerie ability to move among people unnoticed. It wasn't that he was invisible; more that he could redirect people's thoughts elsewhere so that their eyes simply didn't register him. He had only to think, *Don't see me*, and the person wouldn't. He was quick, too, moving with catlike speed. In those moments, all he heard was his own rhythmic breathing as he extricated a wallet from a pocket, snatched a purse from a restaurant table, or stole bread from a store shelf. He didn't know why it worked, or how—only that it did. It was how he had survived on his own for the past two years.

He had a clear memory of the first time it had happened. He'd been young—ten or eleven, maybe; it was sometime after his mother had left. His father had a watch, which had belonged to Sam's grandfather. Sam had been told not to touch it, and it was precisely that edict that made the watch so appealing. One day he'd sneaked it out of his father's drawer and smuggled the treasure in his coat to show the other boys in the schoolyard in the hope that they would understand its value and stop teasing him for his accent, his clothes, his smallness. Instead, they'd ridiculed him. "This? It's just a cheap watch," the leader said, and he smashed it on the ground. Sam had been afraid to go home and face his father. As he sat on the sofa waiting, he wished for a place to hide. When his father came home, Sam's fear was so great that he felt like a small child again, imagining that he could simply close his eyes in a game of hide-and-seek and the other person wouldn't see him. He heard his father's footsteps coming closer, heard him calling Sam's name. *Don't see me*, Sam thought. "Don't see me," he whispered over and over, like a prayer. And then, oddly, his father looked right at him and kept walking, calling his name as if he were a ghost.

Sam was at a loss to explain it. He remembered something strange his mother had said to him once. They were in the bathroom, and she was cleaning the scrapes he'd gotten after the school bullies chased him home and pushed him down on the street. "Don't worry, *lyubimiy*. You have gifts they do not." "What do you mean?" he'd asked, wincing as she pressed a damp cloth to his scraped chin. "In time, you will see." In time, he did see, but he wondered if that was what she had meant after all and, if so, how she could have known.

Trying to keep warm in the slight chill, Sam had watched the sailor carefully and thought of his jacket. It wasn't the wool peacoat itself but the postcard hidden inside his pocket that mattered. It wouldn't seem like much to anyone else—just a worn drawing of majestic, snow-capped mountains and tall trees. No helpful postmark accompanied it. On the back were three words scrawled in Russian. That postcard was the only thing Sam had brought with him from his father's house in Chicago when he ran away, taking refuge in a traveling circus heading east. In the six months since he'd arrived in New York, he'd barely been able to survive. But fortunes could change quickly. The papers were full of stories of self-made men, like Henry Ford and Jake Marlowe. Sam, too, would make his fortune, and then he'd find the place in the postcard. He'd find *her*.

Evie, her uncle, and the Teutonic giant had obviously left for good, so Sam flicked open his Swiss Army knife and easily picked the lock on the museum's door. For an egghead, that professor was pretty dumb about safeguarding his treasures. Street light pressed against the museum's stained-glass windows. It gave the gloom inside a warm amber glow. Sam waited for his eyes to adjust, then slipped through the quiet old mansion looking for his jacket. This whole affair could've been avoided if he'd used his skill on Evie O'Neill back at Penn Station. But for some reason, he'd wanted her to see him. He'd wanted to talk to her. And when the time came, he'd wanted to kiss her as much as he'd wanted her money. That had been his undoing. Now here he was in the Museum of the Creepy Crawlies, searching in the dim light for his jacket.

It had been so much simpler with the sailor. The man had

idled on the corner, confused about whether to go forward or turn right or left, and in that moment, Sam had read the poor chump perfectly. When the sailor had finally crossed the street, Sam had come from the other direction. *Don't see me*, he'd thought, and even when someone looked in his direction, it was with a hazy, unfocused glance. Sam moved seamlessly through the crowd and lifted the sailor's wallet from his pants pocket with ease, then walked away without being noticed.

Where was his jacket? Sam chanced turning on a desk lamp. The light fell onto a stack of newspaper clippings a good two inches thick. He riffled through the stories, dismissing them with a smirk. Ghost stories. Spooky tales invented by folks who were afraid of living. Or who wanted attention. He knew the type. Then Sam's smirk faded as his eyes fell on a small article from a Kansas paper that told of a fifteen-year-old girl who fell ill with the sleeping sickness. Just before she died, she repeated a phrase that baffled her family. It was only the same two words, over and over: *Project Buffalo*.

Sam returned the article to the stack with suddenly shaking hands. If this Professor Fitzgerald knew something about it, then he needed to find a way to stick close to him, maybe by staying cozy with his niece, which sounded like a pretty swell proposition. Unless she killed him in a fit of pique. She certainly seemed like the sort of doll who could do it. Sam smiled at the thought; he liked a challenge. And that one was definitely a challenge. All he needed was a way in.

He spied it hanging on the wall in the collections room: CER-EMONIAL MASONIC KNIGHTS TEMPLAR DAGGER AND SCABBARD OWNED BY CORNELIUS T. RATHBONE, D. 1855. *That ought to do it*, Sam thought, tucking it into his shirt. He left the museum as he'd found it. By this time tomorrow, he'd have his jacket, and maybe a little reward money, too.

THINGS NOT SAID

Evie went straight to Mabel's apartment and the girls scooted past the cigarette smoke–filled parlor, where Mabel's parents were hosting a political meeting. As they shut the door to Mabel's bedroom, they could hear the adults arguing about workers' rights over cups of coffee.

"What's the matter? You look terrible," Mabel said.

"It's been a real lulu of a day, old girl." Evie told Mabel about Ruta Badowski's grisly murder, leaving out the part about the shoe buckle. She knew Mabel—she was as much of a crusader as her parents. She'd probably march Evie down to the police station and make her confess. But Evie didn't want to relive a minute of the terrible things she'd seen.

"How awful! Do you think your uncle Will can help them find the killer?"

"If anyone can, it's Unc. He's a genius."

"Are you going to help?"

Evie shuddered. "Not on your life-ski."

In the other room, the arguments escalated into shouting.

Someone pounded the table and yelled, "We must do more!" while Mrs. Rose shushed and soothed.

"Mabel, could I sleep here tonight?"

Mabel's eyes widened. "You want to sleep through *that*?"

Evie nodded. She needed the noise. It might be enough to drown out the nightmares.

Mabel shrugged. "Suit yourself. Here, have a nightgown."

Evie held up the chaste, high-necked gown, examining it with a scowl. "If I should die in the night, please remove this."

"Could you please remind me why we're friends?"

"Because you need me."

"I think you have that reversed, Evie O'Neill."

"Probably." Evie kissed Mabel's cheek. "You are an absolute doll of a pal, Mabesie, my girl."

"Don't you forget it."

They crawled into Mabel's bed and watched the light make patterns on the ceiling in the dark. They talked of Operation Jericho and poor dead Rudolph Valentino, and they talked, too, of their futures, as if they could shape the glittering course of their destinies with secret confessions offered like prayers to the room's benevolent hush. They talked until their words grew sparse with their drowsiness.

"Have you ever known something that you were afraid to tell?" Evie asked. She was more tired than she ever remembered being.

"Whaddaya mean?" Mabel slurred.

"I'm not sure," Evie murmured. She wanted to say more, but wasn't sure how to begin, and Mabel was already fast asleep.

※

Under a crumbling eave in the old house, a spider waited and watched as a hapless fly ventured into its web. When it became clear that the fly was hopelessly trapped, the spider scuttled forward, entombing the creature in a shroud of silk.

Like the spider, the house was also watching. Waiting. It had waited for many years, through the deaths of presidents and the fighting of wars. It had waited as the first motorcar roared down dirt roads and the aeroplane defied gravity. Now the wait was over.

Deep in the bowels of the old cellar, the furnace flame coughed to life. Behind the furnace lay a secret passageway to a hidden room whose walls glimmered faintly with symbols painted long ago in preparation. The stranger turned a crank and, high above, a metal grate, rusty with neglect, screeched open to reveal a night sky untouched by the phosphorescence of city lights. It was the perfect place to watch listless clouds drift by. To gaze at the stars. Or to catch the full glory of a prophecied comet as it burned past. The stranger stood naked beneath that sky. His shimmering skin was also a tapestry of symbols. He placed the eyes upon the altar and bowed his head, waiting, like the spider, like the house.

Whispers filled the room, soft at first, then louder, like the sound of a thousand devils loosed upon a desert. The gloom moved. The shadows surged, pressing against the stranger and the offering while the cold distant stars looked away.

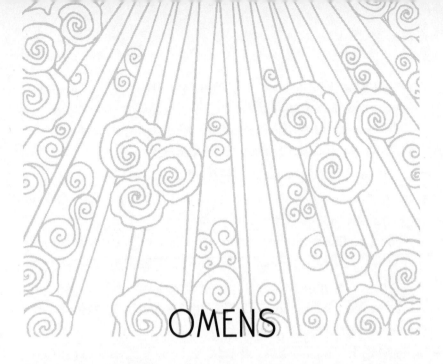

OMENS

The morning's *Daily News* sold the story of Ruta Badowski's death with a three-inch headline—MURDER IN MANHATTAN!—atop a grainy photograph of her grieving parents. Evie read the accounts in every newspaper while she waited for Will to come back from the police precinct. The stories mentioned that it was a ritual murder and that the killer had left a note with a Bible quotation and occult symbols, but didn't divulge what the symbols were. Detective Malloy had obviously held back details. Evie wished she didn't know the details. She'd woken with that terrible whistling melody in her head.

None of the newspaper accounts mentioned that Will had been consulted, and Evie wished that they had. It was terrible, she knew, but there was no such thing as bad publicity, and a mention of Uncle Will in connection to a murder investigation might bring people to the museum. It was nearly one o'clock. They'd been open since half past ten, and the only visitor they'd had was a man from Texas who'd really wanted to sell them cemetery plots. Evie had seen the bills piling up on Uncle Will's desk, along with the letter from the tax office and another from a realty company. If they didn't start getting a steady flow of visitors, they'd all be out on the streets. And Evie would be back in Ohio.

"It is always like this?" Evie asked Jericho, who was absorbed in some religious text that smelled of dust.

Jericho looked up, puzzled. "Always like what?"

"Dead."

"It's a little slow," Jericho allowed.

Evie couldn't do much about the museum just then, but she could do something about Operation Jericho. She scooted her chair closer to him and put on her best pensive face.

"Do you know who would be pos-i-tute-ly wonderful at this sort of thing? Mabel."

"Mabel?" Jericho's eyes had the faraway look of a man trying to place something.

"Mabel Rose! Lives downstairs in the Bennington?" Evie prompted. Jericho still looked lost. "Often comes to visit and speaks aloud in whole sentences. You've heard her voice. Try to remember."

"Oh, that Mabel."

"Right. Now that we've sorted out our Mabels, what do you think of her? *I* think she's a swell girl. And so bright! Did you know that she can read Latin? She can conjugate while she cogitates!" Evie laughed.

"Who?" Jericho said, turning a page.

"Mabel!" Evie said with irritation. "And she has an adorable figure. Granted, it's hidden beneath the most tragic dresses, but that figure is there, I tell you."

"Do you mean Mabel from sixteen-E?"

"Yes, I do!"

Jericho shrugged. "She seems a nice enough sort of girl."

Evie brightened. "Yes, she does, doesn't she? Very, very nice. Why don't the three of us have dinner together some evening?"

"Fine," Jericho said absently.

Evie smiled. At least Operation Jericho was off to a rousing start. She'd figure out a plan for the museum later.

"What you gonna do, writer man?"

Gabe stood between Memphis and the net, arms spread, fingers ready for the steal. Their shoes squeaked on the wooden floors of the church's gymnasium. Overhead, ceiling fans whirred, but they couldn't keep up with the boys' sweat. Memphis wiped a forearm across his eyes, planning his move.

"Gonna stay there all day?" Gabe taunted.

Memphis faked to his left. Gabe took the bait and lunged, allowing Memphis to surge past him on the right. Fast and sweet, he moved down the court and sank the ball with ease.

Gabe fell to the floor. "I surrender."

Memphis helped him up. "Good game."

Gabe laughed as they walked off the court. "'Course it was a good game for you. You won."

They dressed and headed to the drugstore for a snack.

Gabe cleared his throat. "I hear Jo's ankle is only sprained."

"That's good," Memphis said. He didn't want to get into it.

"Still, she's out of work for another two weeks."

"That's a shame."

"That all you got to say?"

"What else should I say?"

"You ever just try—"

Memphis stopped cold. "I told you. I can't do it anymore. Not since my mother."

Gabe put up his hands. "Okay, okay. Don't get hot. If you can't, you can't."

They walked a block in silence. Memphis saw a crow flitting from post to post, keeping pace. "I swear that bird is following me," he said.

Gabe laughed and twirled his lucky rabbit's foot, which hung by its chain from his finger. He swore it was his good-luck charm, and he never played a gig without it. "I told you, Casanova, you've got to stop giving those birds candy and flowers. Then they never leave you alone."

"I'm not kidding. I've seen it every day for the past two weeks."

Gabe raised his eyebrows and his lips pulled into a smile. "And you know it's the same crow? She got a name? Alice, maybe. Or Berenice! Yes, sir, looks like a Berenice to me."

Memphis could see that this would be a joke for Gabe for weeks to come.

"Memphis—it's just a bird. Birds fly around, brother. It's what they do. It's not following you, and it's not a sign. Unless you really did give it candy and flowers, in which case you are one strange brother."

Memphis laughed, shrugging off the bad feeling like an unneeded coat. Gabe was right—he was letting himself get spooked for nothing. It was that crazy dream that wouldn't let him alone. No wonder he saw omens around every corner.

They settled into a booth at Mr. Reggie's and ordered sandwiches and coffee.

"I wrote a new poem last night," Memphis said.

"When're you gonna show those poems to somebody other than the dead folks up in the graveyard?"

"They're not good enough yet."

Gabe reached across the table and took the pickle from Memphis's plate. "How do you know, if nobody's read 'em? One of these days, you just need to walk yourself right up to Miss A'Lelia Walker's town house and say, 'How do you do, ma'am? I'm Memphis Campbell, and I'd be much obliged if you'd read my work.'" Gabe finished the pickle and wiped his hands on Memphis's napkin. "Life don't come to you, Memphis. You gotta take it. We have to take it. Because ain't nobody handing it to us. You understand? Now"—Gabe leaned back against the back of the small booth and spread his arms—"ask me why I'm grinning,"

Memphis rolled his eyes. "Why are you grinning, Gabe?"

"Guess who's playing trumpet on Mamie Smith's new record?"

"Hey, brother!"

"Heard from Clarence Williams at Okeh Records last night in the club. They want me to come in tomorrow." Gabe shook his head. "Me, playing for Miss Mamie Smith."

"What about Mamie Smith?" Alma dropped into the seat next to Gabe and helped herself to some of his potato salad.

"Did I invite you?" Gabe teased.

"I invited myself. Thought this table needed some class."

"Mr. Gabriel Rolly Johnson here is now a recording artist for Okeh Records, blowing his horn for none other than Miss Mamie Smith."

Alma let out a little squeal of excitement and threw her arms around Gabe. "You know what this means, baby?"

"What?"

"It means you can buy my lunch. Hey, Mr. Reggie!" she shouted. "I'll take a meat-loaf sandwich, and you can put it on Gabe's tab. And add a milk shake!" She squinted at Memphis. "What's eating you?"

"Just haven't been sleeping much."

"Oh?" Alma said and pursed her lips playfully. "What's her name?"

"Her name is Berenice, and she's a very persistent bird," Gabe joked, breaking himself up. He slapped the table, making the rabbit's foot jump.

"There's nobody," Memphis said quickly.

"That's your trouble, brother," Gabe said, wiping his eyes. He doused his sandwich with hot salt-and-pepper pickles that made Memphis's nose run. "You need to get your head out of that notebook and come with me to the club Saturday night. We'll find you a girl."

Alma made a face. "How can you eat that, Gabriel?"

"Helps me keep my pucker, baby."

Memphis stirred the tiny mound of sugar at the bottom of his coffee cup. "Don't want *a* girl. I want *the* girl."

Alma put her pinkie in the air and tilted her chin up. "Oh. *The* girl."

Gabe matched her imperious tone. "I say, old boy. Do give her my best."

Alma and Gabe fell into a routine, mocking Memphis like he was high-hat. Memphis knew better than to let on that he was irritated by their teasing, so he put on the big smile and grabbed his knapsack. "Gotta go to San Juan Hill and see about some business for Papa Charles. Oh, and thank you for lunch, Gabriel."

He could hear Gabe saying, "Hey, now!" as he walked out the door and left him with the check.

"Hey, hey—Mr. Campbell! 'Zat you?" Blind Bill called from a chair in front of Floyd's Barbershop. Sometimes Floyd put out an old chair and let him sit and play for the customers, or just soak up the sun. "I know it's you. Don't play with old Bill now. My number come in today?"

"No, sir. Sorry. Better luck next time."

"Heard people got them some numbers they playing for that murder down under the bridge."

"Yes, sir. Some people do have a gig for it."

"Hmph." Blind Bill spat. "Nothin' good can come from that. You don't play a number on a murder, if you want my opinion."

"I just write the slips."

"I keep seeing this number. In my dreams, you know. I see a house, and there's a number, but I cain't never make it out."

Memphis had never thought about the dreams of the blind. How could old Bill see a house and a number if he couldn't see at all? But there were rumors about Bill: He'd lost his sight when he got some bad whiskey. He'd been beaten and left for dead over an unpaid gambling debt. He'd done a woman wrong and she'd gotten her revenge with a curse. Some people said he'd lost his sight in a card game with the Devil and now he was on the run to keep his soul. People said all kinds of things.

The crow chattered again. Blind Bill angled his ear toward it. "Got ourselves a messenger, seem like. Question is, who'd it come for, you or me?"

Bill laughed his big, gravelly laugh. It threaded with the crow's insistent caw, a discordant symphony.

※

Theta blew into the Globe Theatre with her leopard-spot coat hanging from one shoulder and a cigarette dangling from her painted lips. She kept her sunglasses on, feeling her way down the aisle through the rows of seats. The rest of the company was in mid-rehearsal for the Geisha Girl number, which Theta thought was one of the stupidest, most insulting routines they'd ever done—and there had been plenty of stupid, insulting numbers.

The stage manager glared. "Well, well, well. If it isn't Her Highness, come to grace us with her presence at last. You're an hour late, Theta!"

"Keep your shirt on, Wally. I'm here." Theta exchanged a furtive glance with Henry at the piano. He shook his head and she shrugged.

"She thinks she's better than everybody else," one of the chorines, a dim little witch named Daisy, griped.

Theta ignored her. She dropped her coat in the front row, doused her cigarette in the stage manager's cup of coffee, and took her place onstage.

"One of these days, Theta," he fumed. "You're going to do something even Flo Ziegfeld won't tolerate, and it will be my pleasure to toss you out on your—"

"You gonna beat your gums all day, or are we gonna work?" Theta snapped.

Theta executed her steps perfectly. She could do the number in her sleep. For good measure, though, she bumped into Daisy, just to rattle her. Daisy was sore because Theta had gotten a nice write-up in the papers for a number that was supposed to be Daisy's. "That was my specialty dance," Daisy had fumed in the dressing room the next night. "And you stole it out from under me."

"I can't steal what you don't own," Theta had said, and Daisy had hurled a pot of cold cream, missing Theta by a mile—her aim being as questionable as her dancing. As usual, Daisy had gone with her sob story to Flo, who had broken down and given her the spotlight for the Worship of Ba'al number that closed the show. Theta was tired of standing in somebody else's shadow—especially when that somebody was half the performer Theta was.

They broke for five, and Theta sat on the piano bench next to

Henry. "You look like you ran away from a prep school," she teased. He was wearing a cardigan and a straw boater.

"It's all about the style, darlin'."

"We're both bigger than this lousy show, Hen."

Henry played softly, almost reflexively. He was always happiest with his fingers on the keys and some song pouring out of him. "Agreed, darlin'. But we still gotta pay rent."

Theta adjusted the seam on her stockings so it ran straight. "How'd it go when you gave Flo your new tune?"

Henry's perpetual smirk turned to a frown. He plunked out a sour chord and stopped. "About how I 'spected it would."

Theta tugged on the boater's brim. "The Ziegfeld only likes 'em dumb and hummable, kiddo."

"'The people pay to be entertained, kid,'" Henry said in perfect imitation of the great showman. "'They want to leave happy and humming. Above all, they don't want to think too hard!'" He sighed. "I swear I could write a song about constipation, and as long as it rhymed *girl* with *pearl*, Mr. Ziegfeld would like it." Henry struck up a jaunty melody on the keys. He sang with exaggerated romantic bravado in his soft, sweet tenor. "Darling girl, I'd be your fool, if I could only pass this stool, oh the curse of CON-STI-PAAAA-TION!"

Theta dissolved into laughter.

"What's so funny?" Daisy loomed over them.

"I just got a joke Henry told me last Wednesday." Theta cupped a match to her cigarette and blew the smoke toward Daisy, who didn't take the hint.

"Whatcha reading?" The chorine sneered at Theta's copy of *The Weary Blues*, which sat on top of her bag. "Negro poetry?"

"I wouldn't expect you to get it, Daisy. You don't look at

anything besides *Photoplay*—and even then somebody's gotta explain the pictures to you."

Daisy's mouth hung open in outrage. "Well, I never!"

"Yeah, that's what you tell all your fellas, but the rest of us aren't buying it. Go away, now, Daisy. Shoo, little fly!" Theta flicked her fingers dismissively at Daisy, who stormed off and started dishing out an earful about how high-hat Theta was to any of the dancers who would listen.

Henry's fingers found their place on the keys again. "You sure know how to make pals, honey."

"Not interested in making pals. I already got a best pal," she said, patting his knee. She reached into her brassiere and pulled out a fifty-dollar bill, which she tucked into Henry's shirt pocket. "Here. For the piano fund."

"I told you to forget that."

Theta's voice went soft. "I never forget a favor. You know that."

"Where'd you get that kale?"

"Some Wall Street broker with more money than sense. He bought me a fur just to be seen with him at dinner. And that's all he got—dinner company."

"They all wanna marry you."

"Just once I'd like to meet a fella who isn't a phony. Somebody who doesn't wanna buy me a fur so he can show me off to his boys."

"When you meet that fella, see if he's got a brother," Henry joked.

"I thought you were carrying a torch for Lionel?" Theta teased.

Henry grimaced. "More like a matchstick. He giggles when I kiss him."

"So maybe you kiss funny." Theta smirked. She loved the way Henry always found some picky reason to send his beaus packing.

"*I met you on the street in Ohio. We were married at the Kansas state fair. You left me lonely in Florida. Now I'm in a state of despair. . . .*" Henry sang.

"Someday, Henry DuBois, you're gonna meet a fella who sends you, and you won't know what to do," Theta teased.

The stage manager reappeared, clapping for attention. "All right, everyone. The Ba'al number from the top. Places, please. Miss Knight, that means you, too."

"Wouldn't miss it for the world, Wally." She smiled as sweetly as a show poster for the glorified, all-American Ziegfeld girl just before dumping her second cigarette into Wally's fresh cup of coffee.

THE ETERNAL RECURRENCE

Evie and Jericho sat at a long table with stacks of books, police reports, drawings, and assorted papers before them. Jericho had lit a fire in the library's massive stone fireplace. It crackled and spit as it bit into the dry wood. They'd been at it for an hour, searching through musty books for some clue that might shed light on the baffling occult nature of the murder. Evie was tired and irritable. She didn't want to think about what she'd seen the day before, much less wallow in it. But Will showed no sign of stopping. As he spoke, he walked the perimeter of the room, trailing ash from his cigarette.

"Right. Let's review: What do we know so far?" Will asked.

"The killer has a fascination with the occult and with religion, possibly the Book of Revelation," Jericho answered from his perch at the head of the table.

"How do we know this?"

"His note mentions the Harlot, the Whore of Babylon, and the Beast, possibly a reference to the anti-Christ."

"Indeed," Will said. "But the passage is only partially from the Bible. They don't correspond neatly."

"They're close," Jericho said.

"Any librarian or scholar will tell you: Close is not the same as accurate. And don't forget that there are sigils as well. That's more indicative of some ceremonial magic or mysticism than of Christianity." Will indicated the scribblings running around the edges of the note. To Evie they just looked like scribbles—stylized crosses, squiggles, fancy letters, and geometric patterns.

"Now..." Will stubbed out his cigarette in an overflowing ashtray and immediately reached into his silver cigarette case for another without breaking his stride. "We have a symbol, do we not?"

"A pentacle," Evie answered.

"Yes. I've no artistic skill. Evie, could you...?" Will handed her a nub of chalk fished from an old cigar box full of odds and ends. It took Evie a moment to understand that he expected her to draw the symbol on the slate. "No, you've drawn it right side up. *Inverted*, please."

With a sigh, Evie erased her five-pointed star and drew it again with the two points up and the one down. "What's the difference?" she grumbled.

"I've told you: Inverted means matter over God. Spirit becoming flesh rather than the other way 'round. And now the snake, if you would, please."

Evie finished off the sketch. It was a rather nice likeness of a snake, if she did say so herself. Not that Will said thank you. Evie brushed the chalk dust from her hands. "What is the meaning of the snake?"

"Ah. That is a very old symbol, indeed. The snake devouring its tail, no beginning and no end. It exists across time and cultures. We see it in the Norse Jormungandr, the Greek Ouroboros, Gnosticism, the Ashanti, the Egyptian. It represents cycles, the idea that the universe is neither created nor destroyed but returns infinitely, to be played out again and again."

"The eternal recurrence, Nietzsche calls it," Jericho said.

"Does that mean I'll be forced to live through this afternoon again?" Evie joked. No one laughed, and she occupied herself by chalking in a fashionable hat on the snake's head.

Will grabbed a handful of mints from a dish and jiggled them in his palm as he resumed his pacing, the cigarette still in his other hand. "We may assume, then, that our killer has some passing knowledge of the occult, of magical and religious symbolism, most likely the Book of Revelation. But he references the Whore of Babylon as the 'Harlot Adorned upon the Sea.'" Will paused for a second. "Strange phrase, that. Baffling. Possibly from a religion of the killer's own making."

"How do you invent a religion?" Evie asked.

Will looked over the top of his spectacles. "You say, 'God told me the following,' and then wait for people to sign up."

Evie hadn't given religion much thought before. Her parents were Catholics turned Episcopalian. They attended services on Sunday, but it was all pretty rote, like brushing your teeth and bathing. Just something you did because it was expected. Evie hadn't always felt that way. For a year after James had died, she'd cupped his half-dollar pendant between her pressed palms and prayed fervently for a miracle, for a telegram that would say GOOD NEWS! IT WAS A TERRIBLE MISTAKE, AND PRIVATE JAMES XAVIER O'NEILL HAS BEEN FOUND, SAFE, IN A FARMHOUSE IN FRANCE. But no such telegram ever arrived, and whatever possible faith might have bloomed in Evie withered and died. Now she saw it as just another advertisement for a life that belonged to a previous generation and held no meaning for hers.

"We haven't answered the most basic question of all: Why?

What purpose is served by these murders?" Jericho asked, jolting Evie from her thoughts.

"He's a monster," Evie said. "Isn't he?"

Will reached into a bowl of bridge mix. He juggled the candies in his hand without eating them. "Indeed. But that's a what, not a why. Nothing is done without purpose, however twisted that purpose may be."

"Why did he take her eyes?" Evie asked.

"He might be keeping them as souvenirs."

Evie made a face. "A pinwheel from Coney Island is a souvenir, Unc."

"To us, yes. To a madman? Perhaps not. But he might need them in some way for the ritual. Some cultures believe that ingesting the flesh of your victims makes you immortal. The Aghori of India eat the flesh of the dead in the belief that it confers supernatural powers, whereas members of the Algonquin tribe believe that anyone who eats human flesh will become a demonic spirit called the Wendigo."

Evie's stomach turned. "Well, there's nothing in the Bible about holy cannibalism."

"Transubstantiation?" Jericho said. "'Eat of my body, drink of my blood'?"

"Right," Evie conceded. "I'll certainly never feel the same way about Communion again."

"As I've said before—America is a young country comprising all sorts of people. Beliefs converge and become something new all the time." Will finished his second cigarette and Evie could see his fingers twitching for a third, which, thankfully, he resisted. The cigarette smoke hung thickly in the air as it was.

"There's something I don't understand. The note..." Evie searched through the mess of papers on the table and retrieved the photograph of the note left with Ruta's body. "The note says, 'This was the fifth offering.' Why the fifth? Why not the first?"

"Yes. Troubling." Will paced around the table, his cigarette case still clutched in his palm. "Jericho, could you telephone Detective Malloy and ask if there are any unsolved murders that might be similar in nature?"

"Don't you think he would have mentioned that?" Evie said.

"Never assume," Uncle Will said, and it was clear that it was his final word on the matter.

"It's almost time for your lecture at the Women's Association's Ancient Order of the Phoenix club," Jericho reminded Will.

Will squinted at the mantel clock as if he meant to rebuke it for displaying the wrong time, then gave two curt nods, like a headmaster finally accepting a student's scholarly argument in class. "So it is. I'd best gather my lecture notes."

"You left them upstairs," Jericho said.

"Ah. Good. Good." Will paused for a moment longer, his eyes scanning the room. "I can't help feeling that there's something we're missing here. Something important."

The fire cast Will's face in shadows. He shook off his misgiving and was gone.

There was a knock at the door. Finally, a customer! Jericho was up first. From the way he bolted, Evie figured she wasn't the only person worried about the museum. She heard voices, and a moment later Jericho returned with none other than Sam Lloyd in tow.

Evie's eyes narrowed. "Well, well, well. I suppose you've got my twenty bucks."

Jericho glanced from Evie to Sam and back again. "Do you two know each other?"

"Actually, I've come to see Mr. William Fitzgerald. Is he here?" Sam craned his neck.

"*Dr.* Fitzgerald. And what business do you have with my uncle?"

"Your...your uncle?" Sam smiled in surprise. "You don't say! Now, isn't that a coincidence."

"Isn't what a coincidence?" Uncle Will said, stepping into the room. He wore his hat and carried his briefcase. An umbrella hung from his left arm even though it was a sunny day.

Sam marched forward and shook Will's hand with gusto. "How do you do, sir? Sam Lloyd. I have something I believe belongs to you."

"Indeed?"

"Well, sir, I'm afraid it's a story that won't make me look like too swell of a fella. See, I was at the pawnbroker's last night, hoping to get a few rubes for my watch—times are a bit hard. And I hear this fella saying he's got some merchandise to sell. Rare treasures from the Museum of the Creepy Crawlies." Sam gave an apologetic shrug. "That's just what they call it, Professor."

"Go on," Uncle Will said. If he was put out, he didn't show it.

Sam opened his bag and retrieved Cornelius Rathbone's Masonic dagger. Will held it up to the light and peered at it. "That's ours, all right."

"I offered the fella my last twenty bucks for it, and he took it, seeing as the pawnbroker wasn't too keen on taking it for more than ten. I didn't know if there might be a reward for its safe return." Sam paused, glancing quickly up at Will, then back down at his hands. "I just thought, well, it's one thing to take what you need so's you can eat, or to pinch from a bootlegger. It's another thing to steal treasures from a museum. Why, that's just bad form."

Evie stared, her mouth hanging slightly open. Sam winked and said, "Hey, sister, careful there—wouldn't want your tongue to fall out."

Evie glared. "If my tongue goes missing I'll know whose pockets to check first! Of all the cockeyed stories! Unc, you need to give him the bum's rush. He's a cheat, a liar, a thief, a liar—"

"You said that already," Sam noted.

"Well, I'm saying it again! This is the son of a bitch who stole my twenty dollars in Penn Station!"

"Evangeline, not everyone is accustomed to your gangland charm," Uncle Will chided after a pause. "Is that true, young man?"

Sam offered a reassuring smile. "Now, see, that's all a big mix-up, Professor."

"So's your old man," Evie spat out.

Sam adopted a pained expression. "I didn't want to say this and get the young lady in trouble, but she stole my coat."

"And you're not getting it back until I have my twenty dollars."

Jericho came to stand beside Evie, looming over Sam.

"Hi there, big fella. You her brother?" Sam asked.

"No."

Sam glanced from Jericho to Evie. "You *married?*"

"No!" Evie and Jericho said, but not before Sam noted the blush creeping into Jericho's cheeks.

"Listen, sister, I don't know what kind of situation you've got going on here. I'm not the judging type. I'm glad to see you're safe and sound here with your uncle and your"—he nodded to Jericho—"large friend. I was only trying to do a good deed, but I see that no good deed goes unpunished. So if you'll just hand over my coat, we'll call it even and I'll beat it. I won't even charge you with stealing my property."

Evie sputtered for a second, then took off after Sam, chasing him around the long table, knocking over stacks of books as she did. "I'm going to kill him. Who wants to watch?"

Jericho raised his hand.

Will stepped into Evie's path, stopping her. "Pardon me, but I'm rather confused, and I am also"—Will checked his watch again—"six and a half minutes late for my lecture. I don't mind thieves, but I do abhor liars and people who keep me from conducting my affairs in an efficient manner. Now. Did you, in fact, steal her twenty dollars? Answer carefully, young man."

For the first time, Sam appeared nervous, raking a hand through his hair and inching just a bit closer to the door. "Well, sir, a great man once said, 'Subjectivity is truth; truth is subjectivity.'"

"Kierkegaard," Will said, surprised. His tone softened. "Still. Facts are facts."

Sam looked down at his shoes. "I'm sorry. I was planning on paying her back when I saw that fella at the pawnbroker's and gave him my last dime to get that knife back. I thought maybe it could be a peace offering."

"Oh, dry up," Evie muttered. "He probably stole it himself."

Sam forced himself not to look up. "I'm so broke I had to jump the turnstile to take the train. You can call a cop if you want to. In fact, I wouldn't blame you a bit. But I'm as honest as a senator about finding your fenced goods, sir. I hope that counts for something."

"I hear they feed you in Sing Sing," Evie muttered. "Three squares a day."

"Evangeline," Will said with a sigh. "Charity begins at home."

"So does mental illness."

Will drummed his fingers on the back of a chair. "It was wrong to take Evangeline's money, no matter how dire your straits at the time. However, you acted quite nobly in returning the museum's property when you didn't have to. I'd never thought about security for the museum before." Will scratched his head, looking around at the precious books.

"If you don't mind my saying, sir, you can't be too careful these days."

"I'll say." Evie glared at Sam.

Will nodded, thinking it over. "Very well. How would you like an honest job at the museum? There's plenty to be done, and you could stay here at night to thwart any unwanted thieves."

Evie whirled around to face Will. "Unc! *He's* a thief!"

"Yes. So he is. Are you a good thief, Sam?"

Sam smiled. "The best, sir."

"A good thief in need of a job," Will mused. "I suppose you may start right away."

"Will, Evie's right. You don't know him, and he'll only be in the way," Jericho said quietly. "I could keep watch if you need me to."

"I don't think that's wise, Jericho," Will answered quietly. Evie didn't know what he meant by that, but Jericho's face went stony. "We can always use an extra hand, especially now that we're investigating a murder."

"A murder?" Sam said. "Sounds exciting."

"They might be investigating *yours* pretty soon, pal," Evie warned.

"Yes, well, I do hope you're not averse to hard work," Will said.

"Nothing better than an honest day's work, I always say, sir."

Will checked his watch again. "I am now nine minutes late. Jericho, could you return Mr. Lloyd's coat and show him to the filing, please?"

A thoroughly irritated Jericho retrieved Sam's coat from the closet and handed it over a bit roughly.

"He is *enormous,*" Sam whispered to Evie. "What do you feed him?"

Evie leaned close. "I'm on to you, pal. You so much as whistle off-key and I promise I will personally give you the bum's rush. You won't even have time to grab your hat."

"Well." Sam nodded, slipping on the coat. "I *am* pretty fond of this hat. Nice to see you again, Sister."

"The pleasure was all yours," Evie said and ran to catch Will. Behind her, she could hear Sam whistling "Am I Wasting My Time on You?" He was whistling off-key, and Evie had the distinct impression he was doing it deliberately.

"Unc!" Evie called. She caught up with Will at the front door.

"Evie, can this wait? The ladies of the Ancient Order of the whatever-it-is—"

"Phoenix," Evie supplied.

"*Phoenix* are expecting me, and if I can't hail a taxicab, I'll go from being forgivably late to being egregiously late."

"Unc, you can't let Sam Lloyd work here. Not with all those priceless artifacts! He's likely to rob you blind."

"It's precisely those qualities that could prove useful."

"What do you mean?"

"From time to time, the museum has to be...clever in ferreting out objects, stories, and people before anyone else gets there. It's delicate."

"You expect me to believe that there are other people who want those creepy things?"

"You'd be surprised."

"He's still a thief."

"A thief who reads Kierkegaard is an interesting thief, indeed."

"But Unc—"

"Evangeline, not everyone starts life in a comfortable house on a comfortable street in Ohio," Will said pointedly.

The comment stung. Why was Will defending Sam Lloyd, a common criminal, over her? After all, Sam was a stranger; she was family. Weren't family supposed to protect their own? But he'd sided with the opponent, just like her father and mother had sided with Harold Brodie instead of defending their own daughter. If Uncle Will wanted to be foolish, well, that was his affair. She'd been stupid to try to intervene.

"I hope you're right about him," Evie said and went back to the library. She glowered at Sam once for good measure and then settled in at the long table, checking through stacks of newspaper reports and books, searching for anything that might shed light on the strange murder of Ruta Badowski.

When she'd had enough, she sneaked out her copy of *Photoplay*.

"So, is Clara Bow running away with Charlie Chaplin?" Sam read over her shoulder.

Evie did not look up. "Why don't you take it and read it for yourself? You seem to be skilled at taking things. In fact, why don't you carry it with you on your way out?"

Sam snickered. "Now, why would I leave such a sweet deal? Besides, I'd hate for you to miss me, sister."

"Absence makes the heart grow fonder. Let's put that phrase to the test, shall we? I'll get your hat."

"No can do. Your uncle needs my help. Look at all this stuff— who knew there were so many superstitious charms? Like this— love charm of the Hopi. Oh, I better not let you hold this, sister. You might get goofy for me."

"That'll be the day."

"I'm counting on that day."

"I hope you can count pretty high, then," Evie said.

He leaned in a little closer. Evie could see the flecks of amber in his eyes. "Admit it—you liked that kiss."

"You owe me twenty dollars."

"Cash or check?" he said cheekily. Even the dullest Ohio girls knew that bit of lingo: *Kiss now or kiss later?*

"Bank's closed, pal."

Sam nodded. "Check, then." Whistling, he headed for the library doors. Evie followed him up the wide, curving staircase that led to the museum's second floor.

"Can I help you, sister?"

"I'm making sure you don't leave with half the museum."

"Just have to iron my shoelaces," he said, nodding toward the men's room at the top of the stairs. When he reached the men's room door, Evie stood outside, her arms folded across her chest.

"Honestly, I'd invite you in, but I've managed to avoid getting arrested for petty theft. I'd hate to go to the Tombs for perversion."

"Whatever it takes to get you out of my uncle's museum," Evie quipped. "I'll wait."

"Suit yourself, doll."

In the museum's musty lavatory, Sam washed his hands and left the tap running. Whistling, he sat on the cracked tile floor and watched the shadow of Evie's feet under the slit of the door as she paced. She'd get bored eventually. He opened Jericho's wallet, which he had lifted while the blond giant was occupied in the stacks. Trusting fella. That was a dangerous habit—trust. Sam removed a five-dollar bill, replacing it with two singles. It was the oldest trick in the book: If you stole the Abe's cabe outright, the other fella could make you for a thief. But if you took a large bill and left some singles, the mark would think he'd spent the big dough and just didn't remember getting change.

From his jacket pockets, Sam removed two small silver ashtrays, which he'd managed to take from the library unnoticed. These he hoped to sell later to a disreputable pawnbroker on the Bowery for a few bucks. For now, he wrapped them in one of the bathroom's hand towels and hid them behind the toilet bowl. He had big plans, and plans took time and money.

Evie's shadow disappeared. Sam opened the door a crack and saw that the hallway was empty. He closed the men's room door again, turned off the tap, and stared at his reflection in the tall wooden mirror. Two shocks of his dark hair hung down on either side of his gold-flecked eyes. The devil-may-care expression was gone, and in its place was one of hard determination.

"Nice to meet you. I'm Sam Lloyd. Tell me where she is, or . . ."

Sam stopped. Though he'd played the scene over in his mind many times, he was never really sure what he would say when that day came. He only knew that he wouldn't be going in blind. Sam pulled up his pants leg and removed the gun strapped there, turning it over in his hands, examining the barrel, feeling the tension in the trigger. He opened the chamber and spun it around. There were no bullets yet. The ashtrays would bring enough for those. This job at the museum had been a stroke of good luck, easier than hustling magic tricks on the streets of Times Square. All he had to do was hold on for a little while—long enough to find out who needed to pay for what had happened to his family. And they *would* pay.

In the mirror, Sam was scowling. He looked older than his seventeen years. He straightened his collar, eased the scowl into a hard smile, and raised the gun, taking aim at his reflection.

"Nice to meet you. I'm Sam Lloyd. Tell me where she is, and I might let you live."

Sam heard footsteps and hurriedly replaced the gun in its holster. The door swung open and Jericho came in. Sam made a show of washing his hands. "Something the matter?"

"I seem to have lost my wallet."

"Aw, gee. Tough break, pal," Sam said. "Want me to help you look?"

Jericho squinted at Sam, evaluating the offer. "Thanks."

Sam accompanied Jericho through the museum, making a show of looking, pointing out spots where a wallet could possibly hide. When they reached the library, he shook it free from his pants leg near one of the many bookcases. It wouldn't do for Sam to suddenly find the wallet; he needed to make Jericho think he'd found it himself.

"Did you look up here, big fella?"

Jericho frowned at the phrase *big fella*. He took the spiral staircase to the second floor and walked the stacks until he spied his wallet on the floor. "I found it," he called. He opened the wallet and frowned. "I could've sworn I had five dollars. But there's only two here."

"Gee, that's rough. Better hold on to those rubes," Sam said evenly.

Evie skimmed the pages of a book titled *Religious Fervor and Fanaticism in the Burned-Over District*. The author appeared to have written the book with the express purpose of putting his audience to sleep, and Evie had difficulty retaining anything she read. She resorted to skimming the pages, stopping suddenly when she came to an illustration near the back. There was the same symbol used in the murder. The inscription read THE PENTACLE OF THE BRETHREN, BRETHREN, NY, C. 1832.

The telephone rang, echoing through the empty museum. Evie turned down the corner of the page to show Will later and ran for the phone.

"Hold a moment. I'll connect you," the operator said. There was a click and a hiss, and then Theta's voice crackled over the wires.

"Hiya, Evil. It's Theta. Listen, you still want to catch the show?"

"And how!"

"Swell. I'll leave a pair of tickets for you and Mabel at the theater for tonight's show. There's a party in Greenwich Village after, if it's not past your bedtime."

"I never go to bed before dawn."

"Attagirl! And Evil, wear your best glad rags."

"They'll be the gladdest rags you ever saw."

In the privacy of Will's office, Evie jumped up and down. Finally! Tonight, she and Mabel would be out with Theta and her smart set. She danced back into the library, humming a jazzy number.

"What just happened to you? You win the Miss America contest or something?" Sam said. He gathered Evie's book into a tall stack of volumes to be reshelved.

"I will be the guest of Miss Theta Knight at the Globe Theatre for Mr. Ziegfeld's latest revue tonight, and at a private party afterward."

"Swanky. Need a date?"

"Private party!" Evie sang out. She reached up and grabbed her scarf and hat from the giant stuffed bear's paw, where she'd hung them earlier.

"Say, I was wondering, either of you know anything about this?" He pointed to the newspaper clipping on top of the stack, about the girl with the sleeping sickness.

Evie glanced at it as she tied the scarf into a loose bow at her neck. "It's one of Unc's strange scraps. He collects these odd little ghost stories. That's his job, I suppose. Why do you ask?" Evie said.

Sam forced a smile. "No reason. Just trying to keep up."

Evie patted his cheek. "Good luck, Lloyd."

Evie left the museum and walked along Central Park West. Ten blocks farther up, she could see the gothic spires of the Bennington peeking above the roofs and trees. It was a pleasant late afternoon, and a sudden optimism seized Evie—the feeling that all good things were possible, and that she could pull her deepest wishes from the air like a magician with a coin.

At a newsstand, a young boy hawked the late-edition paper by calling out the headlines, but Evie was too preoccupied with thoughts of the perfect evening awaiting her to pay any attention. Dreaming of what she would wear, she passed harried mothers corralling children on the edges of the park as well as an organ-grinder who was accompanied by a tiny monkey dressed as a bellhop. It clicked its teeth and screeched at passersby until they rewarded him with pennies for his small tin cup. Two girls in matching capes advertising a nightclub offered her a flyer.

"What's this?" Evie asked.

"For the Nighthawks Club. We're having a Solomon's Comet party!"

"A what?"

"Jeepers, the comet?" the taller of the girls said in a thick New York accent. "It's comin' t'rough New York in a coupla weeks. It comes once every fifty years or somethin'. 'Posed to be a— whaddaya call it, Bess?"

"Event of heavenly significance," the other girl enunciated carefully. "Like magic or something. All them magicians and holy rollers thought it was a sign. Anyhow, the club's having a real swell party for it. You should come. Oh, your coat is the cat's meow!"

"Thank you," Evie said, pleased. She looked over the flyer. It was a caricature drawing of a flapper dancing up a storm, her cocktail glass sloshing its contents. Above her, a magnificent comet arced over the skyline of New York City. The artist had given the comet a face, and it smiled down at the fetching girl. Its fiery tail showered sparkles on the city.

"You don't wanna miss out on the most magical night of the year, do you?" the taller girl asked.

"Not on your life-ski," Evie said.

Solomon's Comet. An event of heavenly significance. Perhaps it would bring her luck. At any rate, it was a dandy reason for a party, and thinking of the night ahead and the nights to come, she went merrily on her way, clutching the flyer. At the corner, she waited for the traffic cop to signal the all clear with his white-gloved hands. He blew his whistle, spurring the crowd into action again, and Evie turned toward home.

Behind her, the newsboy held the late-edition paper aloft, shouting the headline to anyone who might have a nickel. "Extra! Extra! Madman threatens to kill again!"

SMOKE AND MIRRORS

Outside the Globe Theatre on Forty-second Street, the lighted marquee blazed FLORENZ ZIEGFELD PRESENTS NO FOOLIN': A MUSICAL REVUE GLORIFYING THE AMERICAN GIRL in tall letters. People in eveningwear drifted into the grand beaux arts theater, excited to see stars like Fanny Brice, Will Rogers, and W. C. Fields, along with the talented singing, dancing chorines and the celebrated Ziegfeld girls, beautiful models who crossed the stage in elaborate headdresses and elegant, barely-there costumes. It was the epitome of glamour, and Evie could scarcely believe they were taking their very own seats up in the curved balcony beside all the swells in their furs and jewels.

Evie nudged Mabel. "Oh, look, there's Gloria Swanson." She nodded toward the lower level, where the seductive motion-picture starlet, draped in ermine and velvet, enjoyed the stares of admirers. "She is the elephant's eyebrows," Evie whispered appreciatively. "Those jewels! How her neck must ache."

"That's why Bayer makes aspirin," Mabel whispered back, and

Evie smiled, knowing that even a socialist wasn't immune to the dazzle of a movie star.

The lights dimmed and the girls squeezed each other's hands in excitement. The conductor lifted his baton and a rousing opening song rose from the orchestra pit. The curtains opened, and a bevy of smiling chorus girls in brightly colored bathing suits tap danced in perfect synchronization while a tuxedo-clad gentleman sang of beautiful girls. Evie had never been so excited. She loved everything about the show, from the funny yodeling number set in the Alps to the swirling dance that took place in the harem of a sheik of Araby. She wished it would never end, but she could see from the program that they had come to the finale. It was said that Mr. Ziegfeld always saved the most spectacular number for last. The lights flickered to suggest lightning. From the orchestra pit came the crash of cymbals and the sharp shriek of violins against a violent drumbeat. Smoke pooled near the footlights and crept out into the audience. Onstage, barefoot, skimpily dressed girls wearing tall, beaded headdresses writhed suggestively below a replica of a golden altar. A blond beauty draped provocatively in golden silk stood on top of the altar. She danced as if in a trance while the music swelled and the lightning flashed. The beauty sang sweetly, begging the spirit world not to take her as a sacrifice to the golden idol. Along a catwalk, elegant Ziegfeld girls promenaded like ghosts. It was mesmerizing, and Evie sat forward, rapt.

"There's Theta," Mabel whispered. From her lap, she gestured discreetly to a chorus girl, second from the right. Even though she was dressed and made up to look like all the other girls, there was something special about Theta, Evie thought. The other dancers' placid expressions suggested they were thinking about nothing more exciting than washing out their stockings after the show. But

Theta made you believe she was a worshipper of Ba'al, lost to the frenzy.

Just as the action reached a fever pitch and the priest was about to plunge the knife into the heart of the sacrificial blond, the hero rushed the altar, fighting off the worshippers. He knocked the priest back, smashed the idol, and carried the bewitched girl down the lighted steps to safety. A bevy of chorus girls glissaded across the stage with huge feather fans, and suddenly the scene transformed into a wedding. The dancing girls tossed red rose petals as the now husband and wife, clad in virtuous white, sang to each other a pledge of eternal love before the curtains snapped shut on the whole affair and the show was ended.

"You were wonderful," Evie exclaimed a short while later, as the four of them—Evie, Mabel, Theta, and Henry—walked the tree-shaded, narrow bend of Bedford Street in Greenwich Village on their way to a party one of the girls was hosting.

"Yeah. 'Second girl from stage left' is my specialty," Theta deadpanned.

Henry took her arm in his. "Keep working, darlin', and you just might be 'first girl from stage left.'"

"Well, I thought you were the duck's quack," Evie said. "Mabel and I noticed you right away. Didn't we, Mabesie?"

"And how!"

"You're sweet to say so, kid. This is the joint, here."

They'd stopped at a redbrick building. The party had spilled out onto the stoop, where a girl in a feather boa, a long cigarette holder angled between two fingers, was already drunk. She blocked their way with her leg. "What's the password?"

"Long Island," Henry said.

"You have to say it like this: *Lawn Guy-land*," she instructed.

"Lawn Guy-land," they all said.

"*Entrez!*" The girl let her leg drop with a thump and the four of them pushed their way into the foyer and up three flights of stairs dotted with birdlike clusters of people till they came to an apartment whose door was propped open by an ice bucket. Inside, the radio played a jazzy number. The hostess shimmied past them with a loud "You've arrived!" before disappearing into another room as if riding an unseen tide. There was a lamp on the floor, and a bust of Thomas Jefferson topped by someone's cloche gazed at the four of them from one of the burners on the tiny kitchen's even tinier stove. A fella crooned "I'll Take Manhattan" for a few of the chorus girls and their friends, who sat at his feet singing along.

Mabel tugged on Evie's sleeve. "I'm not really dressed for this party."

"Nothing we can't fix with a little smoke and mirrors, Pie Face," Evie said. With a sigh, she removed her rhinestone headband with the peacock feathers and placed it on Mabel's head. "Here, you go, Mabesie. You look like the Christmas windows at Gimbels. And who doesn't love those?"

"Thanks, Evie."

"Bottom's up," Theta said, handing them each a drink.

Mabel stared at hers. "I don't really drink."

"First sip's the roughest," Henry advised.

She took a sip and winced. "That's awful."

"The drunker you get, the better it tastes."

Evie was so nervous that she downed her cocktail in two stiff swigs, then refilled her glass.

Henry arched an eyebrow. "A pro, I see."

"What else is there to do in Ohio?"

An argument was heating up in the parlor, and a woman's

shrill voice rang out. "If you don't pipe down about that, I'm going to call that occult killer myself and ask him to do you in, Freddie!"

Everyone began chattering about the murder under the bridge and the latest warning.

"A pal of mine who has a cousin who's a cop told me it was a sex crime."

"I heard it's a beef between the Italians and the Irish mobsters, and she was somebody's moll who got too friendly with the wrong fella."

"It's definitely some kind of old-country hoodoo. They shouldn't keep letting these foreigners into the country. This is what happens."

"Evil's uncle is helping the bulls try to find the killer," Theta informed them.

Everyone crowded around Evie, badgering her with questions: Did they have any suspects? Had the victim lost her eyes, like the papers said? Was it true the girl who'd been murdered was a prostitute? Evie had barely had a chance to answer even one of their questions when a girl shouted from the doorway, "Ronnie's got the ukulele out! Boop-boop-a-deet-deet-doh-doh-da!"

And just like that, they were on to the next thing, from one thrill to the next with no time to stop. Evie felt small and dull beside their wattage. They were all so glamorous and exciting. Theater people who could sing and dance and act, who knew bankers and high rollers. What could Evie do? What talents did she have that made her stand out?

Evie was vaguely aware that she had one toe over the line of drunk. A tiny, urgent voice of reason told her to slow down and keep quiet. That what she was about to do was probably a bad idea.

But since when had she ever listened to reason? Reason was for suckers and Presbyterians. Evie downed the rest of her martini and slithered closer to the smart set singing along with the ukulele.

"You'll never guess what I can do," Evie said brightly as they finished a round of "If You Knew Susie." "I'll give you a hint: It's like a magic trick, only better." Ronnie paused his fingers on the strings of the ukulele. She had their attention now, and she liked it. "I can read secrets from just any old thing. Boop-boop-a-ding-dong...ding-dong."

Theta swiped Evie's glass and sniffed it.

"Really, I can! Here." She reached over and grabbed a girl's earring, ignoring her protests. For dramatic effect, Evie pressed the earring against her forehead. For a moment she hesitated—what if she heard that horrible whistling, like she had with Ruta Badowski? But the second she thought that, the more determined she was to take that image from under the bridge right out of her mind, and soon the earring gave up its confessions. "Your real name is Bertha. You changed it to Billie before you moved here from...Delaware?"

The girl's mouth opened. She clapped in glee. "Well, isn't that just the berries! Oh, do something of Ronnie's!"

Evie went from person to person, grabbing up little tidbits, getting better as she went. "Your birthday is June first and your best girl's name is Mae." "For dinner, you went to Sardi's and had the corned beef." "You have a parakeet named Gladys."

"Say, that's swell—you oughta have an act, kid!" Ronnie the ukulele player said.

"I *will* have an act!" Evie said loudly, letting the gin do the talking. "I'll turn my living room into a salon, and every night, people will come up and I'll tell them what they had to eat. All the columns will write me up. I'll be the Sandwich Swami."

Everyone laughed, and their laughter tucked itself around Evie like the warmest of blankets. This was the best city in the world, and Evie was diving right into the thick of it now. Within the hour, she'd gotten a read from about a dozen objects, and she was positively woozy. The hour was late—or early, depending on how you read it. Some fella had wrapped his striped tie around her head and tied it off in a half bow. Mabel had fallen asleep on the sofa. The hostess had left a tray of sandwiches balanced on Mabel's stomach, and from time to time a partygoer would stagger by and steal one. Near her feet, a passionate couple embraced in a never-ending lip-lock.

Henry settled next to Evie. "Say, sugar, that's some party trick you've got. Tell me the truth: You were a magician's assistant."

"Uh-uh," Evie said, grinning.

"Well, how *did* you learn how to do that?" Henry pressed. "Have you always been able to..." He put his fingers on her forehead and mimed reading her thoughts, making Evie laugh. She was drunk enough to tell him the truth, but some tiny voice inside told her not to. The evening had been so perfect. What if it turned sour, like the last party?

"A lady never tells," Evie slurred.

Henry seemed like he was on the verge of asking her something else. Evie could feel it. But then he got that smirk again. "Of course she doesn't."

"Do you want me to tell you *your* secrets, Henry?"

"No thanks, darlin'. I love living in suspense. Besides, if I told myself all my secrets, I'd lose my mystery." He raised one eyebrow and pursed his lips like John Barrymore in *Don Juan*, and Evie felt she'd made the right call.

She giggled. "I like you, Henry."

"I like you, too, Evil."

"Are we pals-ski?"

"You bet-ski."

Theta crashed next to them on the thick zebra-skin rug. "I'm embalmed."

"Potted and splificated?"

"Ossified to the gills. Time for night-night."

"Whatever you say, baby vamp."

"Theta." Evie waved a finger in Theta's general direction. "You didn't let me tell your secrets."

Theta wavered for a minute, but she was too drunk to say no. "Here ya go, Evil," she said, passing over an onyx bracelet shaped like a jaguar. "My birthday is February twenty-third, and I had one of those limp sandwiches in the kitchen for dinner a million hours ago."

Evie squeezed the bracelet and felt an overpowering sensation of sadness, and a trace of fear. She saw Theta running in the dead of night, her dress torn and her face a wreck. Theta was afraid, so very afraid.

Evie had to let go. When she opened her eyes, Theta was looking at her strangely, and all Evie could see was the other Theta, the scared girl running for her life. "S-sorry. I couldn't get anything," Evie lied.

"Just as well," Theta said, taking the bracelet back. But she gave Evie a wary glance, and Evie hoped she hadn't gone too far. Maybe it was best to keep her party trick under wraps for now.

A vase flew just over their heads and smashed against a wall, thrown by the blond from the Ba'al number. Daisy somebody. Now she was shouting. "Nobody 'preciates what I do for the show! Not Flo, not anybody! I'm a star and I could go out to Hollywood and be in the pictures anytime I wanted!"

"Good old Daisy," Henry said knowingly.

"Time to blow," Theta said.

Evie roused the sleepy Mabel, and Henry grabbed their coats. Evie kept diving for her sleeve with her left arm but missed it each time, and Henry finally had to put the coat on her.

Evie patted his face. "Send me the bill for your services, Henry."

"Free of charge."

Arm in arm, the four of them wound through the bohemian streets of Greenwich Village, past the tiny nightclubs and artists' garrets. As they did, they sang a song Henry had made up, a ridiculous ditty that rhymed "she sat her fanny on a boy named Danny," which broke Theta up every time. The first tentacles of a monstrous headache were creeping up the back of Evie's neck, tightening across her skull and making her eyes hurt. She couldn't quite shake what she'd experienced while holding Theta's bracelet. She didn't know what terror Theta had been running from, and she wasn't sure she wanted to know, so she sang louder to drown out the voices in her head. At the edge of Washington Square Park, Henry stopped and hopped onto a park bench.

"Did you know this used to be a potter's field? There are thousands of bodies buried under this land."

"I might be one of 'em soon," Theta said on a yawn.

"Look at that," Henry said, gazing up at the golden moon bleeding its pale light into the inky spread of sky over the Washington Square arch. They tipped their heads back to take in the full beauty of it.

"Pretty," Evie said.

"You said it," Theta agreed.

"Oh, god," Mabel whined. She turned toward the gutter and threw up.

GRIEF LIKE FEATHERS

Memphis sat in the graveyard, near a headstone that read EZEKIEL TIMOTHY. BORN 1821. DIED FREE 1892. He took his lantern from its hiding place, and beside its yellow glow, he set to work on a new poem. *She wears her grief like a coat of feathers too heavy for flight.* He crossed out *heavy*, wrote *weighted* instead, then decided that was downright pretentious and put *heavy* back in. Out on the Hudson, a boat skimmed the surface, trailing streamers of light. Memphis watched it for a while, gathering inspiration, but he was tired, and at last he rested his head on his arms and fell asleep.

In the familiar dream, Memphis stood at a crossroads. The land was flat and golden brown. On the road ahead, the dust kicked up into a brumous wall that turned the day dark. There were a farmhouse and a barn and a tree. A windmill turned wildly with the billowing dust. The crow called from the field and beat its frantic wings just ahead of the tall, spindly man bending the wheat into ash with his every step.

Memphis jolted awake. The candle in his lantern had burned out. It was very dark. He put the lantern back in its secret tree hold, gathered his things, and walked past the house on the hill. *Don't look; keep walking past,* Memphis thought as he reached the gate. Now, why had he thought that? Why were his arms breaking out into goose pimples? Superstition. Dumb, backward superstition. He wasn't having it, and as if to challenge himself, to separate himself from a long line of fearful ancestors, he purposely walked through the gate and stood on the cracked, weed-choked path that led to the ruined mansion. He willed himself to walk, drawing closer and closer to the scarred front doors. Maybe he'd even go inside, put this foolishness to rest once and for all. He was nearly there. Only five more steps. Four. Three...

The doors swung open, releasing a sound Memphis could only describe as a hellish groan. Memphis fell back, scrambled to his feet, and set off running at full speed, not slowing until he reached the bright lights of Harlem.

It was the wind; that was all, Memphis reasoned as he crept into Octavia's house. He'd allowed himself to be spooked by a gust of wind. He shook his head at his softness, then stifled a yelp as he came upon Isaiah standing in the doorway to their room. "Lord almighty, Ice Man!" he whispered. "You almost gave me a heart attack. What're you doing out of bed? You need a glass of water?"

Isaiah stared straight ahead. "Anoint thy flesh and prepare ye the walls of your houses. The Lord will brook no weakness in his chosen."

"Ice Man?"

"And the sixth offering shall be an offering of obedience."

A chill skipped up Memphis's arms and neck. He didn't recognize what Isaiah was saying. It was almost like he was *receiving* those words. Memphis wasn't sure what to do. If he went to Octavia, she'd drag Isaiah and Memphis down to church and keep them there all day and night praying.

Sister Walker. Maybe Sister Walker would know. He'd ask her about it tomorrow. Memphis took Isaiah's hand and led him back to bed. The boy was still staring into the distance.

"The time is now. They are coming," Isaiah said, drifting back into dreams, his last word barely a whisper: "Diviners." And then he was asleep.

A RIND OF MOONLIGHT

Several blocks and a thousand years from the city's ritzy nightclubs and theaters, a rind of moon sweated in the sky, but its glow did not reach the gloom of the tenements along Tenth Avenue, where Tommy Duffy and his friends welcomed the feel of the cool night air as they swaggered through Hell's Kitchen. They called themselves the Street Kings, for they were rulers of the rubble piles and the railyards. Makers of mischief. Sultans of the goddamned West Side.

"...I heard dere's a cellar 'round here where dey take snitches," one of the boys crowed. "I heard 'a floors is covered wit teeth 'at you can pry da gold right outta and sell it over to da pawnbroker on Eighth and Forty."

"You're as full of it as yer old man."

"You take back what you said about my da."

"Yeah, the only thing his old man's full of is Owney's whiskey!"

The two boys fell on each other with fists and curses, more out of habit than a sense of honor, until Paddy Holleran broke them apart.

"Save it," he ordered. "We might need our knuckles for what we're doin' tonight."

Paddy was fourteen and already running some small rackets for Owney Madden's gang, so the boys followed him without question, shouting "Street Kings!" and toppling garbage cans and throwing rocks at windows. No one could touch them. This was what it meant to be in a gang. Without your boys, you were nothing. A chump. A nobody.

When they reached the empty yards along the Hudson where the warehouses stood sentry, Paddy shushed them. "Gotta be looking out. Dey got a guard dog, a big German shepherd with teeth a foot long dat keeps watch. He'll eat your face off."

"What's the plan, Paddy?" Tommy asked. He was only twelve and looked up to the older boy.

"See dat warehouse at the end? I heard Luciano's men got their whiskey from Canada hidden in there. Got a distillery in dere, too. We steal some whiskey, bust up the still, I bet Owney'd be chuffed. Bet we'd look good to him. We'll let dem Italian bastards know we Irish was here first."

"Didn't Columbus discover America?" Tommy said. He'd learned that in school, before he'd quit in fifth grade.

Paddy thumped Tommy's nose. "Whatsa matter wit you? You wanna run wit the Italians now? Is 'at it?"

"N-no."

"Hey! Tommy Gun here wants to be Italian! He's too good for us!"

"Am not!" Tommy shouted over their insults.

"Yeah? Prove it." Paddy had a mean glint in his eye. "You go in first. Stay in for five minutes, then come out with somethin' and we'll believe you."

Tommy glanced down toward the shadowy end of the yards,

where the warehouse sat. Winos slept there. Perverts, too. Sometimes rival gangs patrolled with lead pipes. And there was the threat of the guard dog Paddy had mentioned. Tommy's stomach knotted in fear.

"Do it or you ain't part of the Street Kings no more."

There was no worse fate. Even the thought of some geezer showing his bits was better than being left out of the gang, a nobody.

"Okay, okay," Tommy said. He walked on shaky legs toward the looming warehouse on the river. Feral cats slunk through the weeds, carrying things in their teeth. One hissed, its eyes gone to glass in the dark. *King of the Streets, King of the Streets,* Tommy chanted to himself. At the warehouse's big doors, he hesitated for a second. It wasn't padlocked. There was only a wooden bar looped through the handles. One of the boys howled like a dog and Tommy's heart beat fast at the thought of what might be on the other side of those doors.

King of the Streets . . .

Tommy slipped inside and saw at once that it was not a secret distillery but a slaughterhouse. The place had a terrible smell of river water and dead flesh. Behind him, Tommy heard the wooden bar being slipped back through the handles. He fell against the doors, pounding with his fists. "Lemme out! I'll kill youse!"

"Give our regards to the Italians, chump," Paddy yelled from the other side, and the other boys joined in with their own insults. Tommy could hear their laughter moving away from the warehouse, along with their quick footsteps. Tommy threw himself against the doors, with no luck. Unless he could find another way out, he was stuck there till somebody came. That somebody might be one of Lucky Luciano's men, which was a scarier thought than spending the night alone in the old warehouse. From the riverside, the moon pushed through the building's high, narrow windows. Its fractured light fell first on the chains and hooks suspended from the ceiling, then across the pale carcasses of the pigs hanging in a long line to the back of the warehouse. A rat scuttled across his foot and he shouted.

"Big fellow, wasn't he?" a man's voice said.

Tommy whipped around. "Who's there? Who said that?"

The man stepped out of the shadows. He was as big as a boxer, and he looked important and out of place in his full suit and bowler hat. Tommy swallowed hard. What if this man was one of Lucky Luciano's goons?

"It was a dare. M-my friends locked me in," Tommy managed to say. "I swear, mister. I don't want no trouble."

"What is your name?" the man asked.

"Tommy."

"Tommy," the man said, tasting the name. There was something about his eyes that didn't seem right. Tommy chalked it up to the weak moonlight. "Thomas the disciple. Doubting Thomas, who had to be shown before he could believe."

"Huh?"

The stranger smiled. It was an unsettling smile, but Tommy felt drawn to it. "Since you seem to be in a bargaining mood, Thomas, I will also make you a bargain. Tonight is the sort of night in which men of great daring can be made. But you will have to put your doubts aside, Thomas."

The man pulled a crisp hundred-dollar bill out of his pocket and snapped it taut between fingers blue-black with markings. Tommy's eyes widened.

"Whaddoo I gotta do?" he asked warily.

"All you have to do is walk to the far end of the warehouse and retrieve my walking stick. It has a silver tip."

The man waved his hand and Tommy saw the walking stick's silver knob glinting in the distance on the other side of the pigs.

"What's the catch?"

"Ah. That would be telling, wouldn't it? Life is a game of chance for men of daring, Thomas. You must be willing to risk in order to be rewarded. What say you?"

Tommy thought it over. In his brief life, he'd found that most bargains weren't bargains at all. And the thought of walking through those pale dead pig bodies to get to the stick at the far end seemed daunting. Then he remembered that he was there because his so-called friends had locked him in for laughs. He would not show up without that hundred dollars to rub in their faces.

"Okay, mister. I'll do it."

The man smiled his discomfiting smile. "A man of daring after all. May I see your hands?"

Tommy frowned. "What for?"

"A man in my position must take precautions. Hands, please."

Tommy held out his hands, turning them palms up, then palms down. The stranger's eyes gleamed.

"You may put them down now." The man reached into his pocket and produced a leather pouch, shaking what looked like dust into his palm. He blew it into Tommy's face.

"Wha-what'd you do that for?" Tommy sputtered, wiping at his nose and mouth.

"Upping the ante," the stranger said, holding the hundred-dollar bill between his second and third fingers like an offering. "Game of chance. Men of daring."

Tommy snatched the bill from the man's fingers and stuffed it into his own pocket. The man's eyes seemed to burn with a strange fire, and Tommy looked away quickly. He focused instead on the walking stick at the far end of the warehouse. He took a deep breath and entered the long, dark tunnel between the butchered pigs. All those dangling dead bodies, the eyes fixed and staring, the mouths open in a final silent scream, made him feel a little sick and woozy, and he struggled to keep his own eyes on the silver tip, which seemed a million miles away. Tommy chanted to himself quietly, *King of the Streets, King of the Streets, King of the Streets.*

"That's it, Thomas. Keep walking. You're doing very well. Soon you'll put all those doubts to rest."

Tommy kept moving. A hundred bucks was a world of money. When he showed up at Paddy's in new clothes, his hair freshly oiled and green in his pocket, he'd show the others who was really the chump. Nobody'd be locking him in a warehouse again.

The stranger sang an unnerving song: "*Naughty John, Naughty John, does his work with his apron on. . . .*"

The song made Tommy break out in a cold sweat and he took the last few steps at a clip till he reached the stick. It had been shoved into the ground like a sword. Beside it was a pamphlet for something called *The Good* something or other—the last word started with C, but Tommy had always had a hard time reading; the letters got mixed up in his head. Tommy gripped the stick with both hands and tugged, but it would not yank free, and the stranger's song was starting to work on his nerves. It seemed to come from everywhere, and under the melody he could swear he heard, very faintly, terrible growls and hisses, like voices released from the very depths of hell. He had the money in his pocket. He could run. But something told him he'd better see this through. Tommy positioned himself over the stick, wiped his hands on his filthy trousers, and tried again. It wouldn't budge. He made a third attempt, pulling so hard that he fell backward into the wood shavings. It was wet where he fell, and a drop of something hit his cheek, followed by another. Tommy wiped at his face. His hand came away smeared with blood. Still on his back, he looked up to see a German shepherd dangling on the hook above him, the kill so fresh the animal still twitched. Its belly had been slit open and its insides pulled out.

Tommy scrambled quickly to his feet. The stranger's laughter startled him. He was suddenly right there in front of Tommy, who backed into one of the pigs and sent it swinging against the others. With shaking hands, Tommy patted the dead pig into stillness, as if he could bring order to this nightmarish turn of events. The stranger was *right there. How is that possible? How could he have gotten all the way over here?*

"I...I can't get it out," Tommy whispered. He was not aware that he was backing up.

"Shame. Maybe he could help you?" the stranger said, nodding gently toward the dead dog. Then he frowned playfully. "No. I suppose not." He drew the stick from the ground without effort.

Tommy felt his head swim. He wasn't seeing so clearly anymore. The pigs' legs jerked like marionettes. They were *moving*, writhing on their hooks and squealing till Tommy, too, was screaming. The man's eyes burned with a terrible fire and he seemed to be even bigger than before.

"Game of chance, my boy. You've already rolled your dice."

"Paddy! Liam!" Tommy screamed. "Johnny! I'm in here!"

"Your friends have deserted you."

Tommy cut his eyes in the direction of the barred door at the other end of the warehouse, which was now slightly ajar. How far was it from here to there? Two hundred yards? Three hundred?

"Ah, one last game, I see," the stranger said, as if reading Tommy's thoughts. "Go on, then, Thomas. Place your bets. Roll the dice." His voice echoed in the cavernous slaughterhouse. "Run!"

Tommy was off. His knees moved like pistons, his elbows

jabbing back against the dead air. The door bounced in his vision as his legs gobbled ground. It was known that he was the fastest boy on Tenth Avenue. He'd outrun cops, priests, gangs, and his own mother, who was quick with a belt when he made her angry, which was most of the time. A hanging chain clanged into him and he batted it away, feeling the sting as it hit his wrist, but he did not slow down. Far behind him, he could hear the stranger's voice ringing out above the clang of the slaughterhouse chains. "'And the sixth offering was an offering of obedience....'"

Tommy could see the door. It was maybe sixty yards away, and still there was no sign of the stranger. A frantic chorus pounded in Tommy's head as he cleared the last carcass: *King of the Streets, King of the Streets, King of the Streets!* Fifty yards. Forty. Beautiful moonlight peeked through the crack where the door was slightly open. Tommy didn't stop to ask himself how it had been opened. All he could think about was pushing through it to freedom, racing for the shortcut to Thirty-ninth Street.

Thirty yards. Twenty...

Tommy no longer saw the door. One minute it had been within reach, and now it was gone. Instead, the stranger stood before him. It took Tommy a moment to slow down, for his brain to signal to his legs that there was trouble ahead—a cliff's edge in the shape of a man with burning eyes. He had run in the wrong direction. How was that possible? How had he gotten so turned around? Nothing looked right to him anymore. Tommy turned the other way and saw hideous shadows crawling along the walls and ceiling of the slaughterhouse, as if devouring it whole, the stranger walking just ahead of the movement like a carnival barker leading a parade of darkness.

How? Tommy thought. He dashed left, fighting through the smothering pigs only to find himself facing a brick wall that surely hadn't been there a minute ago. He went right, and there was another wall. When he faced forward again, the stranger was once more before him, standing in a patch of terrible moonlight. He was stripped to the waist, and Tommy stared at the glowing skin, the tattoos like brands, crawling across the man's flesh and underneath it as well, as if his skin were a false one and the thing underneath was waiting to come out.

"You lose, Thomas."

Devilish growls filled the warehouse. The darkness swirled behind the stranger, blotting out the walls and any hope of escape.

"'I am he, the Great Beast, the Dragon of Old. And all will look upon me and tremble. . . .'"

The stranger kept talking, but Tommy was beyond hearing. He kept his eyes on the moving dark and the unspeakable things inside it, on the changing form of the stranger who loomed above him.

"P-please . . ." he croaked.

The stranger only smiled.

"Such perfect hands," he said as the darkness descended.

AND DEATH SHALL FLEE

Evie sat in the tub, two fat cucumber slices placed over her swollen eyes, and sang in contempt of her throbbing head. *"We'll have Manhattan, the Bronx and Staten Island, too. . . .* I had Manhattan, all right," Evie mumbled. "And it . . . had . . . me." She slipped under the water and let it carry her until a fierce pounding made her surface.

"I'm *bathing,*" she yelled.

"Will you be long?" Jericho answered.

Evie let a prune-ish toe play at the hot-water tap. "Hard to say."

"I need the . . . the, ah . . ."

"Oh, applesauce," Evie said on a sigh. "Okay, okay. I don't want you to die of peritonitis like Valentino. Just a minute." Evie rinsed the cucumber slices under the tap and popped them into her mouth. She pulled the plug and let the water swirl down the drain while she slipped on her robe and opened the door with a flourish. "All yours," she said as Jericho pushed past her.

In the kitchen, Evie squeezed an orange into a glass, fished out the seeds, and gulped down the precious juice along with two aspirin. "Oh, sweet Mary."

A moment later, Jericho emerged from the bathroom, scowling. "What's eating you?"

"Nothing."

He sat on the couch and quietly laced up a shoe, but his disapproval hung in the room like the lingering scent of Evie's perfumed bath salts. Evie didn't mind yelling, but she hated feeling judged. It got under her skin and made her feel small and ugly and unfixable. She sang cheerily in rebuke of both Jericho and her throbbing skull. *"You're the berries, my bowl of cream, a dream come true, dear..."*

"I was only wondering if this is going to be your usual routine," Jericho said at last.

"Usual routine. Hmm, well, I might add a trained monkey. Everyone loves those."

"Is that all this is to you? One big party?"

Evie was angry now. At least she wasn't afraid to get out and live. Jericho didn't seem to know life beyond the pages of a musty old book, and he didn't seem interested in knowing anything beyond that, either.

"It's better than spending every night *brooding* like Byron's long-lost brother. Don't make that injured face—you *are* a brooder! And what good does it do you? You're eighteen, not eighty, kiddo. Live a little."

Jericho got up from the couch. "Live a little? Live a little!" He let out a bitter *ha!* "If you only knew..." He stopped suddenly, and Evie could see him force an almost mechanical calm to descend. "Never mind. You wouldn't understand. I have to get to the museum." He grabbed his dog-eared copy of Nietzsche and slammed the door behind him.

Evie sat on Mabel's bed. The aspirin hadn't helped much, but like a true modern girl, she wasn't about to lie in bed all day, unlike poor Mabel, who had succumbed to a terrible hangover. She lay curled in her bed, clutching a bowl in case she felt the need to vomit.

"Hot off the presses, today's headlines: The love of your life does not approve of my wanton flapper ways," Evie said in a voice of affected mystery. "Really, Mabesie. You might want to reconsider—he *is* a bit of a killjoy."

"My stomach doesn't approve of our wanton ways, either," Mabel said miserably. She hadn't lifted her head from her pillow. "I am never drinking again."

"That's what they all say, Pie Face."

Mabel moaned. "I mean it. I feel dreadful. I am ending my association with liquor." She raised her right hand. "You may be the notary public to this announcement."

"Noted. Public'd."

Mabel dropped her hand, her face screwed into an expression of fresh misery. Evie jumped off the bed.

"What is it? Are you about to blow?"

Mabel reached under her bed and pulled out what was left of Evie's headache band. It was bent in the middle, where someone had obviously stepped on it. Several of the rhinestones were missing, and the peacock feathers drooped like spent chorus girls. "I'm sorry."

"Oh..." Evie swallowed down a curse word. Mabel's mouth twitched and Evie could tell she was on the verge of a legendary weep. She tossed the headache band aside as if it were rubbish. "That old thing? I was tired of it, anyway. You've done me a favor, old girl, putting it out of its misery like that."

Mabel cocked an eyebrow. "You're lying, aren't you?"

"Yes."

"Just to make me feel better?"

"No. To make *me* feel better. Otherwise I'll cry."

"Thanks." Mabel managed a weak smile. She crooked her pinkie. "Pals for life-ski?"

Evie hooked her pinkie with Mabel's. "For life-ski." Evie kissed Mabel's forehead and turned off the bedside lamp. "Get some sleep, Pie Face."

Evie left the Bennington and walked down Broadway, past the shops. A radio store played its latest model, letting the sound drift out onto the sidewalks to entice customers. Evie idled for a moment, listening as she painted her lips in the window's reflection.

"...This is Cedric Donaldson, reporting from Roosevelt Field, Long Island, where just moments ago Jake Marlowe landed his American Flyer, an aeroplane of his own invention. You can hear the enthusiasm of the crowds who've gathered here on this fine autumn day to give the millionaire inventor and industrialist a hero's welcome! And here is the Bayside High School marching band playing 'The Stars and Stripes Forever.'"

The man in the shop peered disapprovingly at Evie through the glass. She pumped her arms and legs up and down in imitation of a marching band, gave the man a salute, and continued her meandering walk to the museum. At the newsstand, Evie stopped cold. The front page of the *New York Daily Mirror* trumpeted MAD-MAN OF MANHATTAN STRIKES AGAIN! She grabbed the paper and flipped past a store advertisement for Solomon's Comet binoculars to the story on page two.

"Hey, doll, you gonna pay for that?" The newspaperman held out his palm.

Evie tossed him a nickel and, clutching the paper, ran the rest of the way to the museum.

Will was sitting in the library with Sam and Jericho. He looked pale.

"I...I just heard...." Evie said, out of breath. She held up the newspaper.

"Tommy Duffy. Twelve years old," Will said quietly. "The killer took his hands."

The horror of it made Evie's stomach roil. "Is it the same killer?"

Will nodded. "First he posted a warning note to the papers."

Jericho opened the previous evening's late-edition *Daily News*. "'And in those days shall men seek death, and shall not find it; and shall desire to die, and death shall flee from them. For the Beast will rise when the comet flies.'"

"He seems to like attention, this fellow," Will said. "He left another note with the body."

Evie unscrolled the thin parchment, which resembled the first, with strange sigils along the bottom.

"Careful with that—it's on loan from Detective Malloy," Will explained.

"'And in those times, the young were idle. Their hands were absent from their plows and they did not raise them in prayer and praise to the Lord our God. And the Lord was angry and commanded of the Beast a sixth offering, an offering of obedience.'" Evie read. "The hands. With Ruta, he took the eyes, and with Tommy Duffy, the hands. Why?"

"It doesn't make any sense," Will agreed.

"The murder of a child could never make sense."

"I meant the symbology." Will was up and pacing the room. "Tommy Duffy was posed. He was hung upside down with one leg bent. That's not a Christian symbol. It's pagan. The Hanged Man, as seen on the tarot. It hints at magic or mysticism. Yet, *this* was found shoved into the boy's back pocket."

Will slapped a pamphlet down on the table. On its cover, a man in white robes and a pointed hat stood below an open Bible and a cross, ringing a liberty bell, while the ghostly face of George Washington looked on in approval.

"*The Good Citizen*," Evie read. "What's that?"

"It is a monthly publication of the Pillar of Fire Church," Will said. "It's also a strong endorsement of the Ku Klux Klan."

"You think the Klan might have killed that boy?"

"It's possible. Of course, it's also possible it was on the scene before the murder. However, it's worth nothing that Tommy Duffy was Irish. Ruta Badowski was Polish. The killer could harbor a hatred of foreigners."

"He could be anti-Catholic," Jericho said.

"They don't need much reason," Sam grumbled.

There were men back in Zenith who were Klansmen, Evie knew. People like Harold Brodie's father supported them. But Evie's father and mother had been Catholic once. The Irish O'Neills. And her father had repeatedly railed against the Klan and the thuggish bigotry for which they stood.

"When do we leave?" Evie asked.

"Leave for what, doll?" Sam said.

"We *are* going to this Pillar of Fire Church to sniff around, aren't we?"

"I can't," Will said. "I once helped bring charges against the Grand Dragon of the Klan out there. I'm known to them."

"What about Detective Malloy?" Jericho asked.

Will let out a long sigh. "He sent some men out this morning, but I understand that they were stonewalled. Alma Bridwell White, the bishop of Pillar of Fire, threatens a lawsuit anytime someone breathes a word against her church."

Evie sat up. "What if Jericho and I posed as newlyweds

interested in joining the church? Then we could snoop around and see what we could find."

Jericho looked up. "You . . . and me?"

"You pulling my leg?" Sam said. "Frederick the Giant here will get eaten alive."

"I can handle myself just fine, thanks."

"Don't get sore, Freddy. You're a fine fella. But what you need on this is somebody who can work the angles. You need a con man. Besides, somebody's gotta drive."

"I can drive," Evie said.

"Evie can drive," Jericho said. There was challenge in his stare.

"Fine. We'll all go," Sam said. "But if I get us a car, *I* get the wheel."

"As you wish," Will said. "Evie, may I see you for a moment in my study, please?"

"No one ever lets me drive. I'm a fine driver," Evie grumbled as she followed Will into the study. He retrieved a silver flask from a desk drawer and took a belt from it. "So you *do* have hooch," Evie said.

"I'm sorry to disappoint you; this is Phillips' Milk of Magnesia. My stomach is unsettled—not surprisingly, after what I witnessed this morning. You needn't sit. I shall be brief. Evangeline, I am not your mother, but that doesn't mean I have no standards of behavior. Coming home intoxicated at all hours will no longer be tolerated." Will looked directly at her. It occurred to Evie that she had never been looked at with such scrutiny before.

"But Unc—"

Will held up a hand to stop her protest before it could gather steam. "I might remind you that the trains travel in both directions between New York and Ohio, Evangeline. Is that understood?"

Evie swallowed hard. "I'm on the trolley."

"I don't mind if you enjoy what New York has to offer, but I do think you should be smart and safe. After all, there is a killer loose in our city."

Evie suddenly remembered the page she'd marked to show Will the previous day. "Applesauce! I meant to tell you—I think I found our symbol in a book in the library. Something about a religious order—the Brothers, the Brotherhood...oh, what was it?"

Back in the library, Evie searched the stacks, making a mess of Jericho's careful work as he moved behind her, righting things.

"Here it is!" Evie raced down the spiral staircase. "*Religious Fervor and Fanaticism in the Burned-Over District.* The book is pos-i-tute-ly a cure for insomnia, but it does have this." She opened to the page with the drawing of the pentacle-and-snake emblem. "The Brethren! That's it! Do you know what this is?"

"No, but I know someone who might: Dr. Georg Poblocki at Columbia University. He's a professor of religion, and an old friend. I'll telephone him right away," Will said, walking briskly from the library.

Jericho cleared his throat. "Would you like to take first shift, or shall I?" he asked, as if at any moment they'd be flooded with visitors.

"Where's Sam?" Evie asked.

"He went to call a friend about a motorcar."

"I'll bet he did," Evie scoffed.

"I could take first shift, if you like," Jericho offered.

"No, I will," Evie said. She was still miffed about Jericho's little lecture that morning and wasn't about to let him take the martyr points.

Evie wandered the rooms of the museum, thinking about the murder as well as the previous night's party. She probably shouldn't have been so public about her object-reading. What if they expected her to do that every time? What if, in the sober light of day, they thought of her as strange or frightening, somebody who might be able to divine the secrets they'd worked hard to hide? She made a vow that she'd be more careful in the future.

But she was curious about the Diviners Will had mentioned on her first day at the museum, so she sought out Liberty Anne Rathbone's book and curled up by the woodstove in the collections room to read it.

The Prophecies of Liberty Anne Rathbone,
as recorded by her brother and faithful servant, Cornelius T. Rathbone.

To-day, sweet Liberty Anne lay in that same state of which she has been bewitched since her walk into the woods. A'times, she speaks in soft awe at the wonders she beholds; other times, she is troubled and murmurs warnings of terrible things to come. It is as if she sees into that vast, heavenly abyss of which only the angels and the all-seeing eye of Providence are visitors. I have recorded her words forthwith.

"We are the Diviners. We have been and we will be. It is a power that comes from the great energy of the land and its people, a realm shared for a spell, for as long as is needed. We see the dead. We speak to restless spirits. We walk in dreams. We read meaning from every held thing. The future unfolds for us like the navigator's map, showing seas we have yet to travel."

Evie turned the pages excitedly.

"There can be no security at the cost of liberty. The heart of the union will not abide....The skies alight with strange fire. The eternal door is opened. The man in the stovepipe hat will come again with the storm....The eye cannot see."

At the bottom of the page was a small sketch of an eye surrounded by the rays of the sun, with a lightning bolt beneath it.

"The Diviners must stand, or all shall fall."

Evie closed the book and put it aside. Cornelius Rathbone had obviously loved his sister. Did he dream of her when she was gone, as Evie dreamed of James? Her hand sought the comfort of her half-dollar pendant. She was exhausted from her late evening. The afternoon sun beat through the windows, and combined with the warmth from the woodstove turned the room stuffy. Evie rested her head on her arms and fell asleep.

She dreamed of the city. The canyonlike streets were empty, the setting sun turning the windows orange, but in the distance, a mass of dark clouds threatened. She called out, but there was no one. Newspapers swept across the street and skittered up the sides of the quiet buildings. She became aware of others. Shades just out of sight. Shadow people. She'd turn her head just in time to see them retreat into the growing gloom. Whispering, "She's one. She's one of them. You can't stop us. Nothing can stop us."

Evie turned a corner and was surprised to see Henry also walking the streets, as if looking for someone. His eyes widened when he saw her. "Evie, what are you doing here? Don't remember me," he said, and when she looked again, he was gone. But someone else was running toward her, and Evie found she couldn't move at all. She was paralyzed with fear. The figure came closer. It was a girl with shining black hair and bottle-green eyes. There was something vaguely familiar about the girl; Evie could swear they'd met before. Then it came to her—the hostess from the restaurant in Chinatown. The girl carried a strange dagger in one hand. She looked angry, alarmed, as she shouted, "You shouldn't be here! Wake up!"

"Evie, wake up!" Sam was shaking her shoulder. Evie blinked

awake in the museum. Sunlight still streamed through the stained-glass windows of the collections room. "You were dreaming."

"I was?" Evie said, stretching. Her heart still beat fast.

"Must've been a real lulu of a dream. You called out."

Evie nodded. "A real nightmare."

"Aw, doll. Not surprising with all this murder talk. Tell your pal Sam all about it. I'll keep you safe." Sam moved into the chair beside her. He brushed a curl out of her eyes gently, but his smile had that same wolfish quality she'd first seen in Penn Station.

Evie gave him the big, innocent peepers. "Well, I dreamed I was in New York, all alone...."

"Poor baby." Sam put his arm around her shoulders.

"I walked the streets searching for people...but there was no one...."

"Terrible..." Sam was so close she could smell the musk of him.

"Suddenly, I found myself in Penn Station...." Evie paused. "And the most terrible thing happened next."

"What's that, doll?" Sam purred.

"Some absolute louse stole my twenty dollars." She pushed hard against Sam's chest. He nearly toppled backward but righted himself at the last minute.

Sam smirked. "Well, that's a fine thank-you to the fella who just got you a spiffy wash for the ball."

Evie gave him a little bow.

"I just came back to tell you that we've got a real live paying customer in the joint who wants a tour."

"Send Jericho," Evie said, stretching.

"This fella asked for your uncle, but I told him you were in charge, Your Highness." Sam returned the bow.

Evie replied with an eye-roll. "Do you think you can manage to not steal anything while I'm gone?"

"The only thing I'm trying to steal is your heart, doll." Sam smirked.

"You're not that talented a thief, Sam Lloyd."

Evie arrived in the foyer to find a young man in a rumpled suit standing by the front doors, twirling his hat in his hands. A notebook peeked out of his breast pocket.

"Can I help you?" Evie said, giving her friendliest smile.

The man stopped twirling his hat and stuck out his hand like a salesman. "How do you do? Harry Snyder. I'm visiting from Wisconsin. Heard about your museum and just *had* to take a look for myself. I can't wait to tell the folks back home all about it."

If Harry Snyder was from Wisconsin, Evie would eat her hat. If his name was Harry Snyder, she'd eat a second hat.

"Welcome to the Museum of American Folklore, Superstition, and the Occult, Mr. Snyder," Evie said, stretching out his last name. "Right this way, please."

Evie led the man from room to room, explaining the various objects, giving the historical spiel she'd heard from Will numerous times and adding a few of her own flourishes. All the while the man took notes in his notepad and looked around as if he expected some spirit to manifest at any moment.

"I hear from a friend that you folks are helping the police with that murder investigation—that Madman in Manhattan business. Sounds awful. Do you have any clues?" he asked. He picked up a rare figurine from the seventeenth century as if it were a saltshaker.

Evie took it from his hands and placed it back on the table.

"Has your uncle told you anything about it? Is the killer really carrying out a diabolical occult ritual? What's his angle?"

"I'm afraid I'm sworn to secrecy under the orders of Detective Malloy."

The man moved closer. "I couldn't help noticing that the good Officer Malloy isn't here. Say, what did the killer do with that poor girl's peepers? Somebody said he mailed 'em to the police with a note. That true?"

Evie narrowed her eyes. "Who are you really?"

"Harry Snyder, from—"

"Dry up!" Evie snapped.

The man grinned. He wagged a finger at her playfully. "You've got me." He pumped her hand in a firm shake. "I'm T. S. Woodhouse, reporter for the *Daily News*? I've been trying to get your uncle to comment on the case for us, but he's tighter with a quote than Calvin Coolidge. But, ah, maybe I've been barking up the wrong family member?" T. S. Woodhouse's pencil hovered expectantly above his notepad.

"I'm glad I took your money up front, Mr. Woodhouse. I'll show you the way out." She marched toward the door, her heels clicking on the marble. Mr. Woodhouse ran alongside her.

"Call me T.S., please. Come on, wouldn't you like to see your name in the papers? Show all your friends back home? We could even put your picture in, pretty girl like you. Why, you'd be the toast of Manhattan."

Evie paused. With all the work they were doing, why shouldn't they get the credit and the reward? Why shouldn't they be famous for it? Still, if Uncle Will found out, he'd be furious. She'd already promised she wouldn't get into any more trouble. This was courting trouble for sure.

"I'm sorry, Mr. Woodhouse. I can't."

T. S. Woodhouse cradled his hat to his chest. "Listen, I'm going to level with you, Miss O'Neill. I need this story. This could be my ticket to the big time. Did you ever want something that badly?"

T. S. Woodhouse reminded Evie of an overgrown, wayward

schoolboy. He was tall and skinny, full of a palpable coiled energy; his face was sharp-planed but freckled, and beneath his mop of unruly brown hair and straight brows, his narrow blue eyes seemed to be constantly observing, recording. But there was a determination in those eyes that Evie understood all too well.

"That isn't my concern."

"It could be." Those blue eyes focused directly on her. "What do you want? Name it. You want to be written up in all the gossip pages? You want column inches saying that millionaires are fighting to marry you? I can make that happen."

"You can't even make this story happen, Mr. Woodhouse. How will you help me?"

"I hit it big with this story, give the *Daily News* some exclusive dope, I'll be in a position to give you what you need. A favor for a favor. On the level—a square deal."

He stuck out his hand again. Evie ignored it.

"Pretty quiet around here," Mr. Woodhouse said, and there was no mistaking the implication.

"It's just an afternoon lull."

T. S. Woodhouse reshaped his hat as if doing so were his only concern. "From what I hear, there's a lot of lull time. In fact, I hear the city might shut this place down come spring. Unless, of course, it starts turning a profit."

Evie bit her lip, thinking it over. She'd been wondering how they could make the museum a big deal, and now the opportunity had just fallen into her lap. Will was a genius, but he wasn't much of a businessman. It was clear that if someone was going to save the joint, it was going to have to be Evie. She'd help the museum—and if she helped herself along the way, well, what was the matter with that?

"*I'll* make a deal with *you*, Mr. Woodhouse. We need bodies in this joint. I'll tell you what I know—as an anonymous source—and you keep writing about how swell the museum is, how everybody who's anybody comes here. Of course, you can mention that Uncle Will is being helped in the investigation of these heinous murders by his niece, Miss Evie O'Neill. And if my picture just happened to make it into the papers, too, well, I couldn't help that, could I?"

"No. Of course not." Mr. Woodhouse smiled broadly and dropped his hat onto the back of his head. "It's a known fact that newspapers sell better when pretty girls grace their pages."

"We have a deal, then?"

"We have a deal." They shook on it. T. S. Woodhouse's pencil hovered over his notepad once again. "Ready when you are. We know the killer leaves occult symbols. What are they?"

"It's a pentacle surrounded by a snake that's eating its tail. The killer brands it onto their bodies. And he leaves religious notes. Unc thinks it might have to do with the Book of Revelation."

T. S. Woodhouse's pencil scribbled across the notepad. "That's good. Revelations Killer! I like it."

"We don't know if that's true yet...."

"Doesn't matter." T. S. Woodhouse's expression was all grim determination. "I'm the press. I'll make it true. What else?"

"That's all for now. I'll expect that story, Mr. Woodhouse."

T. S. Woodhouse stuck his pencil behind his ear, shoved the notepad into his suit pocket, and pumped Evie's hand again. "You've been swell, Evie. Don't worry—I always keep my promises."

Evie hoped that was true. If Will couldn't make the museum into a destination, perhaps she could. And if she wanted to stay in Manhattan when her three months were up, she needed to start making a place and a name for herself now. Having a friend like T. S. Woodhouse could be very helpful.

FUNNY HOW THINGS WORK OUT

Henry woke from his dream with a gasp. He'd gone in with the hope of finding Louis. Instead, he'd seen Evie—and she had clearly seen him. That was odd, and Henry knew from odd. He'd been walking in dreams for two years now, and that had never happened.

Henry went to the cracked washstand. He slapped water on his face from the bowl and smoothed his hair back with his wet hands. Then he put the old straw boater back on his head and stared at his pale reflection in the mirror. He rested his forehead against the glass and closed his eyes.

"Louis, where are you?" he asked the empty room, not expecting an answer.

☀

"Sister," Memphis said quietly. "Could I ask you something? Privately?"

"You talking about me?" Isaiah piped up from Sister Walker's dining room table, where he was adding sums now that his work with Sister Walker and the cards was finished for the day. Memphis was always amazed by his little brother's talent for picking up on just which conversations were none of his business.

"Now, why would I be talking about you? Sister and I have more important things to talk about."

Isaiah scowled. "I am too important!"

"Yes, you are," Sister Walker assured him. "Why don't you help yourself to another piece of candy, Isaiah? Memphis, let's step out to the kitchen."

Memphis followed Sister Walker to the back of the railroad flat into a small, cheerful kitchen with flowered curtains framing a window that looked out into a common courtyard strung with laundry. She offered him a cookie as she took a seat across from him at the table. Memphis nibbled at the cookie. Sister wasn't much of a baker; her cookies were always too dry and not sweet enough, but he took them out of politeness.

"Something on your mind, Memphis?"

"I'm worried about Isaiah."

"Has something happened?"

Memphis wasn't sure how much he should say. What if Sister Walker didn't want to work with Isaiah anymore? Isaiah would be crushed. Still, if something wasn't right, he needed to let somebody know, and he certainly couldn't tell Octavia.

"He's been waking up in the night. It's like he's in a trance. And he's saying strange things."

Sister Walker's brow furrowed. "What sorts of things?"

"'I am the Beast. The Dragon of Old.' And something that sounded like scripture, but nothing I was familiar with."

"'I am the Beast, the Dragon of Old,'" Sister Walker repeated. "That's from Revelation, if I recall my Sunday school. I don't like to cast aspersions, but might it be Octavia?" she offered kindly.

Memphis frowned. It would be just like Octavia to scare Isaiah with visions of God's judgment.

"He said something else curious. Just one word over and over: *Diviners.*"

The warmth went out of Sister Walker's face and Memphis was afraid he'd said something wrong.

"What is it? Is it something bad?"

"I haven't heard that word used in a long time," she said, and Memphis thought she sounded a bit sad. "It's a name for people with rare gifts."

"Gifts like Isaiah's?"

Sister Walker gave a small shrug. "It depends on what you believe, I suppose. But yes, some people would call Isaiah a Diviner."

Memphis broke the cookie into smaller bits. "But where would he hear that?"

"Children hear all sorts of things, I suppose." Sister Walker swirled the ice in her glass of water ever so slowly. "The name comes from the accounts of a seer from the eighteen hundreds, Liberty Anne Rathbone. Just a girl, really. Her brother, Cornelius, built a big mansion over near Central Park. Now it's the Museum of American Folklore, Superstition, and the Occult. Some folks call it the Museum of the Creepy Crawlies."

"Oh. I've heard of it. But why would Isaiah know about these Diviners?"

Sister Walker stepped into the other room and returned with the day's newspaper, which she spread out on the table. "The murders. The man who runs the museum, Dr. Fitzgerald, is helping the police try to find the killer. I'll bet Isaiah heard people talking about it. Probably terrified him, too, and he took that right into his sleep. It's not uncommon for children to sleepwalk or talk in their sleep when they're frightened by something during the day.

And Isaiah's gifts make him even more sensitive. He's almost like a radio, picking up signals from everywhere."

There had been a lot of talk in the neighborhood about the killings, and even Aunt Octavia had brought it up. Memphis wanted to believe that was the case, but what Isaiah had said was so oddly specific, and the way he went trancelike... it was unsettling. But he'd already taken up too much of Sister Walker's time and he didn't want to bother her with vague notions of things not being right.

"I'll bet that's what it is. Thank you, Sister Walker."

"I didn't do much. Is there anything else?"

Memphis thought of his own recurring dream, but he couldn't bring himself to tell Sister Walker about it. It seemed so silly, not at all the sort of thing someone who was grown should be asking about.

"No, ma'am. Nothing else."

Sister Walker nodded slowly. "All right, then. Memphis, how old are you, again?"

"Seventeen."

"Seventeen," Sister Walker said, as if it meant something, though Memphis couldn't imagine what that would be. "And have you ever been able to read cards like Isaiah? Anything like that?"

Memphis wasn't sure if Sister Walker knew about his past as a healer. They'd never discussed it, and he couldn't see the sense in telling her now. It wasn't the same as Isaiah's talents, and besides, it was gone. "No, ma'am. I guess all the gifts went to Isaiah," he said without bitterness, just as a statement of fact. "Thank you for the cookie."

Sister Walker laughed. "Memphis, it doesn't take a Diviner to tell me you didn't like that cookie one bit."

"Just not very hungry, ma'am. That's all." Memphis gave her

the smile even though he was pretty sure Sister Walker could see through that, too.

Back in the dining room, Memphis rubbed the top of Isaiah's head and said, "Time to get going, Shrimpy."

"Isaiah," Sister Walker called. "You been having any interesting dreams lately?" She gave Memphis a surreptitious wink.

"Yes, ma'am! I dreamed I caught a frog. It was the biggest frog you ever seen, and it let me ride on its back—just me and nobody else!"

Sister Walker gave Memphis a look as if to say, *You see? Nothing to worry about.* "Well, it's a shame that frog isn't here to give you a ride home. Oh, don't forget your book, now."

She handed Isaiah the book and gave his narrow shoulders a gentle squeeze. Isaiah took her hands in his and looked up at her in worry. "You should be careful with that chair, Sister."

"What chair is that?"

"The kitchen chair."

"Isaiah, let's *go*." Memphis yanked on his brother's sleeve.

"All right, then. I'll be careful. You go on home now, before you get us into trouble with your auntie."

Sister Walker waved in farewell as she watched the boys walking away, arguing about silly things the way brothers do. Memphis was hiding something from her; she could sense it. The old Margaret would've been able to find out what it was without too much trouble. But that was the past, and she was concerned with the future. When she'd come to Harlem six months ago, hunting for Memphis Campbell, she'd thought he was that future. Funny how things worked out. But now she had Isaiah. And if she was right about what lay ahead, she needed to prepare him for what was coming.

Much later, she went to retrieve a dish she needed from the

tall cabinet, pulling the kitchen chair over so that she could reach it. As she stood reaching, the leg gave way and she crashed to the kitchen floor, banging her shoulder and knee. She was fine—just shaky and sore—but the chair was ruined. And with a chill, she remembered Isaiah's words to her: *You should be careful with that chair, Sister.*

THE GOOD CITIZEN

The Pillar of Fire Church was situated on eighty bucolic acres of former farmland in Zarephath, New Jersey. Evangelist Alma Bridwell White had established a community there along the Millstone River, far from what she saw as the corrupting influence of the world. Her followers had all they needed—communal living, a college, and a church. Outsiders were discouraged.

Sam drove up a long dirt driveway bordered by neat, fat rows of firs, which gave way to a cluster of white two-story buildings on a pretty, parklike campus. Men and women in modest clothing walked about, greeting one another with pleasant smiles.

"They don't look much like killers," Evie remarked.

"They never do," Sam muttered.

They were met at the administration building by a Mr. Adkins, a beefy, balding man with a square jaw and a very firm handshake. "The Pillar of Fire Church welcomes you." Jericho and Evie introduced themselves as Mr. and Mrs. Jones, and Sam was Mr. Smith, Jericho's cousin who had graciously offered to drive them in his car.

"What a fine family," Mr. Adkins said. "Just our sort of people."

He led them briefly around the grounds and took them through the church with its enormous pipe organ. Back in the administration building, they passed through a dining hall, where several ladies in identical blue skirts and white blouses sat at a long table assembling pamphlets. They smiled and waved as if it were a church supper and Evie, Sam, and Jericho were their invited guests, and Evie couldn't help imagining those same welcoming faces illuminated by the flames of a burning cross in the night. A bead of sweat trickled down her back under her dress.

Mr. Adkins ushered them into a small, spare office. A simple cross-stitched panel hung on the wall: ETERNAL VIGILANCE IS THE PRICE OF FREEDOM. Evie perched on the very edge of an offered chair. Jericho sat beside her. Sam stood behind them, his hands in his pockets, his eyes searching.

"What may the Pillar of Fire Church do for you today, Mr. and Mrs. Jones?"

"Mr. Jones and I are so very impressed with your godly way of life. We're thinking of moving away from Manhattan, what with those terrible murders going on." Evie shuddered for effect. "We just don't feel safe, do we, Mr. Jones?"

"I...uh..."

Evie patted his hand. "We don't. Don't you think it's simply awful, Mr. Adkins?"

"Indeed I do. But I can't say I'm surprised. It's this foreign element coming in, you know—it's polluting our white race and way of life. The Jewish anarchists. The Bolsheviks. The Italians and Irish Catholics. The Negroes, with their music and dancing. They don't hold to our same moral code. They don't share our American values. We believe in one hundred percent Americanism."

"Which tribe?" Sam said under his breath.

Evie faked a coughing fit. She made it sound as if she were losing a lung. "Mr. Adkins, could I have a glass of water, please?" Evie coughed again for effect.

"Certainly. I'll, uh, I'll have to go to the kitchen for it. I won't be but a minute. Please make yourselves at home."

As soon as he was gone, Evie leaped up. "That's just what I intend to do. You fellas search this room. I'm snooping around."

Jericho shook his head. "That isn't a good idea, Evie. What if he comes back?"

"Tell him I went to the *lavatory*," Evie said with a roll of her eyes. "Men are pos-i-tute-ly *paralyzed* by the mention of females in lavatories."

Evie sneaked down the hall, opening doors, searching for anything that might be a clue. A new batch of *Good Citizen* pamphlets sat in a stack on a table by the staircase. The cover image showed the same hooded man hanging a Catholic upside down in the way that Tommy Duffy's body had been posed. Evie pocketed the pamphlet to show to Will later.

"Psst!" Sam hissed at Evie from the doorway of an office.

"Sam! What are you doing?" Evie whispered.

"Same thing you are. Snooping around."

Evie ran to the end of the hall. Seeing no one, she hurried inside the office and shut the door. "You were supposed to stay with Jericho!"

"You should know by now, doll, that I never do what I'm supposed to do."

"Never mind that. Did you find anything?"

"Not yet. I'll look here. You look over there."

Evie searched the drawers of an end table and glanced at a bookcase but found nothing of value. She moved on to the closet.

Inside, white robes and hoods hung from hooks like the hollowed skins of ghosts. Evie shut the door quickly and ran to Sam, who was opening drawers in a large oak rolltop desk.

"Check the bottom drawers," he said. Sam pulled open the right-side drawer, which was a mishmash of papers and letters. He lifted a notice about a meeting of the American Eugenics Society. Beneath it lay a photograph of a grand castle shrouded in fog. Something about the castle was familiar to Sam, though he couldn't say why. He shoved the photograph into his pocket just as the door opened with a *click*.

A tall, rangy man stood uncertainly in the doorway. He wore a dark hat, farmer's coveralls, and a denim work shirt. From his neck hung a flat, round pendant on a strip of leather.

"Looking for Missus White," the man said in a clipped tone. "You seen her?"

Carefully, Evie slid the drawer closed. "Whom shall I say is calling?" she asked.

"Brother Jacob Call." The man took two tentative steps into the room. Evie's gaze was drawn to the pendant: a five-pointed star encircled by a snake eating its tail. Her heart raced. Behind her back, she signaled to Sam. He squeezed her fingers in response.

"My, that's an interesting pendant you're wearing. Is it very old?"

The man placed a palm over it. "It's the Lord's mark. A protection to his people in the time of the Beast."

A cold tickle crept from Evie's neck down her arm. The pendant, the mention of the Beast—it was very possible she and Sam were in a room with the Pentacle Killer.

"Wh-what did you say your name was again?" Evie asked.

The man looked suddenly suspicious. He turned away briskly, nearly upending a big-boned woman in a sober black dress who gaped at Sam and Evie from behind wire-rimmed glasses.

"What on earth are you doing in here?" the woman demanded. Her voice was pulpit-worthy.

"Who wants to know, sister?" Sam challenged.

The woman's eyes narrowed. "I am Mrs. Alma Bridwell White. Head of the Pillar of Fire Church. And *you* are in my office, uninvited."

She summoned two large, unhappy men to escort Evie and Sam rather roughly back to Mr. Adkins's office, where Jericho still sat. His eyes widened and Evie shot him a warning glance to keep quiet.

"Mr. Adkins, can you explain what these two interlopers were doing in my office, uninvited and unsupervised?"

"I'm sorry, Mrs. White. They came to ask about membership. I went to get Mrs. Jones a glass of water, and when I got back, Mr. Jones told me both she and Mr. Smith there had gone to the lavatory."

"Spies! That's what they are. What, pray tell, were you two doing in my office?" Mrs. White pressed. "I demand an answer!"

A few men had pushed into the room. All of them looked ready for a fight. Evie swallowed hard. If they couldn't think of something, they were done for.

"I didn't want to do this, but the lies have gone on long enough," Sam said suddenly. Evie could tell by the way his hand shook the change in his pocket that he was nervous.

"They...they have?" Evie searched his face for some clue about what game they were playing now.

"Yes, they have. I can't hide anymore, Honey Pie." Sam put his arm around Evie's shoulder, pulling her close. He kissed her on the cheek while Jericho looked on, astonished. "I'm sorry that this is the way you had to find out, cousin. We went into that office to be alone. I'm gone for her, and she's got it bad for me. Don'tcha, doll face? We're going to Reno for the annulment, and then we're getting hitched. Why, I wouldn't blame you if you socked me right here and now for what I've done."

Murmurs of astonishment and judgment rippled through the assembled Pillar of Fire crowd. Hidden by the largeness of Jericho, Sam made a small fist motion, hoping that Jericho would take the hint.

Finally, Jericho's eyes widened in understanding. "Well, that's my wife, and you can't have her," he announced awkwardly. He pulled back and socked Sam, catching him across the jaw and bottom lip. Sam tottered and sank to his knees, his mouth bloody.

"Son of a—" Sam croaked.

"Oh, Sam!" Evie dropped beside Sam. She put her handkerchief to his mouth. "I never wanted this to happen."

Mrs. White was steely-eyed. "I think you'd best leave. We are an honorable organization and want no part of your sordid city affairs."

❋

"An 'honorable organization,'" Sam scoffed from behind the wheel as they made their way down the long drive. A welt was already rising on his cheek, and there was dried blood on his shirt. Evie dabbed at his wound and he winced. "Ow."

"Sorry for that," Jericho said from the backseat, but he looked pretty pleased with himself.

"That punch got us out of there. Good work, Freddie. Though next time, go easy on me, not-so-gentle giant."

At the bottom of the drive, a group of men stood across the road, blocking their escape. Evie gripped the door handle as the men surrounded the car. Sam's hands remained fixed on the wheel, and for the second time, Evie wished she were driving.

A broad-chested man in a straw hat leaned both arms on Evie's open window. "You people from the city, we know what you get up to over there, and we don't want any part of it. You understand?"

Evie nodded gravely. Her heart pounded in her chest. She kept her eyes on the road ahead.

"Don't come back here no more. We don't need your kind."

One of the men angled his face close to Jericho's. He smiled at him in a convivial way, as if they were two old friends on a fishing trip, one giving advice to the other. "If it were me, son, I'd take that one out to the woods and show him what happens to fellas what try to take what's rightfully yours." He took a book of matches from his pocket and struck one, watching it flare into an orange diamond, then flicked it into the front seat at Sam. Evie gave a small shriek as it landed on his pants, but he patted it out quickly. He looked terrified, though. The usual Sam swagger was nowhere to be seen. The men stepped back. The fellow in front took his hand off the hood, and Sam jerked the car forward, spraying small pebbles from the back tires as he drove. They came around the next bend so quickly that they didn't see the man until they were nearly upon him.

"Sam, watch out!" Evie yelled.

Sam hit the brakes and the car shuddered to a stop and quit. In front of them, Brother Jacob Call had both hands up, as if waiting to be hit. He pointed a long finger at them.

"What was started long ago will now be finished when the fire burns in the sky," he said. "Repent, for the Beast is come."

Then he turned away, walking up the hill in long, quick strides.

It was afternoon by the time Evie, Jericho, and Sam returned to the museum and told Will of their narrow escape from the Pillar of Fire Church and their curious encounter with Brother Jacob Call.

"Do you think he could be our killer?" Jericho asked.

"I'll certainly report it to Detective Malloy right away," Will answered. "You did very well. This may be the break we've needed."

"He said something else very curious." Evie rested her stocking feet on a stack of books on the floor. "He said something about 'what was started long ago would now be finished.' What was started long ago? When?"

The phone rang and Will answered it. "William Fitzgerald. I see. Whom may I say is calling, please? Just a moment." Will held out the receiver. "It's for you, Evie. A Mr. Daily Newsenhauser?"

Evie took the phone and said, "I don't need an Electrolux, and I'm already a Colgate customer, so unless you're giving away a mink, I'm afraid—"

"Heya, Sheba. How's the Creepy Crawly?" T. S. Woodhouse said.

Evie turned her back on Will and the boys. "Spiffing. Mr. Lincoln's ghost just asked me to tea. I do love a polite ghost. Clever moniker."

"Daily Newsenhauser? I thought so."

Evie placed a hand over the receiver. "An order I placed with a salesman at B. Altman. I won't be a minute."

"I don't like your appropriating the museum's telephone for personal calls, Evangeline," Will said, but he didn't look up from his stack of clippings.

"I take it you can't speak freely?" Woodhouse said.

"You're on the trolley."

"Maybe we could meet."

"Not likely."

"Come on, Sheba. Play along with your old pal T.S. Got anything for me?"

"That depends. What do you have for me?"

"A story about the museum in tomorrow's papers. A mention of one Miss Evie O'Neill. The very comely Miss O'Neill."

Evie smiled. "Hold on a minute. Jericho," she called. "I need to order unmentionables. Be a dear and hang this one up for me, and I'll take it in Will's office." Evie scurried past Sam, who waggled his eyebrows in response to the word *unmentionables*. Evie gave him an irritated eye-roll and raced to the phone in Will's office. "I've got it, Jericho dear." She waited for the telltale *click*, then spoke in a hushed voice. "They think the killer might be involved with the Klan. A copy of *The Good Citizen* was found with Tommy Duffy's body."

"No kidding? Wouldn't put it past those pond scum."

"I know. Why, they're even worse than reporters."

"I like you, Sheba."

"And I like what you can do for me, Mr. Woodhouse."

"What else?"

"Nothing doing. I'll expect that article first."

"Evie, please do say good-bye," Will instructed from the doorway.

Evie spoke cheerfully and loudly into the receiver. "Get yourself a mustard plaster and stay in bed, Mabesie darling, and you'll be as good as new! I have to dash now. Ta!" Evie put the phone back in its cradle and turned to Will with a heavy sigh. "Poor lamb would simply be lost without me."

Will looked puzzled. "I thought you were speaking to a sales-man at B. Altman."

"There were two calls!" Evie lied, smiling brightly. "Oh, Unc, honestly! Didn't you hear it ring the second time? The sound in these old mansions isn't what it could be, I suppose. Well, no mat-ter. *I* heard it. What did you want, Unc?"

Will threaded his arms through the sleeves of his trench coat and put on his hat. "I've just received word from my colleague Dr. Poblocki at Columbia. That page you discovered has proved help-ful. He's found something significant after all. Well?"

Evie grabbed her coat.

THE ELEVEN OFFERINGS

Evie and Will crossed the long green of Columbia, heading toward the Low Memorial Library, an enormous marble building whose ionic columns gave it the countenance of a Greek temple. To their right, the crooked-tooth rooftops of the apartment buildings of Morningside Heights stood in relief against the gray autumnal sky. Somewhere, a church bell tolled. The day was blustery, but students still sat on the library steps leading up from the green. Heads turned as Evie passed. She allowed herself to think it was because she was devastatingly pretty in her rose silk dress and peacock-patterned stockings, and not because she was one of the only girls on campus.

Dr. Georg Poblocki's office sat at the end of a long hall in a building that smelled of old books and yearning. Dr. Poblocki himself was a large man with craggy cheeks and puffy eyes overshadowed by unruly brows that Evie had the urge to trim.

"The full story behind that drawing you sent was rather hard to find, William," Dr. Poblocki said in a faint German accent. He smiled with an almost mischievous glee. "But find it I did."

He drew a book from a stack and opened it to a marked page showing the familiar star-encircled-by-a-snake emblem. "Behold: the Pentacle of the Beast."

"The police should have consulted you instead of me, Georg."

Dr. Poblocki shrugged. "I don't have a museum." To Evie he said, "Your uncle was my student at Yale before he started working for the government."

"That was a long time ago." Will tapped the page. "Tell me more about this Pentacle of the Beast, Georg. What is it? What does it mean?"

"It is the sacred emblem of the Brethren, a vanished religious cult in upstate New York."

"I forget New York even has an upstate. Seems unnecessary after Manhattan," Evie quipped.

"Delightful!" Dr. Poblocki smiled. "I like this one."

"The Brethren?" Will prompted as if waiting out an unruly student.

"The Most Holy Covenant of the Brethren of God. They were formed during the Second Great Awakening, in the early nineteenth century."

"The second what?" Evie asked.

"The Second Great Awakening was a time when religious fervor gripped the nation. Preachers would cross the country giving fiery sermons about hellfire and damnation, warning of the Devil's temptations while saving souls during revivals and tent meetings," Dr. Poblocki said, slipping into the sort of lecturing mode Evie imagined he used with his students. "It gave rise to new religions such as the Church of Latter-Day Saints, the Church of Christ, and the Seventh-Day Adventists, as well as this one." Dr. Poblocki tapped the book with his finger. "The Brethren was formed by a young preacher named John Joseph Algoode. Reverend Algoode was tending sheep—very biblical, that—when he saw a great fire in the sky. It was Solomon's Comet coming through the northern hemisphere."

Evie suddenly remembered the two girls handing her the flyer on the street. "The same Solomon's Comet..."

"On its way to us now in its fifty-year return. Indeed." Dr. Poblocki finished. He settled into a chair, wincing as he did so. "This dreadful knee of mine. Old age comes for us all, I'm afraid."

"I'll be old before you tell us the story, Georg," Will pressed, and Evie felt a bit embarrassed by his rudeness.

"Your uncle. He could never wait for anything. That impatience will cost you in the end, I fear, William," Dr. Poblocki said, peering up at Will darkly, and it seemed to Evie that her uncle looked just a bit chastened. "Pastor Algoode claimed to have had a vision: that the old churches of Europe were a corruption of God's word. There needed to be a new American faith, he said. Only this great experiment of a country could produce believers pure and devout enough to submit wholly to God's word and judgment. The Brethren would be that faith. They would rule the new America. The true America. They would fulfill its great promise." Dr. Poblocki removed his glasses, fogging the lenses with his breath and wiping them clean with a cloth until he was satisfied, then settled the hooks of them over his ears again. "Pastor Algoode brought his small flock to the Catskill Mountains in 1832. They settled on fifteen acres and built a church in an old barn, where they would meet each evening for prayers by candlelight and all day on Sundays. They painted their homes and church with religious signs in accordance with their holy book, and they farmed their land. They had an odd belief system, cobbled together from the Bible—particularly Revelation—and the occult. Their Book of the Holy Brethren was believed to be part religious doctrine, part grimoire."

"Grimoire?" Evie said.

"A book of sorcery," Dr. Poblocki explained.

"That explains the sigils, I suppose," Will mused.

Dr. Poblocki nodded. "Indeed. There were rumors, as there always are in such cases, that the Brethren practiced everything from unsavory sexual practices to cannibalism and human sacrifice. It's one of the reasons they were so insular and lived up in the mountains—to escape persecution. They did have extensive knowledge of hallucinogens, most likely learned from native tribes who used such things in their religious worship to achieve transcendence. The account of a French-Canadian fur trapper visiting the area tells of 'a magnificent smoke and a sweet wine which, when consumed, cause the mind to imagine all sorts of angels and devils.' Now. The Brethren were an eschatology cult."

"Is that even legal?" Evie said.

"Charming lady!" Dr. Poblocki laughed and patted Evie's hand. "Are you certain you're related to *that* one?" He nodded at Will, and Evie had to fight the urge to giggle.

"Eschatology," Dr. Poblocki continued, "from the Greek *eschatos*, meaning 'the last,' is about the end of the world and the second coming of Jesus Christ. Ah, but here is where things become quite interesting!"

Evie's eyes widened. "More interesting than dope and sorcery?"

"Indeed! You see, the Brethren didn't just believe that the end of the world was nigh; they thought it their God-given duty to help bring it about."

"How did they plan to do that?" Will asked.

"By raising the anti-Christ. The Beast himself." Dr. Poblocki paused to allow his words time to settle. Evie's skin prickled with goose bumps.

"Why would they do that if they were Christians?" Evie asked.

"The line between faith and fanaticism is a constantly shifting one," Dr. Poblocki said. "When does belief become justification? When does right become rationale and crusade become crime?"

"How did they intend to raise the Beast, Georg?" Will asked.

"With this." Dr. Poblocki reached into his pile of books and produced a gnarled, leather-bound volume. "The eleven offerings. It's a sacrificial ritual, both magical and religious in origin, for manifesting the Beast here on earth."

The book was very old, and the thin, veined paper felt leathery against Evie's fingers. It reminded her very much of some macabre illuminated Bible. Each page featured a small, colorful illustration of a ritual murder, accompanied by a scripture-like passage. The same sigils found on the killer's notes also ran along the edges of the book's entries.

Evie read the offerings aloud in order. "The Sacrifice of the Faithful. The Tribute of the Ten Servants of the Master. The Pale Horseman Riding Death Before the Stars. The Death of the Virgin. The Harlot Adorned and Cast upon the Sea..." The drawing was of a sightless, bejeweled woman arranged on water, surrounded by pearls. Above her head was an eye symbol. "Unc," Evie said, shivering. "It's just the way Ruta Badowski's body was found."

Will reached over Evie and turned to the next page. "The sixth offering, the Sacrifice of the Idle Son..." The illustration showed a boy hung upside down with one leg bent, like the Hanging Man of the tarot. The boy's hands were missing, and a pair of hands bent in prayer was the symbol above the drawing. "Tommy Duffy."

Evie read on. "The seventh offering, the Turning Out of the Deceitful Brethren from the Temple of Solomon." She raised her head, thinking. "It's a template for the murders." She continued. "The eighth offering, the Veneration of the Angelic Herald.

The ninth, the Destruction of the Golden Idol. The tenth, the Lamentation of the Widow. The eleventh offering, the Marriage of the Beast and the Woman Clothed in the Sun."

The last page was a drawing of a bestial, horned man with the feet of a goat, two enormous wings, and a tail. He sat upon a throne and his eyes burned. In his hand was a dripping heart. At his feet was a woman wearing a golden crown and dress, her chest torn open. The symbol at the bottom was a comet. It made Evie shudder.

"Does it say how the Beast was supposed to come into this world?"

"It's unclear. It says only that they needed a chosen one."

"A chosen one to commit the murders?" Evie clarified.

Dr. Poblocki gave a small shrug. "There, I'm afraid, I can only conjecture."

"What is this?" Evie pointed to a page near the back. It showed a man kneeling before another man in dark robes, possibly a minister. The Pentacle of the Beast hung over them both like a sun, and heavenly spirits floated nearby. Piles of kindling had been gathered. The minister placed a pendant around the kneeling man's neck.

"That's just like the pendant Jacob Call was wearing," Evie said. "What is the pendant for?"

"Possibly to signify to others that they are members of the same tribe, much like a cross or a Star of David," Dr. Poblocki said. "Though I cannot say that for certain."

"What is the next offering?" Will asked.

Evie flipped back. "'The seventh offering: the Turning Out of the Deceitful Brethren from the Temple of Solomon.' Whatever that means." Evie turned to Dr. Poblocki. "Do you suppose our killer believes the comet is some sort of sign?"

"Comets were often thought to be holy portents. God's messengers. When Lucifer, the light-bringer, fell, he streaked through the sky just like a tail of fire, it is said."

"When will the comet be overhead in New York?"

"October eighth, about midnight," Will said.

"That's less than two weeks away." Evie bit her lip, thinking. "You said that the Brethren is a vanished cult. What happened to them?"

"The entire sect burned to death in 1848." Dr. Poblocki opened a groaning file drawer overstuffed with papers. "There had been an outbreak of smallpox, you see. Several of the Brethren died from it. Apparently Pastor Algoode became convinced it was a sign of God's judgment and that they should prepare themselves to bring on Armageddon. No one knows exactly what happened, but they think that Algoode gathered his followers and doused the meetinghouse in kerosene—a jar of it was found in the ruins. The doors were barred. A hunter nearby saw the flames and smoke. He said you could hear prayers and hymns turning to screams."

Evie shuddered. "How awful. Did no one survive?"

"Not a soul," he said solemnly. "The town of New Brethren was built in the valley below, about five miles from the original camp on the hill. They say that unquiet spirits still haunt the woods of the original Brethren. They've heard terrible sounds and seen lights in the trees up on the mountain. No one ventures there, not even the hunters."

Evie tried to imagine all those souls locked inside the meetinghouse, singing and praying, the mothers clutching their children while the flames raged. "Burned to death. Why would they do such a thing?"

"Why does anyone do anything? Belief. A belief that they are right and just in their actions. Abraham was willing to sacrifice his son, Isaac, because he believed that God had commanded it. To kill your son is unthinkable. A crime. But if you are acting in the belief that your God, your supreme deity whom you must obey, has demanded it of you, is it still a crime?"

"Yes," Will said.

Dr. Poblocki smiled. "I know you do not believe, Will. But imagine for a moment that you believe fervently that this is truth. In this framework, your actions are justified. Glorified, even. They are *inculpatus*—without blame. If this is the case with your killer, then he is on a holy mission, and nothing will stop him from seeing it through."

"What is this?" Evie asked. She had turned to the last page in the Book of the Brethren, which had been torn out. Only the ripped edges remained.

Dr. Poblocki moved in close and peered over the tops of his glasses, squinting. "Ah. That. I can tell you what it is supposed to be. According to the accounts, the Book of the Brethren contained a spell for trapping the spirit of the Beast in an object—a holy relic of some sort—and then destroying the object, casting the Beast back to hell once the mission of the faithful had been accomplished."

"I don't understand," Evie said.

"It's like the Arabic jinn, or genie. A spirit or demon can be contained in an object and then destroyed," Will said. He looked troubled.

"Doesn't seem like much to hang your hat on," Evie said. "Not that it matters, since the page is missing."

"Not just missing, but deliberately torn out," Dr. Poblocki reminded her.

"But who would do that, and why?"

"It seems someone didn't want the Beast to be destroyed after all."

"Georg, may I keep this?" Will said, holding up the book.

"Be my guest. Just promise me you won't start your own doomsday cult with it."

Engrossed in the book's illuminated pages, Will didn't respond.

"And now, it is high time I joined Mrs. Poblocki for our Sunday repast." Dr. Poblocki gave Evie's hand a courtly kiss. "I wish you the best with your investigation. Do keep your uncle in line."

Outside, it had begun to rain. Will opened the day's paper and offered half to Evie. They cupped the flimsy sheets over their heads and walked quickly across the lawn toward Broadway.

"If our killer is following the eleven offerings of this Brethren cult, he had to hear about them somehow. Is it possible he's from that region?" Evie gazed at the vast expanse of city. "Don't you think? Will? Unc, are you listening to me?"

"Hmm? Yes," he answered absently. His brow was furrowed and his eyes looked tired. This case was obviously bothering him far more than he'd let on. "A solid observation, Evie."

Evie couldn't help but smile. From Will, this was quite a compliment.

"I'll let Detective Malloy know that we might have a lead, that the killer could be from the New Brethren region. Perhaps they can ask around upstate and see if there has been anything out of the ordinary happening in or around New Brethren. But we do have something on our side now."

"What's that?" Evie asked. The rain was coming down harder now. The newspaper sagged and the back of her neck was wet.

"If we're correct and our killer is working from this Book of the Brethren, then his next offering will be the seventh—the

Turning Out of the Deceitful Brethren from the Temple of Solomon."

"But what does that even mean?"

"It will be our job to try to figure that out in time," Will said.

A taxi swerved into view and Uncle Will raised his hand for it, edging out two students. "Sorry. My niece is ill," he told them, and Evie thrilled a bit at this small lie. They settled into the taxi just as the clouds unleashed a gully washer.

Evie leaned her head against the seat and watched the rain come down. "Unc, what happens when the killer has completed all eleven offerings? He isn't *really* raising some mythical biblical demon from the deep. So what is he after?"

"But he *believes* that he is. Such strong belief is a powerful force."

"Then what sort of powerful belief does it take to stop someone like that?"

"Turn left here, please, and don't take the avenue," Will instructed the driver, who decided to argue, in true New Yorker fashion, about which route was the best to take at this hour. It wasn't until well after they'd returned to the museum that Evie realized he had never answered her question.

ÜBERMENSCH

Jericho sat in the private dining room of the Waldorf-Astoria Hotel on Fifth Avenue. He'd noted on the way over that the edges of the leaves were changing from green to a faint red and gold. It reminded Jericho of the farm and harvest. Thinking about that always made him melancholy, so he turned his attention to stirring milk into his tea. A moment later, a white-gloved attendant opened the doors, and Jake Marlowe swept into the room like a benevolent prince.

"Don't get up," Marlowe said, taking his seat at the table. He was considered handsome. The papers spilled as much ink on his dark good looks, strong jaw, and tall, athletic build as they did discussing his latest industrial invention or scientific breakthrough. "How are you, Jericho?"

"Fine, sir."

"Good. That's good. You look healthy."

"Yes, sir."

Marlowe pointed to Jericho's battered volume of *Thus Spoke Zarathustra*. "Any good?"

"It passes the time."

"I understand you have a lot of time to pass working at the museum. How is our friend Will?"

"Fine, sir."

"Good. Will and I may have had our differences, but I've always admired him. And I'm concerned about him and his... obsessions."

The silent attendant in white gloves reappeared and poured coffee into Marlowe's china cup. "I'll have the Waldorf salad. Jericho?"

"I'll have the same, please."

The attendant nodded, then vanished.

"How's business, sir?" Jericho asked with no trace of real interest.

"Business is good. Business is terrific, in fact. We're doing exciting things at Marlowe Industries. And California's beautiful— you'd love it there."

Jericho bit back the urge to tell Marlowe he had no idea about what Jericho loved.

"The offer's open—if you get tired of shelving books on magic and ghosts, you can always come work for me."

Jericho examined the spoon on his saucer. It was real silver, with the stamp of the hotel on the handle. "I have a job, sir."

"Yes. You have a job. I'm talking about a profession. A chance to be part of the future, not wither away in some dusty museum."

"You know that Mr. Fitzgerald is quite brilliant."

"Once," Marlowe said and let the word linger. "He was never quite the same after what happened with Rotke." Marlowe shook his head. "All that brilliance spent chasing ghost stories. And for what?"

"It's part of our history."

"We're not a country with a past, Jericho. We're a country of the future. And I mean to shape that future." Marlowe put his elbows on the table and leaned forward, his expression serious. His blue-eyed gaze was penetrating. "How are you, Jericho?"

"I told you, sir. I'm fine."

Marlowe lowered his voice. "And you've experienced no symptoms?"

"None."

Marlowe sat back with a satisfied smile. "Well. That's promising. Very promising."

"Yes, sir." In the spoon, Jericho's face was distorted.

Marlowe rose and stood beside one of the tall windows. "Look out there. What a city! And growing all the time. This is the best country in the world, Jericho. A place where a man can be anything he dreams of being. Can you imagine if other countries had the same democratic ideals and freedoms we enjoy? What would that world look like?"

"Idealism is just an escape from reality. There is no utopia."

Marlowe grinned. "That so? I couldn't disagree more. Is that Nietzsche talking? Ah, the Germans. We have a factory in Germany, you know. Actually, Germany is a fine example, so let's take Germany: They were crushed in the Great War. Their debt was staggering. A pound of bread cost nearly three billion Marks! The Reichsmark was practically worthless—you'd have better luck papering your house with it than trying to buy goods or pay your bills. But Marlowe Industries is going to help them get on their feet. We're going to change the world." Marlowe smiled brightly, the smile that made the newspapers rhapsodize over his can-do qualities. "*You* might change the world, Jericho."

"No one would choose this," Jericho said bitterly.

"Oh, come now. It isn't as bad as all that, is it?" Marlowe

returned to his seat opposite Jericho. "Look at you, Jericho. You're a walking miracle. The great hope."

"I am not one of your dreams." Jericho banged his fist on the table, shattering a saucer.

"Careful," Marlowe said.

"I...I'm sorry." Jericho began gathering the pieces, but at a gesture from Marlowe the attendant appeared to whisk the table clean with a small hand broom.

"You have to be careful," Marlowe said again.

Jericho nodded. Under the table, he clenched his fist, unclenched it. When he felt calmer, he folded his napkin, set it on the table, and rose. "Thank you for the tea, sir. I should be getting back to the museum."

"Oh, come now. Let's start this over—"

"I-I have a lot of work to do," Jericho said. He stood, waiting.

"But you haven't eaten anything."

"I should be getting back."

"Certainly," Marlowe said after a pause. He walked to the other side of the room, where his briefcase sat with his umbrella. He took a small brown bag from inside the case. "You're sure you're fine?"

"Yes, sir."

Marlowe handed the brown bag to Jericho, who looked down at the floor.

"Thank you," Jericho mumbled. He hated this. Hated that once a year, he had to submit to this ritual. Had to pretend to be grateful for what Marlowe had done for him. *To* him.

Marlowe clapped a hand on his shoulder. "I'm glad to see you're doing so well, Jericho."

"Yes, sir." He shook off Marlowe's hand and left him standing there.

Alone in the hallway, Jericho made a fist with his right hand, then flexed his fingers, open, closed, open, closed. They moved flawlessly. He unsealed the bag Marlowe had given him. Inside was a brown glass bottle of pills marked MARLOWE INDUSTRIES VITA-MIN TONIC. Nestled beside it was a silver case loaded with ten vials of a bright blue serum. For a moment, he imagined dropping the bag into the nearest wastebasket and walking away. Instead, he slid the silver case into his inside jacket pocket for safekeeping and settled the vitamin tonic into his outside pocket. He tucked Nietzsche's *Zarathustra* under his arm and walked out into the cool fall day.

※

Mabel had no time to note the grace of the fall leaves as she walked through the crowd assembled in Union Square. She knew she needed to be on her guard—Pinkerton Detectives posing as workers would often disrupt a peaceful protest, giving the police an excuse to move in, break it up, and make arrests. Sometimes it turned ugly.

The rain had stopped, and Mabel's mother stood on a make-shift speaker's platform, inspiring the crowd with her command-ing oratorical skills and dark-haired beauty. She was born Virginia Newell, daughter of the famous Newell clan, one of New York's elite families. At twenty, she'd thrown it all away to elope with Mabel's father, Daniel Rose, a firebrand Jewish journalist and socialist. Her family had cut her off without a cent. But the Newell glamour remained. They called Mabel's mother the "Social Regis-ter Rebel." And in some ways, her mother's throwing it all away for love had made her even more famous than she ever would have been as a society wife. It was the reason they'd been able to move into the Bennington; no one would refuse a Newell girl—even a disgraced one.

But it was hard for Mabel to live in her mother's shadow. No one was writing about Mabel in the papers. And to add insult to injury, Mabel had taken after her father in the looks department—the round face and strong nose, deep brown eyes, and curly, auburn-tinged hair. "You must take after your father," people would say, and there would follow an awkward silence. But when her mother smiled and hugged her and called her "My darling, daring girl!" Mabel was suffused with such warmth. And when her mother inevitably got caught up in this cause or that injustice to be righted, Mabel would stand at her side, playing the dutiful daughter, proving just how indispensable she was. People who were helpful and indispensable were loved. Weren't they?

The only person who didn't seem to regard Mabel's mother with awe was Evie. More than once, Evie had imitated her mother perfectly: "Mabel, daaaahling, how can you complain that you haven't had dinner when the *huddled masses* have yet to breathe free!" "Mabel, daaaahling, tell me: Which dress says Savior of the Poor and Saint of the Lower East Side to you?" And as much as Mabel felt called to chide Evie and defend her mother, she had to admit that it was one of the things she loved about her old friend: No matter what, Evie always took Mabel's side. "You're the real star of the Rose family," Evie would insist. "One day, everyone will know your name." She only hoped that Evie could make Jericho see Mabel that way, too.

Jericho. It embarrassed her how often she thought of him. All those romantic fantasies! She was supposed to be so sensible, but when it came to that boy, she was lost to storybook notions. He was so smart and studious and soulful—not some drugstore cowboy, like that Sam Lloyd, all flattery and promises to any girl who'd fall for it. No. Jericho's affections meant something. That was the challenge, wasn't it? If you could make a fellow like Jericho fall for you, well, didn't it prove just how desirable you were?

Mabel thought of all of these things as she moved through Union Square, handing copies of *The Proletariat* to workers. She waved at the folks manning the table for the Wobblies, but they didn't notice her, and so she moved on, feeling lost in the crowd. If she decided to disappear, would anyone feel her absence?

"Who are your leaders?" Mabel's mother called from the platform.

"We are all leaders!" the crowd answered.

Mabel felt a hand on her arm. She turned to see a young woman holding a baby, accompanied by an older woman in a head scarf.

The young woman spoke in fractured English. "You are the great Mrs. Rose's daughter?"

I have a name. It's Mabel. Mabel Rose. "Yes, I am," she answered irritably.

"Please, can you help? They took my sister from the factory."

"Who took her?"

The woman spoke with the grandmotherly woman in Italian before turning back to Mabel.

"The men," she said.

"What men? The police?"

The woman looked around to be sure no one was listening, and then said softly, "The men who move like shadows."

Mabel didn't understand what the woman meant by that. It was probably a nuance of language that didn't translate quite right. "Why would someone take your sister? Was she organizing at the factory?"

Again, the girl looked to the older woman, who nodded. "She

is . . . *profeta*." The girl seemed to search for the right words. "She . . . talks to the dead. She says they are coming."

Mabel frowned. "Who is coming?"

The shriek of police whistles sounded on the edges of the park, along with shouts and cries from the crowd. A tear-gas canister landed in the crowd, and the park was subsumed in a chemical fog that burned the eyes and throat. Mabel could hear her mother pleading for calm over the microphone, and then the microphone was cut off. The crowd pushed and shoved. People ran screaming as the police descended on the workers. Someone bumped Mabel hard and sent her newspapers to the ground, where they were immediately trod into bits. Mabel couldn't see her parents through the gas and surging crowd. Coughing and disoriented, she pushed her way through the chaotic crowd and took off running, coming face-to-face with a policeman.

"Gotcha!" he said.

Panicked, Mabel darted up Fifteenth Street toward Irving Place, the policeman's whistle blasting to alert others. There were easily five cops chasing her now. She started toward the iron gates of Gramercy, but strong hands yanked her into a service doorway behind a restaurant. She started to yell, and a hand clapped over her mouth.

"Not that way, Miss. It's crawling with cops," a man's voice whispered in her ear, and Mabel quieted. A moment later the police marched past, clubs drawn. She watched from her hiding place as they gave up and headed back to Union Square.

"Thank you," Mabel said. She looked at her savior for the first time. He was young—not much older than she was.

He shepherded her away. "You're the Roses' daughter, aren't you?"

Even here she couldn't escape it. "My name is Mabel," she said, as if daring him to contradict her.

"Mabel. Mabel Rose. I won't forget it." He gave her hand a firm shake. "Well, Mabel Rose. Get home safely."

An explosion came from somewhere nearby. "Go now," her mysterious savior said and ran swiftly down the alley, vaulting up the fire escape and disappearing over the rooftops.

Back at the Bennington, Mabel took the elevator to the sixth floor. Two of the hallway lamps had burned out ages ago, casting the passage in constant shadows, which always gave Mabel a bit of the heebie-jeebies. Mabel heard whispering at the far end of the darkened corridor and froze. What if the police had followed her after all?

Against her better judgment, she crept forward. Miss Addie stood at the narrow window in her nightgown. Her long gray hair hung in tangles. She cradled a bag of salt, which she was pouring out onto the windowsill in a fat line. Salt seeped from a hole in the bag and pooled on the carpet below.

"Miss Addie? What are you doing?"

"I have to keep them out," Miss Addie said without looking up.

"Keep who out?"

"There are awful events unfolding. Something unholy is at hand."

"Do you mean the murders?" Mabel asked.

"It's begun. I can feel it. In my dreams, I have seen the man in the tall hat with his coat of crows. A terrible choice is at hand." Miss Addie's hand fluttered about her face like a wounded bird. She seemed confused, like a woman waking from ether. "Where is my door? I can't find it."

"You're on the sixth floor, Miss Adelaide. You need the tenth. Here, I'll take you."

225

Mabel took the bag of salt from the old woman and helped her into the elevator, securing the troublesome latch on the gate.

"When the cunning folk stood accused of the 'craft as if it were a game, and our gallows bloomed with the dead, the man was there. When the Choctaw were marched to their ruin on the Trail of Tears, the man was there."

Mabel counted the floors, willing the elevator to go faster.

"They say he appeared to Mr. Lincoln upon an evening before the War Between the States. It was as if a hand had come down and pulled out the heart of the nation, and the very rivers bled, and the land's wounds would not heal." Miss Addie suddenly turned and stared right at Mabel. "Terrible what people can do to one another, isn't it?"

Mabel hurriedly slid back the gate to let Miss Addie out of the elevator. She knew she should help her to her door, but she was too spooked. "It's just down the hall on the left, Miss Adelaide."

"Yes, thank you." Miss Addie took the bag of salt from Mabel and stepped out into the dim hallway. "We're not safe, you know. Not at all."

But Mabel had closed the gate and the elevator was already descending.

"Terrible what people can do," Miss Addie said again.

From the elevator, Mabel watched the old woman's bare feet hobbling away, a trail of salt and the lace hem of her nightgown left in her wake like sea foam.

OPERATION JERICHO

"Good evening, ladies and gentlemen of our radio audience, and welcome to the *Gerard Whittington Hour*, brought to you by Marlowe Industries. Yes, Marlowe Industries—Bringing You Tomorrow, Today. From the very latest innovations in aviation and security to helpful household appliances for the housewife, Marlowe Industries..."

"I still don't understand," Evie said over the soft croon of the radio. She lay on the sofa with the illustrated book in her hands. "None of this answers the mystery of the first four offerings. If the Pentacle Killer is truly following the rituals in this Book of the Brethren in order to raise some anti-Christ and bring about Armageddon, why start with the fifth offering? It doesn't make sense."

"Detective Malloy reports no similar murders prior to the discovery of Ruta Badowski's body," Jericho said. He was seated at the dining room table with his notes.

Will, as usual, was pacing. "It is mysterious. But this much we do know: If the killer is following the offerings in the Book of the

Brethren, and it certainly seems he is, we may be able to prevent the next attempt...."

Evie read the seventh offering aloud.

"What does it mean? Who are the deceitful brethren?" Will mused. He walked from bay window to kitchenette and back again till Evie thought he would wear a path in the Persian rug.

"Maybe we're going about this the wrong way. What if we find the temple he mentions? That way, the police can be there to stop him," Evie mused. She snapped her fingers. "There's the Egyptian temple at the Metropolitan Museum of Art."

"It could mean a synagogue, especially if this is somehow connected to the Klan," Jericho suggested.

"What about temples of finance—the stock exchange, or the banks!" Evie shouted. It was as if they were playing a strange parlor game, like charades, but with deadly serious stakes.

"Good, very good," Will said. They discussed it further, making a list of other possible meanings for the temple mentioned in the seventh offering, with Jericho writing each one down.

"I'll alert Terrence that our killer may strike at any of those places. Now, Evie, can you see if there is anything in the Hale book about religious iconography?" Will commanded from his momentary post near the bay windows.

The street lamps had come on in Central Park. It was just after eight o'clock. They'd been at the books for some time and had missed dinner entirely. Evie's stomach grumbled.

"Unc, I'm starved. Can't we come back to it?" Evie begged.

Will looked up at the clock, then at the dark outside the windows. His expression was one of complete surprise. "Oh. So you must be. Why don't you and Jericho go down to the dining room? I'll fix myself a sandwich here."

"I'll do the same," Jericho said.

"Then I'll be all alone," Evie said. "Jericho, it will do us both good to get out of here."

"She's right, Jericho," Will said. "Go downstairs for a bit."

Reluctantly, Jericho closed his books and followed Evie to the elevator. She stopped it on the sixth floor and threw open the gate.

"Why are we stopping here?"

"It just occurred to me that Mabel must be starved! Her parents are at a rally tonight, and the poor dear is all alone."

"She's probably already had her supper."

"Oh, no! I know my Mabel. She's a night owl. Doesn't eat until late—like a Parisian. It won't take a minute-ski."

Evie knocked her special knock and Mabel threw the door open, wearing her bathrobe and already talking: "I hope you've brought me the man of my dreams....Oh."

Evie cleared her throat. "Good evening, Mabel. Jericho and I were just going to have dinner downstairs, if you'd care to join us." Evie cut her eyes at Jericho beside her.

"Oh. Oh!" Mabel said, looking down at her bathrobe in horror. "Let me just get dressed."

"Hello, Evie," Mr. Rose called from the kitchen table, where he sat banging out a story on a typewriter. Evie waved back.

Jericho glowered. "I thought you said they were at a rally."

"Did I? I must have confused my days. Silly me. Mabesie, darling, do hurry!"

A few minutes later the three of them sat in the dining hall at a banquette under a chandelier that blinked every now and then due to some fault in the wiring. Evie filled Mabel in on the details of the murders and what they'd discovered courtesy of Dr. Poblocki. "This fellow seems to be enacting some sort of strange ancient ritual from a vanished cult. It's pos-i-tute-ly macabre. What a monster he is!"

"That's what happens when society neglects and abuses children," Mabel said, fidgeting with her silverware. "They grow up to be monsters."

"What an *interesting* theory! Mabel, you are so clever!" Evie said. "Isn't she smart, Jericho?"

Jericho did not look up from his chicken and dumplings. Across the table, Mabel mouthed an urgent *What are you doing?*

Operation Jericho, Evie mouthed back.

"How do you know that's what happens?" Jericho challenged.

"What do you mean?" Mabel asked.

"How do you know that it's society that makes monsters?"

"Well, my mother says that when—"

"I didn't ask what your mother thought," Jericho interrupted. "Everyone who can read a newspaper knows what your mother thinks. I asked how *you* know that happens."

Mabel chased the noodles in her cup of soup with a spoon. She'd eaten an hour earlier and wasn't the slightest bit hungry. "Well, I've been to the slums with my mother and father. I've seen the horrors wrought by poverty and ignorance."

"Then how do you account for the poor, abused soul who grows up to achieve greatness?"

"There are always exceptions."

"What if that isn't true at all? What if evil exists? What if it has always existed and will continue to exist, an eternal battle between good and evil, always and forever?"

"You mean, like God and the Devil?" Mabel shook her head. "I don't believe in that. I'm an atheist. Religion is the opiate of the masses."

"Karl Marx," Jericho said. "Also not your own opinion. Do you believe that because you actually believe it, or do you believe it because you heard it from them first?"

"I believe it," Mabel answered. "Evil is a human invention. A choice."

"Jericho believes we are doomed to repeat our existence," Evie said, waggling her eyebrows to show just how seriously she took this theory. "Nietzsche."

"I guess I'm not the only one influenced by other people's opinions." Mabel sniffed.

Evie tried to hide her laugh with a cough. She glanced at Mabel and tapped the side of her nose surreptitiously, a signal. "Oh, dear!" Evie said with mock concern. "I seem to have lost my bracelet."

"No, you haven't!" Mabel blurted out. She went to kick Evie under the table and got Jericho by mistake.

"Ow," he said, eyeing her.

"Sorry." Mabel's eyes went wide in horror. She looked to Evie with a *Please do something quickly* expression.

"Do you know what I believe? I believe we should have pie," Evie announced and signaled for the server.

They fell into near silence, the only sounds around the table the chewing and slurping of food. Evie tried to have a conversation with Mabel, but everything felt forced and awkward. Afterward, they rode the elevator together in uncomfortable silence, all of them watching its gold arrow tick the floors off one by one.

Mabel practically leaped from the elevator when the gate opened on her floor. "Good night," she said without turning around, and Evie knew she'd hear all about it later. The first stage of Operation Jericho had been a certified failure.

When they reached their own floor they found that Uncle Will had tacked a note to the door: *Gone to see Malloy—WF.* It was pure Uncle Will, from the brevity to the initials. Evie crumpled the note and slammed the apartment door behind her. She glared at Jericho, who had just made himself at home in Will's chair with his book.

She moved to the couch and glared at him from there. "You didn't need to be so rude, you know."

"I have no idea what you're talking about," Jericho mumbled.

"To Mabel! You could at least *try* to be polite."

"I'm not interested in being polite. It's false. Nietzsche says—"

"Leave Nietzsche out of this. He's dead, and for all I know he died of rudeness." Evie fumed. "She's very smart, you know. As smart as you are."

Jericho deigned to look up from his book. "She's under her parents' thumbs. She thinks what they think. What she said tonight about society making monsters—that was her mother talking."

"So you *were* listening!"

"She needs her own opinions. She needs to learn to think for herself, not just parrot what other people say."

"You mean the way you hang on Uncle Will's and Nietzsche's every word?" Evie swiped the book away from him.

"I do not," Jericho said, taking it back. "And why are we having a conversation about Mabel? Why is it so important to you?"

"Because..." Evie trailed off. She couldn't very well say, *Because Mabel's goofy over you. Because for the past three years, I've gotten letters full of her longing. Because every time you walk into the room, she takes a breath and holds it.* "Because she's my friend. And nobody is rude to my friends. Got it?"

Jericho let out a sigh of irritation. "From now on I will be the picture of politeness to Mabel."

"Thank you," Evie said with a bow. Jericho ignored her.

LIFE AND DEATH

Memphis tore out the page from his notebook and crumpled it in disgust. He'd tried working on the poem again, the one about his mother and her coat of grief, but it wouldn't come, and he wondered if he was doomed to be a failed writer as well as healer.

The wind whistled through the fall leaves. It had been April when his mother died, the trees budding into flowers like girls turning shyly into young ladies. Spring, when nothing should be dying. Memphis's father had roused him from sleep. His eyes were shadowed. "It's time, son," he'd said, and he led the sleepy Memphis through the dark house and into his mother's room, where a lone candle burned. His mother lay shivering under a thin blanket.

"Please, son. You've got to do it. You've got to keep her here."

His father, leading him to the bed. Memphis's mother wasn't much more than bones, her hair thinned to candy floss. Beneath the blanket, her body was still. She stared up at the ceiling, her eyes tracking something beyond Memphis's vision. He was fourteen years old.

"Go on, now, son," his father said, his voice breaking. "Please."

Memphis was afraid. His mother seemed so close to death that he didn't see how he could stop it. He'd wanted to heal her before, but she wouldn't let him. "I won't have my son responsible for that," she'd said firmly. "What's meant to be is meant to be, good or bad." But Memphis didn't want his mother to die. He put his hands on her. His mother's eyes widened and she tried to shake her head, to duck his hands, but she was too weak.

"I'm going to help you, Mama."

His mother parted her cracked lips to speak, but no sound came out. Memphis felt the healing grip take hold, and then he was under, pulled along by currents he couldn't control and did not understand, the two of them carried out to a larger, unknown sea. In his healing trances, he always felt the presence of the spirits around him. It was a calm, protective presence, and he was never afraid. But it was different this time. The place he found himself was a dark graveyard, heavy with mist. The shades did not feel quite so benevolent as they pressed close to him. A skinny gray man in a tall hat sat upon a rock, his hands made into fists.

"What would you give me for her, healer?" the man asked, and it seemed to Memphis as if the wind itself had whispered the question. The man nodded to his fists. "In one hand is life; in the other, death. Choose. Choose and you might have her back."

Memphis stepped forward, his finger inching closer. Right or left?

Suddenly he saw his mother, gaunt and weak, in the graveyard. "You can't bring me back, Memphis. Don't ever try to bring back what's gone!"

The man grinned at her with teeth like tiny daggers. "The choice is his!"

His mother looked frightened, but she did not back down. "He's just a boy."

"The choice. Is. His."

Memphis concentrated on the man's fists once more. He tapped the right one. The man smiled and opened his palm, and a shiny black baby bird squeaked at him.

Memphis's mother shook her head. "Oh, my son, my son. What have you done?"

Memphis had no memory after that. He'd fallen ill with a fever, Octavia told him, and his father had put him to bed. The next morning, he woke to see Octavia covering the mirrors with sheets. His father sat in his chair, his shirt matted to him with sweat. "She's gone," he whispered, and in his eyes, Memphis saw the accusation: *Why couldn't you save her? All that gift, and you couldn't save the one person who mattered?*

Now Memphis wiped the graveyard dirt from his hands. He smoothed out the page and stuck it back in his notebook. Then he headed toward home. As he passed the old house on the hill, he thought he heard something. Was that…whistling? Couldn't be. But yes, there it was, just under the roar of the wind. Or was it only the wind itself? Memphis opened the gate and took two steps on the broken path. How many times he had read ghost stories and thought to himself, *Don't go up those stairs! Stay away from that old house!* Yet here he was, standing in the yard of the oldest, most forbidding house he knew, contemplating going inside. The folly of standing at the boarded-over window of a decrepit house suddenly dawned fully on Memphis, and he backed away. He was immediately reminded of the murders taking place in the city. Why had that thought occurred to him now, here? Again he heard the sound of some faint whistling echoing from the empty chambers of the old house. Memphis ran, leaving the front gate screaming on its rusted hinges.

Back in Harlem, Memphis walked along Lenox Avenue feeling

out of step with the people out for a good time. He wandered until he found himself standing across the street from Miss A'Lelia Walker's grand town house on 136th Street. Several nice cars were parked outside, and a butler stood at the door. The lights were ablaze, and inside, Memphis knew, she was probably hosting one of her famous salons visited by the likes of Harlem's greatest talents—musicians, artists, writers, scholars. Memphis imagined himself at one of her parties, reading his poetry to an elegant audience. But the path from the sidewalk where he stood to the lighted salon seemed an impossible distance, and Memphis turned away. He thought about going to the Hotsy Totsy or the Tomb of the Fallen Angels to see what was going on. There was almost always a party somewhere. But instead, he headed toward home, the memory of his mother fresh in his mind. Blind Bill Johnson was sitting on the stoop of a brownstone playing his guitar softly, even though there was no one to hear it. Memphis tried to sneak past.

"Who's there? Who's walking past old Blind Bill without saying nothing?"

"It's Memphis Campbell, sir."

Bill's mouth relaxed into a toothy smile. "Good evening, Mr. Campbell. I'm mighty relieved it's you and not some lou-lou come for me."

"What's a lou-lou?"

"Old Cajun word. What you call it? A bogeyman."

"No, sir. No bogeyman. Just me."

Blind Bill pursed his lips like he'd taken a shot of bathtub gin mixed with spit. "Not a good night to be roaming. Can't you feel that on the back of your neck? The *fifolet*? Like the swamp gas rising up, the evil spirits following you."

Between the business up at the house and Blind Bill's Cajun superstitions, Memphis was feeling spooked. He didn't want to talk about ghosts and hobgoblins. "My aunt says I'm thick as a brick. I'd be the last person to feel spirits moving."

Blind Bill turned his face toward Memphis, almost as if he could see him standing there. "Heard me something real interesting over at Floyd's shop today. Heard you used to be a healer."

"Once upon a time."

"You still got the healing spirit in you? Could you put dem hands on old Blind Bill and gimme back my sight?"

"I don't have that gift anymore." Memphis was suddenly very tired, too tired to keep his words inside. They tumbled out to the old man. "It left me when my mother... She was real sick. And I laid hands on her, and..." Memphis's throat ached. He swallowed against the tightness. "She died. She died right there under my hands. And whatever healing I had died with her."

"That's a real sad story, Mr. Campbell," Blind Bill said after a pause.

Memphis's nose ran with his tears and he was glad the old man couldn't see him crying. He didn't say anything else.

Blind Bill nodded as if in some private conversation. "But you didn't do nothin' to your mama 'cepting try to ease her pain. You hear me? Sometimes, it's a mercy," he said quietly, and Memphis was grateful for the old man's kindness. "I'ma give you something."

Bill rummaged in his pocket and came up with a butterscotch candy. He felt for Memphis's hand and pressed it into his palm with his dry, scratchy fingers. "Here. You keep that. 'Case you ever need to ask Papa Legba's protection."

"Papa who?"

"Papa Legba. He's the gatekeeper of the Vilokan—the spirit realm. He stands at the crossroads. If you're lost, he can help you find your way. Just leave him a little something sweet."

Aunt Octavia would have a fit if she heard Bill talking that way. Once, she'd made them cross the street to avoid a nearly hidden matchbox of a store whose plate-glass windows were draped in red and black, with candles and figurines of saints with African faces. A small sign advertised CURSES LIFTED AND OBSTACLES TO HAPPINESS REMOVED. "Don't you go anywhere near that voodoo," she'd said when Isaiah demanded to know why they were going a block out of their way. Under her breath, she'd recited the Lord's Prayer.

Memphis held the candy uncertainly. It felt strangely heavy in his palm. "My aunt says you should pray only to Jesus."

Blind Bill grunted and spat. "You think the white folks' god is gonna help you? You think he's on our side?"

"I don't think anybody's god is on our side."

Memphis readied himself for some rebuke. Instead, the old man nodded knowingly, the corners of his mouth twisting into a smile of bitter agreement. "That might be the most honest thing you ever said, Mr. Campbell. Damn sight better than that charm and hair oil you usually putting on." He laughed then—a big, wheezing cough of a laugh—and slapped his leg, and the whole thing—the conversation, the candy, the earlier adventure at the house—struck Memphis as so completely ridiculous that he couldn't stop himself from joining in. The two of them were doubled over like fools.

"Oh, law, law, law," Blind Bill said, patting his chest. "Ain't that the way of the world, now? Good luck turns bad. Bad luck turns good. Just a big rolling craps game played between this world and the next, and we the dice getting tossed around. You go on home now, Mr. Campbell. Get you some rest. Live to fight another day. Plenty of time for regrettin'. Go out and have you some good times while you still young."

"I'll do that, sir." He'd changed his mind about going home.

Blind Bill was right—Memphis was young, and so was the night. And so he charted his course for the Hotsy Totsy.

Bill listened to Memphis Campbell's footsteps fading away. He wanted to tell Memphis how lucky he was that the gift had left him when it did. What a mercy that was. How grateful he should be that the wrong people hadn't found out about it. Bill felt in his pocket for some money for a bite to eat. He rubbed the dime and nickel between his fingers. Not much. If only he could stop gambling. But that was his curse; he couldn't stay away from risk and chance, whether it was cards, the numbers game, craps, cockfighting, or horse racing. But he kept seeing that house in his dreams with the clouds and crossroads. He hadn't worked out the gig for any of it yet, but he would. There was a number on the side of the house's mailbox. If only he could see it, he felt sure, that number would be the key to winning big. And once he had his money, he could set about getting revenge.

THE HOUSE ON THE HILL

The house sat on the windswept hill like a sentinel. Ivy sprawled across the exterior, spreading like a stain. The windows were shuttered and nailed closed. The engraved cherrywood doors were a dull brown. If anyone could have seen inside, they'd have noted that cobwebs draped from doorways and spiders secreted their web-wrapped prey into crevices. Warped floorboards bowed dangerously in spots.

In its day, the house had been magnificent. There had been celebrations and dances. On Sundays, carriages had passed by to admire the house's commanding presence, a symbol of everything that was right and good and hopeful about the country. The house was a dream realized. The man who had built the house, Jacob Knowles, had made his fortune in steel, the very steel used to build the city. He and his wife had only one surviving child, a daughter named Ida, who was their greatest joy. Ida was small and prone to colds, and for this reason, her anxious parents indulged the girl's every whim. There were piano lessons and pony rides and a small spaniel named Chester. When Ida played tea party on the lawn, servants waited nearby to pour tea for her dolls. Many were the days she pretended to be an Arabian princess surveying her kingdom. She would climb the stairs to the very top room of the house, an attic room with a small terrace. In 1863 she watched the smoke from the Draft Riot fires from there, daydreaming that she looked upon the lairs of distant dragons and not the simmering frustrations of a class and race war erupting into brutal mob violence. While the Civil War raged on, Ida grew into a young woman. She dreamed of marrying some handsome officer so that they might become the next master and mistress of the grand house. Months after the Civil War ended, Union soldiers joined General Grant himself for a party at the house that spilled out onto the lawn for fireworks as the strains of a waltz echoed along the rafters. But Ida had a cold and was confined to her bed with a mustard plaster on her chest, sobbing at her misfortune though her mother patted her cheek and told her not to worry, that there would be another ball and a young man waiting for her, and besides, they were not ready to have their only daughter, their dear Ida, leave them just yet.

But it was Ida's mother who was to leave. A year after that ball, Mrs. Knowles fell sick with dysentery and was buried within a week. One year later, Jacob Knowles died of a sudden brain hemorrhage. It fell to twenty-year-old Ida to maintain Knowles' End. Running a household was a far cry from playing princess, and though a distant cousin admonished Ida to be prudent with her spending, she did not heed his advice. Grief-stricken at the loss of her parents, Ida turned to the new Spiritualism for comfort. She opened Knowles' End to Theosophists, card readers, and spirit mediums. The most gifted of these mediums was a wealthy widow named Mary White, who had an uncanny ability to put Ida in communication with her relatives on the other side. There was no rapping of the table, nor cheap levitation tricks, as so many attempted. No,

Mary White had a genuine gift and a warm demeanor, and Mary and Ida became quite close, with Ida calling her "sister." Once again, the house was filled with activity, and Knowles' End became a place for spiritual meetings, card readings, séances, and all sorts of esoteric and occult gatherings. Ida felt certain it was only a matter of time before Knowles' End was restored to its former glory. Mary had all but told her that the spirits assured it.

Mary had a companion in these endeavors, a most charismatic man with transfixing eyes, a Mr. Hobbes. He was, she promised, a prophet. A holy man. Certainly, he spent many hours alone in the library reading, and sometimes, during their séances, he fell into strange trances and spoke in words Ida did not comprehend—proof, Mary told her, of his connection to the spirit realm.

But Ida's expenses were many—spirit mediums were costly—and the Knowles fortune dwindled quickly. Ida would be socially humiliated if her debts were to become known. It was Mary who offered to buy Knowles' End and take Ida on as a boarder in order to spare her reputation. Mary agreed to let Ida have her favorite room, the attic room with the view of the city, and told her not to worry, that she would pay the back taxes and Mr. Hobbes would take on the hard work needed to make Knowles' End, which had fallen into disrepair, beautiful again.

That he did. Such a clamor! A crew would work for a week, then be curtly dismissed, only to be replaced by a new crew who would last perhaps five or six days before Mr. Hobbes sent them packing as well. Finally, he himself set about working in the old cellar, building a storeroom for canned goods and supplies—or so he said, for Ida was not allowed below. "Too dangerous," he'd told her with a smile that did not reach his eyes. (His eyes, those cold and mesmerizing eyes.) "Wouldn't want you to catch your death down there." There were other peculiar changes in the house.

Doors that went nowhere. Decorative rosettes that framed holes in the walls which produced a strange smoke that Mr. Hobbes insisted was good for the lungs and necessary for higher spiritual work. A long laundry chute that Mrs. White assured her would help the poor laundress. They were down to only three servants— a laundress, a housemaid, and a groomsman who doubled as a driver. It was disgraceful, and Ida hoped no one knew how bad things were. But then Mary would smile and tell her she'd been visited by the spectral form of Ida's father, and he was holding rosemary, for remembrance, a sure sign that he was watching over them all, and Ida would feel grateful for this small comfort. For Ida's nervous state, Mary offered her sweet wine, which sometimes gave Ida the strangest dreams of fire and destruction and the ghostly visages of sober-faced men and women.

Things began to turn sour. Strange meetings were held late into the night. Once or twice a month, Ida heard music and chanting from downstairs. People came and went.

"What do you do at these meetings?" Ida asked anxiously one evening when they dined. She only picked at her food; the roast beef was far too bloody for her taste.

"Why don't you join us, my dear?" Mrs. White suggested.

"Babylon, that great city, is fallen. It is time for a cleansing. A rebirth. Wouldn't you say, Miss Knowles?" Mr. Hobbes asked, smiling. His eyes were so very blue that Ida felt quite undone. For a moment, staring at him, she wondered what it would be like to dance with Mr. Hobbes. To feel his kiss. His caress. And as soon as she thought it, she was overcome with revulsion.

"I'm sure I don't know what you mean," she said. Her hands trembled. The blood from the roast beef formed a small, sickening pool on her plate. "I . . . I'm not well. If you'll excuse me, I shall go to bed."

That night, she heard strange sounds coming from inside the house, the most terrible bestial noises and whispers. She was too afraid to leave her bedroom. She lay awake shivering under her covers till morning.

In a cabinet in the formal parlor, Mr. Hobbes kept a large leather-bound book, rather like a Bible. But when Ida tried to get at it, she discovered that the cabinet was locked. Her own cabinet in her own house, locked against her! Shaking with anger, she confronted Mrs. White (for she no longer regarded her with the sisterly affection of "Mary.") "I won't have it, Mrs. White. I won't," Ida sniped.

"It isn't your house any longer, my dear," Mrs. White answered, and her smile was cruel.

It was a Tuesday when Ida discovered a pile of bloodied clothing scraps that Mr. Hobbes assured her, in as delicate a fashion as was proper, belonged to the laundress and which was due to the girl's monthly curse. (*The poor dear, how embarrassing for her. Of course we offered her fresh clothing and sent her home to rest. The poor, poor dear. I fear she is too overcome by shame to return to us.*") Ida wrote a desperate letter to her cousin in Boston, who sent the authorities, but when they came Ida was in such a torpor that Mrs. White told them she was not well but was being cared for, and that she hoped even this effort to descend the stairs and submit to their questions had not put her health in danger. The authorities retreated, mumbling apologies.

The last remaining servant, Emily, left in the dead of night without so much as a good-bye. She didn't even stop to collect her wages.

Ida had had enough. She'd stopped drinking the wine. Her body, though weakened, was strong enough to carry her down the stairs, for she intended to know what was happening in her own home. Yes, *her* home! It had been built by her father, for their family! She was a Knowles, not like these Johnny-come-latelies with their new money and airs: that charlatan Mrs. White, who had left to conduct a séance at the country house of some poor soul with more money than sense. And Mr. Hobbes. Mr. Hobbes, with his cold eyes and arrogant air, his lies and secrets. Wicked man! Ida needed to know what was happening in her house, and she would begin by looking in the forbidden cellar.

She took the long, narrow staircase down into the dank, dark space. It smelled of earth and something else. Ida gagged at the foulness of it. She'd have a quick look around and, hopefully, she'd find what she needed to go to the authorities and have these horrid people thrown out of her house. Then she'd look for a proper tenant, or even—dare she think it?—a husband. A knight noble who would share her life. Together, they'd make the house glorious again. Host parties attended by decent people, people of consequence and status. Knowles' End would reign once more.

Ida's hand trembled on the lantern's handle. Light flickered over the walls and corners. Ida had come for knowledge, and now she knew. Knew beyond a doubt that she faced a terrible evil. There was no scream as the candle sputtered and the whispers began. And just as Ida found the scream she'd held at bay, her candle gave out, and she was plunged into darkness.

THE HOTSY TOTSY

It had been a thudding bore of a day; rain had kept Evie inside at the museum, where she amused herself by rearranging the books on one shelf according to a taxonomy only she understood. When she thought she'd lose her mind listening to the rain and plodding through the boredom, she was cheered by the thought that—if she survived the afternoon—she'd enjoy what promised to be an exciting evening out with her friends. Now the evening had come at last. Evie had bathed, perfumed herself, and gone through every ensemble in her closet before settling on a silver bugle-bead dress that shimmered over her body like rain. She wore a long string of pearls wrapped twice around her neck. On her feet were a pair of gray satin Mary Janes with curved black heels and saucer-shaped rhinestone buckles. She painted her lips deep red, ringed her eyes in black, and topped it all off with a black velvet coat with a fur collar. She slipped twenty dollars of her dwindling reserves into a mesh tile purse, spritzed herself with a blast from her atomizer, and breezed into the parlor. Jericho sat at the kitchen table, painting miniatures for a battle-scene model. Uncle Will sat at his messy desk by the bay windows, surrounded by piles of paper and books.

Hearing Evie, he raised his head for a second, studied her, and went back to his work. "You're rather done up."

Evie pulled on her opera-length, fingerless lace gloves. "I'm going dancing with Theta and Henry at the most darling night-club."

"Not tonight, I'm afraid," Will said.

Evie stopped mid-glove. "But Unc, Theta's expecting me. If I don't go, it will pos-i-tute-ly be an insult. She'll never ask me to do anything again!"

"If you haven't heard the news, there's a brutal murderer roaming the streets of Manhattan."

"But Unc—"

"I'm sorry, Evie. It simply isn't safe. There'll be another time. I'm sure Athena will understand."

"It's Theta. And no, she won't." Evie could feel the tears threatening. She'd spent ages dolling up her eyes, and she blinked hard to keep them from smearing. "Please, Unc."

"I'm sorry, but my decision is final." Will bowed his head over his book, final judgment, case dismissed.

On the radio, the announcer extolled the merits of the Parker Dental System, "Because your dental health is too important to leave to chance."

Jericho cleared his throat. "We could play cards if you like. Or listen to the radio. There's a new show coming on at nine."

"Swell," Evie said bitterly, storming back to her room. She slammed the door and threw herself on the bed. Her new faux-pearl headpiece shifted down over her brows and she had to push it back up. Why of all nights had Will chosen this one to act just like, well, like a parent? They couldn't live in fear behind the walls of the

Bennington, never venturing farther than the museum. Evie lay on her back, staring out her window at the world beyond the fire escape.

The fire escape.

Evie sat straight up. She blotted at her eyes with her fingers and pulled on her gloves again. She opened her door a crack. "I'm retiring for the evening," she announced. Very carefully, she pushed open her window and stepped out onto the fire escape. If there was one truth Evie had learned in her short life, it was that forgiveness was easier to seek than permission. She didn't plan to ask for either one.

Several floors below, Mabel screamed as Evie came in through her bedroom window, saying, "Pipe down. It's only me."

"I thought you might be the Pentacle Killer, come to slit my throat."

"You and Unc. Sorry to disappoint you." Evie smoothed her dress into place.

"Mabel darling, what's the matter?" Mrs. Rose called from the other side of the door.

"Nothing, Mother! I thought I saw a spider, but I was mistaken," Mabel yelled. "I thought I was meeting you upstairs," she whispered to Evie.

"Change of plans. Unc's forbidden me from going out. I swear, he's behaving just like a parent!" Evie scrutinized Mabel's plain white organza dress. "Gee whiz, did you lose your sheep, Pie Face?"

"What's wrong with it?"

"You need lipstick."

"I do not need lipstick."

Evie shrugged. "Suit yourself, Mabesie. I can't fight two battles tonight."

Evie and Mabel tiptoed toward the door. The Roses were hosting another of their political meetings—something about the appeal of Sacco and Vanzetti, the anarchists. Mrs. Rose called to them. "Hello, Evangeline."

"Hello, Mrs. Rose."

"It's very nice of your uncle to take you girls to a poetry reading. It's important to tend to your education rather than fritter away time in bourgeois, immoral pastimes such as dancing in nightclubs."

Evie slid her eyes in Mabel's direction. She fought hard to keep the smile from her lips.

"We have to go, Mother. Wouldn't want to be late for the reading," Mabel said and dragged Evie away.

"Guess I'm not the only one on the lam tonight," Evie said as they ran for the elevator.

Mabel grinned. "Guess you're not."

*

"And then *I* said to him, 'The pleasure was all yours.' I said it just like that, too. I had the last word," Evie said, recounting Sam Lloyd's first visit to the museum.

"Sure ya did." Theta laughed. "You shouldn't let that Sam fella get under your skin."

"Did I say he was under my skin?"

"No. I can see you've really let it go, Evil," Theta said, and Henry smirked.

The four of them had taken a taxi to Harlem, which Theta had been nice enough to pay for, and they were making their way to a nightclub called the Hotsy Totsy, which was supposed to be the latest thing.

"It's over. Finished. The bum's rush to him," Evie said, brushing away the wind for effect.

"Good, because we're here. And I'm pretty sure the password isn't *Sam* or *Lloyd*."

Henry knocked a quick rhythm—*bum-da-BUM-bum*—and a moment later, a door cracked open. A man in a white dinner jacket and bow tie smiled. "Evenin', folks. This is a private residence."

"We're pals of the Sultan of Siam," Henry said.

"What is the sultan's favorite flower?"

"Edelweiss sure is nice."

A moment later, the door opened wide. "Right this way."

The tuxedo-clad man led them through a bustling kitchen hot with steam and down a spiral staircase to an underground tunnel. "Connects to the next building," Henry whispered to Evie and Mabel. "That way, if there's a raid in the club, most of the booze is safe somewhere in this building."

The tuxedoed man opened another door and ushered them into a room decorated like a sultan's palace. Enormous ferns spilled over the golden rims of giant pots. Panels of champagne-colored silk draped the ceiling, and the walls had been painted a deep crimson. White damask cloths covered tables topped by small amber lanterns. On the stage, the orchestra played a jazzy number that had the flappers shimmying on the dance floor while the men shouted, "Go, go, GO!" and "Get hot!" Well-heeled patrons, cocktails in hand, hopped from table to table, waving down the cigarette girls who made their rounds offering Lucky Strikes, Camels, Chesterfields, and Old Golds from enameled trays. A huge sign promised a special Solomon's Comet–watching party, and Evie tried not to think about the comet's more sinister meaning for a madman.

"This is the cat's meow," Evie said, taking it all in. This was what she had been waiting for. Clubs like this didn't exist anywhere outside Manhattan. "And the orchestra is the berries."

Henry nodded. "They're the best. I heard 'em play at the Cotton Club once. But I don't like to go there because they've got a color line." Seeing Evie's confusion, Henry explained. "Down at the Cotton Club, the orchestra could perform for the white folks just fine. But they couldn't sit at the tables out front and order a drink or mingle. Papa Charles King runs this joint. He serves everybody."

In the corner, a white woman sat talking with a black man. It never would've happened in Ohio, and Evie wondered what her parents would have to say about it. Nothing complimentary, she was pretty sure.

Theta elbowed Henry. "There's Jimmy D'Angelo. Go sweet-talk him into letting you sit in."

Henry excused himself and sauntered toward a table near the stage area where a man in a top hat and monocle sat smoking a cigar, a bright green parrot perched on his tuxedoed shoulder.

"Henry's a big talent, but Flo—Mr. Ziegfeld—doesn't see it," Theta said. "Henry's sold a few songs to Tin Pan Alley—enough to keep him in socks, and not much more. They're okay ditties, but his good songs nobody gets. Poor kiddo."

"I'd love to hear them," Mabel said.

"I hope you'll get to. Kid just needs his lucky break is all." Theta held her wrap on one shoulder. "Showtime, dolls. Give the place a look like you're too good for the dump. Just follow me."

Theta sauntered past the tables, not deigning to look at anyone. Heads turned as Theta, Evie, and Mabel followed the host through the crowded tables. They were Shebas in their flapper finery, and they drew appreciative gazes. A few people recognized Theta from the Follies.

"Must be the duck's quack to be famous," Evie said.

Theta shrugged. "They think they know me, but they don't."

The host seated them at a table in a corner and handed them menus printed on heavy cream-colored paper. Mabel's eyes widened. "I can't believe these prices!"

"Believe it," Theta said. "Make sure you like whatever you order, 'cause you'll be nursing it all night long."

"My mother would cast a kitten over the excess," Mabel said guiltily.

"Your mother isn't here."

"Thank heavens for that," Evie muttered.

A waiter appeared with a bottle of champagne and a silver bucket of ice. "Sorry, pal. We didn't order bubbly," Theta said.

"For the ladies. From an appreciative gentleman," the waiter said.

"Which one?" Evie said, craning her neck.

"Mr. Samson at table fifteen," the waiter said, indicating delicately with a nod.

"Oh, brother," Theta said.

"What is it?" Evie couldn't see too well in the dark.

"See that fella across the way? Don't be obvious about it."

The girls peeked over the tops of their menus. Four tables over sat a heavyset man with a very full mustache and the smug air of Wall Street success. "The one who looks like a walrus without a zoo?" Evie asked.

"The same. He's one of those chumps who wants to feel like he's young and exciting. Probably got a wife and three brats up in Bedford and thinks we'll show him a good time. Oh, he's looking at us. Smile, girls."

Evie flashed her teeth, and the older man raised his glass. The girls raised theirs in reply. The man blew a kiss and motioned for them to join him.

"What now?" Evie asked through still-smiling teeth.

"Now it's really showtime." Theta knocked back her champagne and let loose an enormous belch that drew disgusted stares from people nearby. "Nothing like a good glass of giggle water to help a girl's insides!" Theta said loudly and patted her stomach.

Across the floor, the older man's glass hung in midair. He looked quickly away.

"He's scandalized!" Evie said on a giggle.

"Now he can go home to his wife in Bedford and *we* can enjoy his grape juice in peace."

"How'd you get so smart?"

"Hard knocks," Theta said. She and Evie toasted and sipped the man's champagne.

Mabel signaled for a waiter. "Could I have a Sloe Gin Fizz, without the gin?"

"What's the point of that, Miss?" the waiter said.

"Tomorrow morning," Mabel said.

"If you say so, Miss."

"How's Henry making out?" Theta asked, craning her head. Several tables away, Henry lounged in a chair wearing an expression of beautiful, bored elegance as he listened to the man with the parrot.

"He's not really your brother, is he?" Evie said.

Theta smirked. "Now you've done it. People will talk."

Theta was so deadpan that it took Evie a second to realize she was kidding.

"How did you meet?"

"On the street. I was starving, and he gave me part of his sandwich. He's a real pal."

"If you don't mind my asking, why didn't the two of you...?"

Theta narrowed her eyes and blew out a thin stream of smoke. It felt to Evie as if she were weighing her answer. "We just didn't go for each other. He may not be my real brother, but he feels like one to me. I'd do anything for him."

Henry sauntered toward them and Theta scooted over to make room.

"What did I miss?" he asked. "Say, where did the champagne come from?"

"Lonely walrus," Evie explained and giggled. She was already feeling a little tipsy, more from excitement and optimism than from the champagne. She liked Theta and Henry. They were so sophisticated—not like anybody she'd known back home. She hoped they liked her, too.

"You're just in time. We're about to make a toast," Theta said.

Henry raised his glass. "To what?"

"To us. To the future," Theta said.

"To the future," Henry, Evie, and Mabel echoed.

The orchestra segued into a hot, sensual number, and Evie leaned her head against Theta's shoulder. "Don't you feel like anything could happen tonight?"

"It's Manhattan. Anything can happen at any time."

"But what if you met the man of your dreams tonight?"

Theta blew out another plume of cigarette smoke. "Not interested. Love's messy, kiddo. Let those other girls get moony-eyed and goofy. Me? I got plans."

"What plans?" Mabel asked. A waiter had brought pâte on toast, which she ate with delight.

"Pictures. *That's* the future. I hear they're gonna start making talking pictures."

Evie laughed. "Talking pictures? How awful!"

"'S gonna be swell. When my contract's up, I'm heading to California with Henry. Right, Henry?"

"Anything you say, beautiful."

"I hear they have lemon trees, and you can pick 'em right off and make fresh lemonade. We'll get a house with a lemon tree in the backyard. Maybe even have a dog. I always wanted a dog."

Evie wanted to laugh, but Theta seemed so serious, and even a little sad, so she just choked back her drink instead. "Sounds ducky." She clinked glasses with Theta. "To lemon trees and dogs!"

"Lemon trees and dogs," Theta and Henry said, laughing.

"Lemon trees and dogs," Mabel slurred, her mouth full.

Evie leaned forward, resting her chin on her upturned palm. "What about you, Henry?"

"Me? I'm going to write songs for the pictures. Real songs. Not that gooey bushwa Flo Ziegfeld likes," Henry drawled.

"To real songs!" Evie toasted. "Mabesie?"

"I'm going to help the poor. But first, I'm going to eat every bit of this." Mabel swooned. "Heavenly."

Theta cocked her head. "What about you, Evil?"

Evie turned her glass around slowly on the table. What could she say? *I'm going to stop having nightmares about my dead brother. I'm going to let the past stop haunting me like a vengeful ghost. I'm going to find my place in the world and show everyone what I'm made of.* She'd felt it from the moment she stepped off the train at Penn Station, a sense that she belonged here, that Manhattan was her true home. "This probably sounds silly. . . ."

Henry let out a loud, dramatic laugh, then shrugged. "I just wanted to get it out of the way, darling."

Evie grinned. Oh, she liked them both so much! "Ever since I got here, I've had the craziest feeling of destiny—that whatever is supposed to happen, whoever it is I'm going to be, is waiting just around the next corner. I want to be ready for it. I want to meet it headlong." Evie raised her glass. "To whatever's around the next corner."

"I sure hope it's not a car bearing down," Mabel joked.

"To the good stuff just out of sight," Theta echoed.

"To Evie's destiny," Henry said and touched his glass to theirs in a satisfying chime.

Evie paused, her glass in midair. "I don't believe it. Of all the gall!"

"What's eating you?" Theta asked.

Evie slammed her glass down, sloshing champagne onto the tablecloth. "Theta, take my purse. It's got twenty bucks in it. You might need it to bail me out."

"For the last time, what is it?"

"*Sam Lloyd,*" Evie hissed. She marched over to where he stood, leaning against a marble column, talking up a blond with a red Cupid's bow mouth.

"Excuse me, Miss." Evie sandwiched herself between them.

"Hey!" the girl objected, but Evie stood firm.

"What are *you* doing here?" she demanded.

"What am I doing here? I come here all the time. What are *you* doing here?"

"Who's she—your mother?" the blonde said in a voice so high it could break glass.

Evie turned. "I'm from the health department. You've heard of Typhoid Mary? This fella's got enough typhoid to start his own colony."

The girl's eyes widened. "Holy smokes!"

"You said it. Just to be safe, you might want to burn those glad rags you've got on. In fact, you might wanna burn them on principle."

"Huh?"

Evie raised an eyebrow at Sam. "Why, Sam, she's charming." Evie turned back to the blonde, leaned in close and whispered, "You see that fella with the mustache over there?" Evie pointed to the walrus man. "He's so rich he could buy Wool and Worth's and still have enough left over for a steak dinner. Why don't you go get him to buy you a drink?"

"You on the level?"

"And how. He's a real Big Cheese. Trust me."

The girl smiled. "Say, thanks for the tip, honey."

"We Janes have to stick together."

The girl looked worried. "You gonna be okay with his... typhoid?"

"It's okay," Evie said, glaring at Sam. "I'm immune to what he's got."

Sam watched the alluring blond wiggle her way toward the walrus man and shook his head. "Anybody ever tell you your timing is lousy, sister?"

"Where did you get that dinner jacket? It looks expensive."

Sam grinned. "Back of a chair."

"You *stole* it?"

"Let's just say I borrowed it for the duration of my stay."

"I oughta tell Uncle Will."

"Be my guest. Of course, then you've gotta explain what you were doing here at a speakeasy in Harlem at eleven thirty in the PM."

Evie opened her mouth to give Sam an earful just as the tuxedo-clad emcee stepped to the microphone. His white shirt was so stiff it looked bulletproof. "And now the Hotsy Totsy presents the Famous Hotsy Totsy Girls dancing that forbidden dance, the Black Bottom!"

The orchestra launched into the jazzy, uptempo dance tune.

With a loud whoop, the young and beautiful chorines strutted their way across the stage. They swayed their hips and stamped out a hard, quick rhythm with their silver shoes. With each shimmy, the bugle beads on their scandalously revealing costumes swung and shook. It was the sort of display Evie knew her mother would have found appalling—an example of the moral decay of the young generation. It was sexual and dangerous and thrilling, and Evie wanted more of it.

The piano player called out to the girls, and they shuffled forward, hips first. They crooked their fingers and everyone raced onto the dance floor below the stage, caught up in the dance and the night.

☼

Theta sat at the table, alone, behind an inscrutable cloud of cigarette smoke, watching. Henry had started up a conversation with a handsome waiter named Billy, and she wondered if he'd be coming home tonight. She watched the spoiled debutantes getting their kicks by coming uptown to hear jazz in forbidden clubs, just to make their mothers fret. She watched the bartenders filling glasses but keeping their eyes on the doors. She watched the lonely hearts mooning over the fellas who, oblivious, mooned over other dolls. She watched a fight break out between a couple who were now sitting in miserable silence. She watched the cigarette girls smiling at each table, extolling the health benefits of Lucky Strikes or Chesterfields, whichever company paid them a little more. She watched the girls dance onstage and wondered how old they'd been when they started. Had they been dragged from town to town on the circuit from the age of four? Had they lain awake on fleabag motel floors, then made the rounds of booking agents the next morning, half-dead from exhaustion? Had any of them made a daring escape from a small town in the middle of the night? Had they changed their names and their looks, becoming someone completely new, someone who couldn't be found? Did any of them have a power so frightening it had to be kept locked down tight?

A good-looking fella with a fraternity pin on his lapel stepped in front of Theta's table, blocking her view. "Mind if I join you?"

Theta stubbed out her cigarette. "Sorry, pal. I was just leaving." She grabbed her wrap and Evie's purse and went in search of the ladies' lounge.

☀

Memphis had finished his rounds for the night. On his way through the Hotsy Totsy's kitchen, he pocketed a few cookies for Isaiah, then set off to check out the action in the club. A drunk girl whose curls drooped from dancing called to him as he passed: "Oh, boy— get my coat, will ya?" She dropped a quarter in his hand.

"Do I look like I work for you? Get your own damn coat." Memphis tossed the quarter back, and it fell at her feet.

"Well, I never…"

"And you never will," Memphis grumbled. Off the hallway was a sitting room with club chairs and Persian rugs where couples went to neck or smoke. Memphis walked past a petting couple and settled into his favorite chair to read.

"Do you mind?" the man called.

"A little. But I'll be just fine," Memphis shot back, along with his widest smile. He opened his book. The man swore under his breath and called him a name Memphis didn't like. Memphis stayed put, and after a moment, the couple left. Alone in the room, Memphis lost himself to the pleasure of the book.

"Let's dance," Sam said.

"With you?" Evie scoffed. "Just so you know, I left my money with Theta for safekeeping."

"Come on, doll, I'll be as good as a Boy Scout." He laced his fingers through hers. "Feel that rhythm, kid. Doesn't it work on you?"

Evie looked in the direction of the dance floor. A crowd of flappers, lost to the booze and the beat, were tearing it up. Evie wanted to be in the thick of it. To let herself go under the lights.

"One dance," Evie said and dragged him toward the gyrating crowd. Sam pulled Evie into a waltz. His hand was warm at the small of her back.

"What are you doing?" she said as they twirled softly in place.

"Going against the grain," Sam answered.

"Maybe I like going *with* the grain."

"You? I don't see it."

"Maybe you don't know me as well as you think you do," Evie yelled close to his ear. It was hard to hear over the orchestra and the dancers.

"We could work on that," Sam said, pulling her into a twirl. He was a good dancer. Graceful and quick-footed, he knew how to lead without being overbearing. On the dance floor, at least, they were swell together.

"You smell good enough to eat," Sam said so close to her ear that it made the skin along her jaw buzz.

"Just like the Big Bad Wolf," Evie murmured.

"Say, about that ghost business—does your uncle believe in that, or is he just making a buck?"

"How should I know?" Evie asked. She didn't want to think about Will just now. "Why? Do you believe it?"

Sam forced a smile. "Man's gotta believe in something."

He twirled Evie around and around under the lights.

Mabel had gone to the restroom and returned to an empty table. A minute later, she'd been corralled into dancing with a fella named Scotty who had managed to step on both of her feet three times and who insisted on calling her by the wrong name. Now she sat at the table vacated by the others listening to him prattle on about stocks and bonds and finding the right sort of girl to take home to Mother. She guessed the right sort of girl was not the daughter of a Jewish socialist and a society girl turned rabble-rouser.

"You're a swell listener, May Belle," Scotty said. His tongue was thick from Scotch.

"Mabel," she corrected. She squinted in the club's atmospheric glow and allowed herself to pretend this boring idiot was Jericho. Out on the floor, Evie danced with Sam—and after swearing to deck him.

"Why, you're just like..."

"A sister," Mabel finished for him.

"Exactly so!"

"Swell." She sighed. The Scotty fellow continued rambling, making Mabel feel smaller and plainer. Her dress was all wrong; she looked like she was auditioning for a Christmas pageant somewhere. She was tired of being overlooked or compared to someone's sister or passed off as a sweet, harmless girl, the sort nobody minded but nobody sought out, either. How had she allowed herself to be talked into this misery? It was different for Evie. Evie was born to play the role of carefree flapper. Mabel wasn't. In nightclubs or at dances, she was out of her element. Just once, she'd like to be the exciting one, the girl somebody wanted.

"Isn't that right, May Belle?" the idiot said, finishing some painful thought about fishing or motorcars, no doubt. He clapped her on the arm a little hard.

"That's it," Mabel said, getting up. She tossed her napkin on the table. "No. That is not right. I don't know what you just said, but whatever it was, I'm pretty certain it was pure hokum. I don't want to dance. I don't want to hear about your plans for a summer house. I am not your sister. And if I *were* your sister, I'd have to tell people you'd been adopted as an act of charity. Please, don't get up."

"I wasn't," Scotty said.

Mabel marched up to Evie and tapped her on the shoulder. "Evie, I want to go home."

"Oh, Mabel, no. Why, we're just getting started!"

"You're just getting started. *I* am finished."

Evie stepped to the side with Mabel. "What's wrong, Pie Face?"

"Nobody wants to dance with me."

"I'll get Sam to dance with you."

"I don't want you to make someone dance with me. You know perfectly well what I mean. It might be different if Jericho were here."

"I tried to get him to come, Pie Face, honestly I did. But he's pos-i-tute-ly *allergic* to having a good time. Why don't you order another Orange Juice Jazz Baby?"

"They're five dollars!"

"Come on, Mabesie. Live a little. It won't kill you. Oh, they're playing my favorite song!" Evie dashed out onto the dance floor before Mabel could stop her. It probably wasn't her favorite song; she just needed an excuse to get away and avoid Mabel. Sometimes Evie could be so selfish.

Mabel saw the drunken Scotty lurching toward her with a

sloppy "Heyyy, Maybeline, honey," and ran and hid behind an enormous potted fern, plotting all the ways she was going to kill Evie when this evening was finally over.

※

Theta walked the corridors of the club, dragging her fur wrap behind her. Some people recognized her with a "Hey, aren't you...?" To which Theta would say, "Sorry. You must have me confused with another party."

Behind her, a man called out "Betty!" and Theta turned quickly, her heart beating fast. But he was calling to a redhead, who yelled back, "Hold your horses! I need the little girls' room."

Theta had had enough. She didn't want to go home, but she didn't want to stay, either. She wasn't sure what she wanted except something new, something that made her feel anchored to her life. She felt like she could float away at any moment. Sure, she had Henry, wonderful Henry. He was like a brother to her. It was Henry who had saved her life when she'd first come to the city, desperate and starving. And it was Henry who'd saved her life a second time. They'd always be together. But lately, she'd felt a hunger for more. It had the shape of destiny about it, this feeling, though she couldn't begin to put a name on it.

A crowd of revelers caromed down the hall, and Theta ducked into the first room she saw. It appeared empty, but as she came around the side of a green wingback chair, she saw that it was occupied by a handsome young man with a book of poems. He was so absorbed in his reading that he didn't even notice her.

"Must be some book," she said, startling him.

Memphis looked up to see a striking girl with jet-black hair smoking a cigarette and watching him.

"Walt Whitman."

"Mmm," Theta said.

"I'm a poet myself," Memphis said. He held up his small leather journal. Theta took it and flipped through the pages, opening to a series of numbers written in the back. She raised an eyebrow. "Doesn't look like poetry to me. More like a bookie's tab."

Quickly, Memphis grabbed the book back. He gave her the full-dazzle smile that worked on chorus girls and jumpy gangsters. "I'm just holding that for a friend."

"Mm-hmm."

"My name's Memphis. Memphis Campbell. And you are?"

"Just a girl in a nightclub." Theta blew out a stream of smoke.

"You shouldn't smoke those. Sister says they're poison."

"Your sister's a barrel of laughs."

Memphis laughed. "She's not my sister. We call her sister. Sister Walker. And she could rival a pickle for pucker." That got a smirk from Theta. It was all the encouragement Memphis needed. "You French? Got a French look to you. Maybe even a little Creole."

Theta shrugged and tapped the end of her cigarette into a tall silver ashtray. "I look like everybody."

"Well, I'm gonna call you Creole Princess."

"You can call me whatever you like. Doesn't mean I'll answer."

"I'm still gonna keep calling."

"You're persistent, Memphis Campbell, I'll give you that. What are you doing here besides reading library books?"

"Oh, you know. A little of this, little of that."

Theta arched one thin brow. "Sounds like trouble."

Memphis spread his arms in a gesture of innocence. "Me? I'm the farthest thing from trouble you'll ever know."

"Mmm," Theta said, walking around the room.

"Why aren't you upstairs in the club?"

Theta shrugged. "I was bored."

"Bored! That's a first. Don't you know the Hotsy Totsy is supposed to be the swankiest club in town?"

Theta shrugged again. "I've been to a lot of clubs."

"That a fact?"

"Yep." She dragged on her cigarette. "Poet, huh? Why don't you read me something?"

"Whatever you say, Creole Princess." Memphis opened the book and read while Theta once again flipped casually through his journal. He had a nice voice, one well suited to poetry. "'I sing the body electric/The armies of those I love engirth me and I engirth them/They will not let me off till I go with them, respond to them/ And discorrupt them, and charge them full with the charge of the soul. . . .' That's Mr. Walt Whitman. One of our finest poets."

Theta had turned another page. Now she stared at the radiant eye-and-lightning bolt symbol somebody had doodled in the corner of the page. Her heart beat faster. "Did you draw this?" She tried to keep her voice even.

"That? Oh, just something I saw in a dream."

"In . . . a dream?" Theta repeated. She felt hot and dizzy. "What is it? What do you know about it?"

"Nothing. Like I said, just something I saw in a dream."

The drawing seemed to have upset the girl for some reason. Memphis wanted to ask her why, but he also didn't want to scare her off. "Here, let me show you around the club." He reached for his notebook, but Theta held on to it. She looked right at him, but she didn't seem angry; she seemed astonished, maybe even a little scared.

"I've seen that same symbol in my own dreams," she said.

Memphis didn't know where to start. "Do you know what it is or where it comes from? Have you seen it somewhere before?"

Theta shook her head. "Only in my dreams."

"When did it start?"

"I don't know. About six months ago? You?"

"'Round about then."

"How often do you dream it?" she asked.

"Twice a week, maybe more. Used to be only here and there, but lately, it's happening more often."

Theta nodded. "I'm having it more often, too."

She dreamed of the same symbol. Memphis dealt with odds every day, and he knew the odds on this were staggering. It had to mean something, didn't it? "Tell me exactly what you dream."

Theta sank into a chair. She was shaking. "It's always the same. I'm somewhere a long way from New York. I don't know where. No place I know. I'm standing on a road, and the sky's lousy with storm clouds—"

Memphis could feel his heart thundering in his chest. "Is there a farmhouse? An old white farmhouse with a porch?"

Theta's eyes widened. "Yes," she whispered. "And wheat fields, or corn. Some kind of fields. And in the distance there's this tree—"

"With no leaves on it. Just a big old gnarled tree, with limbs as thick as a giant's arms."

Goose bumps rose on Theta's back and neck. "And something's coming on the road. . . ."

"Just behind a wall of dust," Memphis finished for her.

Theta nodded. She felt cold all over. What was happening? "The worst part is the feeling," she said softly. "Like something terrible is coming. Something I don't want to see."

"Something you'll be called to do something about," Memphis said.

"What does it mean?"

A loud crash came from above, followed by screams and the sounds of police whistles being blown. Frantic footsteps thudded across the ceiling. Memphis ran to the door and poked his head out, only to see a full squad of policeman barging their way into the kitchen.

Theta's eyes widened. "Holy smokes! It's a raid."

"Can't be," Memphis said, throwing his knapsack over his shoulder. He still held the book in his hand. "Papa Charles has the cops in his pocket."

"That pocket's got a hole, Poet." The terror of the shared dream was replaced by the real fear of being arrested. "How do I get out of here? I can't afford to get pinched."

"This way!" Memphis offered his hand. "I know this place like my own skin. I'll get you out of here. Trust me."

Theta grabbed his hand and they set off running down the narrow hall.

※

Mabel gasped as the doors to the club were broken down and two lines of police stormed the club. One grabbed her by the wrist. She tugged, but his grip was strong.

"Right this way, Miss. I've got a car waiting," the officer said, smiling.

"My mother will kill me," Mabel wailed as he dragged her away from the chaos unfolding behind her.

※

Theta and Memphis ran. Behind them, the police stormed the place, breaking open walls, knocking chairs over. Two flappers and their beaus screamed and stumbled drunkenly into the wall of cops. A clearly intoxicated man whose face was covered in lipstick pulled out a gun and fired off shots indiscriminately. One of his bullets passed through the book of poetry in Memphis's hand. Memphis stuck his finger through the hole. "That was a library book," he said, gasping.

"Poet, we've gotta scram!"

Memphis ran with Theta around a corner, where he pulled her into a telephone booth. She looked up through heavy lashes into Memphis's handsome face. She'd seen plenty of handsome fellas before, but none who wrote poetry and shared the same strange nightmare. Deep down, Theta felt stirrings she'd guarded against since Roy and Kansas and what had happened there.

"You pull me in here to hide or to neck, Poet?" Theta joked, trying to catch her breath.

"Trust me," Memphis said. He turned the crank on the telephone three times and gave a hard push on the back wall, which opened onto a secret passageway.

☼

Upstairs in the club, it was chaos as the police stormed the doors. The bartenders moved quickly. They flipped the bar over, sending about two dozen bottles of good hooch down a chute to their untimely end, then pulled a lever on the bar itself, emptying the bottles and glasses there down another chute and wiping the evidence away with rags. Patrons screamed and climbed over tables, knocking one another over in their panic to get out. Some of the flappers continued dancing, thrilled to be arrested and make the papers. "You sure you gents don't need a drink?" the club manager quipped as the cops walked him toward the door. In the midst of the hysteria, Henry walked calmly to the piano, took a seat, and began to play.

"Don't look at me, officer. I'm just the piano player," he said, but the man in blue cuffed him anyway.

In the melee, Sam and Evie were separated. Evie dodged and wove her way toward an exit just as a fresh wave of cops barged in. She doubled back, passing the dim blond from earlier, who was pouring her heart out to the cop arresting her: "These chumps are all the same—one minute they're trying to get you into the struggle buggy, the next, they're giving you their typhoid."

Trapped, Evie dove under a table and hid beneath its white cloth, watching. She reached up just high enough to grab an open bottle of champagne and pull it down with her. It seemed a shame to let good hooch go to waste, and if she was going down, she was going in style. After a few minutes, she peeked out and saw Sam gliding easily out the door, untouched. Or rather, she thought she saw him. He moved so quickly she couldn't be sure. She only knew she was angry again. She bolted after him, calling his name, but a second wave of policemen rounded the corner. Evie ran back into the club room, keeping low. She spied a dumbwaiter hidden behind the bar and made a break for it, wriggling herself in. Her long necklace caught on the hook, scattering pearls all over the floor, which tripped an officer heading her way. There was no time to mourn the jewels, so she slammed the door shut and hoisted herself toward freedom.

※

"Didn't I tell you to trust me?" Memphis said. He and Theta stood in the dank wine cellar beneath the club. A lone worker's bulb over the door cast dim light across the dirt floor and the barrels stored in the deep room.

"What is this place?"

"It's where they store the hooch when it comes in from Canada," Memphis explained. "Come on. Be careful—the steps are tricky."

"Where to now?"

Memphis stood for a moment, trying to get his bearings. He didn't spend a lot of time down here, and he wasn't certain of the room. He only knew there had to be a door somewhere. Up the steps, the doorknob jangled. There were shouts.

"Cops," Theta whispered.

"Hold on, hold on," Memphis whispered back. "Let's see if they go away."

It was quiet for a spell; all they heard was their own breathing. Then a loud *thwack* broke the silence, and Theta yelped as a policeman's ax splintered a slit in the cellar's big wooden door.

"Tell me you know a way out of here!" Theta said.

"This way!" Memphis said, and hoped he was right. They threaded through barrels of liquor. Behind them, the door gave way, and someone shot into the air, shouting, "Stop right there!"

"Should we . . . ?" Theta panted.

"Not on your life, Princess," Memphis said, pulling her on.

Footsteps echoed in the cavernous space. The cops had made it in and were gaining on them. Memphis had paid off some of these men for Papa Charles; most would look the other way and let him go. But a few were quick with their clubs, and finding a black man with a white woman in a cellar full of booze didn't bode well for Memphis's case. The shouts of "Stop! Stop!" came again, this time punctuated by gunfire. Where was the way out?

Against the far wall, Memphis saw the silhouette of stairs. He followed them up and saw the outline of a door. It had to lead to a fire escape.

"This way," Memphis gasped out as he half dragged Theta up the rickety staircase.

"There they are!" a cop yelled from below.

Memphis tried the knob but it was stuck. He threw himself against the door, once, twice, and it finally swung open on rusted hinges. He pushed Theta out onto the fire escape. Down below, two officers stood smoking cigarettes. "Go up!" he whispered.

Theta nodded and started the climb up to the roof. A rotting cafe chair rested against the railing. Memphis lodged it under the doorknob, and while the cops banged against the door, he climbed after Theta. The harsh glare of a neon sign advertising Lucky Strike cigarettes turned the roof into a white haze. They ran to the edge of the roof, stepping over the half wall to the next roof, and then the next, climbing at last down another fire escape into an alley. Memphis jumped first, then helped Theta, enjoying for that brief second the feel of her against his chest. The two of them ran out and joined the nighthawks still walking the city streets.

☀

The dumbwaiter had reached the top. Grunting, Evie pushed against the door with her fists, then her feet, but it was hopelessly stuck.

"Hello?" she whispered. "Hello? Anybody there?"

A moment later, the door opened. A man's hand appeared and Evie took it gratefully, slowly unbending her arms and legs and stepping out of the cramped box, still holding fast to the champagne bottle.

"Oh, swell! Thank you, baby!"

"You're welcome, sweetheart," the policeman said, slapping handcuffs on her. "You're also under arrest."

Sam slipped easily through the crowd and back through the corridor into the building next door. Whenever a policeman looked his way, Sam would think that same thought—*Don't see me*—and before the cop could figure out what had happened, Sam would have moved on, leaving him to shake his head and chase after someone else. He hoped Evie had managed to escape. He had to hand it to her, she had moxie. He liked girls with moxie. They were trouble. And Sam liked trouble even more than moxie.

✳

"Did we lose them?" Theta panted. Her legs shook and the white fur of her coat was grimed with dirt.

"I think so." Memphis held up the pulp of the book and sighed. "Mrs. Andrews is gonna kill me."

"At least you'll have something to write about," Theta said and laughed. It was a solid bray of a laugh, completely at odds with her jaded demeanor. The cool she'd shown him earlier was gone. Their narrow escape had made them giddy, and they stood on the corner of Seventh Avenue laughing at their good fortune like a couple of kids on Christmas morning. Theta tilted her head back and caught the breeze. In that moment, she was so beautiful that Memphis wished they could keep running.

"You jake, Poet? You look like someone slipped you a mickey," Theta said.

Memphis forced a smile and spread his arms wide. "Me? I don't wear worry."

"Let's go sneak a peek."

They crept down the block and crossed the street to where they had a good lookout for the action at the club. Sirens wailed on the street and police wagons lined the block in a long line. The men in blue pulled patrons from the club while the neighborhood looked on. The press had arrived, and the flashlamps popped; they could smell the burning magnesium in the night air.

"Papa Charles isn't gonna like this," Memphis said. "He pays the cops enough not to raid his clubs. I hope your friends got out all right."

"Me, too," Theta said. She still held Evie's handbag. "I suppose I'd better blow home and see if they did."

Memphis felt his heart sink. He didn't want the evening to end. "I could take you for a cup of coffee first, if you like. I know *I* could sure use one."

Theta smiled. It was a sweet smile, almost shy. "Thanks, Poet. But I should get my beauty sleep."

Memphis started to say something clever—"Why? You're already the best-looking girl in town"—but didn't. It would seem like charm, and he didn't want to charm this girl. He wanted to know her. But the magic of their escape couldn't extend everywhere.

"Maybe I'll see you in my dreams tonight," he said instead. "On that road."

Theta's smile faltered just a bit. "I suppose I'd feel less scared if you were there."

The cops patted the doors of one of the wagons and sent it on its way. The streets were clogged with people now. Theta stuck out her hand. "Thanks for the daring escape, Poet."

Memphis shook Theta's hand, marveling at the softness of it. "Anytime, Creole Princess."

Theta ran toward the subway. At the corner, she turned to see

Memphis still watching her. He wasn't watching her the way that audiences or the occasional fan on the street did. It didn't make her feel odd or imagined; on the contrary, she had never felt more real. "Hey, Poet!" she called back to him. "It's Theta!"

"Pardon?" he shouted.

"My name. It's Theta—"

The crowd thickened between them just as someone pulled Memphis into a choke hold from behind. He whipped around, ready for a fight. Laughing, Gabe put his hands up in surrender, backing away. "Easy, brother. Just me. Can you believe they raided the club? Somebody's putting the squeeze on Papa Charles. I'd gone out back for a smoke or I'd be in one of those wagons, too. Hey, Memphis—you even listening to me?"

Memphis had turned away from Gabe and was craning his head, searching for some sign of Theta, but she was already gone. How would he find her again? Beside him, Gabe was talking a mile a minute, but Memphis wasn't listening. Something had shifted in the cosmos. His future seemed to have thinned to a point of destiny, and it had a name: Theta.

※

When Memphis let himself into Octavia's apartment, he found Isaiah standing at the foot of the bed in a pale wash of bluish moonlight. The boy stared into the gloom of the bedroom, his head shaking slightly.

"Hey, Ice Man. Whatcha doin' up?" The boy didn't answer. "Isaiah? You all right?"

Isaiah's eyes rolled back until only the whites were visible. His eyelids fluttered wildly.

"The seventh offering is vengeance. Turn the heretics from

the Temple of Solomon. And their sins shall be purified by blood and fire."

"Isaiah?" Memphis whispered. Hearing these strange words coming out of his brother's mouth made him cold with fear.

"Anoint thy flesh and prepare ye the walls of your houses to receive him." Isaiah's thin body jerked with small spasms.

Memphis gripped his arms. Should he run for Octavia? The doctor? He didn't know. "Isaiah, what are you talking about?" he whispered urgently.

"They're coming. The time is now."

"Isaiah, wake up now. You're having a nightmare. Wake up, I say!"

Isaiah went limp and calm in Memphis's hands. His eyelids closed as if he might drift back to sleep. Suddenly, he stiffened. His eyes snapped wide open. He stared at Memphis as his small body shook. His words were a choked whisper: "Oh, my son, my son. What have you done?"

Isaiah swayed, but Memphis caught him in time and put his little brother into his bed, where he resumed sleeping as if nothing had happened.

Memphis sat shivering on his own bed. Unable to rest, he watched the rise and fall of his brother's chest for some time, until early dawn filled the room with a weak, milky light. How could Isaiah have known? No one knew except Memphis. It was what he'd seen when he was under the healing trance in those last moments with their mother on her deathbed. As he'd walked in that other place, a misty land between waking and death, he'd seen her spirit, mournful and afraid, her hands reaching out toward him just before she was swallowed by some vast dark, her last words both a benediction and a warning:

Oh, my son, my son. What have you done?

BLOOD AND FIRE

Eugene Meriwether let himself into the imposing white edifice of the Grand Masonic Lodge on West Twenty-third Street, near the rattling thunder of the Sixth Avenue El, and climbed the steps to a small office on the third floor. He'd enjoyed a dinner out with his Brothers following a meeting on a charity endeavor they hoped to get under way. Now, by the soft glow of his banker's lamp, he worked up a proposal for the Grand Master to review.

In the quiet of the office, he opened the jeweler's box secreted inside his jacket and brushed a finger across the cuff links nestled into the dark velvet. Tomorrow was Edward's birthday. He smiled, imagining Edward saying, "What is this?" as he opened the box and beheld the fine workmanship of the cuff links, which featured a scrolled *E*, the initial they shared. He could practically feel Edward's sweet kiss on his lips. Edward, his great love; Edward, his great secret.

A sudden sound drew Eugene's attention—a jovial whistling. He thought with consternation of old Mr. Saunders, who liked to drink and might have stumbled in.

He called out: "Saunders, old boy, is that you?"

The whistling stopped. Satisfied, Eugene went back to his work. But a few moments later, there it was—an irritating ditty echoing through the empty lodge. More than irritating... uncomfortable. There was a telephone on the desk, and Eugene struggled with whether or not to call the police. How foolish would he feel if it turned out to be old Saunders after all? And how humiliating for Saunders, who was very close friends with the Grand Master himself. Why, Eugene might ruin his own standing in the Brotherhood and never rise above Junior Warden. No, he couldn't risk the taint of shame or ridicule. He'd like to be Grand Master himself one day. Yes, better to handle this on his own. If he took care of this trouble with Saunders carefully, discreetly, the old man might take a shine to him. This was the sort of opportunity disguised as obstacle the inspirational books talked about! He would meet the challenge head-on. How proud Edward would be when he told him later.

Again he called out: "Saunders? Can you hear me?"

Nothing but that damned whistling.

Straightening his tie, Eugene Meriwether left the comfort of his desk and poked his head out of the office. At the far end of the darkened hall, golden, shimmering light spilled out from around the slightly open door of the Gothic Room. Curious, the Mason moved toward it, passing the framed portraits of departed Masonic brothers. As he walked the dim corridor, something in Eugene Meriwether's belly sounded a silent alarm that pulsed through his blood. Something that snaked back to his primitive ancestors and their need to huddle in caves around fires, the kind of warning that no amount of civilization could ever completely eradicate. He almost wished he had called the police, but his ambition kept him moving forward, toward the glowing room. He grabbed the knob and pushed open the door.

Fire. The golden glow had come from a fire burning on the center altar. And as he tried to piece together what was happening—*A fire? In the Gothic Room? How?*—the door slammed shut behind him. He pulled on the doorknob, his mind whirring with logical explanations: *It's a prank. Some hooligans in need of a lesson. They'll be very, very sorry for this. Holding this door shut from the outside, they are. Youth today—no respect. Hooligans, all.*

The whistling stopped. A deep, resonant voice echoed in the room. "'For they did not walk in the path of righteousness and lo, was the Lord's anger sorely provoked.'"

A dark shadow passed across the wall. It seemed at first glance to be the long shadow of a man. But as the shadow drew closer, it became clear that whatever lurked behind Eugene Meriwether was far from human.

"'And for the seventh offering, it was commanded: Turn the heretics from the Temple of Solomon under the watchful eye of God and purify their sins with an offering of blood and fire. For there is no expiation of sin but by blood....'"

Eugene Meriwether put a hand to his chest, feeling the furious beating of his heart beneath the small square box meant for Edward. Clinging to thoughts of his love, Eugene slowly turned. And as the walls began to whisper, he lost his footing on the precipice of reason and began the terrible fall into a hell beyond imagining.

RECKONING

Evie and Mabel spent the entire night in a cell of the city's notorious downtown jail, the Tombs, surrounded by drunken flappers, prostitutes, and a large woman who growled like a dog whenever anyone got too near. Mabel's mother arrived first, sweeping down the hall with her characteristic hauteur. "I do hope you girls have had time to reflect upon your evening," she said, but it was Evie she glared at and it was clear who she thought should shoulder the blame.

"So long, Evie," Mabel said as her mother escorted her out. She looked like a prisoner being led to the electric chair without a last meal.

By the time Uncle Will posted bail for Evie, it was just past seven o'clock. They city was rumbling to life, another morning in Manhattan, as she and Will emerged onto White Street.

"I should have let you sit there longer," Will snapped. He was walking so quickly that Evie could barely keep up. Her head thudded with each step.

"I'm awfully sorry, Unc."

"We had an agreement: I give you your freedom, and you keep out of trouble."

"I know, and I feel like a real Dumb Dora, getting pinched like that."

Will wagged a finger. "That is not the point, Evangeline. You deliberately disobeyed my quite reasonable request that you stay at home last night. You lied to me."

"I didn't *lie*, exactly. . . ."

"Sneaking away is lying."

"Yes, but . . . could you slow down, please, Unc? My head's killing me." The morning sun made her eyes feel bruised.

Uncle Will stopped near a newsstand and ran a hand through his hair. A street urchin waved a newspaper at him and he shooed the boy away. "This was a terrible idea. I'm a bachelor; I haven't a clue how to be a parent, or even an uncle."

"That isn't true. You're terribly uncle-ish. Why, you're the most uncle-ish person I know."

"*Uncle-ish* isn't a word."

"Well, it should be. And it should have your picture beside it in the dictionary."

"The charm won't work, Evie. I forbade you from going out last night for a very good reason. Yet, you chose to disregard my reasonable request."

"Oh, but Unc—"

"And I specifically warned you about getting into trouble, did I not? Well, I believe it's quite clear that this arrangement will not work."

"Wh-what do you mean?" Evie asked. Her stomach had begun to hurt.

"It's best if you return to Ohio. I'll ring your mother tomorrow"— he looked at his watch—"today, and make the arrangements."

"But... it's only the first time I've been in trouble!" As soon as it was out of her mouth, Evie realized how ridiculous an argument it was—almost a promise of more trouble to come—and she wished she could take it back. "Please, Unc. I'm very sorry. I won't ever disobey you again."

Will sagged against a lamppost. He was softening, she could tell, so she kept up her attack. "I'll do anything. Sweep the floors. Dust the knickknacks. Make sandwiches every night. But please, please, please don't send me back."

"I do not intend to have this discussion on White Street with someone who smells like a distillery. I will take you back to the Bennington and you may have a nap, and—I might suggest—a bath."

Evie gave her coat a sniff and grimaced.

"I will expect you at the museum at three o'clock. I'll deliver my verdict then. Don't be late."

※

A long, hot bath washed the stench of the Tombs away, but despite her exhaustion, Evie was too nervous to sleep. Instead, she went to Mabel's flat and used her special knock.

"Hey, old girl. I'm in trouble. Unc's threatening to send me back to Ohio because of last night, and I've got to find a way to win him over. I think he was softening up a little, but maybe if you tell him that it was *your* idea he'll go easier on me, and yes, I know that's not *entirely* true, Pie Face, but this is *absolument* an emergency of the first order and... gee, Mabesie, aren't you going to invite me in?"

With a furtive glance into the apartment behind her, Mabel slipped into the hallway and shut the door.

"Uh-oh. I know that face. What aren't you telling me? Did somebody die?"

"Mother blames you for my arrest. She's banned you from the house," Mabel said.

Evie's mouth opened in outrage. "Your mother's been arrested more times than I have!"

"For the *cause*. She thinks getting arrested for drinking in a nightclub is amoral and a sign of capitalist greed," Mabel whispered. "She says you're a bad influence."

"Golly, I hope so. Tell your mother that if it weren't for me you'd still be wearing black stockings and reading dire Russian novels about doomed aristocrats."

Mabel lifted her chin. "What's wrong with *Anna Karenina?*"

"Everything from A to *enina*. Oh, look, Pie Face, just let me in, and I'll charm her."

"Evie, don't—"

"Five minutes of a sob story about how I'm a product of middle-class bourgeois values lost in the machinery of a corrupt world and she'll be organizing a rally on my behalf—"

"Don't you ever know when to stop?" Mabel snapped. "You're so selfish sometimes, Evie! It's all a game to you—and you want to rig it in your favor all the time, and damn what anybody else wants."

"That's not true, Mabel!"

"It isn't? I wanted to leave last night...."

"But then you would've missed out on all the fun. And once you got home, you'd grumble that you should've stayed. You'd regret it. I know you, Mabesie—"

"Do you?" Mabel shot back.

Evie felt slapped. She'd just wanted Mabel to get out from under her mother's control and kick up her heels. To live it up like a real swell. Hadn't she?

"I've had enough, Evie. I'm tired, and I'm going back to bed."

Evie took in a shaky breath. "Mabesie, I . . . I didn't think. . . ."

"You never do. That's the trouble."

On the other side of the door, Mrs. Rose's voice rang out. "Mabel, darling? Where are you?"

"Coming," Mabel called. She went back inside and shut the door.

Evie stared at the door for a moment longer. She used her secret knock again, but Mabel still didn't answer, so she left to meet with Will. On the walk to the museum, Evie tried to shrug off her fight with Mabel, but doing so proved impossible. She and Mabel had never had a fight. And Mabel's words stung. That was what other people, the dim-witted Normas of the world, said about her. But not Mabel. Not her best friend.

In the museum, Evie heard voices. Jericho was showing a rare couple of visitors the collection in his quiet, scholarly way, a twin of Will. The couple looked bored. "Can these doodads haunt you if you touch them?" the woman asked.

"Oh, no. They're quite harmless," she heard Jericho answer. It was a missed opportunity. If Evie had been giving the tour, she'd have made up a story they'd never forget, something to keep them coming back.

Sam breezed past her in the long hallway, on his way to the collections room. He smiled brightly. "Hey, sister, glad to see your uncle sprang you from the clink."

Evie scowled. "You left me there in that club, you fink. Very unchivalrous of you."

"You weren't thinking of me when you shimmied into that dumbwaiter by yourself. Don't pretend you're better than I am, Sheba. You got a little thief in you, too."

Evie slammed the door on Sam and sat in Will's office

awaiting her fate. What if Will really did decide to send her home? She hadn't allowed herself to really think about it; she just assumed she'd win him over. Now that thought crawled under her skin and left her feeling unsettled.

At precisely one minute before three o'clock, Will marched in. He hung his hat and coat on the coatrack and took his time taking off his gloves while Evie squirmed in the silence. At last he settled into his wingback chair behind the desk, templed his fingers, and fixed her with a pensive stare. Evie swallowed. The saliva caught in her throat and she suppressed a cough.

"Your mother was at a luncheon at her club when I telephoned earlier. I've left a message that she should ring me back. There's a train to Zenith tomorrow evening. You will be on it."

Evie gasped. "Oh, Unc, please. You can't send me home. Not yet." She could feel the tears burning at the corners of her eyes.

"What's done is done." Will rubbed the bridge of his nose. "It was foolish of me to think that I could take this on. I'm an old bachelor, set in my ways."

"No, you're not," Evie said, sniffling. "I'm sorry. Everything will be the berries. You'll see. Just give me another chance. Please," Evie's voice thinned to a whispery pleading.

"My decision is final, Evangeline," Will said gently, and his sympathy was worse than his anger. "You'll be better off back at home with your friends."

"No, I won't." Evie wiped the backs of her hands across her cheeks, but the tears kept falling.

Will was making a speech, something about having been young and careless once, the sort of thing old-timers said when they issued a deathblow, as if they thought their sanctimonious ramblings disguised as empathy would be welcomed, but Evie was only half listening. She'd never told him about the object reading, she realized. He didn't know. He didn't know what she could do—that she might be able to use her skills to help him find the Pentacle Killer. After all, she'd gotten a glimpse from Ruta Badowski's shoe buckle. Maybe what she'd heard wasn't so irrelevant after all.

"There's something I need to tell you," Evie blurted out, interrupting Will's soliloquy on responsibility. "I never told you what happened back in Zenith. The trouble I got into."

"Something about a party game and slander," Will said. "Your mother told—"

"It wasn't a party game."

"Really, Evie, there's no need—"

"Yes, there is. Please."

Will relented and Evie summoned her courage.

"The night of the party, I got into trouble for divining. I believe I may be a Diviner, Unc, like Liberty Anne Rathbone. And if I'm right, I could use my powers to help you solve this case."

Will stared at her openmouthed, but Evie didn't give him a chance to say anything just yet.

"Do you remember at the first murder scene, when I was ill?" Evie said, her words coming in a rush. "It wasn't the sight of that girl, though it was gruesome. There was a buckle that had come loose from her shoe. I simply wanted to put it back, to make something... right. I must have been holding it very tightly—tighter than I meant to—and..." Evie let out a whoosh of breath. "I saw things. Just from holding something of hers."

Will's sympathy had hardened into a tight-lipped disgust. "I suspected this would be a ploy on your part to remain in New York, but I didn't think you'd stoop so low as to capitalize on the murders of two innocent—"

"I'm trying to tell you something important!" Evie practically shouted, stunning him into silence. "Please. Just give me five minutes of your time. That's all I ask."

Will flipped open his pocket watch. "Very well. You have five minutes of my time, starting...now."

This was it. If she couldn't convince Uncle Will, she'd be on the first train back to Ohio. She needed to give him proof.

"It'll be quicker if I just show you. Let me have something of yours—a handkerchief or hat. And don't tell me anything about it."

"Evie," Uncle Will said with a sigh. Evie knew that sigh. It was often paired with her name and disappointment, and she had to fight the tears that wanted to come. Because why should he take her seriously? The party girl, the flapper with the ready quip and the closet full of rhinestones and embroidered stockings.

"Please, Unc," she said softly. "Please."

"Very well." Uncle Will looked around before settling on a glove. "Here. You have exactly four and a half minutes left."

Evie pressed the glove between her palms and concentrated. The *tick-tick-tick* of the second hand on Will's watch was distracting. She tried to block it out and concentrate on the glove, but there was nothing, and the first cold fingers of panic seized her.

"Three minutes," Will said.

Evie gritted her teeth. She didn't understand how or why her object reading worked, only that it did—in its own way, and in its own time.

"Two and a half minutes remaining..."

Images unspooled slowly for Evie now. "These were in a bin at Woolworth's, marked down to seventy-eight cents. It was cold that day and you'd lost one glove of the last pair. You've lost the right glove of this one, too. You keep taking it off and forgetting it."

Evie opened her eyes. Will was still looking at his watch. "That could be a lucky guess. Or cleverness. Gloves at Woolworth's

286

at that price aren't uncommon. You often observe me misplacing my right one. Not proof. One minute remaining."

Evie was tired and desperate and more than a little angry. She closed her eyes again. This time, the scene was strong. She saw a laughing woman with dark hair and eyes, her hands encased in a fur muff. "'That's you all over, William. Always a glove short,'" Evie repeated after the woman.

"Stop," Will said coldly, but Evie was truly there now. She could almost sense the wind. A much younger Will wobbled on ice skates while the pretty woman laughed. Evie smiled unconsciously.

"I can see her. She's standing by an ice rink...in a dark green coat...in the snow...."

"Stop, Evie."

"She's very pretty and...and she's happy...so very happy...it might be the happiest day of her li—"

Will yanked the glove from Evie's hands hard, startling her. He loomed over her, red-cheeked and angry. "I said stop!" he thundered.

Evie turned and ran from the museum, ignoring Sam as he called out after her.

GOD IS DEAD

Evie walked the streets of the city until she was too tired to continue. In Central Park, she found a bench by the pond and sat to watch a rowboat with two couples in it. They laughed easily, enjoying the day's sun. They seemed carefree and unbothered, and Evie hated them for it. She'd hoped Uncle Will of all people would understand. Evie wiped her tears with the back of her hand. Ordinarily, she'd go to Mabel for comfort. But that was out of the question, and Evie felt lost and alone.

She wandered back to the Bennington and climbed the stairs to the roof, where she sat with the pigeons. She had that coiled tightness ballooning in her chest, like her skin was on too tight. Like she'd come around a blind corner, and every demon she kept at bay had been there waiting. Will lectured about belief in the supernatural, but the only ghosts that frightened Evie were the very real ghosts inside her. Some mornings, she'd wake and vow, *Today, I will get it right. I won't be such an awful mess of a girl. I won't lose my temper or make unkind remarks. I won't go too far with a joke and feel the room go quiet with disapproval. I'll be good and kind and sensible and patient. The sort everyone loves.* But by evening, her good intentions would have unraveled. She'd say the wrong thing or talk a little too loudly. She'd take a dare she shouldn't, just to be noticed. Perhaps Mabel was right, and she was selfish. But what was the point of living so quietly you made no noise at all? "Oh, Evie, you're too much," people said, and it wasn't complimentary. Yes, she was too much. She felt like too much inside all the time.

So why wasn't she ever enough?

Evie stared at the long columns of windows cut into the building across the street. So many windows. Who lived behind them? Were they happy? Or did they sometimes sit on a rooftop haunted by a deep loneliness for which there seemed to be no cure?

The door creaked open on its hinges and Jericho angled his broad shoulders through the opening. "Thought I might find you here. What happened with your uncle Will?"

Evie turned her face away and wiped her eyes. "I stirred the tea counterclockwise."

Jericho slid down the wall, keeping a respectable distance between them. "You don't have to tell me."

Evie said nothing. To the south, the sun glinted off the steel tip of a building. Smoke belched from rooftop chimneys in fat, sooty puffs. A billboard advertised Wrigley's Spearmint Gum in giant iron letters. On the roof's edge, the pigeons arched their necks, hunting for food.

"You asked me about how I came to live with your uncle Will. I didn't answer you right away," Jericho started. He pulled a heel of bread from his pocket and unwrapped it.

"No, you didn't," Evie said. Once, she'd been very curious about that. She couldn't see that it mattered now, with her expulsion imminent. But she was grateful to Jericho for coming after her, for trying to comfort her in his way. She just wanted him to keep talking. "Will you tell me now?"

He squinted in the sun. "I was raised on a farm in Pennsylvania. Cows and pastures. Rolling farmland. Mornings seem newly born there. It's about as far from here as you can get."

"Sounds swell," Evie said, hoping her words didn't sound as hollow as they felt.

Jericho waited for a spell, as if gathering words. "There was an epidemic. Infantile paralysis. It took my sister first. And then I woke up with a fever. By the time they got me to the hospital in Philadelphia, I couldn't feel my legs and arms, and I was having trouble breathing. I was nine."

As he spoke, Jericho tore the bread into tiny pieces, which he tossed onto the flat tar roof for the birds, who swarmed the food.

"They put me in a machine, a prototype of something they were working on called an iron lung. It breathes for you. Of course, you're trapped inside it—like a metal coffin. I spent whole days staring up at the ceiling, watching the light from the windows behind me shift like a sundial. My mother would come up from Lancaster by horse and wagon every Sunday and pray for me. But there's a lot to do on a farm, and there were two other children back home and another on the way. Soon it was every other Sunday. Then she just stopped coming." Jericho broke up more of the bread and tossed it into the scrum of squawking birds. "I told myself it was the snow—she couldn't possibly get to Philadelphia on the roads. I told myself a hundred lies. Children do that. It's amazing the sorts of things you'll make yourself believe."

Evie wasn't sure what she should say, so she kept quiet and watched the birds clustering around the food, fighting for it.

"Then I heard a bird chirping on the windowsill, signaling

spring. I knew that if the bird could get there, so could she. I knew the minute I heard that bird outside my window that she wasn't coming back. Even before the doctors told me my parents had signed the papers that made me a ward of the state, I knew."

Jericho wiped his hands on his handkerchief.

"How could your parents just leave you?" Evie asked after a while.

"Invalids don't grow up to work plows or threshing machines. I was beyond their care. And they had other mouths to feed."

"How can you forgive them so easily?"

"What would not forgiving them do for me?"

"But you're strong and healthy now. How . . . ?"

Jericho tossed a small rock from the roof with a baseball player's power. "They tried something new. I was lucky; it worked. And after some time, I recovered."

"Why, that's a miracle!"

"There are no miracles," he said. His face was unreadable. "Will agreed to be my guardian. He needed an assistant, and I needed a home. He's a good man. Better than most."

"He only cares about his work and that damned museum," Evie said, not caring that she swore.

"That isn't true. I don't know what happened today, but he was awfully worried. Talk to him, Evie."

Evie wanted to tell Jericho what had happened, but she couldn't seem to open herself to scrutiny again.

"He's already made up his mind to send me back to Ohio," Evie said. "Perhaps if I were a ghost he'd listen."

"There are no such things as ghosts, either. But don't tell your uncle that," Jericho said. It made Evie smile for a moment.

She knew she should start packing, but she wanted to forestall the inevitable just a little longer, to etch the skyline of the city forever in her mind. It had been a wonderful few weeks. It was a shame it was over.

Jericho took out his dog-eared book, and Evie nodded to it. "May I?"

Jericho handed it over, and Evie read from the bookmarked page: "'God is dead. God remains dead. And we have killed him. How shall we comfort ourselves, the murderers of all murderers?'" Evie narrowed her eyes at him. "You sure know how to have a good time, don't you?" She handed it back to him. "Will you read to me?"

"You want me to read Nietzsche to you?"

"The way I'm feeling, it couldn't hurt."

Jericho cleared his throat and found his place. "'What was holiest and mightiest of all that the world has yet owned has bled to death under our knives: Who will wipe this blood off us? What water is there for us to clean ourselves...'"

Jericho's voice lulled Evie. She watched the sun glint off the side of a water tower on the roof of a building to the west. Nearby, the pigeons hopped about in their constant quest for food.

"'What festivals of atonement, what sacred games shall we have to invent? Is not the greatness of this deed too great for us? Must we ourselves not become gods simply to appear worthy of it?'"

"Jericho, have they tried your miracle cure on anyone else?"

"I told you," Jericho said. "There are no miracles."

A STAY OF EXECUTION

Will returned home around suppertime and summoned Evie to his office. He sat stiffly in his chair, fidgeting with an unlit cigarette. The radio played softly.

"Evangeline, I shouldn't have lost my temper earlier. I apologize."

Evie shrugged. "Everybody gets sore sometimes."

"It took me rather by surprise, I'm afraid." Will lit the Chesterfield in his hand. He dragged on it, then blew out a thin stream of smoke. "Tell me more about this talent of yours."

"It started two years ago, when the dreams about James began."

"Your brother, James?"

"No. James the doorman," Evie snapped, and instantly regretted it. The last thing she needed to do was to aggravate Will.

"There was no antecedent. I'm a curator and scholar. I must have sourcing," Will said matter-of-factly. "How did you come to discover it?"

"The first time, it was a brooch of Mother's. I wanted to wear it, but she wouldn't let me. She'd left it on her dressing table, and I picked it up, but I couldn't seem to work up the nerve to pin it to my dress. I kept turning it over in my hands, and I got the funniest feeling. The brooch felt warm. My hands warmed, too, and my palms tingled." Evie paused. She'd wanted to talk about it, but now she felt exposed.

"Go on. What did you see? Were you privy to only an hour of the object's history, or could you see back farther? Did it come on you as more of a feeling, a suggestion, or did you feel as if you were with the person, living that moment?"

"So . . . you believe me?"

Will nodded. "I believe you."

Evie sat forward, hopeful. "It was just like sitting at the picture show, but a picture show where the projector light isn't terribly strong. It was only a moment. I could see Mother sitting at her dressing table, and I could feel what she had been feeling when she'd worn the brooch."

"What was that?"

Evie looked him in the eyes. "She wished I'd been the one to die instead of James."

Will broke the gaze. "Mothers love all their children equally."

"No, they don't. That's just what we all agree to say."

"And that was the first time?"

"Yes. I tested it. Whenever I concentrated on an object, I could sense some of its history. It isn't always in order. Sometimes the pictures I see are faint; other times, they're stronger. I think when the emotion is strong, I feel and see more."

"Has it gotten stronger, would you say? Or weaker?"

"I don't know. I haven't practiced it like the castanets," Evie said. "Can you practice it like the castanets?"

"Have you met anyone else who can do what you do?" Will asked, ignoring her question.

"*Are* there others like me?"

"If so, they haven't announced themselves. Have you told your parents about this?"

"It was hard enough telling you after what happened in Ohio. They think it was one of my little pranks."

"Good, good," Will said.

"Why are you asking all these questions?"

"I'm trying to understand," Will said.

No one had ever said anything like that to Evie. Her parents always wanted to advise or instruct or command. They were good people, but they needed the world to bend to them, to fit into their order of things. Evie had never really quite fit, and when she tried, she'd just pop back out, like a doll squeezed into a too-small box.

"So no one knows," Will murmured.

"Well, I did show off a bit at that party Theta took me to," Evie said uncertainly.

"You did this at a party?" Will sounded alarmed.

"It was nothing important! Just telling people what they'd had for dinner or the names of their dogs when they were kids. Most of the people there were fried." Evie was careful not to mention her own drinking. "It was only in fun. Why shouldn't I?"

"Isn't that what got you in trouble in the first place?"

"But that was Ohio! This is New York City. If girls can dance half-naked in nightclubs, I don't see why I can't do a little divining."

"People aren't afraid of half-dressed girls in nightclubs."

"You think people would be afraid of me, then?"

"People always fear what they don't understand, Evangeline. History proves that. I suppose if people were drinking…" Will didn't finish his thought. "And you say you had one of these… episodes with Ruta Badowski's shoe buckle?"

Evie nodded. "I saw a terrible room and a large furnace and the outline of a man, I think. But it was only a silhouette, a shadow. I can't be sure." She shook her head. "Do you think what I saw was related to the murder?"

Will's expression was grim. "I don't know."

"Do you think I should tell the police?" Evie asked.

"Certainly not."

"But why not? If it would help..."

"Most likely they'd think you were some sort of crackpot. Or worse—a fame-seeker trying to get her name in the papers. Terrence and I have been friends for some time. I know how the police think."

"But if I could read something else from the murders, something belonging to Tommy Duffy, for instance..."

"Absolutely not," Will commanded. "I don't think you should touch anything having to do with these murders." Will sprang up from his chair and paced the length of the parlor. Midway, he stopped to tap his ash into a tall silver ashtray beside a navy-striped wingback chair that looked as if it had never been sat in. It was as if Will's coiled energy didn't allow him to sit long enough to make an impression on the cushion. "We are going to catch our killer with good old-fashioned detective work, even if we have to go through every occult book in the museum's library."

"So...I can stay?" Evie asked.

"Yes. You can stay. For now. But there will be new rules. There will be no further cavorting in speakeasies. And you will be expected to help out around the museum."

"Of course." It was better than a train back to Ohio. And once she proved to Will how indispensable she was, he'd have to keep her on for the long run. "Thank you, Unc." Evie threw her arms around Will, who stiffened and waited for her to withdraw.

In the doorway, Jericho cleared his throat and waited to be recognized. He dropped the late-edition paper on Will's desk. "You might want to read this."

"'Exclusive to the *New York Daily News*, by T. S. Woodhouse. Museum Makes a Pentacle Killing,'" Will read aloud. He frowned and waved the paper about. "What's this?"

Evie snatched the paper away and kept reading. "'New York City, that bustling metropolis, is no stranger to violence. Bugsy Siegel, Meyer Lansky, and the rest of the Brownsville Boys of Murder, Inc., have kept the bodies piling up faster than the cops can take bribes to look the other way. But the Pentacle Murders have given even hardened New Yorkers the heebie-jeebies. Mothers won't let their children play stickball on the streets after dark. Shopgirls spend their hard-earned dough on taxis straight home to their cold-water flats in Murray Hill and Orchard Street. The Sultan of Swing, Mr. Babe Ruth himself, has promised a five-hundred-dollar reward for information leading to the capture of the foul fiend. But in the midst of this Manhattan murder mania, there is one joint that's raking it in—the Museum of American Folklore, Superstition, and the Occult. That's the Museum of the Creepy Crawlies to you folks in the know.' Unc, the museum made the papers!"

Evie continued. "'Their business is anything spooky, and anything spooky is good for business. On a recent Friday, this reporter witnessed a mob scene parked outside the doors of the old Cornelius T. Rathbone mansion near Central Park. That's because the curator of the museum, Professor William Fitzgerald'—oh, Unc! That's you!" Evie exclaimed. "'...is helping the New York boys in blue figure out what makes this diabolical killer tick in the hope of finding him before he strikes again. He's aided in his work by his niece, Miss Evie O'Neill, late of Zenith, Ohio, a comely seventeen-year-old Sheba who knows her onions about everything from witches' coifs to the bones of Chinese conjurers. But when this reporter tried to get the goods on the hunt for a killer, the dame played coy. "I'm afraid I can't comment on that," she said and batted those baby blues. Fellas, start lining up. There's more than one killer in this town.'"

Evie tried to keep the grin from her face. T. S. Woodhouse had come through after all.

"Evangeline, did you speak to this Woodhouse fellow?" Will demanded.

Evie's eyes went wide. "Unc, I had *no idea* he was a reporter! He was a paying customer. I gave him the tour. When he started asking questions, I stonewalled him. He played me for a chump, that cad!"

"You have to be more careful. Develop a New Yorker's skin." Will tapped a second cigarette against the table, packing down the tobacco before lighting it. "Whatever happened to objective, truthful reporting?"

"Haven't you heard? It doesn't sell papers," Jericho said.

"You're so right, Unc. That Woodhouse is a rat. But he *did* mention the museum, at least," Evie said. "Do you know what this means?"

Will blew twin streams of smoke from his nostrils. "Trouble," he said.

The phone rang, startling them all. Will took the call, his expression hardening. "We'll meet you there."

"What is it?" Evie asked.

"The Pentacle Killer has struck again."

THE BOGEYMAN

Will and Evie were met at the front door of the Grand Masonic Lodge by a small man with a thin mustache whose round black spectacles magnified his eyes into two large, blinking blue orbs that made Evie think of an owl.

"This way," the man said nervously. "The police are already here, of course." He led them through a wood-paneled hallway to a plain door. A brass plaque designated it the Gothic Room. The small man opened the door into a stuffy antechamber before opening a second door into a large room like a church's sanctuary. The smell hit Evie right away—a terrible, cloying odor of smoke and cooked flesh that sat at the back of her throat.

Evie's eyes focused first on the grandeur of the room: the high, wood-beamed ceilings and large chandeliers. At one end was a pipe organ; at the other was the letter G placed inside a sun. In the center of the room, a phalanx of cops and a coroner surrounded a small altar. They moved aside and Evie gasped. On the altar was the badly burned body of the Pentacle Killer's latest victim.

"One of our Brotherhood found the body this morning around ten o'clock," the blinking man said. He stumbled over the word *body* and his mustache crinkled in distaste. "The Most Worshipful Grand Master has been notified by cable. He is away with his family."

"The deceased is Brother Eugene Meriwether—" Malloy said.

"He is a Junior Warden," the owlish man interrupted.

"Was," Malloy said, letting the little man know just who was in charge here. "He was working late in the office last night. Left around eight to have dinner with a coupla Masons at a restaurant over on Eighth Ave. They said good-bye at about ten or so, and Mr. Meriwether came back here alone. The killer took the feet this time."

Evie's eyes reflexively glanced at the rounded nubs of the man's legs, and she felt a wave of light-headedness roll over her. She grabbed the edge of a chair to steady herself and shut her eyes, but the afterimage remained.

"He left the victim with the same pentacle brand. It's the only part of his body not burned." He pointed to a spared circle of flesh on the man's torso.

"May the Great Architect watch over us all," the owlish man said solemnly.

"Doors were locked from the inside." Malloy pinched the bridge of his nose. He squinted at the owlish man. "You got anyone in the Brotherhood who's got a score to settle? Or maybe somebody who's a little over the edge?"

"Certainly not." The man's giant eyes did not blink behind his spectacles. "George Washington, Benjamin Franklin, John Jacob Astor, Henry Ford, Harry Houdini, Francis Bellamy—the author of the Pledge of Allegiance, the very pledge, sir!—these are our

Brothers, great men all. This country could not have been founded, nor would it continue to flourish, without the Masonic influence."

The man and Detective Malloy began to argue, their voices rising in the defiled room.

"We are all a long way from home and weary," Will said at last.

The owlish man stopped his indignant lecture and smiled. "I didn't know you were a fellow traveler, sir. Forgive me, Mr. . . . ?" He moved in for a handshake, which Will avoided, keeping his focus on the body.

"Did the deceased have any enemies?"

"Mr. Meriwether? No. He was highly regarded."

"Well, somebody didn't like him," Malloy grumbled.

"He might have been Most Worshipful Grand Master one day. His speech to the Kiwanis Club last year was very well received. Very well received."

"We've got nothing, Will. Christ." Malloy kicked at a chair in frustration.

Despite their work, they were no closer to catching this madman. A sense of despair lingered in the room, along with the cloying smoke. Evie began inching closer to the dead man. The body had been burned to a blue-black color, with peeks of raw, weeping red flesh beneath. His hands were contorted and his head was arched back, as if to let loose an agonized scream. The fear and pain he must have experienced were unimaginable. And if Evie did what she was thinking of doing, she might very well learn just how awful it was. Her heart raced as she felt the idea hardening into resolve. Eugene Meriwether's Mason's ring had molded to his blackened finger, but it might still give her a reading.

Uncle Will stood talking to the owlish man and Officer Malloy. The other officers canvassed the room, taking notes. No one was paying a bit of attention to her. It was now or never. Evie breathed through her mouth and closed her hand around Meriwether's. As her fingers brushed the Mason's finger, the skin crumbled slightly under her touch, and she bit down on the scream clawing its way up her throat. Tears pricked at her eyes and her breath caught in her chest.

She couldn't do this; it was too awful. She lifted her hand from the victim's and sought the comfort of her coin pendant, and a memory came to her.

"Why do you have to go?" she'd asked James through tears that day in the garden.

"Because, old girl," he'd said, wiping her tears away, "you've got to stand up for what's right. You can't let the bullies win."

Evie took three deep breaths, closed her eyes, and clamped her hand firmly around the partially melted ring and the Mason's crumbling flesh. She was vaguely aware of grinding her teeth as the images came down across her closed eyelids like a spotty rain getting heavier:

Eugene Meriwether polishing the ring with a cloth. His pride in it. A day at the beach with a friend. Sun glinting on sand. A lemonade—Evie could feel its refreshment. But none of these memories would catch a killer. Evie pressed harder, willing the ring to give up more, but the images remained faint and flickering, photographs shown too quickly for the viewer to hold on to anything meaningful in them.

Breathe, Evie told herself. *Slow down. See everything.* But she was distracted both by the horrible condition of the body and by her own nerves. She lost the connection and had to fight to get it back. And then she heard it: whistling. It was the same tune she'd heard when she'd touched Ruta Badowski's shoe buckle. Evie was conscious of her heart rate picking up. In her dreamlike state, she was suddenly with Eugene Meriwether as he made his way down the darkened corridor toward the golden light spilling out from the Gothic Room. His hand reaching. The shining brass of the knob. The door opening…

"What are you doing?" One of the officers took firm hold of Evie's hand, breaking the connection. He stared at her in disgust.

"I…I…" Evie whispered. "I was praying," she managed to say. She'd been so close—one more moment and she might have seen the face of the killer. Tears of frustration streamed down her cheeks, and the cop softened.

He patted her shoulder. "Come away from there, now, sweetheart."

She let herself be led. She'd definitely heard something. Was it important? Had the whistling come from the killer, or from somewhere else? Was it the same tune? It was. She was certain of it.

A crew of cleaning ladies in starched aprons arrived with mops and pails of soapy water. "Don't touch anything!" Malloy and Will yelled at the same time. The owlish man shooed them away with a flick of his soft fingers and they retreated into the gray of the antechamber to await further instruction.

"We got ourselves a bad one, Will," Malloy said.

※

They came out blinking into the hazy light of Twenty-third Street and were rushed by a wave of reporters shouting over one another. A flashlamp went off and Evie blinked away the bright dots dancing in the air.

"Vultures!" Malloy grumbled. "Get away from here!"

T. S. Woodhouse ran forward, notebook and pencil in hand. His unruly brown hair had clearly been oiled back that morning, but now a long chunk of it hung over his left eye like a veil. Evie hoped he wouldn't blow her cover.

"Excuse me! Gentlemen, T. S. Woodhouse, with the *Daily News*. I hear you've got another stiff in there. And this one isn't some marathon dancer from Brooklyn or a kid from the West Side."

"Get lost, Woody," Malloy growled.

The insult didn't seem to make a dent in Mr. Woodhouse. He glanced at Evie, then turned to Will. "What's your bead on this, Professor? Must be pretty bad for them to pull in a civilian. Is it a gangland war? A mob beef? Anarchists? Reds? The Wobblies?" Woodhouse smiled. "The bogeyman?"

"It might be a reporter!" Malloy taunted. "Why don't ya write that down, Woody. Give us a reason to ship you boys out to Russia."

"Freedom of the press, Detective."

"Freedom of the jackals, more like. The way you boys play fast and loose with the facts, we'll all be reading stories that are as reliable as my grandfather's fish tales."

"Anarchists mean to abolish the state," Will said, as if still taking part in the previous conversation. "They want to cause the most chaos, to upend order. This is methodical. Planned out."

The reporter's pencil scratched across the page. "So the bogeyman, then?"

"Pal, aren't you a little young to be on this beat?" Malloy again.

"Time to get rid of some of these old windbags writing careful little stories, Detective. Bring in the new blood, I say. It's a modern world. People need some excitement in their news. A little zip. Wouldn't you agree, Miss O'Neill?"

Evie didn't answer.

"Best of luck," Malloy said.

"I don't believe in luck. I believe in opportunity. You and me,

Professor, we could work together on this one. Put the killer on the ropes. Whaddya say?"

Uncle Will squared his hat and marched toward Sixth Avenue. T.S. sidled up to Evie and tipped his hat. "That must've been some awful scene in there. You poor thing, you're trembling. Let me help you. Excuse me, excuse me, folks, coming through."

T. S. Woodhouse led Evie to a spot behind a police wagon. He opened his jacket to reveal a flask. "You, ah, need a little liquid courage?"

Evie took a swig, and then chased it with a second. "Thank you."

"Don't mention it. What you *can* mention is what the scene was like in there."

Evie filled him in on some of the details, purposely leaving out others.

"You ever need a favor, you just let T.S. know."

"I'll remember that, Mr. Woodhouse."

Evie took one last drink from his flask, then adjusted her scarf. "How do I look?"

T. S. Woodhouse grinned. "Swell, Sheba."

"Have your shutterbug get me from my left side. It's my good one. Oh, and we should make this seem unfriendly. You understand."

T. S. Woodhouse gave a thin-lipped smile. "Purely business."

"There's no worse class of human on earth than cold-blooded murderers. Except for reporters," Evie said loudly as she walked past the human chain of policemen keeping the reporters back. She turned just slightly, holding the pose long enough for the photographer from the *Daily News* to snap her picture. Then, tossing her scarf over one shoulder, she ran toward Will and the waiting car on the corner.

The headache had started. Evie leaned back against the seat

and watched Sixth Avenue fly by from the police car's windows. Down a side street, several boys played stickball, blissfully unaware. She hoped they'd stay that way for a long time. In the front seat, Officer Malloy scribbled in his notebook. The scratching made her head hurt all the more. She closed her eyes. She wasn't aware she was whistling the song she'd heard in the Temple until Malloy said, "I haven't heard that one in a long time."

Evie sat forward. "Do you know that song? What is it?"

"*Naughty John, Naughty John, does his work with his apron on,*" Malloy sang. "*Cuts your throat and takes your bones, sells 'em off for a coupla stones.* They used to sing it on my block to scare us little ones into behaving. They'd say Naughty John would come and get you if you didn't behave."

"Who?"

"Naughty John. John Hobbes. A grave robber, con man, and killer. He kept people's bones in his house, an old mansion uptown."

"Do you think he could be behind *these* killings?"

Malloy's smile was patronizing. "Not likely, Miss O'Neill."

"Why not?"

Malloy stopped writing and looked her in the eyes. "Because John Hobbes is dead, and has been for nearly half a century."

NAUGHTY JOHN

Evie followed Will into the museum, talking quickly despite the pounding in her head. "I heard that song with Ruta Badowski's buckle, and again today with Eugene Meriwether's ring."

"Didn't I specifically ask you not to do that very thing—"

"What if there's some sort of connection we've missed? What if our killer has patterned himself after this Naughty John person?"

"You're basing your assumption upon a song—"

"A song known to be associated with a murderer!"

"That's rather a questionable hunch to go on. . . ."

Jericho and Sam watched the scene unfold like a tennis match gone awry.

"What is this about?" Jericho said at the same time that Sam asked Evie, "Why would you touch a dead man's ring?"

Will and Evie ignored them and continued arguing.

"Would *you* touch a dead man's ring?" Sam asked Jericho, who shrugged.

"Unc, it's the only lead we have," Evie said.

"Very well," Will said after a pause. "If you feel strongly about it—"

"I do."

"Then you may do what scholars do when they feel passionately about a subject."

"What's that?"

"You may visit the library," Will said. "The New York Public should have what you need to know about this John Hobbes fellow."

"I will do just that, then." Evie hung her hat and scarf on the stuffed bear's giant paw.

"What we do know is that the killer *is* playing by the Book of the Brethren," Will said. "The Temple of Solomon: The Freemasons also refer to their lodges as temples, and they consider themselves descendants of King Solomon."

"We had the right idea, but the wrong joint," Sam said.

"What's the next offering?" Sam asked.

Jericho turned to the next page in the Book of the Brethren. "The eighth offering, the Veneration of the Angelic Herald," Jericho said. He immediately began naming possibilities. "Angels...a church, a priest or nun, someone named Angel or Angelica. A herald—a messenger of some sort...postman, radio announcer, reporter, musician..."

"Reporter," Evie repeated. She rubbed her temples.

"What's the matter?" Will asked.

"It's just a headache."

"A headache? When did it start?" Will asked.

"It's nothing but a nuisance. Mother says it's because I need cheaters—um, eyeglasses, but I'm too vain to wear them. I told her my eyesight's just fine. Honestly, two aspirin and I'll be right as rain."

Jericho fetched Evie two aspirin and a glass of water.

"Unc, why are you looking at me like that?" Evie asked.

Will had been watching her, his brow furrowed. He busied himself with a pointless tidying of his desk. "Take your aspirin," was all he said.

THE WRONG PERSON

Memphis was distracted. All day long he replayed his meeting with Theta, the excitement of their narrow escape from the police. The way she'd looked at him when it was clear they'd made it, with gratitude and a little shyness. Memphis had wanted nothing more at that moment than to sweep her up into a romantic kiss. In fact, it was thinking about that kiss that had nearly gotten him in trouble. That morning when he'd gone to Mrs. Jordan's beauty shop to write their slips, he'd mixed up Mrs. Jordan's regular gig with Mrs. Robinson's washerwoman's gig because his mind was elsewhere.

"Memphis, where is your head?" Mrs. Jordan had tutted good-naturedly, and Memphis had apologized and run their numbers to Floyd's Barbershop just ahead of the clearinghouse posting.

Papa Charles had called a meeting at the Dee-Luxe Restaurant, one of his own, to discuss the previous night's disastrous raid. He assured everyone that the situation was minor, a misunderstanding that was already on its way to being worked out, and that the padlock would be off the doors of the Hotsy Totsy very soon. But Memphis could tell that beneath Papa Charles's elegant manners and calm speech, he was nervous. He had that tic in his jaw that Memphis had seen a few times before, when he'd had to deal with a drunken, belligerent customer or a hopped-up bootlegger. But still, Memphis's thoughts were on Theta.

Theta, Theta, Theta. He'd met the girl of his dreams—a girl who had the same dream he did—only to lose her in the crowd. Just as it felt his destiny was shaping up, it was lost again. He didn't know where she lived, where she was from—he didn't even know her last name. And that crazy bird was back, dogging his every step.

"Shoo!" Memphis waved his hands at the crow. "Go on, Berenice! Git!"

Now Memphis was late to pick up Isaiah from school. He entered the classroom with apologies, but Isaiah wasn't having any of it. On the street, his brother's mood was stormy as he kicked a rock ahead, then chased it into the gutter so he could kick it again. "You were 'posed to be here at three o'clock!"

"I had some business to take care of, Ice Man."

"What kind of business?"

"My business. Not yours."

"Next time, I'ma walk myself home."

"I won't be late next time."

"Prolly stepping out with that Creole Princess," Isaiah grumbled.

Memphis stopped. "Where'd you hear that?"

Isaiah laughed. "Saw it written in your book from last night. Memphis got a gir-rl! Memphis got a gir-rl!"

Memphis grabbed Isaiah's arm. "You listen here: That notebook is private. It belongs to me. You understand?"

Isaiah's chin jutted forward. "Leggo my arm!"

"Promise me!"

"Let go!" Isaiah tore away, running ahead on the busy street. He was unpredictable when he was mad, and just as likely to tell Octavia everything as not.

Memphis softened. There was no need to take out his frustration on Isaiah, no matter how annoying he was. He hurried to catch up, saying, "Don't be mad, Ice Man. Come on. Let's go over to Mr. Reggie's for a hamburger. You can sit at the counter, on the stools that turn around. Just don't turn too much and vomit up your hamburger."

Isaiah stopped. His nose was running. "I want chocolate."

"Then you'll have chocolate," Memphis promised.

Memphis worried about Isaiah. It was by accident that Sister Walker had discovered Isaiah's special talents. About six months ago, she'd moved to Harlem and come around to pay a call on Octavia. She said she was an old friend of their mother's and was saddened to hear that she had passed.

"Viola was a fine woman," Sister Walker had said.

Octavia had sized her up and found her wanting. "Funny, she never mentioned you to me. And we were close as can be."

"Well, I expect even sisters keep some secrets," Sister Walker had answered. That hadn't sat well with Octavia, Memphis could tell.

But when Miss Walker offered to tutor Isaiah in arithmetic, a subject that gave him trouble, and to do it for free, Octavia relented. One day, while Sister Walker used the cards to teach him multiplication, Isaiah started calling out the cards ahead of time, and Sister asked if there were other things he could do. She said it was a skill that might help Isaiah in the world, and she started pushing him to work at it like it was a subject in school. Memphis didn't see how Isaiah's skill was something that could move him up in the world, like wailing on a trumpet the way Gabe did or solving mathematical equations like Mrs. Ward up at school could do. And if Octavia ever found out what really went on at Sister Walker's house, she'd pitch a fit the likes of which they'd never seen. But it mattered to Isaiah. It made him feel special and happy like before, when their mama was alive and playing hide-and-seek with them while hanging the laundry from the clothesline in the garden they'd shared with the Touissants in the house on 145th Street. Memphis could still hear his mother's laugh as she'd say, "All right, now. Let's see if you two are as good at putting away these sheets as you are at hiding yourselves in them."

Those had been good times, their father coming home from his job with the Gerard Lockhart Orchestra with a jovial, "Well, well, well, what have the Campbell brothers been up to today?" Memphis missed the smell of his father's pipe in the front parlor. Sometimes he'd walk in front of the tobacco shop on Lenox Avenue just to light the memory of it in his mind.

"Watch out for Isaiah," his mother had said to him. She was skin and bones then, lying in the front room, the sickness robbing her of the playfulness he'd always loved about her. Her eyes had a hollow look. "Promise me." He'd promised. Three days later, they'd buried her out in Woodlawn Cemetery. The Gerard Lockhart Orchestra relocated to Chicago, and Memphis's father with it, until he could save enough to send for Memphis and Isaiah. But there never seemed to be enough, and there they stayed, in the back room at Octavia's. Isaiah was all that was left of those happier times when their family was all together, when you only had to walk through the door to hear somebody laughing or calling out, "Who's that knocking at my door?" and Memphis held tightly to his brother. If anything happened to Isaiah, he wasn't sure he could survive it.

But all that was the past, and he wasn't going to dwell there.

The night before with Theta had given him new hope. She was somewhere out there in that city, and Memphis meant to keep looking until he found her again.

At the pharmacy, he and Isaiah took two seats at the counter and Mr. Reggie put their order on, pressing two hamburgers against the grill with a spatula, making a comforting hiss of grease and heat. He scooped them onto plates and served them up, along with a soda for Memphis and a chocolate shake for Isaiah. Isaiah got to work spooning the thick ice cream into his mouth, dribbling half down his chin.

"Looks like I'm just in time." Gabe dropped onto the stool next to Memphis. He grabbed Memphis's hamburger and took a generous bite from it. "Mr. Campbell. Just the man I wanted to see. Alma's having a rent party. We going. Oh, and get us some good hooch."

Gabe handed him a thick wad of bills.

"Not in front of Isaiah," Memphis whispered.

"He doesn't know what we're talking about. He's enjoying that shake," Gabe said.

"Don't know what?" Isaiah said.

Memphis flashed Gabe a *You see?* look.

Gabe pursed his lips and folded his arms across his chest. "Little man, you got some kind of magic ears over there?"

Isaiah grinned. "No, but I do have powers."

"Isaiah," Memphis warned.

"Oh, do you now? I see how it is," Gabe teased.

"I bet I know how much money you got in your pocket," Isaiah said, turning all the way around on his bar stool.

"Isaiah, Gabe doesn't have time for your games now," Memphis said sharply. "Eat your food."

Isaiah's eyes narrowed. Memphis knew that look well enough to know that trouble generally followed it.

"You got a five, a one, and two quarters. And a address for a lady named Cymbelline."

Gabe emptied his pocket. His eyebrows shot up. "How'd you know that?"

"Told you! I got the gift. I can prophecy, too."

"He can't do any such thing. Isaiah, quit telling stories," Memphis said, flashing his brother another warning look.

"I can say whatever I want," Isaiah snapped back.

"He can say whatever he wants," Gabe said, grinning. "Tell me something else, little man."

"I can see people's futures sometimes."

"Isaiah. Quit it now. We've got to get home, anyway—"

"Hold on, now, brother. Boy's about to tell me my future. Maybe he knows something about the recording. So tell me, Isaiah, am I going to be Okeh Records' newest star?"

"I gotta be touching something of yours."

"Mr. Reggie! Excuse me, Mr. Reggie!" Memphis said quickly. "What do we owe you?"

"Hold on a minute, Memphis," Mr. Reggie called. He carried two plates of food in his hands.

"Tell me," Gabe whispered, extending his hand. Isaiah took it in his own and concentrated. After a long moment, he dropped Gabe's hand very fast and backed away, his eyes big.

"What did you see? Don't tell me—is she ugly?" Gabe joked.

"I didn't see nothing," Isaiah answered, and Memphis didn't even correct him. He looked up at Memphis with very big eyes, and Memphis knew that whatever Isaiah had seen, it had spooked him.

"Get your coat now, Ice Man."

But Gabe wouldn't let it alone. "Come on, now. What do you see for your old pal Gabriel?"

"Under the bridge...don't walk under the bridge," Isaiah said softly. "He's there."

"What bridge? Him who? What's gonna happen to me if I do?"

"You'll die."

"Isaiah!" Memphis growled. "He doesn't mean that, brother. He's just playing around. Say you're sorry, Isaiah."

Eyes big, Isaiah looked from Gabe to Memphis and back again. "Sorry, Gabe," he said in a small voice.

"You just playing, Isaiah?" Gabe asked.

"That's right," Isaiah whispered. He kept his head down.

Gabe's face relaxed into a grin that was part relief, part annoyance. "Little brothers," he said, shaking his head. He clapped Memphis on the back. "Don't forget about that other business, Memphis."

"I won't," he said.

Blind Bill Johnson sat in the corner nursing the cup of soup Reggie had been kind enough to give him. The soup was thin but warm, and he had eaten it slowly while the scene at the counter unfolded. Now, his soup finished, he lifted his guitar onto his back with a grunt and tapped his cane out into the streets of Harlem. The air was scented with coming rain. He didn't like rain. It reminded him of Louisiana, back when he was a sharecropper's son with two good eyes, picking cotton all day, and the rain would about drown a man just trying to make his quota. It reminded him of the day the owner, Mr. Smith, hit him with a strap for playing guitar instead of picking cotton, and how later, the man's half of the crops failed—browned to wisps—and they found Mr. Smith's bloated body in the river, swelled up like a bag of rice gone bad with rot, and the whispers went around that Bill Johnson wasn't a man to be trusted, that there was something of the *Mabouya* about him. That he'd stood at the crossroads at midnight and cursed at

Papa Legba. That he'd spit upon the cross. That he'd sold his soul to the Devil.

It was raining the day the men in the dark suits came to the camp. It was the crops that had caught their attention. Word had spread that Bill Johnson might have done it. That he could put an old dog down when it needed mercy or that, when he was angry, he could hold a butterfly in his hand and it would fall dead. The men in dark suits sat, cool and patient as you please, all bland smiles and quiet courtesy, in Mrs. Tate's parlor, drinking lemonade from sweaty glasses.

Bill was brought to them. He was a strapping man of twenty then, six feet tall, his skin a smooth dark brown and free of the brands his ancestors wore with shame. Bill sat on an old cane chair with his hands on his knees while the men asked questions: Did Bill want to help keep his country safe? Would he like to ride with them and talk?

Bill had wanted out of the fields and out of Louisiana, with its white-hooded men who set the night ablaze with their crosses. He'd gone with the dark-suited men, had ridden in the back of their car with the curtains over the side windows. He'd done the things they'd asked. He'd told them about the toll it was taking on his body, showed them how his spine bowed and his hair grayed. He was only twenty, but he looked fifty. The men had smiled those same bland smiles and said, "Just one more, Bill."

And when his sight shriveled up to tiny points of blurry light that finally faded to black, they sent him away with nothing but his guitar, a raised scar on his skin, and a handshake of warning to keep quiet. His sight was gone, his body used up and broken. And his gift—if that's what it could be called—seemed to have deserted him, too. How many times had he railed to the sky and wished he could have the gift back? And then, suddenly, about three months ago, he'd felt the first stirrings of hope. All he needed was the right spark to get it running again.

Now, as the Campbell brothers barreled out of Reggie's Drugstore, setting the little bell over the door to tolling, Bill could hear them arguing. The younger Campbell brother had the gift—that was perfectly clear—and the older brother wanted to keep it a secret. That was smart. It wasn't good to let on to anyone about secrets like that. The wrong person might find out. Someone you didn't even know was dangerous.

The first raindrops splatted against Bill's dark glasses and he frowned. Damned rain. Without thinking, he rubbed the scar on his left hand and tapped his cane downhill.

A HEAVENLY STAR

Theta was pouting. To anyone else, she probably just looked bored. But Henry knew everything about Theta, and she was most definitely pouting. She was sitting on the edge of the stage in her one-piece shorts outfit and black stockings that showcased her lithe body. She'd tied a green paisley scarf across her forehead in a Bohemian fashion. Her lips were painted red, a bright contrast to her mud-brown eyes and fashionable tan.

Henry sat at the rehearsal piano and watched as she sighed and pouted and swung one leg out and back, out and back.

"Mr. Ziegfeld will be here soon, people," the stage manager yelled. "He wants to work on the Heavenly Star number in the second act. He thinks it's getting stale."

"It *is* stale. Those jokes were old before my mother was born. And the song is lousy," Theta snapped, lighting up a cigarette.

"As always, we thank you for your invaluable opinion, Theta," he shot back. "Perhaps if you spent more time rehearsing your steps and less time complaining, we'd have a show. Take ten, everyone."

"I could do those steps with both legs broken," Theta grumbled as she perched next to Henry on the piano bench.

"Somebody's cranky," Henry said teasingly, low enough that only Theta could hear.

She rested her seal-black head on his shoulder. "Thanks for the sympathy."

"You still pining for your mysterious knight in shining armor?"

"If you'd met him, you'd understand."

"Handsome?" Henry played a sexy trill.

"And how."

"Gallant?" He switched to a galloping, heroic rhythm.

"Very."

Henry's music became soft and romantic. "Charming yet sensitive."

"Uh-huh."

"Rich?"

Theta shook her head. "A poet."

"A poet?" He brought his hands down in a discordant plunk. "Haven't you heard, darlin'? You're supposed to marry for money, not love."

"He has the same dream I do, Hen. He's seen that crazy eye with the lightning bolt, and the crossroads. What are the odds on that?"

"I'll admit that's pretty spooky." Henry lowered his voice. "Do you think he's . . . special, like you and me?"

"I don't know. There was just something about him, like I'd known him my whole life. I can't explain it."

Henry took up a lilting jazz number of his own. "Now you're starting to make me jealous."

Theta kissed his cheek. "Nobody'll ever replace you, Hen. You know that."

"We could go up to Harlem, try to find him."

"The Hotsy Totsy is padlocked."

"Plenty of other clubs to scour. And then you can see which ones are hiring dancers, because you know what Flo would say about your dating a Negro poet numbers runner."

"Flo doesn't have to know."

"Flo knows everything."

Wally came rushing down the aisles, clapping for attention. "Everybody—places! Mr. Ziegfeld has arrived!"

※

The rehearsal was long and dispiriting. Mr. Ziegfeld hated everything. He stopped them during every number, shouting, "No, no, no! That might fly at the Scandals, but this is a Ziegfeld show! We stand for something here."

They'd been running the Heavenly Star number for nearly an hour, and nothing was going right.

"That bit doesn't land," Mr. Ziegfeld yelled from the back of the theater. He was an elegant man with combed-back white hair and a neatly trimmed mustache. His suits—and he always wore a suit—were rumored to be made on Savile Row in London. "We need a laugh. Something."

"Well, we could bring Mr. Rogers back," Wally said.

"I'm not worried about Will Rogers. Will Rogers could gargle and it would be funny! I'm worried about this number!"

Everyone was on edge. When Mr. Ziegfeld wasn't happy, no one was happy. He might fire them all and hire a new chorus, turning the whole thing into a publicity stunt.

"Again!" the great Ziegfeld barked.

Henry launched into the music. The star of the piece, an

arrogant crooner named Don, descended the long, wide staircase, singing with melodramatic vibrato: *"Stars up in heaven, fall from the sky. So tell me, my darling, why can't I fall into your arms like a heavenly star, and live there forever just as you are . . ."*

At the piano, Henry rolled his eyes as Theta looked his way. *Constipaaaation*, he mouthed, and Theta tried not to laugh. Arms out, the girls began their elegant descent. Out in the audience, Flo looked as if he'd been sucking on a dill pickle. They'd end up doing it again, Theta could tell. But no amount of rehearsal could ever make the number work. It was lousy—sentimental and cheap. As her feet felt for each step, she remembered a piece of advice she'd gotten in vaudeville: If you want a laugh, do the unexpected.

As the girls strutted gracefully forward down the long staircase, Theta intentionally went the wrong way, gliding to the left like a deranged Isadora Duncan, screwing up the other girls, who had to scramble to get around her.

"Hey, watch it!" Daisy griped.

"Sorry, Mother," Theta said, eliciting snorts from some of the other girls.

"Theta! What are you doing? Get back in line!" Wally shouted.

Theta kept going. She bumped into a glittery hanging star. "Oh!" she said, petting it as if she were a drunken flapper. "Sorry, Mr. Rogers."

The company glanced nervously at Theta and then out again to Mr. Ziegfeld sitting in the audience. Don, the stick in the mud, picked up the song again, glaring at Theta with a tight smile. Theta stumbled down the stairs, humming loudly. "Don't stop, Don, honey. You're doing swell! Even Mr. Rogers liked it," she said, gesturing to the glittery star. "Oh, Henry!"

Theta raced to Henry's side near the wings and threw her

arms around his neck, giving him a passionate kiss. "Oh, it's okay. He's my brother."

"Just don't tell our mothers," Henry quipped, and this time everyone laughed, except for Don, Daisy, and Wally, whose cheeks reddened.

"Miss Knight! I think we've had quite enough of your bad behavior—"

"Gee, Wally, that's not what you said last night," Theta cracked. She was skirting dangerously close to the edge. She might have even gone over. For all she knew, she'd be out on the street in a minute. Somewhere in the dark, Flo was watching, waiting to pass judgment.

"Mr. Ziegfeld, I can't work under these conditions," Don huffed.

A hush fell over the entire company as the great Florenz Ziegfeld marched down the center aisle. "Fine, Don. You don't have to. I can always get someone else." Mr. Ziegfeld looked at Theta, his eyes narrowed. Slowly, he broke into a grin, applauding her performance. "Now, *that* was entertaining!"

Theta let out the breath she'd been holding.

Ziegfeld pointed at the stage manager, talking as fast as New York traffic. "Wally, add that bit in. Build an act around it. And get me an item planted in the gossip rags: 'Ziegfeld discovers new star in...'" He smiled at Theta.

"Theta. Theta Knight."

"Miss Theta Knight!"

"And her brother, Henry DuBois," Theta added.

The chorus girls giggled anew at this, except for Daisy, who had sided with Don. She stared daggers at Theta.

"And her brother," Flo echoed. "I like this kid. Where you from, honey?"

"Connecticut," Theta lied.

"Connecticut? Who's from Connecticut?" The great Ziegfeld made a face like he'd tasted sour milk. He paced near the orchestra pit, thinking. "You're a long-lost member of the Russian nobility whose parents were killed by communists—that'll win hearts. You were smuggled out of the country by loyal servants in a daring midnight escape and sent on a ship to America, land of dreams. Wally, let's get some shots of her on a ship. Put a bow on her head. A big bow. Blue. No, red! No, blue. Sweetheart, give me a forlorn look."

Theta cast her eyes heavenward and clasped her hands over her chest. "Sad enough for ya?" she asked out of the side of her pitiful pout.

"Perfect! Another minute and I'll need a handkerchief. Now, you were raised by sympathetic nuns in Brooklyn—Wally, find me a convent school in Brooklyn that needs a donation—where my dear wife, Billie, was visiting—make sure the papers get that part about Billie, along with a picture of her holding a baby—and she heard you sing. 'Silent Night.'" Ziegfeld grimaced. "'Silent Night' too much?"

He looked to Henry, who shrugged.

"'Silent Night' it is," the great Ziegfeld continued. "And she brought you straight to me, your Uncle Flo, who knows beauty and talent when he sees it. I like it. You're about to become famous, kid."

"Mr. Ziegfeld, Henry could write you a swell number. He's very talented." Theta shot Henry a *Speak up for yourself* look.

"I could."

"Fine, fine. Hank—"

"Henry, sir."

"Hank, write me that number. Make it…"

"Hummable," Henry finished for him.

"Exactly!"

324

Henry gave Theta an *I told you so* face, and she answered with a tiny shrug that asked, *What can you do?*

"Wally, get this up on its feet. I have to go meet Billie to look at a country house—that woman can spend money. Fortunately, I've got a lot of it."

"Sure thing, Mr. Ziegfeld," Wally said, following the great man out. He looked back at Theta, and she stuck out her tongue at him.

The girls crowded around Theta, congratulating her on her good fortune, while Daisy stomped off, cursing a blue streak.

"Upstaging people isn't very nice," Don sniped as he breezed past.

"If you were any good, I wouldn't be able to upstage you, Don," Theta shouted after him. She hugged Henry. "Do you know what this means?"

"More rehearsal?"

"We can finally afford a piano, Hen. And everybody's gonna walk out of the show singing *your* song."

"Don't you mean humming my song?"

"Don't get cute. It's a start."

"I can see it now," Henry said, sweeping his hand wide. "Florenz Ziegfeld presents Mr. Henry DuBois's memorable melody, 'The Constipation Blues'!"

Theta hit him.

RAISING THE DEVIL

The New York Public Library, that grand beaux arts queen of books, presides over Fifth Avenue between Fortieth and Forty-second streets with a majesty few buildings can match. At exactly eleven o'clock in the morning, Evie arrived at the bottom of the grand marble steps, confident that she would find just what she needed to break open the case of the Pentacle Killer, and that she would find it in roughly a half hour, give or take. She'd pestered Detective Malloy for what he knew about John Hobbes, which wasn't much, but he did tell her that the man was hanged, he believed, sometime in the summer of 1876.

"*Ev'ry morning, ev'ry evening, ain't we got fun? Ba-da-bum-bum, la-la-la-la. Ain't we got fun?*" she sang as she passed one of the pair of sculpted stone lions guarding the entrance. She gave its right paw a pat. "Nice kitty," she said, and went inside. She was directed up three flights of winding stairs into a large, wood-paneled room crammed with bookcases. A librarian whose brass nameplate identified him as a Mr. J. Martin looked up from a copy of Edith Wharton's *House of Mirth.* "May I help you?"

"Pos-i-tute-ly!" Evie beamed. "I have to get the goods on a murderer for my uncle, Dr. William Fitzgerald of the Museum of American Folklore, Superstition, and the Occult. Perhaps you've heard of us?"

Evie waited while Mr. Martin furrowed his brow, thinking. "I can't say that I have."

"Oh," Evie said, deflated. "Well, then. What can you tell me about a man named John Hobbes who went to trial for murder in 1876? Oh, and could you be a doll and make it fast? There's a swell sale over at B. Altman, and I want to get there before the crowd."

"I'm a librarian, not an oracle," Mr. Martin said. He offered her a scrap of paper and a pencil. "Could you write down the name, please?"

Evie scribbled *John Hobbes, murderer,* and *1876* on the paper and slid it back. Mr. Martin disappeared for a bit, then returned with two stacks of newspapers bound on a wooden rod, which he placed on the desk in front of Evie. There had to be a week's worth of work for her in those two volumes. She wouldn't be shopping that day. Or possibly ever.

"All of this?" Evie said.

"Oh, no," Mr. Martin said.

"Thank heavens."

"I'll be back with the others in a moment."

"Others?"

"Yes. All fourteen."

⁂

At half past six Evie staggered back into the museum. She clomped into the library, past the table where Will, Jericho, and Sam sat working, tossed her scarf to the floor, and, with a heavy sigh, collapsed onto the velvet settee, her cloche still on her head. "I'm exhausted."

"I thought you went to the library," Uncle Will said.

Evie cut her eyes at Will, who didn't look up from his book.

"Why do you think I'm so exhausted? If you'd like to know anything at all about this city in 1876, please raise your hand. No show of hands? Pos-i-tute-ly shocking." Evie bunched a pillow into a corner of the settee and rested her face against it. "There is a hideous invention called the Dewey Decimal System. And you have to look up your topic in books and newspapers. Pages upon pages upon pages..."

Uncle Will frowned. "Didn't they teach you how to go about research in that school of yours?"

"No. But I *can* recite 'The Battle Hymn of the Republic' while making martinis."

"I weep for the future."

"There's where the martinis come in." Evie yawned and stretched. "I thought research would be more glamorous, somehow. I'd give the librarian a secret code word and he'd give me the one book I needed and whisper the necessary page numbers. Like a speakeasy. With books."

"I don't see any books," Uncle Will said warily.

"Got it all right here," Evie touched her head. "And here," she said, patting her pocketbook.

"You stole books from the New York Public Library?" Will's voice rose in alarm.

"O ye of little faith, Unc. I took notes." Evie drew a stenographer's notebook from her cluttered bag.

Uncle Will held out a hand. "May I see them?"

Evie clutched them to her chest. "Nothing doing. I've lost hours of my precious youth I'll never get back, and I never made it to B. Altman. I'm playing radio announcer, here." Evie lay on the settee with her feet propped on the back and flipped pages till she found the one she needed. "Naughty John, born John Hobbes, raised in Brooklyn, New York, at the Mother Nova Orphanage, where he was left at the age of nine. A troubled youth, he ran away twice, finally succeeding when he was fifteen. He shows up in police records again at age twenty-nine, when a lady accused him of doping her up and trying to have his way with her—what a bad, bad boy!" Evie waggled her eyebrows, and Sam laughed. "However, the lady in question was a prostitute, and the case was dismissed. Poor bunny." Evie riffled through to another page. "He worked in a foundry, where he was told to beat it when they caught him using company iron to make his own goods. He showed up again in 1865 for peddling dope to returning Union soldiers. In 1871, he worked for an embalmer—that's a real undertaker, not a bootlegger. He set up a profitable side business selling cadavers to medical schools. At some point, he reinvented himself as a Spiritualist, running séances at Knowles' End, a ritzy mansion uptown on the Hudson. Ida Knowles—who owned the joint—ran out of dough and had to sell it to a lady"—Evie traced her finger to the spot she needed—"named Mary White. Naughty John's companion, who was a wealthy widow and medium who got pretty chummy with Ida after Ida's mother and father died. That Ida was a real tomato who was not hitting on all sixes...."

"Beg your pardon?" Will said.

"She was pretty gullible," Sam explained.

"Because she started spending all her clams on séances with Mary and John. Anyway, the chin music was—"

"The what?" Will asked.

"Gossip," Sam said.

"That John Hobbes kept a lot of dope around, and these *Spiritualist* meetings should've been called 'spirits meetings' because everybody was pretty half seas over on some kind of drugged plonk, and what they got up to would've made every Blue Nose and Mrs. Grundy from here to Topeka reach for her smelling salts."

Will held out his hand. "May I, please?"

"Suit yourself." Evie handed over her notes, as well as several newspaper articles, which Will regarded with an expression of alarm.

"How did you get these out of the library?"

Evie shrugged. "I'll take them back tomorrow and tell them I'm awfully sorry for thinking they were my *Daily News*."

"Does your mother know you've a burgeoning criminal mind?"

"That's why she sent me to you."

Sam grinned. "Nice work, Sheba."

"Ishkabibble." Evie reclined against the pillows, closing her eyes. "I might be too tired to go to the pictures tomorrow."

Will paced as he read. "... Mrs. Mary White, a rather colorful widow whose companion was Mr. John Hobbes. Ida continued to live there in the eastern wing, and she and Mary grew very close. Ida was not, however, particularly fond of Mr. Hobbes. In letters to her cousin, she wrote, 'Mary and Mr. Hobbes hosted another of their spiritual meetings in the parlor last night, which went on well past a decent hour. I attended for a spell. Mr. Hobbes offered a sweet wine, which made me feel very odd. I saw and heard such strange visitations that I could not be certain of what was real and what was not. I excused myself and retired to bed, where I was troubled by peculiar dreams.

"'The old book, which he does not allow me to read, he keeps locked in the curio cabinet. "It is the book of my brethren, given to me by my dear departed father before I was sent to the orphanage," he told me with a smile....'"

"The book of my brethren!" Evie exclaimed. "Hot socks!"

"'But I *do not trust a word he says*,'" Will continued. "'For he seems to lie as easily as some laugh. He lies to gain sympathy, or to frighten. Once he told me that he had the power to raise the Devil if he wished. There is a foul stench in the house, as if the very walls are corrupted, and I hear the most terrifying noises. People come and go at all hours of the day and night. Most of the servants have left us. I fear something wicked is at work in this house, dear cousin. Oh, please do send the authorities to investigate, for I am too ill to see to it myself.' "

Will fell silent as he read through Evie's stolen newspaper accounts.

"So how did this Naughty John fella end up?" Sam asked.

"Ida Knowles disappeared," Evie said, relishing the wickedness of the tale. "The fuzz came to investigate. Naughty John tried to give them a wad of chewing gum about Ida running away with some drugstore cowboy. He said that he and Mary White hadn't spilled it for fear of ruining her reputation because"—Evie put a hand to her forehead in melodrama fashion—"they loved her as a sister."

"What a load of bunk," Sam said.

"You said it, brother. The police didn't believe a word of it, either. They searched the house and found ten dead bodies, which Mr. Hobbes confessed were related to his work supplying stiffs to medical schools. But the police couldn't be sure about that, either."

"That's where the song comes about," Jericho said.

"*Cuts your throat and takes your bones, sells 'em off for a coupla stones,*" Evie sang like a saloon chant. "The topper is—"

" 'When they looked further,' " Will read aloud, " 'they found the body of a woman. She happened to be wearing a brooch belonging to Ida Knowles.' "

Evie dropped her hands to her sides in disappointment. "You stole my big finish, Unc."

Will ignored her. " 'Though he and Mary White protested his innocence, John Hobbes was found guilty of her murder on the strength of her letters and the brooch, as well as the ten bodies, and sentenced to hang.' "

"I wonder if they sold *his* body to a medical school," Sam joked.

Will took a cigarette from his silver case and searched his pockets and paper-strewn desk for a lighter. "He was buried in a pauper's grave. No funeral home wanted him, and he had no next of kin to claim him."

"Do you think there could be some connection to our killer? Could our killer be familiar with this story? Is he taking a page from history?" Evie asked.

Sam reached behind a stack of books for the silver lighter with Will's initials etched into it and handed it over. The cigarette sparked and Will blew out a stream of smoke. "I still think you're grasping at straws, Evangeline. I'll allow that there are some correlations...."

Evie ticked them off on her fingers. "The comet. The Book of the Brethren. The song..."

"How *did* you know about that song, anyway?" Jericho asked.

Evie looked to Will, who shot her a warning glance. "Women's intuition," she said.

"The book of *my* brethren, Hobbes said—not the same at all," Will corrected her. "Semantics."

"Gesundheit," Evie said. "Well, here's something that'll put the ice in your shaker." She sat forward, relishing their attention, though in truth Will seemed more impatient than held in suspense. "There was a mention of some missing persons and an unsolved murder that took place in the summer of 1875. A body was found with strange markings on it!"

"Fifty years ago," Will said pointedly. "And you don't know what those markings were. I fail to see what that has to do with our case."

Evie sighed. "I do, too. But it is interesting." Evie drummed her fingers on the end table, trying to make connections that vanished like smoke.

"What happened to John's tomato, Mary White?" Sam asked.

"After John Hobbes swung, she married a showman named Herbert Blodgett in 1879. They moved away from Knowles' End. There's a mention of her falling from a horse and suffering from ill health, but there's no record of her thereafter."

"She probably died," Sam said.

Suddenly a furious knocking sounded through the museum. Evie raced to the door and opened it to find a group of nearly a dozen people lined up outside. The fellow in front held T. S. Woodhouse's *Daily News* article aloft. "We've come to see what all the fuss is about."

※

Within a few days of T. S. Woodhouse's first article, which was followed quickly by a second and a third, the museum was seeing more business than it had in years. Will had been asked to lecture everywhere from private clubs to high-society ladies' luncheons where, try as he might to keep things on a scholarly level, all anyone wanted to know about was the murders. In New York's more fashionable quarters, the smart set, who were too swell to admit fear, organized "Murder Clubs" where they swilled cocktails with names like Pentacle Poison, Voodoo Varnish, and The Killer's Cocktail—a potent mix of whiskey, champagne, orange juice, and crushed cherries said to make anyone wish she were dead the next morning. Murder was just another reason to drink and dance the night away. It was very good for business. Everyone, it seemed, had caught Pentacle Killer fever. And Evie had every intention of capitalizing on it.

During Evie's guided tours of the museum, a simple linen cap became the coif of a Salem witch who'd been accused of dancing with the Devil in the woods. A bowl of water Evie had poured that morning and placed on a table with two lit candles was "a blessing from monks to keep the room free from spiritual corruption." She made a small altar and placed the bone fragment from the Chinese railroad worker alongside a spirit photograph taken in western Massachusetts and told gullible guests it was the bone of the girl in the picture—a girl who still haunted the museum. At that, Sam would blow a hidden bellows, making the curtains move, and the jaded Janes and their dapper dates would gasp and chuckle, thrilled by their close call with a ghost.

It was on one such afternoon that Will returned from a lecture to find the museum crowded with visitors spilling out of the objects room. He tried to get closer and was rebuffed by a young man: "Wait your turn, Father Time." Will peered over the heads of two flappers and saw Evie holding forth: "Of course, you must be very careful around these objects. They're quite powerful. You wouldn't want them to haunt you after you've gone."

"They can do that?" a woman in the front row asked. She looked alarmed.

"Oh, yes!" Evie said. "But that's why we sell the charms in the gift shop. They're replicas of ancient tokens said to ward off evil." Evie held up a small silver disk. "I keep several on me at all times. You can never be too safe, especially with an occult killer loose in the city."

"Evie!" Will barked from the corridor. "May I speak to you in private for a moment?"

Evie forced a smile. "Of course, Dr. Fitzgerald. This is Professor Fitzgerald, the museum's curator and the city's top academic in the field of Things That Go Bump in the Night. As you know, Dr. Fitzgerald is aiding the police in their investigation of the heinous murders terrorizing the city. As am I."

As one, the crowd turned to look at Will, fluttering with excitement.

"Do tell us more about the crimes, won't you, Professor," a young woman called. "Is it true he drinks their blood and wears their clothing? Is he really committing these horrid crimes as a judgment against Prohibition?"

Will glared at Evie, who immediately busied herself with rubbing an imaginary spot of dirt from the wall.

"Evie, in my office. Now, please."

"Certainly, Unc—Dr. Fitzgerald. I'll be with you in a moment, ladies and gentlemen. Please do be careful. I wouldn't want you to disturb the spirits. Anyone who wants to shell out the rubes for some protective charms, please see our associate Mr. Sam Lloyd in the gift shop."

"Evangeline! Now!"

Evie closed the doors of the small office behind her. The wood thrummed with the gossiping of excited customers. "Yes, Unc?"

"What on earth are you doing?" Will demanded. He'd lit a cigarette and grabbed a handful of nuts at the same time and seemed uncertain which he should bring to his mouth first.

"I'm leading a tour."

"I can see that. What sort of nonsense are you telling these people?"

"I am creating an atmosphere! Oh, Unc, we've finally got bodies in this joint! *Paying* bodies. We could have a good racket going here."

"I'm not interested in a 'racket.' I'm an academic."

"That's okay, Unc. I won't hold it against you.

"And since when do we have a gift shop?"

"Since last night. Now don't cast a kitten—there are no precious artifacts being given away. I used your embosser and sealing wax on some tinfoil. Voilà! Instant charms."

"That's dishonest!"

"No, that's business," Evie replied. Will went to speak, but Evie silenced him with pleading hands. "Unc, when Lucky Strike sells you cigarettes, do they say, 'We have a tobacco product in a box for you'? Why, of course not! They say, 'Lucky Strike is the one for me!' and they show you pictures of beautiful people in beautiful places enjoying that cigarette as if...as if they were making love!"

Will coughed out a lungful of smoke. "I beg your pardon?"

"They *make* you want it. You *have* to have it. It's what everyone who's simply anyone has, so you'd better get on the trolley, kiddo, or be left out. *That* is what I'm doing with our museum."

"*Our* museum?" Will put the nuts back in the dish and took another drag on his cigarette. Then he pointed it at Evie. "You will not sell any more 'charms.' And stick to the facts. Do I make myself clear?"

"As you wish," Evie said. She opened the pocket doors onto the crowd. "Right this way, if you please, folks. We're walking to the dining room, where it's *possible* that séances took place and spirits *might* have been conjured," Evie said with a glance back at Will. "And while we don't know for certain, it's rumored that President Abe Lincoln himself may have communed with the other side at this very table."

Will stubbed out his cigarette and immediately lit another.

※

"Ask me how much money we made today." Evie beamed at Sam and Jericho. It was five fifty, and the last person had been pushed out only ten minutes earlier.

"How much?"

"Enough to pay the light bill and still have enough left over for a cup of tea. Well, hot water."

"Good work, you," Sam said.

"Good work, all of us," Evie corrected.

The *thud* of the brass knocker echoed in the empty museum. Evie glanced at the clock. "It's nearly closing time. Go away," she said on an exhausted sigh.

"Want me to get rid of 'em?" Sam said.

"No, I'll do it. Jericho, keep an eye on Sam near the till," Evie teased with a wink.

Just outside, Memphis stood on the front steps of the museum, staring at the massive oak doors. Ever since Sister Walker had mentioned the story of the Diviners and Cornelius Rathbone's sister, Liberty Anne, he'd wondered about the place. He'd wondered if this Dr. Fitzgerald might be able to shed some light on both the business with Isaiah and the strange symbol from his own dreams. Now, though, he wasn't sure that he should have come after all. He didn't even know these people. What could he say that wouldn't make him sound like a fool? And how did he know if he could trust them? For all he knew, the museum wasn't even open to black folks. *Acting like you haven't got a lick of sense*, Memphis chided himself, as if Aunt Octavia were nearby. He was about to turn and walk back to the subway when the massive oak doors opened and a small, doll-like white girl with blond curls and big blue eyes leaned against the door frame.

"I'm afraid the museum is closing in another ten minutes," she said apologetically.

"Oh, I see. I'll come back another day, then. Sorry to have bothered you." Memphis cursed the waste of a subway fare.

"Ah, gee. Come on in. But I warn you, it's been a long day, and I may have to take my shoes off."

Memphis followed her into the grand, dark mansion with its wood-paneled walls and stained-glass windows. It was more like a cathedral than an old house.

"Evie O'Neill, at your service."

"Memphis Campbell."

"Well, Mr. Campbell, seeing as we've only got ten minutes, I could give you a quick peek-a-loo at the collections room, though you may have to specialize. Pick your poison—witches, ghosts, or voodoo priests?"

Memphis opened his knapsack and removed his notebook. "To tell you the truth, Miss, I read about you in the papers, and I was wondering if you might be able to tell me what this symbol means?" Memphis showed her the drawing of the eye and lightning bolt.

Evie studied it. She shook her head. "I haven't the foggiest. I'm awfully sorry, but if you'd like to come back another day, you could look through our library and see if you can find it."

"Thank you. I'll do just that," Memphis said. He was frustrated that he still had no answers. He was almost to the door when he turned back.

"Was there something else, Mr. Campbell?" Evie asked him.

"Yes. Um, no. That is, I feel a little funny asking. You see, there's this old house up north of where I live. It's just an old wreck of a joint, though I hear it used to be a real showplace."

The girl was smiling at him in a patient way, like one might with a feeble-minded grandmother, and Memphis was once again struck by how ridiculous this whole enterprise was. Still, he was compelled to tell somebody, even if it was nothing more than his imagination at work and he looked like a fool for worrying about it. He fidgeted with the buckle on his knapsack.

"You see, sometimes I go up there and, well...there's something funny about that old house lately. It almost seems lived in, and, well..." *You sound like a madman, Memphis.* "I was just wondering if you might have any books on Knowles' End or know anything about it. It's just an old wreck, so—"

"What did you say?" The girl's eyes were wide.

338

"I said it's a wreck...."

"Before that. Did you say Knowles' End?"

"That's the name of the house. Or it was a long time ago. Nothing but spiders and rotting boards now."

She was looking at Memphis in a way that made him very uncomfortable. He saw that her hands were shaking. "Would you mind waiting here, Mr. Campbell? I won't be a bootlegger's second."

Evie O'Neill hurried down the hall, her heels click-clacking against the dingy marble floors. As Memphis stood in the empty foyer, holding tightly to his hat, it dawned on him: What if she thought he was the Pentacle Killer?

Memphis didn't wait for Evie to return. He slipped out the front doors and ran for blocks, slowing only when he realized that he was drawing odd looks from the white people on the street. He forced himself into a stroll, employing the charm of his smile as he walked, as if he didn't have a care in the world even though his heart was racing. Still smiling broadly, Memphis turned a corner and walked smack into a girl. He caught her as she stumbled. "I beg your pardon, Miss!"

"Go on, beg," the girl said in a familiar smoky voice.

Memphis grinned. His heart was racing again, but this time, it was with pure joy. "Well, if it isn't the Creole Princess!"

"We gotta stop meeting like this, Poet," Theta said.

※

Back at the museum, Evie returned with Will, Sam, and Jericho in tow to find an empty foyer and no sign of Memphis Campbell anywhere on the street.

"He was right here!" Evie said on a long exhale. "And, Unc, he was talking about Knowles' End! Don't you think that's peculiar?"

"Are you sure he wasn't a reporter?" Will asked.

"I suppose he could've been," Evie allowed. "But he seemed very sincere. He was asking about a symbol—an eye with...oh, here. I'll draw it for you."

Evie sketched the eye and lightning bolt and held it up for Will. Sam sidled up close to Evie and said, "He was asking about this symbol?"

"What did you say his name was?" Will asked.

"Memphis. Memphis Campbell," Evie replied.

"You know what that symbol means, Professor?" Sam asked. He was looking at the drawing of the eye with keen interest.

Will glanced briefly at the page. "Never seen it before. Now please don't disturb me. I've work to do." He turned on his heel and left them standing in the foyer.

☀

Memphis and Theta sat in Mr. Reggie's drugstore in Harlem with a couple of egg creams, talking and talking. Theta felt like she hadn't talked this much since she first met Henry. She made Memphis laugh with her stories of the petty antics of the showbiz folks, and Memphis told her about playing the numbers and picking gigs, and about how irritating Isaiah could be, but Theta could tell he loved his brother fiercely. They talked so long that they both lost track of time. Theta had missed her call for the show, which she shrugged off.

"I'll tell them there was a subway fire," she said.

"You sure you don't want something else? A sandwich, or some soup?" Memphis asked.

"For the last time, I'm jake," Theta said. She was aware that everyone in the joint was watching them. The minute she looked

up and caught their eyes, they'd look away quickly, busying themselves with their silverware or pretending to be reading a newspaper.

There were so many things he still wanted to ask her. Where
was she from? Did she still dream of the eye? Had she thought of
him at all since the night of the raid? Had she, too, lain awake,
staring at the ceiling, picturing his face as he had hers?

"A Ziegfeld girl, huh?" was all he said.

"I heard the position of poet was already taken," Theta joked.
"Speaking of poetry, have you read *The Weary Blues* by Langston
Hughes?"

"'And far into the night he crooned that tune,'" Memphis
quoted, grinning madly.

"'The stars went out and so did the moon,'" Theta finished. "I
never read anything so beautiful before."

"Me, either."

The rest of the drugstore seemed to fall away—the *clink* of
dishes in the back, the bright *brrring* of the cash register, the low
drone of people talking—and there was only Memphis and Theta
and the moment. Theta's hand slid just slightly toward Memphis's.
He inched his forward, too, just grazing the tips of her fingers
with his.

"There's a rent party this Saturday night at my friend Alma's
place, if you'd like to come," he said.

"I'd like that," Theta answered.

The drugstore seemed to swirl once more into noisy life. An
older man walked past and frowned at them, and Theta and Memphis pulled their hands back and were quiet.

A TERRIBLE CHOICE

Evie and Jericho were having a late lunch in the Bennington's dowdy dining room. Jericho was talking, but Evie was lost in her own thoughts. Her chin balanced on one fist, she stared, unseeing, at her coffee, which she had been stirring mindlessly for a good ten minutes.

"So I shot the man in the back," Jericho said, testing Evie's attention.

"Interesting," Evie said without looking up.

"And then I took his head, which I keep under my bed."

"Of course," Evie muttered.

"Evie. Evie!"

Evie looked up and smiled weakly. "Yes?"

"You're not listening."

"Oh, I pos-i-tute-ly am, Jericho!"

"What did I just say?"

Evie gave him a blank stare. "Well, whatever it was, I'm sure it was very, very smart."

"I just said I shot a man in the back and took his head."

"I'm sure he deserved it. Oh, Jericho, I'm sorry. I can't help thinking there's a connection between this John Hobbes fellow and our murders."

"But why?"

Evie couldn't tell him about the song, and without that, there really wasn't much to go on. "Don't you think it's interesting that there were some unsolved murders fifty years ago that were similar in nature?"

"Interesting but remote. But if you want to know about them, we could go back to the library...."

Evie groaned. "Please don't make me go back there. I'll be good."

Jericho gave her the slightest hint of a smile. "The library is your friend, Evie."

"The library may be *your* friend, Jericho, but it pos-i-tute-ly despises me."

"You just have to know how to use it." Jericho played with his fork. He cleared his throat. "I could show you how to do that sometime."

Evie sat fully upright. "Jericho!" she said, grinning.

Jericho smiled back. "It would be no trouble. We could even go—"

"I know someone who could find out about the old murders for us!"

"Who?" Jericho asked. He hoped she couldn't sense his disappointment.

"Someone who owes me a favor."

Evie ran to the Bennington's telephone box and shut the beveled glass door behind her. "Algonquin four, five, seven, two, please," she said into the receiver and waited for the operator to work her magic.

"T. S. Woodhouse, *Daily News*."

"Mr. Woodhouse, it's Evie O'Neill. I'm calling in that favor you promised."

"Shoot."

"Can you dig up some information on an unsolved murder in Manhattan in the summer of 1875?"

She heard the reporter chuckle on the other end. "You got a history test, Sheba?"

"Just tell me what you find out, please. It's very important. Oh, and Mr. Woodhouse—this is just between you and me and the garden gate. Do you understand?"

"Whatever you say, Sheba."

Feeling very clever, Evie stepped from the telephone box and headed back toward the dining room. As she passed the elevator, the doors opened and a flustered Miss Lillian stood inside. "Oh, dear. I went down instead of up." She was struggling with a bag of groceries, and Evie offered to help her carry the heavy bag to her apartment.

"Come in, come in, dear," Miss Lillian said. "So nice to have a visitor. I'll put the kettle on."

"Oh, please don't go to any trouble," Evie said, but the old woman was already in the kitchen. Evie could hear the strike of the match, the hiss of the gas as it took. She hadn't meant to get trapped in a conversation. That was the trouble with offering help to old people. She nearly tripped over a tabby cat, who meowed in surprise and darted away. A second cat, black with yellow eyes, peeked out from under a table. It was hard to see in the dim light. Miss Lillian reentered the room and turned on a lamp.

"What a charming home you have," Evie managed to say, hoping that her grimace passed for a smile. The place was a dreadful mess, papers and books stacked all about, every surface covered in some sort of bric-a-brac: ornate clocks set to slightly different times, brass candelabras with dark candles burned down to nubs, a bust of Thomas Jefferson, a framed picture of solemn pilgrim ladies on a hill, plants, dead flowers in a glass vase whose water had dried to a film on the sides, and a small painted tintype of what Evie presumed were the young Lillian and Adelaide in their starched pinafores. *If there were an award for hideous taste*, Evie thought, *the Proctor sisters would win, hands down.*

"Here's your tea, dear. Do have a seat," Miss Lillian said.

Miss Lillian indicated a rocking chair beside an old pump organ.

"Thank you," Evie said, already thinking up excuses for why she needed to leave: sick uncle, building on fire, a sudden case of gangrene.

"Addie and I have lived in the Bennington since nearly the beginning. We moved in in the spring of 1875. April." She frowned. "Or perhaps May."

"Spring of 1875," Evie said, thinking. "Miss Lillian, do you remember a story about a man named John Hobbes who was hanged for murder in 1876?"

Miss Lillian pursed her lips, thinking. "I can't say that I do."

"He was accused of murdering a woman named Ida Knowles."

"Oh, Ida Knowles! Yes, I remember that. Ran off with a fortune hunter, they said. And then...yes, yes, I remember now! That man—"

"John Hobbes."

"He was tried for it. Oh, he seemed a bad sort. A grave robber, if I recall correctly. A charlatan."

"Do you remember any details of the case, or anything about him? Anything at all?" Evie sipped her tea. It had an odd taste.

"No, I'm afraid not, dear. I'm an old woman. Ah, here's our Addie now."

Miss Adelaide carried the black cat with the yellow eyes and wore a dress that had probably seen its best days when Teddy

Roosevelt was president. "I found Hawthorne trying to eat my begonias, the little devil," she said, nuzzling the meowing cat.

"Miss O'Neill was just asking about the Ida Knowles case—you remember that, don't you, dear?—and that terrible man who hung for it. But I couldn't remember much, I'm afraid. Hawthorne, come here and have some kibble." She put a bit of chicken salad on a plate at her feet and the cat leaped from Adelaide's arms and ran for it.

"They hanged him the night of the comet," Miss Addie said dreamily.

"Solomon's Comet?" Evie asked carefully.

"Yes, that's it. He told them to. It was his one request."

"John Hobbes asked to be hanged the night of Solomon's Comet?" Evie asked again. She wanted to be sure she had it right. It struck her as important, though she couldn't say why. "Now why would he do that, I wonder?"

"Comets are powerful portents!" Miss Lillian clucked. "The ancients believed them to be times when the veil between this world and the next was thinnest."

"I don't understand."

"If you wanted to open a door into the great spirit realm, to assure your return, what better time to plan your death?"

"But Miss Proctor, that's quite impossible," Evie said as gently as possible.

"It's an impossible world," Miss Lillian said, smiling. "Drink your tea, dear."

Evie swallowed down the rest, spitting up small ends of leaves.

"That is a pretty talisman," Miss Addie said, gazing at Evie's pendant.

"Oh, it was a gift from my brother," Evie replied. She didn't elaborate further. If she told them James had been killed, they might cluck and sympathize, or else draw out the conversation talking about every relative who'd ever died, and she'd be there all day and night. She needed to make her getaway.

Miss Addie reached out a finger and slid it over the surface of the half-dollar, paling as she did. "Such a terrible choice to have to make."

"What do you mean?" Evie asked.

"Addie sees into the eternal soul," Miss Lillian said. "Addie, dear, you'll let your tea go cold, and we've much to do still." Miss Lillian stood rather hastily. "I'm afraid we must bid you good day, Miss O'Neill. Thank you for visiting."

"A terrible choice," Miss Addie said again, looking at Evie with such sympathy that Evie felt quite undone.

Out in the flickering light of the hall—why couldn't they seem to fix the lamps in the old place?—Evie thought about John Hobbes's odd last request. Had he thought he could come back after death? That was ridiculous, of course, the thought of an egotistical madman, which he seemed to be. In two weeks, that same comet would make its return to New York's skies.

As she waited for the wheezing elevator, a shiver passed down her spine, though she couldn't say why. She wished she could talk it over with Mabel, wished they could share a laugh about the Proctor sisters' awful décor, but she and Mabel were still on the outs. They'd never gone this long without talking, and Evie wavered between being angry with Mabel and missing her terribly. When the elevator door opened, her finger hovered over the button for Mabel's floor. At the last possible second, she pressed the button for the lobby instead.

Back in the Proctor sisters' overstuffed apartment, Hawthorne brushed affectionately against Miss Adelaide's leg. In the other room, her sister prattled on about the day's activities. Miss Addie peered into the dregs of Evie's tea, examining the pattern the leaves had left in the bottom of the cup, and frowned.

THE TOMBS

Detective Malloy swept into the museum, pushing gruffly past the curiosity seekers, silencing anyone who tried to ask him about the Pentacle Killer with a terrifying scowl. "Miss O'Neill," he said with a tip of his hat.

"Unc isn't here just now, Detective. Do you have something new?"

He nodded toward the library. Evie had Sam take over and led Detective Malloy to the library, closing the doors behind them. Malloy dropped his hat on the brass statue of an eagle.

"Followed up on that tip your uncle gave us about the Brethren. Turns out there's been a resurgence of that religious cult the past few years. The townspeople've been complaining about 'em. And guess who's the leader?"

"I'm guessing it's not Will Rogers."

"Brother Jacob Call," Malloy said.

Malloy took a handful of nuts from the crystal bowl on Will's desk. "They say he's been preaching about Solomon's Comet coming through, and the Beast coming with it." He let this settle.

"Turns out, he raises livestock and comes down to the city every few weeks to sell to the butchers."

"He's a butcher!"

"Yep. And he was here for every one of the murders. I had the boys pick him up and bring him in. But so far, he's refusing to talk to us. Thought I'd have your uncle take a crack at him."

Evie bit her lip. "Detective, could I have a go-ski?"

Malloy's eyebrows went up. "At questioning a possible killer? I'm afraid not."

"He might open up to a girl. After all, I'm not a threat like the police."

"I admire your spunk, Miss O'Neill, but this is not your job." He tipped his hat and wished her a good day.

Evie raced out into the hall as soon as he left. The museum was packed with people, and for once, she wished it weren't. She hopped up and down, trying to be seen over the heads of the paying customers. "Sam!" she called. "Sam Lloyd! I need you!"

Sam came to her side, grinning. "I knew you'd come around."

Evie rolled her eyes. "Take a shower, pal. I need you to help me get into the Tombs."

"Haven't you already learned your lesson?"

"Oh, Jericho!" Evie called. "Could you take over? I need Sam for a mission of utmost importance."

"I could help you with that," Jericho said.

"You already are!" Evie trilled. She linked her arm through Sam's, dragging him toward the door. "I'll fill you in on the way."

Sam and Evie borrowed Will's old car for the ride from the Upper West Side down to the city's notorious jail. It was a long drive, and Sam was in a chatty mood. "Your friend Mabel still goofy for the giant?"

349

"Jericho? Mm-hmm," Evie said, nearly flinching at the words *your friend Mabel.*

"What is it about that guy?"

"You just don't like him because he hates you."

"That isn't the only reason," Sam said.

"What do you mean?"

"Nothing. I suppose you like the giant, too."

"Jericho? Oh, he's nice enough, I suppose."

"So you don't like him," Sam said, smiling.

"I didn't say that."

They had passed the many music publishing houses of Tin Pan Alley in the West Twenties and were close to the fashionable town houses of Gramercy.

"You have a steady fella?" Sam asked after a bit.

"No fella can hold me for long."

Sam gave her a sideways glance. "That a challenge?"

"No. A statement of fact."

"We'll see."

"You still owe me twenty bucks," Evie said.

"You're a lot more like me than you think, Evie O'Neill."

"Ha!"

"What I meant to say is, you like me a lot more than you think."

"Keep driving, Lloyd."

The car jostled along, past a flock of dark-suited businessmen holding fast to their bowler hats in the stiff wind whipping off the East River and barreling down the canyonlike streets.

"Got a little something for ya," Sam said. His smile was cryptic.

Evie raised an eyebrow. "Yeah? What's that? I already told you the bank's closed."

"Some neck lightning." He pulled a necklace from his pocket and offered it to her.

Evie gasped. "Holy smokes! That looks like a real diamond on there! Where'd you get this?"

"Would you believe a generous aunt?"

"No."

"Didn't think so. Where I got it, they won't miss it. They got plenty."

Evie sighed. "Sam…"

"I know their type. They don't care what happens to anyone but themselves. They buy everything the magazines and billboards tell them to and forget about it when something new comes along."

"And Uncle Will thinks *I'm* cynical!" Evie shoved the necklace back into Sam's jacket pocket. "You can't just go around taking things that don't belong to you, Sam."

"Why not? If captains of industry do it, they're heroes. If little people like me do it, we're criminals."

"Now you sound like a Bolshevik. Say, you're not one of those anarchists, are you?"

"Bombs and revolution? Not my style. I've got my own mission," Sam said, the last part coming out a bit hard.

"What mission is that? Leading girls astray with stolen gems?"

Sam gave her a sideways glance. "You ever hear of something called Project Buffalo?"

"Can't say that I have."

"Well, if you look for any information on it, you won't find it. It was a secret government operation during the war."

"Then how do *you* know about it?"

"My mother went to work on it. She took some kind of test—"

"A test? What…?"

"Don't know. Whatever it was, she scored pretty high. She

and my father had a big fight about it. I heard 'em in the other room. She said she felt she had to go. 'What can we do?' she said. My father said no. My father loves the word *no*." Sam's face clouded. "Anyway, maybe a month later, these fellas from the government showed up. They had my dad's papers. Told him they could send him back to Russia if he didn't cooperate. My dad wasn't going back to Russia to starve or be killed. He had a nice house and a fur business. So that night, my mother packed her things and left. She sent us only one letter. Most of it had been blacked over. But she said they were doing good work, important work for the country. She said it would change mankind. And then we never heard from her again. When my father wrote to them, they said she'd died from influenza. I was eight."

"I'm sorry. That's terrible." In the afternoon sun, the city shimmered like a mirage. "Sam Lloyd doesn't sound very Russian, though."

"Sergei Lubovitch. My father changed our last name to Lloyd when he and my mother came through New York. When I was born, he insisted they name me Sam. As in Uncle."

"I thought you looked familiar," Evie teased. "Where's your father now?"

"Back in Chicago, I suppose."

"You don't know?"

"My father and I didn't get along too well. He likes to say no, and I'm supposed to say yes. He didn't like it when I could say no myself. And he sure didn't like it when I said I wanted to find out what really happened to Mama."

"I thought you said she died."

"That's what they told us. Two years ago, I got this." He pulled the worn postcard of trees and mountains from his pocket. Evie pretended it was the first time she'd seen it.

"Pretty. Where is this?"

"I don't know. That phrase on the back, there. It's Russian."

Evie examined the soft handwriting, obviously feminine.

"It means 'little fox.' It was my mother's nickname for me. She was the only one who ever called me that. That's when I knew my mother was alive, and I was going to find her. So I took off. I joined up with the navy for a bit—till they found out I was only fifteen. Then I fell in with a circus."

"You did not!"

"Scout's honor."

"You're no scout," Evie sniped. They hit a bump and Evie careened into Sam for a second. "Sorry." She sat back, red-faced.

Sam smiled. "No apology necessary. Gee, I might have to hit another."

Evie cleared her throat. "The circus?"

"The circus. I trained as an acrobat. Got pretty good on the high wire. Quick feet. I even worked as a barnstormer, doing aerial tricks out on the wings."

"On a moving aeroplane?"

Sam grinned. "You should try it sometime. Though if you really want to see someone do it up right, you should see Barnstormin' Belle Butler, the aerialist extraordinaire."

"Who is *that*, pray tell?"

"An old friend."

Evie arched an eyebrow. "What sort of friend?"

Sam smiled but didn't satisfy her curiosity. "The circus brought me to Coney Island. When they headed south to Florida for the winter, I decided to stay here for a while, see if I could make enough money so I could find my mother."

Evie looked at the postcard again. It was a beautiful picture of blue skies and tall trees, with mountains in the background. She handed it back to Sam, who secured it inside his jacket pocket once more. "Doesn't seem like much to go on."

"I'm going to find her," Sam said, sounding very determined. "So now you know about me. What about you? How'd you end up with your uncle?"

Should she tell him the truth? Then she might have to admit that she'd tried to read his mother's postcard and gotten nothing from it. He might be furious. Or he might ask her to try again. And when she couldn't get a read, he'd think she was a liar.

"I killed a man for insulting my honor," Evie said blithely.

"Naturally. And?"

"And... I robbed a five-and-dime. I can never have enough paste bracelets."

"Who can? And?"

"And... I accused the town golden boy of knocking up a chambermaid."

Sam let out a low whistle. "For fun?"

Evie looked up. The sun seemed close enough to touch, like a shimmering foil prop in a Broadway show. "I was at a party filled with those 'bright young things' you love to hate. Yes, I was one of them. It was late and I was drunk and... anyway, it was just some gossip I heard," she lied. "But it turned out to be true."

"I don't understand. If it was true, how come you got sent up the river?"

Evie wished she could tell him the truth, but she'd also promised Will she'd stay mum, and she didn't want to do anything to jeopardize her stay in New York. "I really did kill a man in Ohio."

"Hmm. And then these murders started in New York. Coincidence?"

"You're on to me, Lloyd. I'm afraid I'll have to kill *you* now. Be a honey and sit still while I strangle you." Evie reached playfully for his throat and Sam jerked the wheel, making the car swerve and Evie scream.

"I'll go quietly, sister," Sam said, correcting their course. "Just don't wreck us."

They parked Will's old Model T a block away and dodged the trolley rattling up the cobblestones of Centre Street on their way toward the Tombs. The imposing, elliptical jail was anchored by a turret at each end and surrounded by a tall stone wall and an iron railing, which made it seem more like some medieval fortress than a modern New York City building.

"If I give you this signal"—Sam put a finger to the side of his nose—"it means distract the flat foot while I steal what we need. Got it?"

"Got it. But how will we find where they're holding him?" Evie said in despair. They entered the building to find a bedlam of officers and miscreants. It was like opening night at a Broadway show of criminals.

Sam walked up to the officer at the front desk. "Pardon me. The lady here heard you might be holding her brother, Jacob Call?"

The officer conferred with someone over the telephone and came back shaking his head.

"No visitors."

"I see. We just want to be sure he's not being held down below. He had pneumonia just last month, and that swampy air isn't good for his lungs," Sam said.

The officer turned to Evie. "He's in the warden's office on this floor, so you can rest easy, Miss."

Evie batted her lashes and tried to look forlorn. "Thank you. You've been a real doll, sir."

Sam put his finger to his nose in the secret signal, at which Evie's eyes fluttered. She swayed on her feet. "Oh, ohhhh…" She swooned as attractively as she could, and the officer caught her. Through slitted eyes, Evie watched Sam steal his keys.

"Oh, thank you, officer. If I could just sit down somewhere until I feel steadier on my feet?"

The officer led them inside to a waiting bench. Evie winked at Sam and he whispered low in her ear, making her neck tingle. "Sister, together, we could be a hell of a team."

Up front, a commotion broke out among a group of drunks and the officer abandoned Evie and Sam to help out. Evie grabbed Sam's hand and pulled him after her, deep into the building.

"For the record, sister, this isn't my idea of a swell time," Sam whispered as he and Evie sneaked through the labyrinthine corridors of the city's notorious jail.

"How are we going to get past the guards?" Evie said. She could see a policeman sitting on a stool behind a desk, filling out paperwork.

"Leave that to me."

"Sam," Evie warned as they got close.

The officer looked up, and it seemed to Evie that he looked right at them. She heard Sam muttering something under his breath, prayerlike. He put up a hand as if to shield them, and the officer looked back down at his paperwork, almost as though he hadn't seen them. It was very strange, and Evie told herself that he hadn't really seen them after all.

"That was a stroke of luck," she said, letting out her breath.

"Just keep walking," Sam instructed.

They found Jacob Call sitting in a dingy room with only two chairs and a table. He wore the same coveralls and black hat as when they'd last met him. The pendant still hung from his neck.

His sleeves were pushed up some, and Evie could see crude tattoos peeking out from beneath the cuffs.

"Hello again," Evie said. "Do you remember me, Mr. Call?"

Brother Call barely glanced at her. "Yep."

"I hear you won't tell the police anything. Why is that?"

"Won't tell them. Won't tell you," he said.

"That's a shame. I think we'd have just oodles of things to talk about. This, for instance." Evie placed the Book of the Brethren on the table between them.

Jacob Call's expression darkened. "Where'd you get that?"

Evie opened the book and turned the pages but didn't offer him a glimpse. "Fascinating reading. Much better than *Moby-Dick*. Like this passage, for instance."

She'd opened to the page for the eleventh offering, the Marriage of the Beast and the Woman Clothed in the Sun. She laid the book on the table and watched as Jacob Call looked on in awe.

"The ritual of the offerings. It's begun, hasn't it? The rise of the Beast?"

He leaned forward, placing a hand reverently on the page. "Just like the prophet seen," he said. "When the fire burns in the sky, the chosen one will make the final offering. The Beast will rise in him, and Armageddon will begin."

Evie's skin crawled. She fought to keep her composure. "And the Beast comes into this world through the ritual kill—um, the offerings. Is that correct?"

Jacob Call gave a curt nod. "The world has fallen into sin. The Lord will purify it in blood through the chosen one."

"And you are that chosen one," Evie tried.

The man's lip curled in contempt. "Why should I tell you? You ain't the law or a believer. You're just a girl."

"Just like Ruta Badowski was a girl?" Evie snapped. She did

not like Jacob Call one bit. "Tell me, did you really mail her eyes to the police as an offering to the Beast, so that he'd know you'd fulfilled the prophecy?" she bluffed.

"I-I done it. May it please the Lord." *Jacob Call wouldn't make a very good poker player,* Evie thought. In that brief, unguarded moment of surprise, he'd shown his hand—he didn't know she was lying. He didn't know the details of the murder.

"What about Tommy Duffy's hands? What did you do with them?" she pressed.

Jacob Call sat stone-faced. "I've said all I'm a-goin' to. I ain't saying no more."

"All right, then. I just want to know one more thing. That's all, and then I'll leave you alone. Your pendant—what does it mean?"

Jacob Call continued to sit in silence.

"Let's blouse, Evie," Sam said. "I hear somebody coming down the hall."

"It's just darling!" Evie said, deliberately goading him. "I simply must have one for myself. Where did you get it?"

"The Lord will not be mocked!" Jacob said, glaring.

"Who said anything about mocking the Lord? I just want to know the name of your jeweler. Or perhaps you'd let me buy yours...." Evie reached out a finger as if to touch the pendant, and Jacob Call pounded his fists on the table, making her jump back.

"It's for me and me alone! And the Lord said, 'Anoint thy flesh and prepare ye the walls of your houses. Bind your spirit to the Holy Mark and wear it upon your person always and ye shall be protected both in this life and the hereafter. But take care that the Holy Mark be not destroyed. For then shall ye sever the tie to your spirit!'"

"I see," Evie said, trying not to smile. She'd gotten what she needed, though her heart was racing. "I'll just try Tiffany's, then. Thanks all the same."

※

"What was that hooey about binding yourself to the Holy Mark?" Sam asked after they'd slipped out of the Tombs and were walking briskly back to the spot where they'd parked Will's car.

"He seems to believe that you can tie your spirit to that pendant, that it's some sort of magical object that allows you to live on."

Sam let out a whistle. He shook his head. "The things people will believe. So, you think he's our killer?"

Evie shook her head slowly. "I don't think so. The killer didn't send Ruta Badowski's eyes parcel post. I made that up, and he went along with it."

"Maybe he's only pretending not to know."

"Maybe," Evie concurred, but she wasn't convinced.

A newsie hawked the late edition on the curb. "Extra! Extra! *Daily News!* Pentacle Killer exclusive! Read all about it!"

Evie tossed the kid some change and gaped at the headline: COPYCAT KILLER! PENTACLE FIEND TAKING GRUESOME PAGE FROM HISTORY? "That fink!" Evie fumed. "I gave him that tip, and he went and used it to make a name for himself!"

"Never trust the press, doll," Sam said.

Evie flipped to the story and they read it together on the street amid the swirl of pedestrians.

" 'In the summer of 1875, the partially decomposed body of an unidentified man was found at the Belmont racetrack. The body bore traces of strange tattoos, including a five-pointed star, and a note was found pinned to his shirt. Most of the ink had been washed away by the elements, but two words were legible: *horseman* and *stars.*'" Evie gasped. "The Pale Horseman Riding Death Before the Stars. The third offering. He *is* taking a page from history."

They hopped into Will's car and drove quickly back uptown, and while Sam parked, Evie burst into the museum, interrupting Will's class.

She held up the newspaper. "I found the third offering!" and ran out, leaving Will and his students at a loss.

Will barreled into the library a moment later. "Evie, what the devil do you mean by interrupting my class?"

"Unc, listen to this!" She read to him from T. S. Woodhouse's article. "Fifty years ago! The third offering happened fifty years ago...."

"Evie," Will said.

"That's why the killer started with the fifth offering—because the other four have already taken place, and he's just finishing up the job!"

"Evie, Evie!" Will interrupted. "Jacob Call confessed."

"He...what?"

"Just a half hour ago. Terrence phoned me. He confessed to all of it. Said he's the chosen one, meant to bring about the end."

"But he's not the killer. He can't be."

"He is, Evie. The police in New Brethren confirmed that he's been preaching about the coming of the Beast and the arrival of Solomon's Comet for the past six months. He's admitted his crime. It's over," Will said with finality. "Why don't you give yourself a night off to go out dancing with your friends? You've earned it. Now, I must return to my class."

Evie sat on the wide staircase and listened to Will's voice floating out from the classroom as he talked about the nature of evil.

Jericho came to sit beside her. "Murnau's *Faust* is playing at the Palace."

"Swell," Evie said, still turning things over in her mind.

"I was just wondering if you might—"

There was a knock at the door.

"I'll go," Evie said, sighing. "Probably another reporter."

"Want to go with me," Jericho finished as he watched Evie walk away.

The Negro woman standing on the steps of the museum was tall and broad-shouldered and smartly attired in a brown plaid suit and a beige hat with a red band. She didn't seem like a reporter; in fact, she carried herself more like a queen.

"May I help you?" Evie asked.

The woman's smile was polite but formal. "I am looking for Dr. William Fitzgerald."

"I'm afraid he's teaching just now."

"I see." The woman nodded, thinking something over. "May I leave my card?"

"Of course."

From her pocketbook, the woman retrieved a simple cream calling card. Evie rubbed a finger over the lettering. Miss Margaret Walker, with an address uptown. "Do you work for Mr. Fitzgerald?" the woman asked. There was something strange in the way she said "work," with an air of suspicion that left Evie feeling guarded.

"I'm his niece, Evie O'Neill."

"His niece," Miss Walker said in wonder. "Well. Isn't that something?"

Evie didn't quite know what to make of Miss Margaret Walker. It wasn't often that someone left her feeling so undone. "And do *you* work with my uncle, Miss Walker?"

Miss Walker's mouth twitched, flirting with a semblance of

smile before settling into something far harder. "No." The woman started down the steps, then turned back. "Miss O'Neill, if you don't mind my asking, how old are you?"

"I'm seventeen."

"Seventeen." The woman seemed to consider this. "Have a pleasant day, Miss O'Neill."

Evie turned the card over and was surprised to see that Margaret Walker had left a note in script that was as precise and clipped as she appeared to be.

It's coming back.

What was coming back? Who was Margaret Walker? And who was she to Will?

Upon returning to the library, Evie was surprised to find Will there. "Oh, you've finished already. Someone was just calling for you. A woman. She left her card."

Will stared at the name on the card. He turned it over and read the other side.

"Who is she, Unc?"

"No one I know," Will answered and tossed Margaret Walker's card in the wastebasket.

PACK UP YOUR TROUBLES

Evie was dreaming.

In the exotic, looping logic of dreams, she sat on the old wooden swing behind her family's house in Ohio while James pushed her. She felt the desperate need to look behind her, to make sure he was there and to whisper a warning to him, but the swing rose higher and higher and she could do nothing but hold on tightly. On the fourth push, she swung so high that her pendant flew from her neck. Evie reached out a hand to grab it and fell down, down, down into a velvety forever.

A crow snatched it from her grasping fingers and flew with it into a churning, dark-gray sky above a vast wheat field. Lightning shot from the clouds and struck the land. The wheat burned. Evie put up an arm to shield herself from the heat.

When she took her arm away, she found herself on the streets of a deserted Times Square. Under the giant billboard for Marlowe Industries, the hollow-man war veteran sat in his wheelchair, rattling his cup. "The time is now," he said.

The pretty woman in Uncle Will's photograph skated past, laughing. "That's you all over, William," she said. Evie heard laughter and turned to see that it was Will, the young Will of family pictures. But when she looked again, it was James, standing on the edge of the familiar forest in the mist. He was pale. So very pale. Dark shadows lay beneath his vacant eyes. He waved to Evie, and she trailed him through the woods and into the army camp. Atop a barrel, a Victrola played, the record going round and round: *"Pack up your troubles in your old kit bag and smile, smile, smile. . . ."*

Sandbags formed a wall in front of a long trench. A barbed-wire fence stretched for miles. And the fog sat heavily over it all.

"Don't let your joy and laughter hear the snag. Smile, boys, that's the style. . . ."

Above the tree line, a long, serrated roof appeared, like a forgotten fairy castle in the mist. Where was James?

The record spun: *"What's the use of worrying? It never was worthwhile. . . ."*

The soldiers stood around talking, eating from tins, drinking from canteens. She blinked, and for a split second, the boys became skeletal specters. Evie screamed and hid her eyes, and when she looked again, they were just soldiers. One toasted her with his canteen. He smiled, and locusts hopped from his mouth.

"So, pack up your troubles in your old kit bag and smile, smile, s—"

An explosion rattled the ground. A column of fierce white light pierced the sky and spread out in rapid waves, decimating the trees and the soldiers where they stood—flesh peeled back from bone, sockets missing eyes, limbs melting, mouths open in unheard screams while the Victrola turned on a hiss. Evie ran. Her bare feet squished through fields of bloody mud. It splattered her night-gown, face, and arms. The blood became poppies, which rose beside the scorched trees. She saw James up ahead, his back to her. He was alive and unharmed!

James. She called his name, but in the world of the dream, she made no sound. *James, James!* She was close. She would reach him and they would run away from this horrible place. Yes, they would run. They would be all right. They—

He turned slowly toward her and removed his gas mask and she saw that his beautiful face was ghastly pale and skeletal, his teeth garish now that his lips were gone.

And then he was melting, like all the others.

Evie woke shaking. She sat up and pulled her knees to her chest and waited for her breathing to return to normal. She knew there'd be no more sleep tonight. Exhausted, she took herself to the kitchen for a glass of water, then settled into Will's office chair and tried to comfort herself by straightening the mess that was his desk. She picked up a crystal paperweight. A letter opener. A framed picture of the woman she'd seen when she held Will's glove. If she wanted to, she could press any of these things between her palms, concentrate, and draw out Will's secrets. Jericho's, too. And Sam's and Mabel's and Theta's. The list was endless. But it was a form of stealing, knowing people's secrets without their consent. And she wasn't sure she wanted the responsibility of knowing.

She put the photograph back in its protected place and let her palm rest against the half-dollar pendant at her neck, feeling warmed by its presence. She'd never been able to read it; the coin was too imbued with her own memories. But she liked the weight of it against her neck. It was her last connection to James, and James had been her connection to everything good. She remembered the birthday note that had accompanied the gift:

Happy birthday, old girl.

Are you seven already? Before I know it, you'll be pinning gardenias to your frocks and sitting with gentlemen callers on the front porch—under the watchful eye of your dear brother, of course. France is miserably muddy, I'm afraid. You'd have a grand time of it, making mud pies and throwing them at the Germans. Big day tomorrow, so I won't write again for a while. Here is a little something to remember your old brother by. Don't spend it all at Hale's Candy Store.

Fondly, James

A week later, they'd received the horrible telegram that James was dead, and her family had broken and been taped back together, a posed photograph kept behind fractured glass.

On Will's desk, the *Daily News* lay folded open to T. S. Woodhouse's latest article on the Pentacle Killer. Her brother was long dead, and somewhere in this city a murderer was breaking hearts. Evie twirled her pendant and thought about the grieving families of Ruta Badowski, Tommy Duffy, and Eugene Meriwether. She knew what it was to wait for someone who would never come home. She knew that grief, like a scar, faded but never really went away. Uncle Will hadn't wanted her to use her talents to help catch the killer; he thought it too dangerous. He was wrong. It was dangerous *not* to use them. Not that it mattered, now that Jacob Call had confessed. Why couldn't she feel better about that?

Jericho had forgotten to draw the shade before bed, and now the weary neon of the night-owl city woke him. He crossed to the mirror and stood shirtless before it, examining himself. He was tall, six-foot-two, with the broad shoulders of a farmer, which he would have been if he hadn't gotten sick. Silently, he slid his bureau drawer open and took the leather kit from its hiding place under a stack of folded undershirts, unrolled it, and ran a finger along the dark blue vials. He wanted to bring a fist down and crush them all. Instead, he brought his hands out in front of his body and held them there for a few long seconds, watching, before dropping them to his sides again. His hands were steady, his skin smooth, his eyes clear. His heart kept a steady, comforting rhythm. To look at him, you'd never know. Only someone who was very close to him would ever know the truth. And he didn't intend to let anyone get that close.

He sensed movement in the apartment and opened his door a crack to see Evie leaving Will's office, on her way back to her room. The bluish light cutting through the windows silhouetted the shape of her body beneath her nightgown and Jericho felt a stirring deep in his belly. He admonished himself for looking, but didn't stop. When she disappeared from view, he shut the door quietly and dropped into a push-up position, driving himself through a punishing routine of exercises, counting them off in his head: *Thirty . . . fifty . . . one hundred.* When he'd finished, his body glistened with a fine sheen of sweat that gave Jericho a sense of relief. Sweat was good. It was healthy. Normal. He held out his hands again. Steady as a rock. He buried the leather kit under his shirts and closed the drawer.

In a garden apartment in Harlem, Alma's rent party was in full swing. Gabe's trumpet wailed and growled like a man on the prowl. The small flat was packed with bodies dancing and drinking, singing and shouting into the night. When Memphis had first stepped into the packed apartment with Theta on his arm, he'd gotten some raised eyebrows, and one or two stares. That ended when Alma's girlfriend, Rita, walked straight up to Theta and said, in a loud voice, "Got a cigarette?" Theta answered, "I've got ten. Which one do you want?" To which Rita laughed and said, "She's all right," and it was all fine after that. Soon enough, everybody was lost to the good times. Or almost everyone was.

Gabe pulled Memphis into a corner. "Brother, when I said you should find yourself a girl, I didn't mean a white girl."

Memphis didn't want to get into it with Gabe, so he just said, "It's a free country." He walked into the kitchen to buy a couple of drinks, and Gabe followed.

"No, it isn't. You know that."

"Well, it should be."

"*Should* and *is* aren't the same thing. What happens when she gets tired of you, or worse, accuses you of something? You remember Rosewood?"

"Two beers!" Memphis told the man with the liquor. "Why you bringing that town into this, Gabriel?"

"That town got burned to the ground because a white woman said—"

"Gab-ri-el!" Alma called over the din. "You gonna blow that horn or run your mouth all night?"

"Don't get hot, sugar," Gabe called back, smiling. He dropped the smile as he turned back to Memphis. "It's not enough they're slumming it up here and taking the best tables in our own clubs when we can't even get a table in theirs! Or that they're trying to take over our business from the inside, like what happened with the Hotsy Totsy. Now you want to go and parade around with one of them?"

"I am not parading, Gabriel."

"Brother, you are borrowing trouble. Do us all a favor: Escort her out front, help her to a taxi headed downtown, and say good-bye."

"Don't tell me how to run my life, Gabe," Memphis snapped.

Gabe grabbed hold of Memphis's sleeve. "I'm not trying to run it; I'm trying to save it. You get caught by the wrong people, and you won't be able to heal what they'll do to you."

"Told you, I can't heal anymore," Memphis said through gritted teeth. He twisted out of Gabe's grip, paid for his beer, and pushed his way through the dancing party to where Theta sat, swinging her leg along to the Count's crazy piano rolls.

"You copacetic, Poet?" Theta asked.

"Me? I don't wear worry."

"Sure you don't," Theta said, watching his face closely. "Kind of smoky in here, huh? Maybe we should take a breather?"

Alma's flat was jammed with people from where they sat to the door at the far end. It would take forever to try to get through. So Memphis nodded to the window, and he and Theta climbed through it into a neat square of garden crisscrossed with clotheslines hung with the day's washing. The air was brisk but welcome after the close quarters inside.

"Where you from?" Memphis asked Theta.

"Everywhere."

"But where are your people from?"

"People sure like to know where you're from in this country, who 'your people' are," Theta grumbled. "Tell you the truth, I don't know. My father ankled before I was born. My mother left me on some church steps in Kansas when I was a just a baby. When I was three, I was adopted by a lady named Mrs. Bowers. She wasn't what you'd call the motherly type. From the time I could put on tap shoes, I was on the Orpheum Circuit, eight shows a week."

"I can't imagine anybody ever leaving you," Memphis said with such sincerity that Theta felt a catch in her chest.

"Careful there, Poet. I might start to believe you."

"I'm a believable fella."

"Yeah? Prove it. Tell me a secret about yourself."

Memphis thought hard for a moment before answering. "I used to be able to heal," he said at last. "They called me the Harlem Healer. Miracle Memphis. Once a month at church, I'd stand up at the front and lay hands on people, take away their pain, their sickness."

"Are you pulling my leg?" Theta's expression was very serious.

Memphis shook his head. "I wish I were." He told her about his mother dying, about how he lost the gift that night and hadn't ever gotten it back. "Just as well, I guess."

Theta listened closely. She could tell he was on the level about all of it. She wanted to tell him about Kansas. About what she'd done, and why she'd had to run. But what kind of fella would stick around after he'd heard that?

"Come here." Theta crooked a finger and Memphis followed her down the narrow alley between the two rows of laundry. Safely hidden, they shared a kiss while the night raged around them. Their mouths tasted sweetly of Alma's coconut cake and home-brewed beer.

"This is happening pretty fast, isn't it?" Memphis said. He could not remember a time when he didn't know Theta, a time when she didn't occupy his thoughts and dreams.

"Life goes fast, Poet."

Memphis cupped her cheek in his hand and put his mouth on hers. Theta had never been kissed the way Memphis was kissing her now. There had been fumbling boys thrumming with nervous want. There had been theater owners, older "uncles" who pawed at her when she walked past or who wanted to "inspect" her costume to make sure it was decent down to the undergarments, men she granted the occasional kiss in order to stave off something worse. And there was Roy, of course. Beautiful, cruel Roy, whose kisses were declaratory, as if he needed to conquer Theta, to brand her with his mouth. Those men had never really seen Theta. But Memphis's kiss was nothing like theirs. It was passionate, yet tender. A mutual agreement of desire. It was a kiss shared. He was kissing *her*. He was *with* her.

Memphis pulled away. "Everything jake?"

"No," Theta said.

"What's the matter?"

Theta looked up at him through thick, dark lashes. "You stopped."

He drew her to him. She grabbed the clothesline to steady herself, and they fell to the ground, laughing, in a tumble of laundry that would have to be washed all over again.

"Let's just stay right here," Memphis said, and Theta rested her head against his chest, listening to the steady beat of his heart as he held her close.

Outside, the city stirred and sighed in its sleep. Steam hissed up from sewer grates and coiled around a lamppost like the tail of a forgotten god. Deep under the ground, in the half-finished tunnels of the new subway lines, rats scurried along tracks just ahead of something they imagined chased them, something more horrible than their rat dreams ever conjured. A storefront psychic whose connection to the spirits was nothing more than the pull of a string with a toe to make a knocking under the table felt compelled, quite suddenly, to cover her crystal ball with a cloth and lock it up in a wardrobe. In Chinatown, the girl with the dark hair and green eyes bowed reverently to her ancestors, offered her prayers, and readied herself to walk in dreams, among the living and the dead. North along the Hudson, in an abandoned, ruined village, the wind carried the terrible death cries of some ghostly inhabitants, the sound reverberating ever so faintly in the village below so that the men bent over their checkers in the back of the general store glanced nervously at one another, their play suspended, their breath held for several seconds until the wind and the sound were gone. Elsewhere in the country, there were similar stirrings: A mother dreamed of her dead daughter and woke, she could swear, to the chilling sound of the words *Mama, I'm home.* A Klansman who'd left his meeting in the woods to piss by an old tree jumped suddenly, as if he'd felt hanging feet dragging across the tops of his shoulders, marking him. There was nothing there, but he brushed at his shoulders anyway, scurrying back toward the fire and his brothers in white. A young Ojibway man watched a silvery shimmer of a hawk circle overhead and disappear. In an old farmhouse, a young boy nudged his parents awake. "There's two girls calling me to play hide-and-seek with them in the cornfields," he whispered. His father ordered him sleepily back to bed, and when the boy passed by the upstairs window, he saw the incandescent girls in their long skirts and high-necked blouses fading into the edges of the corn, crying mournfully, "Come, come play with us...."

And farther still, in the vast prairies mythologized in the American mind, a figure stood shadowed in the dark, biding his time, a scarecrow awaiting harvest.

THE ANGEL GABRIEL

Gabe didn't feel the press of ghosts as he walked west toward home, his head still buzzing from the reefer he'd smoked at Alma's party. The night had turned chilly, and he blew on his hands to warm them. It had been a good day, as good as any Gabe could remember. Meeting the great Mamie Smith. He was only eighteen, but the other cats treated him like he was one of them, grinning as he took his solos, complimenting him on his chops.

The only cloud had been the fight with Memphis. What was he thinking, bringing that girl to their party? Sure, she was pretty. But there were lots of pretty girls who weren't trouble—or, at least, no more trouble than most women were. He didn't like that they'd left it on such a bad note. Memphis and Theta had breezed on out without even saying good-bye. If that was the way he wanted to play it, fine. When that girl dropped him for some white big shot, who would have to hear the whole sob story? Gabe, that was who.

A sound startled him. *One, two, three; one, two, three.* A three-legged cadence, like an off-tempo waltz. But when he turned around, he saw no one.

He was getting worked up about Memphis and his girl, and it was killing his good feeling. Gabe flipped up the collar of his jacket, a temporary buffer against the wind howling off the Hudson, and kept walking. The wind had to content itself with kicking a tin can down the street. Overhead, the tracks of the Ninth Avenue El groaned in their emptiness. In his head, Gabe replayed the day's best moments. The camaraderie with the other musicians. Shaking hands with Clarence Williams, who promised him a bright future with Okeh Records. "Gonna have you playing for everybody," he'd said, and Gabe felt made.

The sound intruded again—*one, two, three, one, two, three, click, step, step, click, step, step.*

"Somebody there?" Gabe called into the shadows. Something darted out from between the wide tires of a parked Ford and Gabe let out a yelp. As the cat slunk away down an alley, Gabe laughed. "Lord, cat. Announce yourself next time. I don't have no nine lives."

Shaking his head, he carried on, scatting a little bit of Miss Mamie Smith's song under his breath, his hands unconsciously fingering an imaginary trumpet. The latticed tracks of the El bridge left stripes of light on the road, and Isaiah's warning drifted back to him: *The bridge. Don't walk under the bridge.* Gabe never would've said anything to Memphis about it, but there was definitely something not quite right about Isaiah. This business about telling Gabe's future was a good example. Isaiah took the joke too far; Gabe had actually believed the kid was scared, too. Too much imagination—that was the trouble with that boy.

One, two, three, one, two, three, click, step, step.

There was that damned sound again! Gabriel turned around. It had gotten very foggy all of a sudden. The lights of the Whoopee Club were a distant haze.

Don't walk under the bridge. He's there.

Gabe pulled his collar tighter at his throat. Why was he letting that boy's silly words get to him? The sound of footsteps echoed. It seemed to come from all around. The fog was even thicker. How was that possible? How could it have gotten thicker in just a matter of seconds? Was he walking closer to the river? Had he gotten lost? Gabe felt disoriented. Which way was back toward the clubs? The sound of whistling carried through the mist.

"Gabriel…"

Somebody was calling his name. He didn't recognize the voice.

"Who's there?"

"Gabriel, the angel. The messenger…"

"Memphis, that you? Lay off, now…." Gabe looked for something he could use to swing if he needed it, but he couldn't see. *Don't walk under the bridge. He's there.*

If this was a joke, Gabe wasn't laughing. He walked quickly ahead.

The man stepped from the mist as if born of it. His clothes were old-fashioned and he carried a silver walking stick. He was smiling at Gabe. It was a cold, cold smile, and Gabe felt unsteady on his feet.

"Gabriel the Archangel, whose trumpet did rend the sky."

"If you're looking for a horn player, I already play with the Count's outfit," Gabe said. His heartbeat had picked up something fierce. It was just some odd cat with a cane who was probably drunk. Gabe could take him if it came to that. So why was he suddenly so scared?

Don't walk under the bridge. He's there. You'll die.

"Gabriel, whose trumpet announced the birth of John the

Baptist. Of Jesus Christ. And whose call shall bear witness to the coming of the Beast," the strange man continued. His eyes appeared to be swirling with fire, and Gabe found he couldn't look away. "'And the eighth offering was the offering of the angel, the great messenger whose heavenly music aligned the spheres and welcomed the fire in the sky. And lo, he played a sound upon his golden trumpet and heralded the birth of the Beast.'"

The man seemed to be getting bigger. His eyes were twin flames and his skin was crawling. Changing.

"'And the Lord said, let every tongue welcome and praise the Dragon of Old, for His is the path of righteousness.'"

From the fog came the terrible din of demonic whispers, a breath straight from hell itself.

"Will you look upon me, Gabriel? Will you look upon me and be amazed?"

Gabe found he couldn't speak. For the thing before him was beyond words.

KNOWLES' END

The papers reported the arrest of Jacob Call with screaming head-lines: KILLER KAUGHT! OH, BROTHER—CALL THIS ONE SOLVED! EVERYTHING'S JAKE! Though Detective Malloy insisted publicly that Jacob Call was only a person of interest, in the court of public opinion, he had already been tried and found guilty. But Evie had talked to Jacob Call. It was obvious he didn't know much about the murder of Ruta Badowski. It was almost as if he wanted to draw attention to himself once they'd brought him in.

Evie had left a peace offering for Mabel: a photograph of Jeri-cho she'd found lying about. She'd wrapped it inside a letter that simply read, "Sorry, Pie Face. Forgive your bad pal? Evie." Mabel had responded by coming up straightaway and hugging Evie, and they'd promised they'd never be on the outs again. Evie had arranged a lunch with Jericho, and then, at the table, she'd announced that she was awfully sorry but she had to make an important telephone call. When she returned forty minutes later, she found the pair having a pleasant conversation about Tolstoy. It wasn't fireworks and passion, but it wasn't rude, either, and Evie took it as a good sign.

Now, draped in capes, Mabel and Evie sat in chairs at a beauty parlor on Fifty-seventh Street while a pair of beauticians washed and set their hair.

"How would you like an adventure?" Evie called over the rush of water in the sink.

"What sort of adventure?" Mabel shouted back.

"You trust me, don't you?"

"Ha!"

The conversation ceased for a moment as the beauticians patted their hair dry and led them to waiting chairs, getting to work setting Evie's finger waves and combing out Mabel's long mane.

"There are times when one friend requires the blind faith of another, darling girl. This is such a time," Evie said after a long pause. "Besides, when have I ever steered you wrong?"

"Would you like a list?"

"What if I told you this had to do with the Pentacle Killer murders and that we were about to undertake a necessary investigation?" The beautician's comb paused over Mabel's hair, and Evie gave the beautician a sidelong glance. "I'll bet *you'd* go with me, wouldn't you?"

"Absolutely positively! I'd bring a gun and shoot that horrible man with all six bullets. Then I'd stab him to be sure he was dead." The beautician shrugged and resumed combing. "You gotta be sure."

"And how," Evie said.

"Ow!" Mabel said as the comb hit a snag. Her hand flew to her injured scalp.

"Sorry, Miss. That is some head of hair. You ever think of cutting it?"

"Don't even try," Evie said with a sigh. "We've been at her for ages."

"Very well," Mabel said decisively. "I'll do it!"

Evie hugged Mabel. "Mabel, you've joined the twentieth century! Hip, hip, hooray!"

"Carpe diem!" Mabel declared.

The beautician shook her head. "Well, I don't know from nothing about those foreign movie stars, but you'd look swell with Clara Bow's haircut," she said and grabbed her scissors.

✳

The sun was a nice, fat ball as Mabel and Evie stepped off the train at 155th Street and walked north through streets of sprawling Tudor-style apartment houses and smaller brownstones, past the Old Wolf tavern and Johnson's Greengrocer, around a corner anchored by a realty office with flats to let, and on toward the river, where the houses were fewer. A couple of boys in dusty coveralls tossed a baseball back and forth, narrating their play as if it were a Yankees game: "It's Babe Ruth at the plate, the Great Bambino, the King of Swing hitting for the stands...." The boys nodded at the girls, and Evie made a swinging motion. "Clobber it like the Caliph of Clout!" she said. Finally, the girls turned onto Knowles' End, a forgotten side street that wound up a hill overlooking the Hudson. There the house sat on the windswept hill like a gargoyle.

"Please don't say that's where we're headed," Mabel gasped, winded. It had been a climb. "We're likely to be eaten by rats or meet Dr. Frankenstein's monster."

"Wouldn't that be a thrilling afternoon? At least you'll go out with the ritziest coif in town. Your hair is abso-tively the cat's pajamas! I am so happy you decided to bob it!"

Mabel refused to be charmed. "Evie. Why have you brought me here? What does this have to do with the murder investigation?"

"I believe this may be the lair of the Pentacle Killer."

Mabel stared, dumbfounded. "Theta was right to nickname you Evil. I believe you need the services of Sigmund Freud. He's the only person who could possibly understand the workings of your very unhealthy mind."

Evie linked her arm through Mabel's. "I'm going to tell you something confidential about the case. But you must swear on the King James Bible—"

"I'm an atheist."

"You must swear on the atheist Bible not to tell."

"There's no such thing as an atheist Bible."

"We should write one, then. Swear on the grave of the Sheik himself!"

"I swear on the grave of Valentino," Mabel said.

"I have it on good authority that there may be clues inside that house that will prove the identity of the killer." It wasn't lying, exactly.

"I thought the police already had the killer locked up—that Jacob Call fella." Mabel scrutinized Evie's face for a moment. "You don't think he's the Pentacle Killer."

"Call it a hunch."

"Oh, no," Mabel said. "No, no, no!"

"Please, Mabesie. I need to do this." She broke down and told Mabel everything she hadn't about the murder investigation— about holding Ruta's buckle, the whistling, Naughty John's connection to Knowles' End, and Memphis Campbell's strange, brief visit to the museum in which he said the house seemed lived in.

"Jeepers, Evie," Mabel said, shivering, and then she was thinking. Evie knew Mabel's thinking expressions; the old girl was coming up with a plan. "We are not heading in there without taking precautions." Mabel signaled for Evie to follow her as she marched down the hill and back to the boys tossing the baseball. "Do you know that old house on the hill?"

"Yes, Miss," they said.

"Does anyone live there? Have you seen anyone coming or going?"

"Don't nobody go in there. Not even for dares," one boy said emphatically.

Mabel looked at Evie as if to say *You see?*

"Well, we are going in. It's...a dare. For our sorority," Mabel informed them.

The other boy shook his head. "That's your funeral, Miss."

"How would you fellas like to make ten cents?"

The boys followed them to the corner, which was as far as their mothers would allow them to go, they said.

"If Miss O'Neill and I are not out in thirty minutes, bring the law," Mabel instructed.

"We don't get the law for nobody. They're as bad as the house."

"How about if we're not out in thirty minutes, you throw that baseball at the window as hard as you can, then run for your mothers. Can you do that?"

"It's our only baseball."

"Fifty cents," Evie said.

"For fifty cents? Miss, I'll throw like Babe Ruth."

"Spiffy!" Evie placed a quarter in each of their hands. "Now, we're trusting you to be on the square as a couple of regular fellas and keep watch. You are knights entrusted with a quest."

"Huh?"

"Just keep your peepers on that dive, and don't you dare breeze," Evie said. She made them spit and swear on it, and then, arm in arm, she and Mabel walked toward the looming ruin of Knowles' End.

The house had surely been a beauty in its day, with its grand turrets, the terrace, two small chimneys and one very fat one, and the arched windows. But now those windows were boarded over and the only two remaining shutters each hung by a nail, threatening to fall. The double oak doors had grayed with age. Metal scars marked the spot where a large knocker had been, but it was gone now—probably sold or stolen. The door was locked.

"There has to be a way in. Look around the side," Evie said. She tripped over something in the yard and saw that it was a child's doll. Its porcelain face was cracked and mold had settled along the scarlike seams.

At the back was a servants' entrance. Evie removed a hairpin and worked it into the simple lock, springing it. The door creaked open and they found themselves inside a butler's pantry with tall cabinets. It smelled of rot and dust. Weak bars of sunlight showed through the shutters' slats.

Evie drew a flashlight from her pocketbook and the beam showed cracked tin ceilings and dust motes.

"What the devil are you looking for in here, Evie?"

She wasn't sure, exactly. She needed something that would give her a read. "See if you can find an old pendant with a pentacle on the front."

"Pentacle, as in Pentacle Killer?" Mabel said warily.

"It's just a pendant," Evie lied. "Steady, old girl. Oh, my..."

Evie swept into what surely must have been a ballroom in its day. Some of the furniture had been draped in sheets, making it seem more like a graveyard than a home. Beside a large hearth was a velvet settee gone to mold, its stuffing piling onto the floor. Filthy yellow wallpaper hung from the walls in strips. In spots, it had worn away entirely, exposing the rotting beams underneath. Whatever had been of value had been removed from the home long ago. There were no books or silver or knickknacks, nothing to help Evie. Even the light fixtures were gone. A cobweb-strewn grand piano with a handful of keys missing anchored one corner. Evie plinked one and it rang shrilly in the dead space. A small black spider crawled out from between two keys and Evie yanked her hand away. On the far wall hung a cracked mirror. It reflected the room in a fractured tableau. For a moment, Evie thought she saw movement in one of the shards and jumped.

"What is it?" Mabel asked, and Evie realized it had only been her friend coming closer.

"Nothing." Evie took in the whole of the room. "Funny," she said.

"What is?"

"From the outside, I noticed a fat chimney, but this fireplace is very small."

"We don't have time to critique the architecture, Evie. Any minute, those boys are going to run for their mothers. If they haven't already run to the pharmacy for cream sodas. You had no business giving them the money before."

"Keep looking," Evie instructed.

"For what?" Mabel called.

I don't know. "I'm going upstairs."

Mabel raced to her side. "Evangeline Mary O'Neill! You're not leaving me for a moment! I'm sticking with you, just like George and Ira Gershwin."

"Oh, rhapsody. Then I'll never be blue," Evie quipped, though it felt odd to joke in such a tomb.

"Will you keep moving, please?"

A grand central staircase led to a second floor. Its elegantly carved newels were rotted through in spots. The stairs creaked and groaned with each step, and Evie hoped the staircase would bear their weight. She swept the flashlight across austere oil portraits silvery with spiderwebs. At the top was a long hallway branching off left and right with doors all the way down. Evie kept her eyes open for something to take, something that might give her a solid read, something personal.

"This way," Evie said, walking right. She rattled the knobs of several doors, but they were all locked shut. At the back of the house, they came to yet another staircase. This one was narrow and enclosed and led to an attic room whose dormer window had been boarded over. Small slices of sunlight bled through the cracks, but it wasn't enough to cut the gloom. Evie waved her flashlight around the room. Its beam landed on a four-poster bed draped in curtains. A bureau with a tri-fold mirror. A wardrobe. Carefully, Mabel opened the wardrobe's creaking doors. It was empty inside except for a few hats. The bureau held a tarnished hand mirror and brush.

Suddenly Mabel let out a bloodcurdling scream.

"What is it? What is it?" Evie said, heart pounding. Mabel was still squealing as she pointed to the bed, where Evie's flashlight beam caught the scuttling form of a rat as it scurried away, and Evie and Mabel nearly climbed up each other, screaming all the while.

"That is the last straw, Evie!" Mabel choked out. "Can we please go?"

"Very well," Evie said. She couldn't help feeling that she had failed. As she turned to leave, her foot caught and she stumbled into Mabel.

"Evie! Do you want to scare me to death?"

"Sorry, old girl." Evie turned the light beam on the floor. Part of a floorboard had rotted away, and underneath it, she could just make out something hidden. "Hold this steady," she said, handing Mabel the flashlight. With a grunt, she pried away the board.

"Tell me you aren't putting your hand in there," Mabel said.

"All right. I won't tell you." Evie bit down on her scream and inched her fingers under the rotted board into the dark space below, feeling very carefully for the object. When it was in her grasp, she yanked it free with a shout and shuddered all over. "Holy smokes! I never want to do that again."

Mabel crowded next to Evie. "What is it?"

Evie rubbed the layers of dust from the hosiery box and lifted the lid. Inside was a small leather book. While Mabel held the flashlight steady, Evie opened the book to a random page. At the top it was marked with a date: March 22, 1870. "'Tonight, Papa lies upon the dining table in his shroud, ready for burial. I am the last remaining Knowles. Oh, I am lost!'" Evie read aloud. "Ida Knowles' diary," she said in astonishment.

"Is that what you'd hoped for?"

"Better!"

"Swell. Let's beat it. This place gives me the heebie-jeebies."

They tore down the stairs as fast as they could without injuring themselves and Mabel headed toward the kitchen, where they'd come in. But Evie's attention was drawn to a door slowly creaking open at the far end of the corridor behind her. She hadn't noticed it before. What if it held some important clue?

"Evie! Let's go!" Mabel hissed, but Evie was already at the door.

Evie stepped inside and found herself in a small room. There was another door, oddly, in the center of the wall. She turned the knob on that door, and a trap in the floor gave way, sending her barreling down a laundry chute. Screaming, she pawed the smooth sides for something to grab, something to slow her descent. As she was shot out the other end, her coat caught on a sharp edge, suspending her. Carefully, she eased out of the coat, holding fast to it as she lowered herself. The coat ripped at the collar, dropping her the rest of the way. She landed on a dirt floor with an uncomfortable thump that rattled her bones. Nothing was broken, but her flashlight was gone, and her new gold brocade coat was now in tatters; a square of bright cloth stuck to the mouth of the laundry chute.

Evie struggled to her feet. She waited for her eyes to adjust to the gloom, the room beginning to take dim shape. An old furnace. A potting table covered in tools. Linens hanging from a line, gone stiff and dusty with neglect. One moved ever so slightly, and Evie could hear her blood pounding in her ears. There was no one there. But it had moved; she was certain of it. She put up a hand and felt the slightest of breezes. But from where? There were no windows in this dark tomb.

"Evie! Are you all right?" Mabel's panicked voice echoed dully down the laundry chute. "Evie!"

"Mabel, honey, you should see—there's the most darb speakeasy down here, and John Barrymore is fixing me a champagne cocktail," Evie joked to calm her nerves.

"Don't you dare tease me!"

"Everything's copacetic, Pie Face. Looking for the steps. Be up in a minute."

Mabel continued talking. It was what she did when she was nervous, but Evie was grateful for it as she stumbled around in the gloomy basement, her hand up and following the tiny breath of air.

"…can't believe you talked me into this…"

The breath of air led to a wall. That was impossible; air couldn't seep through a wall.

"…will never, ever follow you into the breach again, Evil O'Neill…"

It was so dark. Evie felt along the wall for a seam. In the stillness, she thought she heard whispers, a low, steady tone. Gooseflesh rose on her arms and shot up to her neck. Yes, whispers. Like the scratchings of wings. The drone of insects. The low growl of dogs. A thousand tongues whispering at once.

"Steady, old girl, steady," she said aloud to herself. It was what James had said when he helped her learn to navigate the icy pond on skates, his hands holding hers.

Now her hands shook, along with her breath. She heard a crunch as her foot came down on something hard. She bent to find the object and came up with the pieces of a rhinestone clasp. A shoe buckle. Just like the one missing from Ruta Badowski's shoe. Her mind reeled, and she felt dizzy. She dropped the buckle like an unclean thing. The whispers came again. It felt as if something were moving in the dark. The old furnace flared to life and Evie fell back from the suddenness of it; just as quickly, it died down again.

From above, she heard a loud *thump*, followed by Mabel's quick scream.

"Mabel! Mabel!" Evie cried.

"Those brats have thrown the baseball, after an eternity!" Mabel yelled down through the chute. "We'd better beat it before their mothers come and have us arrested for trespassing."

Evie stumbled across the basement searching for a way out and practically cried with joy when she found the staircase at last. She bolted quickly up the rickety basement stairs and banged on the door until Mabel came to let her out. Arm in arm, they barreled through the front door and into the reassuring sunshine, not bothering with the latch, and not stopping until they reached the subway platform and could see the train rattling down the tracks of the city's long metal spine.

※

Evie knew Will would have a fit when she told him of the day's exploits at Knowles' End, but she hoped he'd be swayed when she showed him Ida's diary, which she had managed to wrest away from Mabel with the promise that they would read it together after she'd shared it with Uncle Will. Now she settled herself at a table on the second floor of the museum library, beside a green banker's lamp, and read the few entries at the end.

September 7, 1874. Tonight was an evening of wonders! In the darkened parlor, my dear Mary communed with the spirits of my departed mother and father. We joined hands, and Mary and Mr. Hobbes spoke in strange tongues. There came a rapping sound and the candle flame flickered above its wax shroud and went out. We were pitched into darkness.

"Do not be afraid, dear pet," Mary said in a trance, and I knew at once it was my dear papa speaking to me through her. Oh, to hear his words to me from such a mysterious distance, the veil lifted for the most precious of moments, was a balm beyond any I have known!

"How do my lilacs fare?" Mother asked, as she had in life. Her darling lilacs! I could scarcely speak for the longing in my breast.

"Beautiful as ever," I replied, and though it was unseemly, I could not stop the flow of my tears.

Too brief was their sojourn on this plane, and I hope to try again as soon as possible.

October 3. Mr. Hobbes is a most peculiar man. He wears the oddest pendant, a round medallion upon which are imprinted a constellation of curious symbols. Mary says that it is a holy relic of a secret order. Sometimes I see him sitting in the cool of the library, studying an ancient text, which he claims the Good Lord directed him to find hidden in the knothole of a twinned oak. The book is a mystical text filled with keys to the next world, which cannot be shared with the uninitiated, he said with apology, and locked the book in the curio cabinet and pocketed the key. I found it rather brash that he would appropriate my curio cabinet so. But Mary tells me that Mr. Hobbes is a spiritual man unbothered by earthly concerns and proprieties, though he is kind enough to oversee, at his own expense, repairs to the house, which is a great comfort to me as I wish Knowles' End to be returned to its former glory.

October 28. Such a clamor! Mr. Hobbes's hammers disturb us night and day. I have moved to the old attic room to avoid the dust and unholy noise.

November 22. Mr. Hobbes would not allow me into my own cellar. When I took umbrage at this, he told me as kindly as possible that there had been a terrible misfortune in the cellar and the old furnace must be replaced, along with most everything else. He smiled as he said this, and I noted that his smile is never quite mirrored in his eyes, which are the coldest shade of blue.

January 15. I am not well and am confined to bed. Mary says I am overwrought by grief at speaking with my dear mother and father so often and by the assessor's continued letters for payment of taxes. I haven't the money. "Sell Knowles' End to me, my dear, and I shall pay the taxes and you will live on as before, with none the wiser that you are not the sole owner of the house. Your good standing need never be in question," Mary said to me. I cannot bear the anguish of selling Knowles' End, but how much worse to lose it to the auction block. I shall think on it. Mary offered me sweet wine and insisted I drink it all to soothe my nerves.

January 20. My sleep is disturbed by the most terrible dreams.

April 21. I found him in the dark of the parlor, naked. "Look on me and be amazed," he growled. And his eyes burned in the dark like twin fires. I remember nothing after but that I woke in my bed well after noon with a headache and Mary insisting that I did not need a physician, only to rest and let her care for me.

May. I know not what day it is, for the days run together as currents in a stream. They hold odd séances below. I can hear them, but I am too weak to go downstairs, and too afraid.

August. It is terribly hot. A foul stench permeates the house, turning my stomach. The boarder has gone, I know not where.

September 1. The beast skulks the halls of the house, frightening all within. The servants, the few remaining, fear him. He tells the most fantastical tales. Once, he claimed to be the last surviving member of a lost, chosen tribe, when I know he was poor as a church mouse, common as dirt, raised in an orphanage in Brooklyn. Every time it is a new tale, until it is impossible to know what is truth and what folly.

September 20. I will have no more of that woman's sweet wine.

September 28. The lack of wine has made me terribly ill. For a week, I have lain upon the bed, writhing and vomiting, attended by our last remaining servant, Emily, the dear girl. She has confessed that she is as frightened as I. It seems she chanced upon a locked room left unlocked and nearly plummeted to her death through a trapdoor and a chute that she surmises can only lead to the cellar.

October 3. I was awakened in the night by screams, but I could not tell where dreams left off and waking began.

October 8. Emily has not come for six days.

October 10. With effort, I roused myself from bed and went downstairs. The shutters were sealed and the house had the feel of a tomb. "Where is Emily?" I inquired of Mr. Hobbes, cool as you please though beneath my dressing gown my knees shook. "She has gone rather suddenly to be with her sister, who was in childbirth," the beast answered. "Strange that she did not mention it to me or collect her wages," I said. "She did not wish to trouble you with such petty concerns," he answered. "Then why has she gone without her purse?" I asked, for I had gone to her room first and found it there, untouched. Mrs. White materialized then at his side, drawn by the tone of my voice, no doubt. "We shall see that it is returned to her, the poor dear. So worried was she about her sister."

What woman leaves behind her purse?

October 13. Once again, I was stopped from entering the cellar by Mr. Hobbes. "It isn't safe," he said, and something in his tone, the cold blue of his gaze, had me scurrying back to my room.

October 15. I hear whispers in the very walls. Oh, some terrible calamity is surely at hand!

October 17. Mrs. White has gone to the country to perform her services as medium. The charlatan! I am alone in the house with him.

October 19. Today, when I saw Mr. Hobbes's carriage pulling from the garage and into the street, I hurried downstairs and, with a hairpin, worked at the lock of the *curio cabinet until I heard it give. Then I read his terrible book. Profane! Obscene! Filled with degradation and filth! It was all I could do not to pitch it into the stove. Oh, I am in danger! I have written to my dear cousin once more and told him as much. Why oh why did I consent to selling the house to that terrible woman? Trickery and deceit! Lies and more lies! I shall take it back. I am Ida Knowles, and this is my house, built by my father. But first, I mean to discover what is happening in the cellar. I must see it for myself.*

"What was happening in the cellar?" Evie said to herself.

Jericho stuck his head through the library's doors. He was breathless. "Evie, some help here? We've got a crowd."

"Coming," she said and put the diary aside.

PRELUDE

Memphis stepped out into a morning that had come up in a bad mood, gray and cold and wet. The night's rain had sent a shower of autumn leaves onto the walk, where they made a matted golden carpet. Octavia had asked Memphis to sweep them up before they left for church, and he did so, brushing them into a dustpan and dumping them into the garbage bin. A police sedan wailed up Broadway, followed by a second and a third. Memphis leaned over the gate, trying to see what was happening. He stopped a neighbor who was rushing past.

"What's going on?"

"Heard they found a body in Trinity Cemetery," the man said.

"There's lots of bodies in Trinity Cemetery. It's a graveyard," Memphis said dryly.

"They think it's the Pentacle Killer," the man said and hurried down the street to join the others. Memphis abandoned his broom and followed.

Outside the tall wrought-iron gates of Trinity Cemetery, a crowd had gathered, some folks still in robes, slippers, and head scarves. Mothers shooed their children back to the sidewalks and told them to stay there unless they wanted a good swat on the bottom. The police swarmed the gentle hills of the old cemetery, which had been the site of a great battle during the Revolutionary War and still sported a marker commemorating that fact. Memphis backed up and climbed a lamppost, trying to see better.

On the street, a cry went up. It was followed by gasps and more cries as word was passed from lips to ears, rippling over the people like a drowning wave. Memphis spied Floyd the barber and hopped down and ran to him.

"What is it, Floyd? What's going on?"

Floyd looked at him with doleful eyes and shook his head. "It's not good, Memphis."

Memphis felt as if he'd swallowed a piece of ice that was melting slowly through him. "Who is it?" he asked, but already his blood pounded in his ears, a prelude.

"It's Gabriel Johnson. They say the killer took his mouth and strung him up like a crucified angel."

DEATH NO LONGER HAS DOMINION

Memphis sat in a crowded pew of the Mother AME Zion Church between Aunt Octavia and Isaiah. Up front, Gabe's coffin gleamed under a blanket of lilies, donated by Mamie Smith herself. Every seat was filled, and a crowd of men stood three deep along the back wall. It was close in the room, and women kept themselves cool with wooden fans provided by the funeral home.

Pastor Brown took the pulpit and hung his head sorrowfully. "A young man, struck down in the prime of his life by an unspeakable violence. It's almost too much to bear...."

People cried and sniffled as Pastor Brown spoke about Memphis's dead friend, about his promising life ended too soon. Memphis swallowed hard thinking about how they'd fought the night he was killed. He wished he could go back, talk it over. He wished he could stop Gabe from leaving the party alone. If they'd left together, would he still be alive? He took out Gabe's lucky rabbit's foot. Mrs. Johnson had given it to him earlier, saying, "He'd want you to have it. You were like a brother to him." Memphis squeezed it tightly in his hand.

"Death no longer has dominion over Brother Johnson," Pastor Brown thundered.

"Amen," a woman called.

"For the Bible assures us, 'as Christ was raised up from the dead by the glory of the Father, even so we also should walk in newness of life. For if we have been planted together in the likeness of his death, certainly we shall be also in the likeness of his resurrection.' Thus sayeth the Lord."

"Hallelujah," several people shouted. And then, "The word of the Lord."

"Pray now for our brother, Gabriel Rolly Johnson, that he may be sheltered in the bosom of Jesus Christ and find everlasting peace. Amen."

"Amen," the congregants answered. The choir began to sing. "Wade in the water, wade in the water, wade in the water, the Lord's gonna trouble the water...."

The sorrowful notes of the familiar spiritual washed over Memphis, dragging him down into terrible depths like stones in his pockets. Aunt Octavia cried into a handkerchief, softly praying "Lord, Lord" under her tears. Every now and then she'd reach a gloved hand over and squeeze Memphis's hand to comfort him, but Memphis remained dry-eyed and numb. He looked down at Isaiah, who hadn't stopped staring at his shoes. He thought about what Isaiah had said to Gabe down at Mr. Reggie's: *You'll die.* Had Isaiah really seen something happening to Gabe? What if somebody had overheard them talking? What if somebody said something to the police? He had to protect Isaiah, no matter what.

After the service, the funeral procession made its slow, mournful passage down Broadway. The Elks Club had paid for the burial, and they'd insisted on a proper good-bye. They walked in front wearing their sashes, Papa Charles leading the way, his hat held to his chest. Behind him, several of Harlem's best musicians played a mournful dirge on their horns and a choir of women in black dresses sang. A flatbed truck carried Gabe's coffin through the streets to its temporary resting place at the Merrick Funeral Home. Later, his family would bury him. Reporters ranged along the sidewalks taking notes and pictures, reaching up in the nick of time to remove their hats as the casket passed by. Memphis walked behind the casket with slow, dutiful steps all the way to the funeral home. He hadn't been inside since his mother's death, and he couldn't face going in now.

"I'm just going to get some air," he explained to Octavia, who patted his cheek, called him poor child, and waved him on. Memphis slipped unnoticed into the throngs of people trying to get a glimpse of the Pentacle Killer's latest victim. Some were just curious onlookers. Some were angry and shouted at the line of police for answers. Hadn't they caught the killer? Wasn't he behind bars? What now? What were they doing to protect the citizens of New York? When would they feel safe again? The police remained silent.

At the corner, Memphis spied the girl from the museum. Weren't they supposed to be helping to catch this killer? Why hadn't *they* caught him yet? Memphis was overcome with anger, and he marched up to Evie O'Neill and tapped her on the shoulder. It took her a second to recognize him.

"It's you. Mr. Campbell."

"You know who the killer is yet?"

"Not yet."

Memphis nodded, his jaw tight.

"Did you...did you know the deceased?" she asked.

"He was my best friend."

"I'm so very sorry," she said, and Memphis thought she sounded sorry, too. Not like these reporters, who would say "sorry for your loss" and then follow with a question about whether your best friend was a dope fiend or ask whether you thought jazz music was to blame.

"Memphis!"

At the sound of Theta's voice, both Evie's and Memphis's heads turned. She was running down the street, her stage makeup still on, a coat thrown over her costume. Evie could see the sequins peeking out. Theta gave Evie a quick hug, then turned to Memphis.

"I came as soon as I heard," she said.

"You . . . you two know each other?" Evie asked.

"He's gone," Memphis said, his voice cracking on the last word. "Gabe's gone."

Theta spoke soft, soothing words to Memphis, and Evie felt odd standing by without saying anything at all.

"I'm so sorry about your friend," she offered, though it seemed hollow.

Memphis turned to her, his face gone hard. "I want to help you find Gabe's killer."

"There is something you can do," Evie began uncertainly. "It would help our investigation if we could have something of the deceased's . . . um, of Gabriel's. Preferably something he had with him the night of his death."

"How's that going to help?" Memphis challenged.

"Please," Evie pleaded. "Please trust me. We want to catch him as much as you do."

Memphis reached into his pocket and pulled out the rabbit's foot. "It was his good-luck charm. He was never without it."

"Thank you. I promise I'll take very good care of it," Evie said, but Memphis wasn't listening. Theta had slipped her hand in his, and they were looking at only each other. Evie walked away, leaving them to their private, silent conversation.

The press jammed against the barricades, calling for comments, trying to tease out quotes, while the cops stood firm, mouths shut. T. S. Woodhouse was front and center. Evie tried to sneak past.

"Well, if it isn't the Sheba," he said, blocking her escape. "We've got to stop meeting like this."

"So why don't you leave?"

"You aren't sore about that story, are ya?"

"And how! I asked for a favor and you repaid me by stealing my tip and printing it in the papers."

T. S. Woodhouse spread his arms in a conciliatory gesture. "I'm a reporter, Miss O'Neill. Let me make it up to you. Tell me what you've got on this and I'll do a whole feature on you. Maybe even give you some column inches to write up whatever you want. You'll be the most famous flapper in Manhattan."

"I'm sorry—I no longer talk to reporters."

She walked away and Woodhouse scurried to keep pace with her. "C'mon, Sheba. The bulls aren't giving us anything but the same wad of chewing gum. We know Jacob Call can't be the Pentacle Killer, unless he can off somebody from behind bars or he's got an accomplice. Say . . . accomplice. That's good."

"Good-bye, Mr. Woodhouse."

T. S. Woodhouse gripped Evie's arm, and she glared at him until he was forced to remove his hand. He jerked his head at the other reporters. "These fellas get the jump, I got no story for today. I've been showering daisies on your Uncle Will's museum. I'm trying to make a name for myself here, too. You understand?"

She did understand. She also understood that T. S. Woodhouse would do anything, say anything, step on anyone to get that story. It had been a mistake to get involved with him. And it was time for T. S. Woodhouse to get his comeuppance.

"Very well, Mr. Woodhouse," Evie said. "We believe the killer is working from an ancient mystical text, the *Ars Mysterium*."

"Yeah?" Woodhouse said, practically salivating at the tip. "That's good."

"Now, don't breathe a word of this to anyone, not even your publisher"—Evie bit her lip and made a show of craning her neck to be sure they weren't overheard—"but we believe the next killing will take place tonight, on Hell Gate Bridge. You'll want to be there with your cameraman."

"You on the level?"

"Would I lie to such an upstanding member of the press?"

T. S. Woodhouse was weighing his ambition against her story. She could tell by the twist of his mouth.

"Thanks, Sheba," he said at last.

"Don't mention it—and I do mean that, Mr. Woodhouse."

It had been a perfectly hideous day, but as she walked away from T. S. Woodhouse, Evie couldn't help but feel a stab of satisfaction at thinking of him later, freezing in the bitter wind on Hell Gate bridge, waiting for a story that would never happen, while all the other reporters got the jump on him.

THE SAME SONG

"Dammit!" Will stubbed his cigarette hard into the ashtray. The four of them—Evie, Jericho, Sam, and Will—sat at one of the library's long tables. Will had closed the museum early despite the crowds clamoring for tours of the supernatural led by Manhattan's foremost expert on the occult. "He's just going to keep killing, and we'll always be one step behind him."

"We don't have to be," Evie said. She held Will's gaze. "I can find out what we need to know."

"How would you do that?" Jericho asked.

"With this." Evie placed Gabe's rabbit's foot on the table.

Sam's eyebrows shot up. "You intend to catch a killer with a hunk of dead fur?"

"It belonged to Gabriel Johnson. It was on him the night he died." Evie looked at Will. "Unc, I can read it. I know I can. Just give me a chance."

"Read what?" Jericho asked.

Will glowered. "Where did you get that?"

"From a friend of his."

Will shook his head. "It's too dangerous, Evangeline."

Evie leaped up from her seat and pounded a fist on the table. She'd had it with Will's reluctance. They'd tried it his way, and all they had to show for it was another dead body. "It's too dangerous not to at least try!"

Jericho looked to Sam, who shrugged. "Don't look at me. I don't know from nothing," Sam said.

"There's a killer out there and we have to stop him, any way we can," Evie pleaded. "Please."

"This is madness," Will whispered. He raked a hand through his hair.

"Will somebody tell me what's going on?" Jericho said.

"I'm a Diviner," Evie said.

"Evangeline!"

"They might as well know, Unc! I'm tired of keeping it a secret." She turned back to Jericho and Sam. "I can read objects. A ring, a letter opener, a glove—they're more than just things to me. Give me your watch and I might be able to tell you what you had for dinner...or I could tell you your deepest secrets. It just depends." She looked to Will again. "What do you say, Unc?"

His hands behind his back, Will walked a full lap of the library. He stopped beside Evie, looking at her for an uncomfortably long time. "We will do this in a controlled manner. Do you understand?"

"Anything you say, Unc."

"I will guide you. Do not go too far under, Evangeline. You are to remain detached. A spectator."

"I'll see what I can find and let go."

"If you feel the least bit threatened, you are to drop it immediately."

"I'm on the trolley, Unc."

"I'm glad somebody is," Sam said, shaking his head.

"It will become evident in just a moment," Will answered. "Evie, come have a seat."

Evie settled into a leather club chair.

"Comfortable?" Will asked.

"Yes." Her heart beat quickly and her mouth was dry. She hoped she was ready for this.

"Remember, if you feel at all frightened..."

"I *understand*, Will," Evie assured him.

"Will, is this safe?" Jericho asked.

"I'll keep her safe," Will assured him. "You may begin whenever you're ready, Evie."

Will placed the rabbit's foot in her waiting hands. Evie closed her eyes and felt along the seams of it, waiting. *Come on*, she thought. *Please*... It took a few seconds for the connection, but once it was made, pictures of Gabe's day came at her in a dizzying jumble. It was like Evie had plunged into a cold lake and was splashing her way up to the surface. "I can't...I can't make them out...."

"Slow down. Take your time. Breathe and concentrate," Will instructed.

Evie's breathing slowed. She could hear that and the gentle coursing of her blood. The earlier, inconsequential scenes of Gabriel's day were gone. She was with him on the night-gloomy streets of Harlem. The scene had a haze to it, like a photograph not fully developed, but she could make out Gabriel walking under the El tracks, and she could feel what he felt.

"He's angry about something...." Evie said haltingly.

"Not too close," Will warned.

Evie took another deep breath. The street became a little less hazy as she concentrated. The flicker of distant neon, even the smell of smoke and garbage began to come alive in her mind. She heard the tread of footsteps, a strange hollow clicking.

"Someone's following him."

"Careful, Evie."

"It's gotten very foggy all of a sudden, but there's someone there." She saw the walking stick first, a silver thing with the head of a wolf. The man carrying it was still shrouded in shadow and mist. Gabe called out, and, hearing nothing, kept walking under the great shadow of the elevated tracks. Evie could only see what he saw. But she could hear the slow, deliberate footsteps on the street. She felt Gabe's first stab of apprehension. And then she heard the whistling.

Evie gasped. "It's the same song!"

"Evie, time to stop," Will instructed, but Evie wasn't about to stop yet. She was close. So very close.

Footsteps. Close. *One, two, click. One, two, click.* The stick glinted in the mist. "It's him. He's coming. . . ."

"Evie. Stop," Will commanded.

Evie clutched the rabbit's foot tightly. The man stepped from the shadows and Evie's pulse accelerated. "I see him!"

"Evie, stop!" Will thundered. He clapped loudly several times and the trance was broken. Evie dropped the charm and blinked, her eyes watering.

"I know him! I've seen him before!" Evie said.

She ran to their vast collection of notes and files, pushing aside papers until she found what she was after. Her stomach was fluttery with excitement and incomprehension. "It's him," she said, slapping the newspaper photograph of John Hobbes onto the table. "The man under the bridge was John Hobbes. Gabriel Johnson was murdered by a dead man."

JUST STORIES

Will stared into the fire. His jaw was clenched.

"How is that possible, Uncle Will? How is it possible that a man who's been dead for fifty years killed these people?"

"You saw somebody who looked like him, doll. That's all," Sam said.

"I know what I saw!"

"I'm telling you—it's the power of suggestion. We've been all over the legend of John Hobbes. You'd seen his mug in the papers, so that was already in your mind when you went under. You supplied the killer with the first face that came to mind."

"Will you stop staring at me, please!" Evie said to Jericho, who looked away quickly, blushing. The tiny claws of a new headache raked across Evie's skull. "Unc, you haven't answered my question. How could John Hobbes have killed Gabriel Johnson, and possibly all those others?"

Sam put an arm around Evie's shoulder. "I'm telling you, baby vamp, it wasn't him."

"It's him," Will said, breaking his silence at last.

The room was quiet except for the crackling of the wood as it was consumed by fire.

"Will," Jericho said after a moment, "you're not honestly saying that you believe a ghost is killing these people, are you?"

"Yes," Will said, his voice hoarse.

"I mean no insult, Professor—you've got a swell museum going here—but there are no such things as ghosts," Sam said.

"Sure of that, are you?" Will turned to them. The firelight cast his face in shadows. "There are doorways between this world and the world of the supernatural. Ghosts. Demonic entities. The unexplained and undefined. The mysterious. I've whole books and archives dedicated to it."

"But those are just stories people tell," Evie said. The headache was spreading out behind her eyes.

"There is no greater power on this earth than story." Will paced the length of the room. "People think boundaries and borders build nations. Nonsense—words do. Beliefs, declarations, constitutions—words. Stories. Myths. Lies. Promises. History." Will grabbed the sheaf of newspaper clippings he kept in a stack on his desk. "This, and these"—he gestured to the library's teeming shelves—"they're a testament to the country's rich supernatural history."

"But, Will, you're not just saying ghosts exist; you're saying they can come back from the dead and kill," Jericho said.

Will sank into his chair, but his foot tapped steadily against the floor. "I know. Impossible. They shouldn't be able to...." he said more to himself than to anyone else. "I've been keeping watch."

"Keeping watch over what?" Jericho asked.

The chair couldn't contain him, and Will was again up and pacing. He swiped another handful of newspaper clippings from his desk on the way. "These. Ghost sightings. Supernatural activity. In the past year, it has escalated. Instead of a few reports here and there, there have been hundreds, something reported every day."

"And you think it's related to our case, that Naughty John has come back from the dead?" Evie sneaked a hand up to rub at her temple.

"I'm sure of it," Will said. "The question is not whether John Hobbes has come back from the dead, but how and why."

"Ghosts exist. Ghosts are real," Evie whispered like a mantra. She looked up and saw Jericho staring at her. "What is it?"

"Nothing," Jericho said, again looking away quickly.

Will gave in and reached for a cigarette. He took several puffs before speaking again. "The parts of the body," he said, blowing out a stream of smoke. "I think he needs to ingest them to become stronger. More corporeal. Spirit made flesh. A perversion of transubstantiation. He's getting stronger with each killing. He's very strong now. Soon, he'll be unstoppable."

Evie shuddered just thinking about it. "And then?"

"Armageddon. Literal hell on earth."

"But he can't really become some anti-Christ, can he?" Jericho asked.

"He believes he can become the Beast through this ritual. Belief is everything. And we don't understand everything about what he can do. These are not the rules of our world we're playing by here, Jericho. They're *his* rules—the rules of the supernatural world."

"So how do we stop him?" Evie asked. "How do we stop a ghost?"

"We have to meet him where he is. We have to dispatch him via his own beliefs. If the last page of the Book of the Brethren contained some sort of spell or incantation for getting rid of John

Hobbes, we need to know what was on that page. And we must solve the mystery of his connection to this book. Why does it matter to him?"

Evie opened the Book of the Brethren, running her hand along the rough seam where the last page had been torn away. There were three offerings remaining: the Destruction of the Golden Idol, the Lamentation of the Widow, and the Marriage of the Beast and the Woman Clothed in the Sun. She flipped back to the previous offerings.

"The dead body found at Belmont in 1875—that had to be the third offering, the Pale Horseman Riding Death Before the Stars," Evie said.

"And besides Ida Knowles, they found exactly ten bodies in the basement of Knowles' End," Jericho said.

"The ten servants of the master," Evie said excitedly. "A laundress and a maid went missing, as did people who boarded there. They could all be considered servants. The second offering. Oh, Unc. It fits!"

"So who was the first offering?" Sam asked. He put up his hands. "I'm just playing along here. I don't go for ghosts."

Evie stared at the picture of what looked like a house or barn. "The first offering—the Sacrifice of the Faithful. Ida Knowles was faithful. For a while, at least."

"But she wasn't first," Jericho said.

"True," Evie said on a sigh.

Uncle Will reached for another cigarette. "I don't like that you went to Knowles' End, Evie. Not with what we know now."

"But it's just a house, Unc."

"An awful, awful house filled with dead bodies once upon a time," Sam said cheerily. "I'm sure it's swell at Christmastime."

"It's *his* house," Will said. "It's his lair, and I imagine he wouldn't take too kindly to trespassers. Evie, you and Mabel didn't leave anything behind, did you?"

Evie thought of the small patch of cloth stuck on the laundry chute. It was so small—too small to be of note. Wasn't it? "No, Unc."

"Why not just go there and burn it to the ground?" Sam asked.

"Because we don't quite know what sort of entity we're dealing with," Will explained. "What if that only made him stronger? No. Until we've satisfied the question of why Naughty John is enacting this ritual, why it matters to him, and we've found what was on that missing page, our only hope is to prevent him from killing again. We know he has to complete the murders by the time of Solomon's Comet—"

"Which is in four days," Jericho reminded everyone.

"If we can stop him from finishing his task on time, he'll lose by default. The timing is key."

Sam played a coin across the tops of his right knuckles, flipped it, and neatly caught it in his left hand. "You planning to tell Detective Malloy you're hunting the ghost of a killer who hung fifty years ago? I don't care how good of a pal he is to you, Professor—he'll lock us all up in the loony bin."

"Sam's right," Jericho said.

Will nodded. "Agreed. We can't let Terrence know. We're on our own. Evie, what's the next offering?"

Evie turned to the correct page. "The Destruction of the Golden Idol. 'And lo, they did not believe but were seduced by the golden calf. They paid tribute to false idols and were damned for it. And the ninth offering sprang from lust and sin. The golden calf was destroyed, stripped of its skin of shame, and placed upon the altar of the Lord. And the Beast was pleased.'" Evie looked up to see that Jericho was still staring at her in that uncomfortable way.

"For crying out loud, Jericho, what is it? Have I grown a second head?"

"Sorry. It's just that . . . you're not what I thought." He hadn't meant to say it like that.

Evie was tired and scared and her headache had really taken hold. And now Jericho thought she was a freak. He was afraid of her. She thought somehow it would be different with Jericho. He was a deep thinker, a philosopher, but he was no different from the small minds of her small town. Angrily, she grabbed his cold hand and clamped her own over his watch.

"That's right, I'm a real sideshow act," she said. He tried to pull away, but she dug her fingers under the watch. "How's about it, Jericho? Would you like me to tell you your secrets? All the little lies you keep hidden from the world?"

"No!" Jericho jerked his hand away from Evie's so quickly that he nearly lost his balance.

Tears stung at the corners of Evie's eyes and a lump rose in her throat. She wasn't about to cry here, and so she ran from the library and shut herself in the bathroom.

"Nice work, Frederick," Sam grumbled and went after her.

Sam sat on the floor outside the bathroom door, hoping Evie could hear him. "Doll, I don't care if you can read every secret I've got. I don't even care if you keep me sitting outside this john all night. Well, my legs would care, but don't mind them—they like to complain."

Evie didn't respond, and Sam blew out a gust of trapped air. He'd never met anyone else with a strange gift. Never. So there were two of them. A pair. A pair was good.

"There's nothing wrong with you. I just want you to know that."

Silence.

"Take your time, doll. You know where to find me. I'll keep your seat warm."

In the bathroom, Evie leaned her head against the door. "Thank you," she whispered, though Sam was no longer there to hear it.

※

The stranger stood in the dark of the basement, listening as the house whispered to him. He could tell something wasn't right. The house felt violated. Unclean. He would have to repaint the symbols to restore it to its purity. *Anoint thy flesh and prepare ye the walls of your houses.* The sacred covenant kept.

Naughty John plucked the scrap of Evie's coat from the edge of the laundry chute. Again, the house whispered to him. A girl. A girl had done this violation. She would pay for her transgression. But first, the house must be prepared in time for tomorrow's offering.

Whistling the old tune, he felt for the secret door. It opened for him, and he was welcomed inside with sighs and whispers.

THE NINTH OFFERING

When Detective Malloy came to call the following afternoon, he didn't look happy. He gestured to the crowds of visitors. "Business is good, I see."

"We've gone from forgotten to fad in a few weeks," Will said. Two giggling college girls asked for Will's autograph and he politely declined, much to their disappointment.

Detective Malloy watched the exchange. "That's the trouble."

"What do you mean?" Evie asked. She'd never seen the detective quite so businesslike. He was uncomfortable—that much was evident. But she had no idea why. After all, shouldn't he be pleased that his old friend's museum was finally in the black?

The detective lowered his voice. "Will, there's talk that you might be involved in the killings."

Will's eyes widened. "What?"

"That's bunk!" Evie protested.

"I know. But it doesn't look good—the fella who knows everything about the occult, who gave us the tip on Jacob Call, whose museum is now the hottest ticket in town, getting written up in all the papers—"

"I had nothing to do with those newspaper articles, I can assure you," Will snapped, and Evie hoped no one could see her blush.

"I'm just saying, you might want to stay out of it. Leave it to the police."

"But we're so close," Evie said. "We're going to find him." She wished they could tell Detective Malloy what they were really up against, but of course that was impossible. How could they confess that they were looking for a ghost? He'd lock them up forever.

"Will, I'm telling you, as a friend, you're off the case. Go back to teaching. I'll handle it from here."

Uncle Will squared his shoulders. "What if I say no?"

"Then you're on your own. I can't protect you." Detective Malloy put his hat back on. "Fitz, don't do anything dumb. Know when to quit."

"Are we going to quit?" Evie asked after the detective had gone.

"Not on your life."

By evening, Evie, Jericho, Sam, and Will were once again crowded around the table in the library.

"The ninth offering, the Destruction of the Golden Idol," Evie said. She swore under her breath. "He's out there ready to kill again, and we don't have any idea where he's going."

She buried her head in her hands.

"Don't let your frustration get the better of you, Evangeline. Think. Golden idols…" Will flicked the wheel on his silver lighter, creating sparks and squelching them with his thumb.

"Gold. Money, greed—Wall Street, a banker or a broker?" Jericho said.

"The Golden Palace in Chinatown?" Sam threw out. Evie could hear the exhaustion in his voice.

"In the Bible, it's a golden calf. But we can't be sure the offering is biblical in reference. The Book of the Brethren is a pastiche, remember?" Will said.

"We'll probably be here all night," Evie said, sighing.

"I don't think we have all night," Jericho said.

"None of you has eaten," Will said suddenly, and Evie knew he must be hungry himself or he'd never have said anything. "I'm going to Wolf's Delicatessen on Broadway for some pastrami sandwiches. Keep working. I won't be gone long."

"Let me see that," Evie said as Will left, taking the Bible from Jericho. They hadn't spoken more than a few words since he'd discovered she was a Diviner. She was still smarting from his comment. Evie read the Bible passage again and again, searching for some clue, but it wasn't coming.

"Worshipping false idols. Worshipping false idols..." Something was trying to take shape in her mind. "What's the name—" She broke off mid-thought, flipping wildly through the Bible. She put her finger on a passage. "Ba'al," she said suddenly. "The worship of Ba'al. Oh, god..."

"What is it, doll?" Sam asked.

"I know where he'll strike next," Evie said, already grabbing for her coat and hat.

"Where are we headed?"

"The Globe Theatre!" Evie yelled.

"What's at the Globe?" Jericho asked.

"The Ziegfeld revue," Sam said and ran after Evie.

LITTLE BETTY SUE BOWERS

Theta sat at her dressing room mirror, cold creaming the last of her makeup. The mirrors were hung with scarves and boas. The wardrobe mistress had already put away the rapidly discarded costumes as the girls hurried to meet their stage-door Johnnies and stockbroker boyfriends. Except for her, the theater was empty. Theta had always liked the feel of an empty theater.

Theta was six when she made her debut in the Peoria, Illinois, musical emporium as Little Betty Sue Bowers in a pinafore dress of red, white, and blue, and silver tap shoes that sparkled under the lights. She sang and danced to "God Bless America" while her overbearing foster mother stood in the wings, mouthing every word. The audience was charmed. "The Ringleted Rascal," they called her, and "Betty Baby Doll." Soon she was playing the Orpheum Circuit throughout the Midwest. Theta hated vaudeville, hated the hours of work, the drafty backstage rooms, the leering "uncles" who invited her to sit on their laps. Crisscrossing the country, all those little towns and their dying music halls. Every night Mrs. Bowers would set her hair on rollers and smack

Theta on the rear with the hairbrush, saying, "Don't you ruin it." Theta had been too terrified to sleep, afraid she'd muss those curls and get another, much harder smack come morning. She'd never been to school. Never had a birthday party or a real friend.

By the time Theta was fourteen, it was clear she was no longer the Ringleted Rascal. She was developing a woman's body and face, with long, shapely legs and a pout of a mouth. She was too old to play the adorable little girl and too young to play the more risqué acts. Theta was on her way to being unemployable. They'd just signed on for a monthlong run at the Palace in Kansas City when Theta met a handsome soda jerk named Roy. She eloped with him two weeks later. That had proven to be an even bigger mistake than staying with Mrs. Bowers. At first, Roy had made her feel protected. But Roy soon became obsessed with her—what she wore, where she went, whom she saw. Once, he'd even locked her in the bathroom all night while he went out with his boys. Theta had picked the lock and crawled out of a second-story window to get away. Roy hadn't liked that. He hadn't liked that at all.

The next morning, with her eye swollen and bruised and her lip split open, she'd tried going home. She stood on the front porch of the boardinghouse with her small plaid felt suitcase. Her tears stung her raw mouth. "Please, Mama. I'm sorry," she'd pleaded.

"You made your bed, you lie in it, Betty Sue," Mrs. Bowers had said and shut the door.

Theta had tried to be what she thought a good wife should be, but every little thing seemed to set Roy off: Her stockings were crooked. The toast was too brown. Her long hair, thick as broom bristles, wasn't put up like a proper lady's, making her look "like some kinda Indian squaw!" The house wasn't tidy enough. If she didn't get a good cut of meat from the butcher, she was a terrible house-keeper. If she did get a good steak, well, then she must have been flirting. The sting of the hairbrush was nothing compared to the smack of Roy's hand. Nights were the worst. She would grit her teeth and stare at the ceiling, waiting for it to be over. Once, she tried to get a part in a sketch at the Palace, but Roy forbade it, and anyway, pictures were the new fashion. The vaudeville theaters and music halls were being refitted as grand movie palaces. The days of vaudeville were coming to an end. Sometimes, when Roy was away at work and the heat from the diner below would rise up through the linoleum, baking the apartment in an afternoon haze, Theta would strip down to her slip, roll back the carpets, and dance to the radio, imagining she was Josephine Baker at the Folies Bergère in Paris. In these fantasies, it was not the imagined love and adulation of the audience, the collective desire, that fueled her. Rather, it was the sense of absolute freedom, of dancing because she could, dancing because she enjoyed the dancing and not because she was expected to do it.

"*Why you gotta be such a mean old Daddy?*" she'd sing along in her husky voice, the fingers of one hand splayed across the slim curve of her belly. With the other, she'd reach higher and higher, as if she might, at any moment, pluck a star from the heavens or punch a hole in the sky and make her escape. It was during one of those sultry, stifling afternoons on the prairie that Theta lost herself to this smallest of escapes, singing along to the radio ("*Love me sweet, honey, like you ought to do*") and reveling in the gyrations of her body so completely—*her* limbs, *her* hips, *hers, hers, hers* only—that she didn't hear Roy's key in the lock.

"Well, well, ain't this a picture?" he growled, and she turned with a gasp to see him taking up the whole of the doorway, chest bowed slightly forward, muscular forearms pressed against the doorjamb like a sinewy slingshot waiting to snap. "This how you spend your time while I'm off working?"

He'd come home drunk and mean. Her mind whirred with preparations, the many small ingratiations, the hopeful peace offerings and distractions from his anger she'd need to have at the ready in order to avoid a beating.

"You want me to get you some dinner, Roy? You just sit and relax and I'll make you a sandwich," she said, hoping the desperation didn't show in her voice.

"A sandwich? That your idea of a home-cooked meal?" Roy shouted.

She'd chosen poorly. It wouldn't matter if she cried out or screamed. She'd done that plenty of times. No one had come to see about it. Shades were drawn and windows closed against her misery. That was the way of the town. She'd learned to bear it in silence. It made the beatings shorter, she'd discovered. His hand had threaded through her hair, as a lover's might, but there was nothing loving in the hard yank that made her eyes water, that bent her neck toward him, crooked her body so that she could only follow like a dog at its master's heel. The first slap was a warning. Her cheek stung with it.

"You want to dance? Huh?" *Slap.* "I like dancing." *Slap.* "Let's dance, then. I want to dance with my girl."

He'd pushed her onto the bed and pinned her arms above her head with one huge hand. She suppressed a cry when she felt him rip away the flimsy protection of her underwear, and again when that same hand rained down blows till her lips bled and her ear rang. Then his thighs were parting hers roughly, and she could only swallow her fear down with the metallic taste of her blood.

Her panic stoked some strange new feeling inside her, something she couldn't control. She remembered her hands growing warmer and warmer, her body getting hot. She remembered the expression on Roy's face: the whites of his eyes getting bigger, his mouth hanging open in surprise just before the scream was torn from him.

Theta shut her eyes tightly. Her mind always went blank after that part, like a motion picture with a reel missing. All she remembered was the train to another train and then New York City, where she'd arrived dirty, broke, and half-starved, then survived by sleeping on a series of park benches, taking refuge in the ladies' room at Grand Central Terminal, and stealing into the picture houses to sleep all day, leaving only when she was chased out. Stealing milk bottles delivered to stoops in the anonymous night. Narrowly avoiding the rough men eyeing her from alleys and slow-moving motorcars. She might have gone on that way far longer if she hadn't seen Henry sitting at a table near the front windows of the Horn & Hardart Automat on Sixth Avenue, scribbling away on thin white paper, uninterested in his food. Theta was close to fainting with hunger. She'd ventured inside and was hovering near his table, hoping to steal his scraps, when, without a word, Henry pushed the other half of his sandwich toward her. She hesitated at first—Theta had street smarts, and street smarts said don't take anything from a stranger. But this sort of hunger was an animal that could eat you up from inside. The hunger beast won out, and she ate so fast she nearly vomited the sandwich back up. Still silent, Henry walked to the gleaming, lighted machines, plunked in two nickels, waited for the tray to revolve, opened the small glass door, and retrieved first a square of rice pudding and then a carton of milk. These he brought back to the crumb-strewn lacquer table, placing them before Theta and then watching her spoon the pudding into her mouth with machinelike precision and wash it down with four quick swallows of milk, not caring when it dribbled down her chin in two white streams. Afterward, she sat, glassy-eyed, in an almost drugged stupor, feeling both full and sick.

"How do you do? I'm Henry Bartholomew DuBois IV," Henry had said in a slow taffy pull of syllables, extending a hand. He had the longest, most elegant fingers Theta had ever seen. Everything about him was fair: His thick, dun-colored hair, kept long. The soft brows and heavy fringe of pale lashes that made the heavy-lidded gaze of his narrow hazel eyes seem permanently sleepy. Faint constellations of freckles on his arms, cheeks, and nose, which only showed themselves in sunlight. Even his mouth, set in a perpetual smirk of amusement, was only a shade darker than his skin. You might look past him completely, except for his eccentric style of dress: a pair of tweed trousers held up by suspenders splayed across a stiff white tuxedo shirt worn under an open vest, and a jaunty straw boater hat with a red-and-blue striped ribbon around it perched on his head at an angle that hinted at mischief—or at least impertinence.

"Betty," she'd managed to say, giving his fingers a quick shake.

Henry tilted his chin and looked down at her, appraising. "That's an awfully dull name for such an interesting girl."

She struggled to keep her eyes open.

"Do you need a place to stay?" Henry had asked quietly.

Theta's eyes snapped open. She palmed the knife. "Try anything funny, fella, and you'll be sorry."

"Well, after everything, I would hate to meet my end with a simple butter knife," Henry said as if he might be saying hello. "I can assure you, Betty, I'm a gentleman, and a man of my word."

Theta was so tired. It was as if the hunger had been the plug holding back her emotions. Now it had been removed, and she sat weeping softly in her seat.

"It's copacetic, darlin'. Come on." Henry told her later that he'd never seen anyone so beautiful cry so ugly.

Theta followed Henry home to his one-room apartment with the leaky roof on St. Mark's Place, where he offered her a pillow and a blanket. While she cradled them both to her middle, still distrustful, he dragged an old cane chair to a battered piano beside an airshaft window. He hummed softly and made notes on those same sheets of paper filled with scratchings and blots of ink. "You're welcome to stay," he said without looking up. "There's no cleaning lady. The pipes leak. The bathroom down the hall is shared with ten very eccentric neighbors. It's cold in the winter and hot as the devil in summer. All in all, it's not much better than the street. But you're welcome all the same."

She figured he'd want something in exchange, but he never tried a thing. Theta slept through the night and well into the next day. When she woke, she found a doughnut on a chipped plate, and beside that, a wobbly daisy stuck into an empty milk bottle, which propped up a note:

Hope you slept well. I'd ask you not to steal anything, but there's nothing to steal. You're welcome to stay as long as you like.
Sincerely, Henry DuBois IV

She had nowhere else to go, so she ate the doughnut and washed the plate. Then she washed the other dishes and put them away. Henry came home to a room so clean he had to leave and come back in to be sure he'd entered the right apartment. "Your name wouldn't happen to be Snow White, would it?" he asked wryly. They shared a bowl of noodles from a shop downstairs and talked until very late.

It was Henry who had convinced her to bob her hair. Arm in arm, they'd walked to the barbershop on Bleecker Street, Theta dressed in Henry's clothes. She sat perfectly still, eyes forward, as the shears bit through her thick ringlets. Hair fell in feathery piles around the barber's chair. Theta felt her head growing lighter, as if she were being shorn of the weight of memory, the ghosts of her past. When the barber swiveled the chair around so she faced the mirror, Theta's mouth opened in an astonished O. Gently, she petted the smooth skin of her neck, reveling in the shock of stubble high up her nape, where her shingle cut formed a provocative V. In the mirror, she caught sight of Henry biting his lip.

"What are you gawking at, Piano Man? You never seen a flapper before?" she said with a wink.

"You are the most beautiful girl on this street," Henry said, and Theta waited for him to kiss her. When he didn't, she felt a strange mix of disappointment and relief.

They'd celebrated with champagne at a bohemian nightclub in Greenwich Village off MacDougal Street where, away from judging eyes, beautiful boys danced elegantly together, chest to chest, holding one another up, exchanging longing looks across tables decorated with decorative men. Theta had heard that such places existed, and she'd known men who favored other men—"sissies," Mrs. Bowers called them with a sneer, and Theta could feel the shame of the word coil around her heart—but she'd never actually been to such a nightclub. She was afraid she wouldn't be welcome there, but she found that she was.

In the dark of the club, Henry leaned back in his chair and watched the scene, his gaze coming to rest again and again on a handsome, dark-haired young man who looked back shyly from time to time. In that moment, Theta understood at last. "I'm on the trolley, kiddo," she'd said. Then, with a performer's flair, she'd sauntered over to the dark-haired young man, pulled up a chair, and said, "My pal, Henry, is going to be the next George Gershwin. You should ask him to dance before he gets rich and famous."

Much later, they all sat in a heap on a velvet sofa, Theta on one side of Henry, the handsome boy on the other, along with two boys from a college in New Jersey and a sailor originally from Kentucky, laughing and drinking, singing songs and trying on one another's ties. They tried to come up with a new name for Theta, who, Henry announced, simply was not a Betty. They'd run through all sorts of names, from the glamorous—Gloria, Hedwig, Natalia, Carlotta—to the silly—Mah Jong, Merry Christmas, Ruby Valentino, Mary Pickaxe.

"Maybe you could be Sigma Chi!" one of the college boys said, breaking them up all over again.

"That's terrible," Henry drawled between laughs. His cheeks had the slightest flush. It made him look like a debauched altar boy.

"Alpha Beta! Delta Upsilon! Phi Beta Kappa! Delta Theta!"

"Wait—what was that last one?" Theta had asked.

"Theta," the college boy said, and his companions all repeated it. They were loud with a contagious drunken happiness.

"Theta," she'd said, liking the feel of it on her tongue. "Theta it is."

She insisted on Knight for her last name. It made her feel strong and bold. A name of armor. For she would defend herself in this new life.

"To Miss Theta Knight," the boys toasted, and Theta drank to her new name. Laughing, they'd danced in a circle under a chandelier that bathed them in dappled light, and she'd hoped the night would never end.

A week later, Theta woke Henry so early that the daylight was no more than a blue-tinged thought bleaching them both of color. Her eyes were puffy and red, her cheeks stained with tears. It had been two months since she'd left Kansas and Roy, since he'd hurt her for the last time.

Henry pushed himself up onto his elbows. His voice was thick with sleep. "What's the matter, darlin'?"

She told him what had happened back in Kansas, managing not to sob until toward the end. She'd been so light these past few weeks, as if she'd been rescued from the drowning current of a rain-sodden river and had warmed herself on the bank under a hot sun, only to wake later and find that the river had risen in the night, pulling her back out and under.

Henry had listened soberly. When she'd finished, he'd scooped her close and held her against his bare, smooth chest. "I'll marry you, if you want," he'd said.

She kissed his palms and brought them to her face. "I can't have this baby, Hen."

Henry nodded slowly. "I know somebody who might be able to help us out."

He'd said it like that—*us*. And Theta knew then that they'd never part, that they'd always be like this, two halves of the same whole, the best of friends.

They had the name of a man, and an address, written on a scrap of paper hidden tightly in Theta's palm. It was raining as they threaded their way down an alley and into a shabby building where two men paced and smoked, looking scared, and then made the heavy climb up five crumbling flights of stairs, past closed doors behind which children squalled and were shushed. The odor of cooking fish wafted down a long, dark hallway, turning Theta's stomach, and she had to will herself not to vomit, and then finally they reached the top floor and knocked at the plain brown door of an apartment that smelled strongly of Lysol. A wiry man with a lined face ushered them into a dirty sitting area with three mismatched chairs. Off to the right was a bathtub half-filled with bloody water and a collection of carving knives. Behind a drape, a woman moaned. Theta gripped Henry's hand so tightly she thought she'd break it off. The wiry man pointed to a cot with a sheet and told her to undress and lie down. The woman cried out again, and Theta bolted down the winding stairs and out into the soggy alley, not caring that she was getting soaked.

"It's okay," Henry said when he caught up. He was out of breath. "We'll find the money."

Henry sold his piano and they found another doctor, expensive but clean. After it was done, Theta lay on Henry's bed, cramping and groggy with ether, promising she'd get him a new piano if it was the last thing she did. Henry squeezed her hand and she drifted into sleep. Two weeks later she'd gotten the job in the chorus at the Follies. She'd had to lie about her name, her history, and her age, but everyone did. It was what she loved about the city—you could be anybody you wanted to be. When their rehearsal accompanist left to play for a nightclub uptown, she suggested they hire Henry. With the extra money, they'd rented a bigger apartment in the Bennington, posing as brother and sister, which was laughable, really, their appearances being as different as their souls were alike. And every week, Theta put a dollar in an old coffee can marked HENRY'S PIANO FUND.

She'd thought it would just go on like that forever, Theta and Henry, neither belonging to anyone but themselves and each other. But she hadn't counted on meeting Memphis. It wasn't just that they dreamed of the same strange symbol, which was certainly big enough. No, it was Memphis himself. He was kind and strong and handsome. Being with him filled her with a lightness and hope, even though the idea of their being together seemed completely hopeless. And if Flo ever found out, she'd be banned from his show.

Daisy had left a pair of ruby earrings on her makeup table, one of her many gifts from this stockbroker or that theater critic. Theta had half a mind to sell them and give the dough to an orphanage, just to teach the frivolous cow a lesson about taking care of her things. Instead, she left them and flipped off the lights, making her way through the darkened theater by the dim glow of the work lights. She had just reached the wings when she heard a sharp whistling somewhere in the theater that stopped her cold.

"Wally? That you?" she called, her heart beating quickly.

The whistling stopped. There was no response.

Theta quickened her steps. If some chump was playing a joke, he just might get a sudden sock in the jaw for it. Theta swung her legs over the stage and leaped nearly into the front row. She heard it again—a jaunty whistle coming from somewhere inside the theater. She wished she'd left all the lights on.

"Who's there?" she cried. "Daisy, if that's you, I swear you won't be able to dance for months after I break your legs."

But the whistling didn't stop, and she couldn't pinpoint its source. It seemed to be coming from everywhere all at once. She raced down the right aisle, banging her leg against the armrest of a chair in the dark, but she didn't stop. She threw herself against the closed theater doors only to discover that they were locked.

Where was the whistling coming from? She backed down the aisle, peering up into the balconies. A spotlight came on suddenly, blinding her. Blinking away the black spots, she turned and ran back toward the dressing rooms, the hollow song following her. Every door was open, and Theta inched her way down the long, ill-lit hallway, fearful that whoever was doing that whistling might leap out from behind any one of those doors. Theta was truly scared now. Beneath her gloves, her skin was very warm and itchy.

"No," she whispered. "No."

A sliver of light shone at the end of the hall; the stage door was ajar. She ran for it. Her fingers burned with unwelcome heat.

The whistling was louder now. It seemed to come from right behind her. The work lights flickered and whiffed out as she passed. She tripped and skidded on her knees, wincing in pain. She placed a palm against the wall and felt the wood grow hot. Gasping, Theta pushed away and raced for the door. The door, the door, the door. The stage door, her means of escape. The stage door, which even now was swinging shut.

THE ONE WHO WORKS WITH BOTH HANDS

Memphis woke to a feeling that something wasn't right. When he looked over and saw that Isaiah's bed was empty, he was immediately up and moving quickly through the apartment, his heart racing. He checked the bathroom and the kitchen. Octavia snored in her bed, and Memphis did his best not to make noise so he wouldn't wake her. He looked out the parlor windows and saw his pajama-clad brother standing in the cold in the garden. He raced to his brother's side.

"Isaiah, what're you doing?" Memphis shook the boy. Isaiah was cold to the touch.

"Talking to Gabriel." Isaiah's teeth chattered. His eyes had the fixed, unseeing quality of a trance. "Memphis, brother," Isaiah whispered. "The storm is coming...the storm is coming...."

"Isaiah! Isaiah!" Memphis shook his brother hard.

"What in heaven's name is going on?" Octavia had wandered out in her nightgown. "What are you doing outside in the middle of the night?"

"Isaiah's having a nightmare. Come on now, Ice Man. Wake up!"

"The ninth offering was an offering of lust and sin. . . ." Isaiah said. His eyes had rolled back in his head and his mouth twitched.

Octavia put a hand to her mouth in shock. "Oh, sweet Jesus. Memphis, help me get him inside."

Together, they carried the shaking Isaiah inside and placed him on his bed. Octavia fell to her knees beside the bed and put one hand on his forehead and the other across her heart. "Get on your knees, Memphis John. Pray with me. We're gonna pray the Devil out of this child."

"There's no devil in Isaiah!" Memphis growled.

"They're coming, brother. . . ." Isaiah whispered. His shaking had become more violent.

"Say it with me," Octavia ordered. "The Lord is my shepherd, I shall not want."

Memphis watched the scene unfolding in the bedroom in horror. His best friend was dead. His brother was sick with visions. His mother lay in an early grave and haunted his sleep, and his father had left and was probably never coming back. Memphis was sick and tired of everything. He wanted to grab Theta and run away from it all.

"He maketh me to lie down in green pastures," Octavia prayed fervently. "He leadeth me beside the still waters. He restoreth my soul—Memphis John, where do you think you're going?"

"Away from here!" Memphis shouted. He threw a coat on over his pajamas, shoved his sockless feet into his shoes, and tore out of the building, walking in an aimless fury. A fog had come up in the night. It hazed the street lamps and turned Harlem into a ghost town. Obscured by mist, the few people out on the streets were like laughing shades. Memphis turned away from them, walking uptown.

Why was this happening? What if Isaiah was sick, like their

mother? They hadn't known how bad things were with her until it was too late. Was this a warning? He remembered what Sister Walker had said about Isaiah being like a radio that picked up signals. What signals was Isaiah getting, and how could he make them stop?

He found himself in front of Trinity Cemetery. The open gate squeaked in the wind. Why was it open? A black cat slunk across the road, giving Memphis pause. "Go on! Git!" he hissed at it. Memphis shivered. It had gotten noticeably colder, though he couldn't say why. It wasn't wind. In fact, it was very still. Not a tree swaying. Not one rustle in the leaves. Gooseflesh tickled up Memphis's arms and neck. He had the sudden thought that he should turn around, go home, and pull his covers up over his head.

"Caw!" Up in the branches of a barren tree, a crow sat watching him.

"Leave me alone!" Memphis howled at it.

In the graveyard, he saw the silhouette of a figure in the fog. The person wasn't moving at all. He was just standing there.

"*Memphis . . .*"

The voice was a rasp, like the scuttling of dried leaves in a gutter. Memphis stood perfectly still except for the quaking of his knees. His breath came out in a foggy Morse code of fear. He tried to speak, but his tongue had gone very dry.

"Gabe?"

The figure beckoned. "*Brother . . .*"

The crow cawed again. Memphis began to laugh. He was losing his mind—that's what was happening. He was trapped in some sort of nightmare and couldn't wake up. With a feeling of fatality, he followed the figure deep into the foggy graveyard, until he came to the mausoleum where Gabe's body had been hung like a broken angel. Now Gabe stood in the mist in his funeral suit. His skin was

431

shiny and tight across his full face, and he shimmered around the edges, transient, phosphorescent, a deep-water fish swimming briefly through the shallows. Memphis was aware of a sound, like a ragged high note held on a trumpet. It rushed into Memphis's ears and made his heart race. His knees gave and he fell to the ground, paralyzed. Above him, Gabe flickered, dreamlike, as if Memphis were seeing a cycle of Gabes passing through: His soulful-eyed friend. A laughing demon. A decaying death mask crawling with flies, eyes stitched shut, the tongue gone.

Gabe's voice came out as a long, labored whisper, as if these were the last sounds he would ever make. "At the crossroads, you will have a choice, brother. Careful of the one who works with both hands. Don't let the eye see you...."

Memphis's entire body shook. The horn reached a pitch that made him want to scream. The fog swirled around Gabe, and the last thing Memphis heard before blacking out was Gabe's faint warning: "The storm is coming.... All are needed...."

※

Sister Walker sat at her kitchen table in her robe, her hair tied in a scarf, an untouched cup of coffee in front of her, and listened to Memphis talk about his dead friend. She kept perfectly still as he spun out his frantic tale, which started with Isaiah's trance and ended in Trinity Cemetery; she didn't even move as he told her about how Gabe had issued a warning—"The storm is coming"— just before he vanished into the fog. When Memphis had finished, there was only the steady ticking of the kitchen clock and the first milky-blue light of dawn at the window.

Finally, Sister Walker spoke. "Memphis, I want you to listen to me very carefully: You've had a terrible shock. I don't know what happened in that graveyard, but for the time being, I would like you to keep this between us. Tell no one—no one, do you understand me?"

Memphis was too tired to do anything other than nod.

"As for Isaiah, I'm going to stop working with him for a small while, till he's better. When he comes over next time, we will work on his arithmetic, and nothing more."

"Isaiah won't like that," Memphis said hollowly.

"You let me worry about Isaiah." She coughed long and hard and popped a lozenge into her mouth. Then she placed Memphis's coat around his shoulders like a mother would do, and Memphis felt a cry ballooning at the back of his throat. "Go on home now, Memphis. Get some rest."

Sister Walker stood at the door watching Memphis trudge toward home. Her cough was bad—too little sleep. A swig of medicine and some hot tea would help for now. As for what she'd just heard, she had no remedy—only a deep sense of dread that some nameless horror was about to sweep its dark wing across the land, and that they might all be lost in its shadow.

FALSE IDOLS

The car screeched to a halt in front of the Globe Theatre, and Evie leaped from it before the engine had quit its sputterings. She tried the front doors. "Locked!" she shouted.

"Stage door!" Jericho said. He took off for the alley with Evie and Sam in hot pursuit. The stage door was ajar. The handle was partially melted, the door frame blackened.

Evie's legs felt in danger of buckling as she crept along a dim backstage hallway past dressing rooms whose mirrors flashed in the dark.

"Jericho?" she whispered urgently. "Sam?"

"Here," Sam said, popping out of a dressing room and making her jump.

Light glowed from the stage, and as Evie drew closer, she could see that the spot was on full. She saw the lighted staircase from the Ba'al worship number, and her heartbeat quickened.

"Theta?" she said. There was no response.

Evie walked out on the stage. She put up a hand to block the blinding spotlight and followed it to the altar at the top of the staircase. The spot threw thousands of sparkles as it reflected off the beaded costume of the dead girl lying there.

"Sam! Jericho!" Evie shouted and, despite her fear, bounded up the stairs. At the sight of the body, she put out a hand to keep herself from tumbling back down.

"Is it her?" Sam shouted, racing up.

"No," Evie said, her voice small. The girl was a blond.

"Her skin..." Sam said. He put a hand on Evie's shoulder and she jumped.

"It's gone," Jericho finished.

The doors flew open, and shouts of "Stay where you are!" and "Don't move!" reached them as a wave of police officers, guns drawn, streamed down the aisles. Evie could see their handcuffs gleaming in the dusky theater. "You're under arrest," an officer said.

Evie offered her hands and allowed herself to be taken to the police station without protest.

Detective Malloy was furious. As Evie sat with Jericho and Sam on the chairs outside his office, she could hear him lighting into Uncle Will. "...contaminating a crime scene...breaking and entering...thought I told you to stay out of this..."

Will caught her eye only once through the half-open office door, and it was enough to make Evie snap her eyes forward again.

"I'll tell him it was my idea," Sam said.

"Swell. I'll tell him it was your idea, too," Evie said.

The officers dragged a protesting T. S. Woodhouse into the precinct and dumped him unceremoniously into a chair beside Evie and the others.

"Hey! I got rights, you know," Woodhouse yelled.

"Yeah?" the officer snapped back. "Not for long. Hey, Sarge— caught this one at the theater, sneaking pictures of the body with a camera he had strapped to his leg. Don't that beat all?"

"That camera is property of the *Daily News*, pal!" T.S. yelled. Then, noticing Evie, he said, "Well, well, well, if it isn't my favorite Sheba." Woodhouse sneered at her. "That was quite a little scavenger hunt you sent me on the other night. *Ars Mysterium*, huh? More like Betty Bunk."

"You got exactly what you deserved, Mr. Woodhouse."

T. S. Woodhouse's eyes flashed. "Yeah? What do you think your uncle would say if he found out you were the one feeding me information on the case?"

"That was you?" Sam said, eyebrows high.

"And how," Woodhouse said, without taking his eyes off Evie's.

"Are you blackmailing me, Mr. Woodhouse?"

He shrugged. "I might be."

"Fine. You want to know who the Pentacle Killer is? It's Naughty John Hobbes himself, come back from the dead to finish the ritual he started in 1875. And when he's finished, he's bringing hell on earth."

"Evie," Jericho cautioned.

Evie stared down T. S. Woodhouse. He responded with a cynical laugh. "You're a hot sketch, Sheba. I'll give you that. But I wouldn't look for any more favorable articles on the museum—or you, if you catch my drift."

Will stepped out into the hallway. "No one is to say a word until we get home."

"So long, Sheba," T. S. Woodhouse said. "It's been good knowing you."

※

Henry was asleep, curled toward the wall. Theta slipped in behind him, matching the arch of him. She draped her arm across his side. He stirred, lacing his fingers in hers. Theta began to cry, and Henry turned to her.

"Theta? What's the matter?"

"I was at the theater. I-I heard noises. Somebody was there, Hen!"

Henry fought off his sleepiness and tried to make sense of what Theta was saying. "Who was there? What are you talking about, darlin'?"

"I went back and Wally was there with the cops. He looked like he'd been punched. I pretended like I was out on the town and just walking by, and I asked him what happened."

Theta buried her face against Henry's side. Henry could feel her trembling.

"It was Daisy," she finally managed. "The Pentacle Killer got Daisy. She must've come back for her earrings and...It could've been me, Henry."

Theta started to cry again. Henry pulled her close. The thought of losing Theta terrified him. "Are you hurt?"

"No. Oh, Hen, I heard this awful whistling coming from everywhere. I was running, but I couldn't get the doors open, and..." Her voice softened to nearly a whisper. "It started to happen again, Hen. Just like Kansas."

Henry knew about what had happened in Kansas. He also knew it hadn't happened since.

"Well, you're safe now. I got you."

"What's happening, Hen?"

"I don't know, cher."

Henry put his arms around Theta; she rested her seal-black head against his chest, and they stayed that way till dawn.

THE WILD MAN OF BORNEO

The morning's papers had a field day with the murder of Daisy Goodwin. FINAL BOW! MURDER AT THE FOLLIES! PENTACLE PERFOR-MANCE! Evie was reading the *Daily News*'s front-page story when Sam ran in waving a piece of official-looking paper overhead. "I've got news!" He trundled quickly up the spiral iron staircase to where Evie stood in the library's tall stacks and preened like a cat who knows there's a dish of cream waiting.

"Okay. I'll bite. What the devil are you so smug about?"

"I found the tax records for Knowles' End." He swung his legs over the railing, hopped onto the rolling ladder, and pushed off.

"When did you become wise in the ways of research?"

"Well, I did rely on my charms," Sam admitted. "You'd be sur-prised how helpful the girl in the records office can be."

Evie took the stairs two at a time to the first floor and trotted alongside Sam as he rode the library ladder. "Well? Did you find anything interesting?"

Sam gave the ladder another push.

"And how. For the past thirty years, the taxes have been paid by a Mrs. Eleanor Joan Ambrosio." He paused dramatically.

Evie rolled her eyes. "And?"

"That name didn't mean anything to me. So I did a little digging. Ambrosio is a married name. *Blodgett* is her maiden name. Ring any bells?"

"No." Evie reached for the ladder and Sam pushed off again, leaving her grasping at the air. He was really enjoying this, she could tell.

"Mary White married a fella named Blodgett. Eleanor was their daughter."

Evie kept pace with the ladder. "So her daughter kept up the taxes on Knowles' End? Why?"

"That's exactly what I said. See? We think alike."

"Will you come down from there, please? You're making me dizzy." Evie stopped the ladder abruptly and Sam leaped down.

"Aw, doll. You say the sweetest things."

"Sam, I'm warning you. You might be the next victim."

Sam settled into a chair and placed his boots up on the table. He laced his fingers behind his neck, and his bent elbows stuck out on either side of his head like wings. "It was pretty ingenious of me to think of going after the tax records, if I do say so myself."

"When you've finished congratulating yourself, could you explain?"

"Seemed odd to me. If the daughter inherited the old place, why keep it? Why not just sell it off and make some dough? Why hold on to an old eyesore?" He paused again.

"Will you keep me in suspense all night?"

Sam grinned. "*All* night?"

"Just get on with it."

Sam tipped the chair onto its back legs, rocking it just slightly. "I did a little more digging and found a record of an offer from Milton and Sons Real Estate to buy the place. Apparently they thought the spot might be perfect for some fancy housing, and they were willing to pay some cabbage for it, too. But the offer was refused, signed by the rightful owner, Mrs. Mary White Blodgett." He popped a grape into his mouth and let that land.

"Our Mary White? Former lover of John Hobbes?"

"Yup. The same."

Evie's heartbeat quickened. "How long ago was the offer made?"

"Three months."

"Mary White is alive?" Evie said, wide-eyed.

"Yes she is. Living in one of those shacks out at Coney and still holding on to that house up on the hill."

"Now why would she do that, I wonder?"

"Maybe we should find out."

Mary White Blodgett lived on Surf Avenue in a wind-and-salt-battered bungalow with a view of the Thunderbolt roller coaster. Mrs. White's daughter, Eleanor, met Will and Evie at the door wearing a housedress, her hair set with bobby pins.

"Mrs. Ambrosio?" Will asked.

"Who wants to know?"

"How do you do? I'm William Fitzgerald. From the museum. We spoke on the phone."

Some spark of recognition showed in the woman's eyes. "Oh, yeah. So we did. My mother's an old lady, and she's real sick. So don't go agitatin' her."

"Of course," Will said, removing his hat.

Mrs. Ambrosio led them through a sitting room littered with empty Whitman's Sampler boxes and a collection of Radithor bottles that hadn't yet made it to the rubbish bin. The place smelled of old beer and salt. "It's the cleaning girl's day off," she said, and it was hard to know if it was a gallows joke or an excuse—or perhaps both. "Wait here in the kitchen a minute."

Evie kept her hands to herself. She didn't want to stand in the place, much less sit. On the messy kitchen table, a bottle marked MORPHINE stood dangerously close to one labeled RAT POISON. A dirty syringe lay on a wad of bloodstained cotton.

Mrs. Ambrosio disappeared behind a curtain, but her voice could still be heard, loud and shrill. "Ma! Those people are here to see you about Mr. Hobbes."

Mrs. Ambrosio reappeared suddenly, moving the bottles hurriedly into a cabinet and shutting the door. "We get rats sometimes," she explained. "Like I said, she's real sick. You can have fifteen minutes. Then it's time for her nap."

Behind the curtain, Mary White's bedroom was tomblike. The roller shades had been pulled down, and the bright beach sunshine bled around the edges. The old woman sat propped in bed against a pillow. She wore a sleep cap and a dirty peach silk boudoir jacket. Under the fragile skin of her arms, her gray-blue veins stood up like a knotty mountain ridge drawn along the folds of an old map.

"You want to know about my John," she said in a voice weak with labored breathing.

"Yes, Mrs. Blodgett. Thank you." Uncle Will sat in the only chair, forcing Evie to sit on the edge of the bed. The old woman smelled of Mentholatum and something sickly sweet, like flowers dying; it made Evie want to bolt from the house and run toward the hard light of the beach.

"Did you know my John?" Mary White smiled, showing teeth gone brownish-gray.

"No. I'm afraid not," Uncle Will said.

"Such a lovely man. He brought me a carnation every week. Sometimes white, sometimes red. Or a pink one for special days."

Evie shivered. From what they knew, John Hobbes had been anything but a lovely man. He'd killed many people and taken body parts from them. He'd terrorized and probably murdered Ida Knowles. And if they were correct, his spirit had come back to finish a macabre ritual and bring forth terrible destruction.

"Yes. Well. Can you tell us about John's beliefs?" Uncle Will asked. "About the cult of the Brethren and—"

"It wasn't a cult!" the old woman coughed out. Evie helped her sip water from a grimy glass. "They tried to make it sound diabolical. But it wasn't. It was beautiful. We were seekers manifesting the spiritual realm on this plane. Jefferson, Washington, Franklin— enlightened men, the founders of our great nation—they knew the secrets of the ancients. Secrets even the Masons in their hallowed halls didn't know. We meant to free people's minds, rid them of their shackles. The world we know would die, and in its place a new world would be born. That was our mission—rebirth. John knew that."

"What about the boarder who went missing? The servant girl?" Will persisted.

"Lies," Mary spat. "The boarder left without paying his rent. The servant was insolent. She left to see her sister and didn't bother to say good-bye."

"And Ida Knowles?"

"Ida?" Mary's hand fluttered about her mouth and her eyes searched. "Who are you? What do you want?" she said in a raised voice. "I did not say I would receive you!"

Evie took Mary White's cold, thin hands in hers. "I understand just what you mean about Mr. Hobbes," Evie started. "The Blue Noses think we flappers are morally indecent. But we're only trying to live life to the fullest." Evie glanced at Will, who nodded slightly for her to continue. "Why, I'll bet if Mr. Hobbes were here today, he'd be celebrated as thoroughly modern."

Mrs. White smiled. Two of her teeth had rotted away entirely. She laid her damp hand on Evie's cheek. "He would have liked you. John always did like a pretty face."

Evie willed the scream in her throat to stay put. "I am just curious, if you don't mind my asking, why did you hold on to Knowles' End? I'm sure you could have made a fortune selling it."

"I would never do that."

"Of course not," Evie agreed, nodding vehemently. "I was just curious why not."

"So that John would have a home to come back to. He said it was very important. 'Don't ever sell the house, Mary, or I can't come back to you.'"

Goose bumps danced up Evie's spine. "But how?"

Mary White laid her head against the worn satin pillowcase and looked toward the light sneaking in around the edges of the window. "Johnny didn't tell me everything. Only he understood the Almighty's infinite plan. His body was anointed, you know, just like a work of art—Botticelli's *Venus*, Michelangelo's *David*. The marks, everywhere. He wore them as a second skin."

"Why?"

"It was all part of the plan, you see. He would come back. He would be reborn. A resurrection. And once he was reborn, he would bring the end times. The world would be cleansed in fire. He would rule it as a god. And we would be by his side." She laughed, a schoolgirl sort of laugh, completely at odds with her

443

sagging face. "He called me his Lady Sun. Oh, he was a prince. Here." With effort, Mary opened her nightstand drawer and removed a tiny black box. "Open it."

A fat gold band dulled with age lay against the black velvet.

"It's beautiful," Evie said.

"It was his," she whispered conspiratorially. "I gave it to him. Husband mine, I called him, though we'd not yet married. He wore it nearly till the end, my Johnny."

Evie's fingers tingled with the desire to take it, to read it. It belonged to him. To John Hobbes.

"Put it back, if you please," Mrs. Blodgett commanded.

Reluctantly, Evie closed the box. "Oh, but you can't be comfortable, Mrs. Blodgett. Dr. Fitzgerald? Could you please help her to a more comfortable position?"

Will looked momentarily flummoxed, but he set about trying to help the old woman, who fought him at every turn. During the distraction, Evie quickly pocketed the ring, then replaced the box and closed the drawer. "Ah. That's better, isn't it?"

"Yes, thank you," Mary said, as if she'd been the one to think of it. Then she continued. "But he had to make the world ready. To purge it of sin. To take it on, like a savior. To eat the sin of the world." Mary White's eyes moistened with tears. "They murdered him. My Johnny. He was so beautiful, and they murdered him. Philistines! Philistines." She hacked again, and Evie helped her to more water. "He never hurt a soul! People were drawn to him— women especially." She smiled and gave Evie's arm a pat. The mere suggestion of touching John Hobbes turned Evie's stomach. "I feel pain. Where is Eleanor with my medicine? Stupid girl. Always late."

"Yes, yes," Evie soothed. "We'll have your medicine in just a moment. But I am ever so curious about something: Did Mr.

Hobbes ever mention a ritual for binding a spirit, or sending it back into the other realm once it had done its work?"

Mary White frowned. "No. Will you call her with my medicine?"

"Of course I will! And Mr. Hobbes wore a special pendant, didn't he?"

"Yes," Mary White answered, her voice thinning with pain. "Always."

"And where is that pendant now?"

"The pendant?" She had a faraway look, and Evie feared they wouldn't get what they needed in time.

"Did he give it to you?" Evie prompted. "As a lover's gift, maybe."

"I told you, he wore it always," the old woman snapped. "He was wearing it when he died. It was buried with him. Eleanor! My medicine!" Mrs. White called out.

"He was buried in a pauper's grave. It's long since gone," Will said quietly to Evie.

"No, no, no! No pauper's grave for my Johnny," Mary White corrected him, her hearing apparently much clearer than her memory.

"I beg your pardon. I thought..."

"We paid a guard to give us the body. In accordance with Johnny's wishes, we buried him at his home."

"Brooklyn or Knowles' End?"

"No," the old woman said, irritated. "His real home."

"Where was that?" Evie asked.

"Why, in Brethren, dear. Up on the old hill, with the faithful."

The room seemed to reel. Evie heard her voice as if from far away. "Mr. Hobbes was *from* Brethren?"

"Yes. Of course."

445

"But there were no survivors of the Brethren fire," Evie said.

"Only one. Could you hand me that hatbox, dear?"

Evie retrieved the hatbox from the dresser. Mary White reached in and removed a false bottom, revealing a leather-bound hymnal underneath. From inside its tissue-thin pages, she retrieved a smaller, folded piece of paper, which she passed to Evie.

It was a county record of birth for the village of Brethren, dated 6 June 1842: Yohanan Hobbeson Algoode, son of Pastor John Joseph Algoode and Ruth Algoode (died in childbirth).

"Such a sacrifice they made for him, the chosen one."

The curtain snapped back. In the doorway, Mary White's daughter held the syringe in one hand and a length of tubing in the other.

"I've been waiting," Mary White barked. "You want me to hurt, don't you? Oh, my life was so good before."

"Yeah, yeah. When you lived in the mansion on the hill. I know. If you hadn't been paying the blasted taxes on that old house, we wouldn't hafta live in this stinkin' hole. You ever think about that?"

Mary White groaned as her daughter plunged the needle into the bruised crook of her arm, then released the tubing. In a moment, the old woman's eyes gleamed with the morphine. "He's coming, you know." Her speech was becoming syrupy. "He said he'd come for me, and I waited. I kept everything as it was for him. He said he'd come, and I knew he would." Her eyes glazed over. "Such a beautiful man." Her eyes closed with the morphine and Evie and Will showed themselves out.

Safe again in the bright sunshine, Evie and Will walked quickly through the strolling families.

"Of course!" Will said. He'd stopped to pace before a colorful sign that advertised the Wild Man of Borneo. Just outside the tent, a man in a red circus master's jacket and top hat tempted the curious to "Come inside and see the savage—part monster, part man!" Behind them, the roller coaster inched up the incline with a steady *click-click-click* before plunging down and around, the riders screaming with a mixture of fear and pleasure. It was the last ride of the year before the boardwalk would shutter its amusements until the next summer.

"Of course," Will said again, admonishing himself. "It all makes sense now."

"Wonderful. Could you explain it to me?"

"Yohanan is the Hebrew name for John. John Hobbeson Algoode. John Hobbes," Will said. "Naughty John Hobbes was Pastor Algoode's son—the chosen one. The prophecied Beast meant to rise. He's come back to finish his father's work, to bring about hell on earth."

They were walking again, Will's words coming as fast as his steps. "Mary said he had to eat the sin of the world. To take on their sins. That why he takes parts of them in accordance with the seals: He ingests parts of them. It's an ancient magic, the idea that eating parts of your enemies makes you stronger. They can't defeat you. Two, please—with relish!" Will had stopped in front of Nathan's Hot Dogs. He fished out two nickels and gave them to the boy behind the counter, taking two hot dogs in return. He handed one to Evie, who held it awkwardly.

"Ugh," she said, grimacing at the food. "Honestly, Unc."

Will wolfed his down, still talking. "In John's case, it is helping him manifest. Giving him strength."

Evie tried a small bite of her hot dog. It was surprisingly delicious, and she found that even the talk of cannibalism couldn't keep her from devouring it. "If that pendant is his connection to this plane, his protection, then all we need to do is destroy it, and we destroy his link to this world. Is that right?"

"It stands to reason."

"But she said it was buried with him."

"Yes," Will said, pausing to think. "That will be messy."

Evie stopped mid-chew. "You can't be serious." She stared at Will. "Oh, sweet Lois Lipstick, you *are* serious."

Will tossed his hot-dog wrapper in a garbage can. "We're going upstate, to Brethren. And we're going to need a shovel."

Jericho returned to the Bennington from the records department, where Will had sent him. He didn't even stop to take his coat off. "I found it! The documentation."

He handed it to Will and nodded grimly at Sam, who was seated at the dining room table with Evie. "Sam. You're here late."

"Just keeping Evie company," Sam said. He smiled triumphantly at Jericho.

Will read aloud from the document. "Yohanan Hobbeson Algoode was taken to the Mother Nova Orphanage, where he was admitted on October 10, 1851. The director's entries on him are brief, but they document Yohanan Algoode as quiet but ill-humored, a bed wetter, arrogant, and prone to small acts of cruelty. When brought before the director for discipline, he said only, 'I am the Dragon of Old, chosen of the Lord our God.' The other children shunned him. He called himself the Beast. After two thwarted attempts, Yohanan successfully ran away in the summer of 1857. No further documentation exists."

"So we know it's him. But we still don't know how we're going

448

to stop him," Jericho said, finally removing his coat and hanging it on the rack. "The last page of the Book of the Brethren—the one with the incantation for binding and destroying the Beast—was torn out. You said yourself that we have to dispatch him according to his beliefs. But how are we going to find that information in time? The comet arrives in two days."

"I need to show you something." Evie unwrapped the tissue covering John Hobbes's ring.

"Is that what I think it is?" Will asked. Evie nodded. "This is becoming a habit, Evangeline."

"Will, if I can see him, understand him, we can be one step ahead of him."

"Do you think that's a good idea, doll?" Sam asked. "This fella's a killer."

"And a ghost," Jericho added.

"What good is it to have this power and not use it?"

"I salute your spunk, but I question your sanity," Sam said.

Will crouched beside Evie. "Evie, this isn't a party trick. This ring belongs to the Beast himself."

"I understand."

"Get in, get what we need, and then get out," Will advised. Evie nodded. "I'll clap three times to help bring you up. If at any time you feel as if you are in danger—"

"I don't like the sound of that. Do you like the sound of that, Frederick?" Sam muttered.

"You will say a code word. Let's decide on one now."

"How's about *no*?" Sam said. "Or *hooey*? Or *stop*?"

"James," Evie said. "The code word is *James*."

Will nodded. "Very well."

"Evie, are you sure you want to do this?" Jericho asked.

"Pos-i-tute-ly." Evie attempted a smile. Her hands shook with both apprehension and excitement; going under was a bigger thrill than a front-row table at the most exclusive nightclub. "Put it in my hand, please."

"I don't like this," Sam grumbled, but he put the ring in her hand anyway.

Evie closed it tightly in her palm and placed her other hand on top, like a seal. It took a moment for her to find her rhythm, and then she was falling through time in her mind.

"I see a town with muddy streets...." Evie said from her trance-like state. "Horses and wagons. I can't... it's speeding up...."

"Concentrate. Breathe," Will instructed.

Evie took three deep breaths and the image stabilized.

"There's a crowd, and a preacher...."

A tall, heavily bearded man in a black suit stood on an over-turned fruit crate as he preached on the edge of a small town. A crowd had gathered. Many ridiculed him. Evie saw their laughing faces as almost satanic. The preacher didn't stop. If anything, his voice gathered strength. "You must arm yourself that when the day of judgment comes, when the Beast brings forth God's justice upon the sinners, you will be counted in the Lord's number and spared. Prepare ye the walls of your houses with his markings to usher in his holy coming and anoint your flesh to bear witness to his glory!" the preacher thundered. At the preacher's side stood a small boy of no more than nine or ten with a pale face and arrest-ing blue eyes.

The boy held up a leather-bound book. "This be the Word of the Lord! The Gospel of the Brethren!"

Someone threw a tomato. It broke apart on the preacher's face and slid down, staining his suit with pulp. Everyone laughed. The preacher wiped his face clean with a handkerchief without stopping his fiery sermon. But the boy stared daggers at the tomato thrower, and something in his gaze stopped the man's laugh cold.

"Evie?" Will asked, for she'd fallen quiet.

"Yes. I'm here," Evie answered. "It's changing. I see wagons by a river. It's cold. The preacher's breath comes out in white puffs. They're praying...."

In her mind, she saw Reverend Algoode raising his hands to heaven as he addressed his small congregation. "You are the chosen, the faithful, the Brethren...."

"The angel of the Lord appeared to me in the heavens as a streak of fire and bid me to part ways with the corruption of the old world and build a new Godly body of heaven in this country...." Evie echoed. "The Blood of the Lamb runs in our veins, and in blood will we vanquish our enemies and bring forth God's true mission on earth."

The connection became uncertain for a moment, and then Evie was falling again. She concentrated with all her might and saw the boy's feet as he ran through leaves, heard the *huff-huff-huff* of his breathing. He lay upon the riverbank and watched lazy clouds overhead, and for a moment Evie felt his loneliness and doubt. A deer ventured out of the trees, sniffing for food. It raised its head, and the boy threw a rock, laughing as the deer startled and broke for the woods.

"Evie, where are you?"

"Inside the church, I think," she answered slowly as the image in her mind shifted again.

The boy with the blue eyes had been stripped to the waist and strapped to a chair. The faithful surrounded him. He squirmed in the chair, his eyes on the preacher as he turned a brand in the coals of the stove. There were twelve brands in all—a pentacle, and one for each of the eleven offerings.

"Your flesh must be strong. The Lord will brook no weakness in his chosen," the preacher said. He drew the red-hot brand from the fire and approached the boy, who screamed and screamed.

"Oh, god," Evie said. She was not aware that tears streamed down her face.

"Will, make her stop," Jericho cautioned.

"I'm with Frederick the Giant," Sam chimed in.

Will hesitated. "Just another moment. We're close."

Sam didn't wait. "Hey, doll? Time to come up for air. Can you hear me?"

"I said just a moment!" Will snapped.

Evie's mind reeled away from the boy's fear. For a moment, she tumbled madly through a fast stream of pictures. She willed herself to breathe and stay calm, not to run away. Soon, the pictures settled in her mind again.

"I'm fine," she said in a calm voice. "I'm fine."

The boy sat by the river with the Book of the Brethren turned to the last page. Evie's heartbeat quickened as she tried to see it.

"The missing page. I've got it," she said, and Will rushed to grab a pen. "'Into this vessel, I bind your spirit. Into the fire, I commend your spirit. Into the darkness, I cast you, Beast, nevermore to rise.'"

Young John Hobbes ripped the page from the book, tearing it into tiny pieces and floating them on the river.

"We've got it, Evie. You can stop now," Will said.

Evie had never gone quite so deep before. She was only vaguely aware of their voices, like a conversation heard in another room when falling asleep. It was almost like a drug, this feeling, and she wasn't ready to stop.

"I'm somewhere else now," Evie said dreamily.

She found herself walking through thick, sodden leaves in a

blue-gray wood toward an encampment. Somber-faced men and women in plain clothes left their modest log cabins and walked with their children toward a white clapboard barn painted with the same sigils John Hobbes had scribbled along the bottom of all his notes. And there across the door was the five-pointed- star-and-snake emblem.

"The Pentacle of the Beast," she murmured.

"Evie, I'm going to clap my hands now," Will said. He did, and Evie pressed harder. She was beyond his reach now.

In her trance, she followed the others into the church. The women sat on one side in simple chairs, the children at their feet, while the men sat on the other side. His face grim, Pastor Algoode stood at the front with his son by his side. "The time has come. I have heard it in the town that even now the authorities ride to Brethren to take us down. Forgive them, Father, for they know not what they do. Yes, the time has come for the chosen one to begin his journey!"

"Hallelujah!" a woman shouted, raising her palms high.

"The time has come for the ritual to begin! For the Beast to rise and bring judgment to the sinners!"

"Hallelujah!" others joined in.

"We are the faithful. We must be strong. The Lord will brook no weakness in his chosen." Pastor Algoode opened the book, finding the page he needed. "And I heard the angel's voice as a voice of thunder saying, 'None of the faithful shall enter the king-dom of the Lord but that they have purified their flesh with oil and the flames of heaven. Their sacrifice shall be the first, the sacrifice of the faithful, and the Beast will take from them the book and bathe in the smoke of their tithe. Thus will the first offering be made and the ritual begun.' Hallelujah!"

Pastor Algoode passed around two jugs, which the faithful

poured over themselves. Evie could smell the strong kerosene. Her heartbeat sped up. Pastor Algoode slipped his pendant around the boy's neck and placed a hand on his forehead. "Take of our flesh and make it yours. Thus sayeth the Lord. Go. Do what you must. Find a dwelling and make it holy. Prepare ye the walls of your house. Do not forget to honor us with tribute."

Calmly and quietly, the boy left the barn, locking it from the outside. On the other side of the door, Pastor Algoode continued praying while the congregation took up a plaintive hymn. Evie smelled smoke. Black wisps curled out from the cracks in the barn. Flames licked at the roof. The boy stood fast, also praying, letting the smoke fill his lungs. "The Lord will brook no weakness in his chosen," he intoned over and over.

Inside, the children screamed and coughed. The women tried to keep the song going. Pastor Algoode's voice was choked with pain; it made his prayers into a fearsome cry. Evie wanted to get away, but she couldn't. She could not command her hand to let go of the ring, nor could she remember the code word. She was too far under, with no idea how to get out or ask for help. The screams had died to isolated moans. The roof caved in. The smoke. Evie coughed; she was smothering. Shouts from the woods—someone was coming up the mountain. The boy opened his eyes quickly. For a second, Evie thought she saw flames reflected in the cool glass of those eyes. The boy walked calmly toward the woods and the sound of a man's voice calling out. Suddenly, he stopped and turned toward Evie. Something about his face—calm, cold, cruel— made Evie's heart beat wildly. He was looking right at her!

"I see you," he said, and his voice was not the voice of a boy; it was a terrible thing, more bestial than human. "I see you now."

"J-James," Evie whispered, suddenly remembering the code word. "Help. James."

The next thing she knew, Jericho was shaking her. Her fingers were cramped but the ring was gone; Sam had taken it from her. "Evie!" Jericho shouted. "Evie!"

She gulped in a huge breath, like a drowning woman breaking a lake's surface. "Oh, god, oh, god!"

"We should have stopped, Will!" Jericho growled.

"It's all right," Will said rather automatically.

"I saw him—I saw the Beast! Horrible, horrible!" She gagged but did not vomit. Her head began to throb and her vision swam.

"I'll get her some water," Sam said, running for the kitchen.

Evie held on to the edge of the desk even though she was sitting. Her cheeks were pale and her forehead bathed in sweat. The room spun. "He...he looked at me! Right at me! He said, 'I see you, I see you'!"

"What the hell does that mean?" Sam asked. He'd returned with the water and tried to get Evie to drink, but she couldn't.

"It's all right," Will said, shaken.

"It's not all right! You can't do this to her. She's not an experiment," Jericho snapped at a stunned Will. He gathered Evie in his arms, carried her to her room, and placed her on the bed.

Evie had never felt so sick. Her head pounded and her stomach roiled as she lay on sweat-drenched sheets in the dark room. Every sound echoed in her skull. She was vaguely aware that she was having the dream about James again, but it kaleidoscoped in and out of the images she'd pulled from John Hobbes's ring till she couldn't be certain what was happening anymore. At one point, she saw Naughty John playing chess with James on the battlefield, the Victrola playing so fast it made a mockery of the song. She saw Henry, too, running through the trees, calling for someone named Louis. A woman stood at the edge of the forest in her nightgown and a gas mask. When she raised the mask, Evie saw that it was

Miss Addie. "Such a terrible choice," she said as the sky lightened and the first waves of the explosion came toward them all.

At half past nine in the evening, Evie woke with a desperate thirst. She wobbled to the kitchen for water and saw that Uncle Will's light was on. The door was ajar, but she knocked softly anyway.

"How are you feeling?" Will greeted her.

"Better." Evie settled into an uncomfortable chair. It seemed to have been designed so that a visitor would not stay long. "What happened today, at the end?"

"You established a psychic link with him. You could see him, but he could also see you. That is the danger of your gift: You may open yourself up to the other side." Will templed his fingers and bounced them gently against his chin. "Are you familiar with the story of the Fox sisters of Hydesville, New York?"

"Are they a radio quartet?"

A smile flickered briefly on Will's lips. "There was no radio in the mid–eighteen hundreds. The Fox sisters lived in Hydesville, New York, in a house that was rumored to be haunted. The youngest Fox sisters, Maggie and Kate, claimed to be in communication with the spirit world. They would ask questions and the spirit, whom they called 'Mr. Splitfoot,' would answer by rapping." Will knocked on the desk for effect. "They became a sensation during the Spiritualism movement, conducting séances for many famous people."

"This is what happens when there's no radio," Evie said.

"Yes, well, later on, the girls had a change of heart. They became religious and confessed that their communication with spirits was all an elaborate fraud, that they had produced the raps by the cracking of their toes. The sisters fell on hard times. They became drunks; some said they drank to dull the phenomena."

Evie stared at her big toe as it noodled a spot in the rug. "Is there a point to this tale?"

"A year later, Margaret Fox recanted. She had a change of heart. She told everyone that it had all happened just as they'd said. I believe her. I think the sisters were frightened, and so they stopped and renounced it all. It was as if they said to the restless spirits, 'Be gone. We are closed to you.' And long after the girls had died, a human skeleton was found in the basement of their home in Hydesville."

Will shuffled the newspaper clippings on his desk. He'd probably been looking at them for hours, Evie guessed.

"Why is this happening now?" Evie asked.

Will templed his fingers again. "I don't know. Something is drawing the likes of John Hobbes. Some energy here. Spirits are attracted to seismic energy shifts, chaos and political upheaval, religious movements, war and invention, industry and innovation. There were said to be a great many ghost sightings and unexplained phenomena reported during the American Revolution, and again during the Civil War. This country is founded on a certain tension." He pressed his fists against each other. "There is a dualism inherent in democracy—opposing forces pushing against each other, always. Culture clashes. Different belief systems. All coming together to create this country. But this balance takes a great deal of energy—and, as I've said, spirits are attracted to energy." He let his hands rest on the desk.

"Can we stop him?"

"I believe we can." Will offered a hint of a smile. "In the morning, we'll drive to Brethren and exhume his body and take the source of his power on this plane—the pendant."

"Then what?"

"Then we'll bring it back to the museum, where we can create a protective circle. Using the incantation, we'll trap his spirit in the pendant and then destroy the pendant before Solomon's Comet passes through."

Will was looking at her with a new appreciation, Evie felt.

"You were very brave today, Evangeline."

"I was, wasn't I?"

"The bravest. Family trait, you know."

Evie felt much better for Will's reassurance. Her stomach had settled and her head was lighter. She found her gaze drawn to the only photograph on Will's desk—the mystery woman she'd seen when she'd held Will's glove that day, just over a week ago. Was it only a week? It seemed like years.

"Who is she, Unc?"

Unconsciously, Will stroked a finger across the woman's face. "Rotke Wasserman. She was my fiancée for a time."

"Why didn't you marry her?" Evie asked, and immediately realized her mistake. What if the woman had jilted Will at the altar? What if she'd left him for a man with more money and position?

"She died," Will said softly.

"Oh."

"It was many years ago," Will said, as if that should soften it. "I haven't been able to keep up with that other glove since. It's always...lost."

For once, Evie didn't know what to say. She hadn't really thought of her uncle as very human. He was more like a textbook who occasionally remembered to put on a tie. But it was clear that he was, indeed, human, with a deep wound named Rotke.

"I'm sorry," she said after a pause.

"Yes. Well. We've both lost someone, I suppose." Will turned the picture toward the wall.

Evie's hand sought the comfort of her coin talisman. There was something she wanted to ask Will, had wanted to ask him since she'd first discovered ghosts were real. Only now did she feel brave enough to do so. "These stories about people communicating with the spirits of the dead, mediums...Could you really contact someone from the other side if you wanted to?"

Will's gaze followed Evie's hand as it held fast to the pendant at her neck. "It's best to let the dead lie in peace," he said gently.

"But what if they aren't at peace? What if they seem to need help? What if they show up in your dreams again and again?" Evie felt tears threatening again. She'd turned into a regular waterworks lately. She fought it. "What if they're trying to get through to you and tell you something, only you're not quite on the trolley?"

"What if they're trying to harm you?" Will said. "Did you ever think of that?"

No. She hadn't. But James? James would never hurt her. Would he?

"People tend to think that hate is the most dangerous emotion. But love is equally dangerous," Will said. "There are many stories of spirits haunting the places and people who meant the most to them. In fact, there are more of those than there are revenge stories."

"Unc, if you believe in ghosts and goblins—"

"I do not believe in *goblins*...."

"The *goblinesque*," Evie said, rolling her eyes. "Why is it you have such trouble believing in God?"

"What sort of god would let this world happen?" he said, holding her gaze a moment too long before checking his pocket watch. "I believe it's just time for *Captain Nightfall and the Secret Brigade.* Shall we catch it?"

"Sounds swell."

Will flipped on the radio. Ominous music swelled. *"Wherever evil lurks, wherever shadows gather, there will you find Captain Nightfall and his Secret Brigade as they fight the forces of iniquity and keep the citizens of this country safe from all manner of villainy. . . ."*

The shadow-painted living room filled with sound effects and music and the well-modulated voices of actors pretending to put the wicked in their place.

But it wasn't enough to chase away the ghosts.

Rain beat gently against the windows. The trees of Central Park bowed with wind. And on the street in the dark, a whistling could be heard as John Hobbes walked the sodden blocks to the Museum of American Folklore, Superstition, and the Occult. He passed easily into the old mansion, with its collections of gris gris bags, witches' letters, and spirit photographs. Mere trifles. Child's play. Umbrellas opened against a typhoon. In two days' time, none of it would matter, anyway. But first, there was work to be done. Whistling, John Hobbes visited the old library. It was cloaked in night's gloom, but he could see the untidy desk with no trouble. He saw very well in the dark now. First he slid open the drawer and left a small present. But he would also need something. There on the desk he saw it, winking out from under a stack of newspaper clippings. That would do. Yes, that would do nicely. He dropped it into his pocket and left the museum, singing softly, *"Naughty John, Naughty John, does his work with his apron on. . . ."*

Upstairs in his bedroom, Sam woke briefly, thinking he heard someone singing, but all was quiet now, and so he rolled over and went back to sleep.

EVERYTHING WILL BE FINE

Memphis walked the leaf-strewn streets of the Upper West Side, pulling his coat closed against the brisk breeze. It was truly fall now. Chimney smoke burned the edges of the air, scenting the wind. The nights had weight. *Everything will be fine, Memphis. Stop your worrying.* Memphis walked faster, eager to get to the Museum of American Folklore, Superstition, and the Occult. Sister Walker had told him to keep the incident with Gabe's ghost to himself, that he was probably seeing things out of grief and weariness. But between Isaiah's trances, Gabe's visitation, and the dream he shared with Theta, it was too much to ignore, and Memphis wanted someone to explain to him what was going on.

In the distance, Memphis saw the gothic towers of the Bennington peeking through the thinning leaves. That was where Theta lived, and for a moment he wished he could just run up and see her, forget this whole crazy world. But her world was just as mysterious as everything else he was worried about. He couldn't do anything about that, and besides, he had answers to get, and so he moved on.

It was around Central Park West and Eighty-eighth Street that Memphis became aware that he was being followed. When he looked over his shoulder, he saw them: two men shadowing him at a respectful but consistent distance. Memphis knew at a glance that they were plainclothes cops. His heart raced, and he told himself to keep calm. He had no slips on him. He was fine. Memphis picked up his pace. So did the men. They were definitely following him, then. Memphis scanned the street, looking for an escape. Along Central Park West, diggers were hollowing out the street for the new subway line. Could he hide down there? No, he'd be trapped for sure, and probably break a leg in the process. But he might be able to outrun them. Memphis waited until he saw a car coming up the street, then darted out in front of it, making the driver swerve and take up the boulevard, momentarily blocking traffic. He sprinted full-out for Central Park. His lungs burned and his shoes clip-clopped loudly on the circuitous path ambling down through trees and sharp black rocks, the sun dappling the path with little fool's-gold promises of light. Over his ragged breathing, Memphis could hear the cops running behind him, shouting. They were faster than they looked, but Memphis aimed to be even faster. He chanced another look behind; he was losing them, he saw, and a sudden joy took flight in his chest. He turned back around just in time to see the nurse and baby carriage directly in his path, and the nurse's expression of horror as she stood, trans-fixed, unable to get out of his way. He had too much momentum on the downhill. He tried to stop and skidded, rolling to a stop in the grass, banged and bruised and dazed. His trousers were torn and bloodied at the knee. Still, he staggered to his feet, ready to run. But it was too late; the men were on him, lifting him vio-lently to his feet and twisting his arms behind his back.

"What do we have here?" one cop gasped out, and Memphis

was glad he'd at least winded them. "Looks like we got ourselves a numbers runner."

"Not me," Memphis said. "No slips on me."

"Oh, yeah? What's this in your pockets, then?" the other cop said. He pulled a wad of slips from his own pocket and shoved them into Memphis's.

"I'd say there's at least twenty-five slips there—enough for a judge to lock you up, boy."

"But those aren't mine!" As soon as the words were out of his mouth, Memphis realized how stupid they were, how futile his protestations. The word of two white cops against a Negro numbers runner? It was a fixed fight.

"Call Papa Charles," Memphis said. "He'll give you whatever you need."

"We don't work for Papa Charles," one cop sneered, and Memphis knew the cop was dirty for Dutch Schultz. "You're going downtown, friend."

The policemen tugged him roughly toward a waiting car that had pulled up alongside the curb. Behind him, Memphis could see the tall points of the Bennington floating behind a scrim of passing clouds, like a mirage.

A GOODLY HERITAGE

It was nearly four o'clock and the day's shadows stretched long over the curved backs of the Catskills as Uncle Will took the turnoff from the main road, just beyond the weather-beaten sign for Brethren. The road wound its way toward the valley, past a small farm whose barn bore a white hex sign on its side. The leaves had slipped into autumnal reds, golds, and oranges. Down below, the small town rolled out like a postcard photo, all gabled roofs, gas street lamps, and church steeples. There was a quaintness to the town, as if it had been stopped in time around the turn of the century. It was the sort of place about which politicians liked to wax nostalgic and hold up as a symbol of all that was American, everything the country was in danger of losing.

Then they'd driven north. The roads were muddy and now they were considerably later than they'd meant to be. They checked into a motel on the edge of town. It was a rustic, cabinlike place with a large lot for cars and wagons. Uncle Will rang the bell. The proprietor, a man with a handlebar mustache but a more modern cut of jacket, greeted them. Will signed the register as Mr.

John Smith and family, from Albany, and secured two rooms—
one for Evie alone and one for him to share with Jericho.

"Come for the county fair?" the innkeeper asked.

"Why, yes. We hear it's the finest in New York," Will answered
with a tight smile. "My son and daughter can't wait to attend."

Evie flashed Will a look of surprise. Still smiling, he gave her a
small head shake of warning: *Play along.*

"Oh, it is at that," the innkeeper said proudly. "I recommend
the First Methodist Church's peach jam. Now that's something
special."

"Evangeline does love peach jam, don't you, dear?"

"Can't get enough of it," Evie answered.

Will took the keys and hurried them to their rooms.

"Why do we have to stay here?" Evie asked in dismay as she
took in the dark, cedar-lined room with its lumpy bed. She'd seen a
perfectly lovely old inn when they'd driven into town. This one
didn't even have a telephone.

"We'll attract less interest," Will said. He spread out a crude
map on the chipped desk. "Now. According to this, the old camp
is up the mountain, about here. John Hobbes's grave should be in
the woods somewhere beyond the old meetinghouse. There's only
one road leading up there—if one can call it a road. It'll probably
be rough going, especially if the weather turns nasty. And unfor-
tunately, we'll need to go close to dark...."

"According to the *Farmers' Almanac*, the sun sets at six
twenty-five," Jericho said.

"Then we'll need to meet back here by quarter to six at the latest."

"Back here? Where are we going?"

"Where are *you* going," Will corrected. "You and Jericho will
attend the fair."

"Oh, Unc. I thought you were only being polite!"

465

"It will be good. Make us seem like friendly tourists. Throw anyone off the scent of our true purpose."

Evie had a particular memory of attending the Ohio State Fair and getting sick from the smell of farm animals and eating too much cotton candy. State fairs were a far cry from Manhattan nightclubs; she and Jericho would probably die of boredom before they even got to the old Brethren site. But she could tell from Will's tone that he was resolute about this.

Evie's sigh was long. "Okay, Unc. I'll go eat peach jam with the yokels. But you owe me."

Will drove Evie and Jericho to the fair before heading to the town hall to see if he could gather additional supplies for their expedition. Evie and Jericho bought their tickets and pushed into the fairgrounds with the rest of the crowd. Several long white tents had been set up, giving the whole fair the feel of some medieval encampment. An Araby of imagined delights awaited them inside: Flimsy wooden vegetable stands were stacked deep and high with fat pumpkins. Hand-painted signs promised THE BEST APPLE PIE IN THE COUNTY and SCHROBSDORFF'S LYE SOAP—NO FINER CLEANING AGENT! as well as sweet pickles, plum preserves, caramel corn in newspaper cones, and lace doilies stitched so fine you could scarcely tell they'd been stitched at all. A jovial din filled the marketplace: "Ferber's Horse Equipment—right this way!" "A game of checkers, only one penny!" "Come to the automobile display and see the motorcars of the future!"

They passed through the long, wide livestock pavilion, where pens teemed with animals groomed to perfection while sober-faced farmers stood nearby, arms crossed, nervously awaiting the verdict of the men judging their worthiness.

They emerged from the pavilion to find that an old-fashioned brass band occupied a center bandstand. The band played "Abide with Me" while gray-haired couples sat in slatted chairs, singing along to the old hymn. Children in their Sunday best ran through smiling and wonder-eyed, their pinwheels spinning madly in the breeze. Despite her earlier grumblings, Evie was enchanted. For a brief moment, she could forget that they had come for a terrible purpose. They stood in line for the hayrides, laughing as the cart's wheels bumped over the rutted field, and then laughing again as they shook the itchy hay from their hair and clothes like dogs shaking off water. At a small wooden counter, they drizzled honey on slabs of fresh bread drenched in melted butter and gobbled it down. Evie laughed as a big drop of honey slid off the side of Jericho's bread and he tried to catch it with his tongue.

"You missed a spot," she said. Without thinking, she wiped her thumb over his mouth. His lips parted slightly, as if he meant to take her thumb in his mouth. He backed away, substituting his hand for hers.

"Thank you, Evie."

"You're welcome," Evie said shyly. Jericho was looking at her in a way she couldn't name. "Oh, look! Let's ride the Ferris wheel," Evie begged, walking quickly toward it.

They bought their tickets for a penny apiece and settled into the metal chair. It swung just slightly as they lifted, and Evie yelped and grabbed Jericho's arm. He responded by taking her hand in his, and as the ride lifted them higher into the air, Evie's stomach fluttered, both from the height and from the nearness of him.

"Look over there! You can see the inn if you try," Evie said, extricating her hand to point. It was impolite to point, but it was even more impolite to hold the hand of the boy your best friend was goofy for, even if he was only being gentlemanly.

"Where?" Jericho leaned over her slightly to see, and Evie's body thrummed again.

"Oh. I...I don't believe you can see it anymore." She settled back against the seat with her hands firmly on the bar.

Exiting the Ferris wheel, they found that it had turned chillier. Wispy clouds drifted in the hazy sky above the red-gold hills.

"Cold?" Jericho asked.

"A little," Evie said. Her teeth chattered. She nodded to a clapboard pavilion off to the side. "That looks warm."

A sign above the door proclaimed FITTER FAMILIES FOR FUTURE FIRESIDES. A fair-haired boy barreled out of the door and down the steps, proudly showing off a bronze medal on a ribbon. "I won!"

"Attaboy! What did you win?" Evie asked, and he let her see the medal's inscription. "'Yea, I have a goodly heritage,'" Evie read. "Well. Good for you, then, I suppose."

Inside, the building had been set up with long tables and curtained-off areas labeled EXAMINATION. Families sat in chairs, waiting their turn, while nurses in starched aprons and stiff white hats moved about, writing down information and escorting them one at a time behind the examination curtains. Fathers filled out surveys and answered questions while mothers bounced fussy babies on their knees and encouraged their children to sit up straight, all in the hope of coming away with one of those bronze medals the boy outside had been so proud of. There was hot cocoa, and Jericho went to get them some while Evie waited.

At a nearby table, a tall, thin, gray-haired man asked a young couple questions. "Has anyone in your family ever had heart trouble? Infantile paralysis? Scoliosis? Rickets?" They shook their heads, and the gray-haired man smiled. "Fine, fine. How about a history of nervous trouble? Have you or any of your family members ever demonstrated any *unusual* abilities? For instance, if I were to hold a card in my hand, might you have a...well, let's call it a *sense* of what that card was? Would you like to be tested for such an ability?"

Evie was only half listening. She was drawn to the far wall, where a large board was suspended. The board, which sported small, flashing lightbulbs, had been divided down the middle. The left side, where an arrow pointed to a fast-flashing light, read EVERY FORTY-EIGHT SECONDS, A PERSON IS BORN IN THE UNITED STATES WHO WILL BE A BURDEN ON SOCIETY. AMERICA NEEDS LESS OF THESE, AND MORE OF THESE. . . .

An arrow on the right side pointed to a lightbulb that rarely flashed. The text read EVERY SEVEN AND A HALF MINUTES, A HIGH-GRADE PERSON IS BORN IN THE UNITED STATES, WHO WILL HAVE THE ABILITY TO WORK AND BE FIT FOR LEADERSHIP. ONLY FOUR PER-CENT OF ALL AMERICANS FALL WITHIN THIS CLASS. LEARN ABOUT HEREDITY. YOU CAN HELP TO CORRECT THESE CONDITIONS.—THE HUMAN BETTERMENT FOUNDATION: MAKING AMERICA STRONG THROUGH THE SCIENCE OF EUGENICS.

Jericho returned with their cocoa. He frowned at the board. A smiling nurse holding a clipboard approached them. "Did you want to be tested?"

"For what?" Evie asked.

"We don't need a medal," Jericho said curtly.

"Do you know about eugenics?" the nurse asked, as if she hadn't heard him. "It's a wonderful scientific movement designed to help America achieve her full potential. It is the self-direction of human evolution.

"Why, every farmer knows that the key to having the best pos-sible livestock is in the breeding," the nurse explained, as if she were imparting a Sunday-school lesson to children. "If you breed inferior animals, you'll have inferior stock. You must maintain the superiority of the bloodlines to have truly superior stock. It's the same with people. How costly is it for America when defective people are born? There are the unfortunates. The degenerates. The unfit, insane, crippled, and feeble-minded. The repeat criminals found in the lower classes. The defects particular to certain of the races. Many of the agitators causing such unrest in our society are an example of the inferior element who are leading to a mongrelization of our American culture. Purity is the cornerstone of our great civilization. Eugenics proposes *corrections* for what is sick in our society."

"Let's go," Jericho urged in Evie's ear, but the nurse was still talking.

"Imagine an America in which both our physical and social ills have been bred out of us. There would be no disease. No war. No poverty or crime. There would be peace, as people of superior, like minds could reason out their differences. A true democracy! All men are not created equal, but they could be. Mankind was meant to reach ever forward, ever upward, ever onward! Corrections," the smiling nurse said again. "Are you certain you wouldn't like to be tested? It won't take but a few moments of your time, and we have some lovely cookies."

"We're not interested," Jericho said crisply and stormed outside.

"Jericho! Jericho, slow down, please," Evie huffed. She had followed him out of the Fitter Families building. He walked briskly, and she was having difficulty keeping up. "What is it? What's wrong?"

"Nothing," Jericho said, though it was clearly anything *but* nothing. She'd never seen him so angry. He was always so cool, so calm. "That isn't science. It's bigotry. And…and I don't like experiments." He took a deep breath, as if he were forcing himself to calm down. "It's time to go back. We're already late."

They came out on the far end of the fairgrounds and walked

toward the jitney that waited to take people back into town. Just beyond the fence, roughly half a dozen men stood on a small, makeshift platform. They wore coveralls, plain black jackets, and black hats. Evie stopped short.

"Look, it's Jacob Call."

Holding his holy book aloft, Brother Jacob Call thundered at the crowd. "Pastor Algoode spoke the truth and the way. Don't you see what's happening in this country? Sin has taken root in our homes. Greed and envy rot the foundation. We've lost our way. Repent, sinners, for the end is near! Hear the word of the Lord God as it was revealed to his prophet, the Right Reverend Algoode, amen!"

"The Brethren," Evie whispered.

"And the Lord spake with the tongue of a thousand serpents, saying, 'Anoint thy flesh and prepare ye the very walls of your houses, for the end will come.' The Lord your God has sent the Beast to rise!"

"The Beast will rise," the men echoed. One of the men shook, and his eyes rolled back in their sockets. He spoke in tongues as his body twitched.

"Solomon's Comet cometh! The Dragon of Old will rise, and only the faithful will be saved to fight God's holy war while the sinners perish!"

Evie and Jericho would have to pass before them to get to the jitney.

"I can't," she said.

"Don't worry. I'm with you," Jericho said, positioning himself between her and the men. Evie felt their gaze on her. Automatically, she crossed her coat over her body. She wished she weren't wearing her patterned stockings and lipstick even as she felt angry that the zealots' contempt made her feel this way. A boy of no more than fourteen or so watched her intently, wearing an expression that wavered between lust and hatred.

"The sin of the world was woman's sin," the boy shouted. His voice hadn't even changed yet; he was younger than she'd thought.

"Just keep walking," Jericho whispered, taking Evie's hand in his.

Evie tried to keep her eyes forward, but she could hear the boy saying something, a word that caught her attention. It was not a nice word. She glanced in his direction. His face was twisted with hate.

"Harlot," the boy hissed. His arm went back, as if for a pitch, and Evie was completely shocked when the mud hit. She gasped as it splayed across the front of her coat.

"Harlot!" the boy yelled again.

People were staring at her—at *her*, as if *she'd* done something wrong. She wanted to scream at them. She wanted to punch the boy as hard as she could. She also wanted to cry.

"Harlot," Jacob Call shouted, and the men joined him, a chorus now. "Harlot!"

Jericho clutched Evie's hand tighter and walked her quickly toward the fairground gates. But she could hear them calling after her.

Harlot, harlot, harlot, harlot!

CROSS MY HEART AND HOPE TO DIE

Memphis was late. He'd told Isaiah that he'd pick him up from Sister Walker's house at five o'clock, but it was coming up on six, and Isaiah was hungry. Aunt Octavia served dinner promptly at six fifteen. If they weren't washed up and sitting at the table by then, they went to bed hungry. Isaiah was already mad that Sister Walker wouldn't let him read the cards. All they'd done that afternoon was sums and computation, and he was pretty sore about it. He did not intend to spend the night tossing and turning on an empty stomach just because of Memphis. Isaiah knew Sister wouldn't let him leave without an adult, so he waited until she went to the kitchen for her tea, then called loudly, "I think I see him now, Sister!" and bolted for the door before she could catch up with him. He'd never walked home from Sister's house by himself before. It was exciting, like he had a secret world to explore. He wished it weren't getting dark, though. He didn't like the dark. His path took him past the funeral home, and he thought of his mama, lying in her coffin in her white Sunday dress, and of Gabe, too, and that made him sad and a little frightened. Now he had to walk past Trinity Cemetery at night. Everybody knew that was when the dead walked. His stomach growled, and he thought about Octavia denying him dinner.

Isaiah held his breath—you were always supposed to hold your breath walking past a graveyard; everybody knew that, too—as he ran through the first fallen leaves of autumn past the high stone-and-iron walls. He hoped his lungs would hold out. It was hard to run and hold his breath at the same time. By the time he reached the end, he was dizzy. He bumped headlong into Blind Bill Johnson and yelped.

"You scared me!"

Bill smiled. "Isaiah Campbell! Didya think I was a ghost?"

"Uh-huh. I don't like walking past the graveyard, but if I don't make it home in time, my aunt Octavia won't give me supper."

"Guess we better hurry, then. Come on, I know a shortcut." Bill's cane *tap-tap-tap*ped down the sidewalk. They stopped at the corner. "Say, do you like magic tricks?"

"I guess so."

"You guess so? What sort of answer is that?" Bill said, pretending to be put out. "You in for a treat. I been practicing my magic act. Wanna see?"

"Sure," Isaiah said. He bounced a ball, catching it neatly each time.

"Behold! In this hand lies a rose." Bill opened his right hand to show the boy, then closed it again. "Alakazam!" He opened his hand. "Whaddaya see?"

Isaiah squinted at the slightly squished rose. "Nothing happened."

"Nothing?"

"Nope."

"Lemme try this again. O great spirits of the land, gimme a

frog in my right hand!" Blind Bill opened his hand again. The rose was still a rose.

Isaiah laughed. "Still ain't no frog," he said.

"Confound it!" Blind Bill said. "I read me a book on magic and everything. I guess I just don't have the touch."

Isaiah wanted to tell the old man what he could do. Memphis always said not to talk about it, but Memphis wasn't there. He'd gone off somewhere and forgotten all about his brother. It made him feel like crying, but boys weren't supposed to cry. Seemed there was a whole list of things Isaiah wasn't supposed to do, and he was tired of it.

"I can do magic," Isaiah blurted out.

"Can you, now?"

"Mm-hmm. Sister says I'm something special." If Memphis was keeping secrets from him, then Isaiah could keep secrets from Memphis. He could tell them, too.

"Does she, now? What makes you so special?"

"Sister says I'm not supposed to tell."

"Well, now, you can tell old Blind Bill, cain't you? Who'm I gonna tell?"

"Sister says no."

"Mm-hmm. I see. You gonna let a woman own you, little man?" Quick as a snake, he grabbed the ball with his left hand and held it up out of reach.

"Hey!"

"You so special, how 'bout you take it from me? Or maybe you not really special after all, is that it?"

"I am!"

"'At's all right, son. We cain't all be special."

"I am special!" Isaiah said, so angry that the tears came.

Blind Bill gave Isaiah his ball and patted his head. "Now, now,

I didn't mean any offense, little man. 'Course you special. I can tell. Blind Bill can tell."

"You can?"

"Yes, sir, yes, sir."

The old man's words settled over Isaiah like a balm. At least somebody cared about his feelings. Isaiah was tired of being small and easily dismissed. He was tired of everybody—Sister, Memphis, Octavia, his teachers, the folks at Mother AME—telling him what he could and couldn't do. What good was it having something special if he couldn't let anybody know about it?

"All right, then. I'll tell you. But you have to promise to keep it a secret."

The old man crossed his heart with a long finger. "Cross my heart and hope to die."

That was the most solemn promise Isaiah knew.

"I can see things in my mind. When Sister's holding the cards, I can tell what shapes she's got without even seeing 'em."

Bill's mouth twitched. "'Zat so? You'd clean up real good at poker."

"Sister won't let me."

"No, I expect she wouldn't."

"And sometimes..." Isaiah paused.

"Yes?"

"Sometimes, I can see things that haven't happened yet."

A tingle started in Bill's stomach, working its way through his blood like a hunger.

With a shaking hand, he patted the top of the boy's head again.

The boy took the blind man's big paw, turning it over. "You got a mark on ya."

"Old cut from back when I used to work the cotton. Them

bristles reach out and GET YA!" Bill spooked Isaiah, who shrieked, then laughed. He liked Bill, liked being teased by the old man. It made him think of his daddy, how he used to swing Isaiah up by both of his arms when they walked down the street, and his mother would scold the both of them, saying, "Now, Marvin, you're going to stretch his arms clean out." Thinking about his mama and daddy made him sad.

They'd reached the small alley Bill had told him to be on the lookout for. "Shortcut," he said to the old man.

"Thank you." Bill's walk slowed. "You all right there, little man? You sound sad."

"Just thinking about my mama. She died."

"Well. That *is* sad." Bill slowed just a hair more. The alley, he knew, would dead-end at a brick wall. He'd slept there a few times. "I could take the sad right out of your head if you want."

"How you gonna do that?"

"Come on over here and I'll show you."

Isaiah was dubious. It wasn't just that his auntie had told him about being careful with strangers; Blind Bill wasn't a stranger, exactly. There was just a moment's pause, something deep down that made him wary, but he followed Bill anyway.

"Not much of a shortcut, Mr. Johnson. Got a brick wall at the other end."

"My mistake. Must've been thinking of another street. Hard for a blind man, you know. Now come on over here. Come on, now."

Isaiah looked back down the alley at the empty street.

"You not scared, are you? Special fella like you?"

"No. I ain't scared," Isaiah said. *Not scared*, Memphis would say. Well, Memphis wasn't there. Isaiah went to the old man.

"I just have to put my hand on your head, like so. That tickle?"

It did just a bit, and Isaiah laughed.

"I take that as a yes. How 'bout here?" Bill moved his hand forward so that the tips of his fingers gripped the front of Isaiah's forehead firmly.

"That's good."

"All right, then. Gonna be a little squeeze, and then you won't feel sad no more."

Anymore, Isaiah silently corrected. Just like Memphis. He had a sudden premonition about his brother, the growing sense that he was in trouble, that something wasn't right.

"I have to go home, Mr. Johnson. Octavia'll be waiting dinner on me."

"Just hold still, son."

"I have to go."

"Don't struggle, now. Don't struggle."

Panic beat its fists against Isaiah's rib cage. The sense of dread bloomed into a terrifying vision: He saw his brother standing at a crossroads under a blackening sky.

"Let me go!" Isaiah shouted, trying in vain to break free from Bill's fierce grip. "Let me go, let me go!"

Bill grunted and held on tightly and was rewarded by the electric jolt.

Under his grip, Isaiah twitched and shook, and if it was anything like the past, when he could see, Bill knew the boy's eyes had rolled back in their sockets. Maybe a small bit of drool foamed in the corners of his mouth. Bill's own heartbeat sped up, and for a second he remembered running through tobacco fields barefoot under skies that stretched in every direction. A number floated before him—one, four, four. A number. He'd gotten a number in the bargain! Another jolt rocked Bill's body, stronger than the first. His tongue curled in his mouth and he tasted metal. He saw a crossroads, and a cloud of dust billowing up on the road as if before a storm, and tall, gray stick of a man in a stovepipe hat. Under his palm, the boy was still and quiet. He dropped to the pavement at Bill's feet and the old man crouched next to him, listening to the sound of his breathing.

"Hey! Hey!" someone yelled from the street.

Bill cursed under his breath and pulled his hand back. "Over here! We need help over here!"

The voice moved toward them and became the dim outline of a man. A shadow. Oh, if only he'd had a few more moments! How much more could he see? How much more power could he taste?

"What happened?" The man's voice was hard, accusatory.

"I don't know. The little man was lost. I was trying to help him find his way, and he started having some kind of fit, I think. I couldn't rightly tell 'cause of my condition." Bill put a hand on his cane. "I been calling out—didn't you hear me?"

"I expect so," the man answered. "I expect that's what brought me. It's lucky you were here."

"The Good Lord musta been looking out."

People were so suggestible.

※

Octavia cried out when she saw the man carrying Isaiah's limp body up the walk, Bill Johnson trailing just behind. The boy was put to bed. A doctor was called.

Plates of spoon bread were offered. Bill cradled his on his lap and gobbled it down. He hadn't tasted home cooking in a long time, and Octavia was a fine cook.

"What happened?" Octavia asked.

"Well, ma'am, the little man was lost, and I was just tryin' to

479

help him out. . . ." Bill told her the same story he'd given before. He was nearly finished when he heard the older Campbell boy bursting through the front door as if he might break it down.

"Where is he? Where's Isaiah?" Panic in his voice.

"Resting." Steel in hers.

"I'm sorry, I—"

"Save your breath for prayer, Memphis John. I already heard from Mrs. Robinson that you were arrested and Papa Charles had to bail you out," she said bitterly.

"Can I see Isaiah?"

Bill didn't hear anything, and he could only assume the communication was a signal—a nod, a gesture. How many such silent conversations had he missed over the years? He could hear Memphis slinking away to some other room—to his brother's side, no doubt. Those two were close, a bond forged by tragedy. That gave Bill the smallest pause, but he pushed it away. It wasn't his job to put the fairness back into the world.

"Don't be too hard on the boy," he said to Octavia, a peace offering. He stood to go, and Octavia gave him his cane plus another piece of spoon bread in waxed paper.

"Thank you, Mr. Johnson."

"Bill."

"Thank you, Bill." He could hear the catch in her voice. "Oh, my sweet Jesus, Lord Jesus. What if you hadn't been with him? What if he'd been alone?"

"The Lord works in mysterious ways, Miss."

"You call anytime," Octavia said after him. He was at the little gate out to the street.

"Thank you. I believe I will."

Bill Johnson turned toward the night, which was not as dark as the place he'd been. He took the rose from his pocket and curled it tightly in his left hand. "I'm sorry, little man. I'm real sorry," Blind Bill whispered. When he opened his hand again, the rose had turned to ash.

In the quiet of the back bedroom, Memphis watched his brother breathing in and out. Each breath felt like an indictment: *Where . . . were . . . you . . . brother?* He swallowed dryly, terrified. What if he had brought this on Isaiah? What if a curse meant for Memphis had reached out and touched his brother instead? He felt sick inside, and sweat beaded on his forehead.

"Don't you worry, Ice Man," he whispered. "I'll make it right. I'll take it on."

Memphis placed his hands on Isaiah's small body, shut his eyes tight, and waited for the warmth and the trance, the strange dreams of healing. But nothing happened. His hands never gained warmth. His brother slept on, like the enchanted resident of a bespelled fairy-tale kingdom, and Memphis, the dragon-slayer, stood on the other side of the kingdom's unassailable walls.

He slunk down by the side of the bed and buried his head in his useless hands.

BRETHREN

The ruins of old Brethren lay up in the heavy woods of Yotahala Mountain, a name the Oneida had given it, meaning "sun." But there was precious little of that as Will's Ford made the steady two-mile climb over the narrow dirt road through heavy woods barely touched by the late-afternoon gloom. A light early-October snow had begun to fall. The wispy flakes danced in the glow of the Model T's headlights. The car hadn't much heat, and Evie shivered as she sat in the backseat, absorbing every bump.

"Close now," Will declared above the steady whine of the engine. "Look for a twined oak. That's the turnoff."

"I wasn't doing a thing but walking past," Evie said, continuing an earlier conversation. She was still shaken up about the encounter with the faithful outside the fairgrounds. "Not a thing."

"It isn't your fault. There's nothing more terrifying than the absoluteness of one who believes he's right," Will said. He was hunched over the wheel, craning his head this way and that, not content to trust Evie and Jericho to do the searching on their own.

"The records keeper told me there's been a resurgence in the Brethren cult in recent years."

"But why on earth?"

"When the world moves forward too fast for some people, they try to pull us all back with their fear," Will explained. "Let's hope they remain at the fair. I'd hate to think what would happen if they should discover us exhuming the body of their prophet's son."

On the right side of the road, where trees with bark like skinned knees stood guard, Evie spied an animal-skin charm branded with the familiar pentacle hanging from a scraggly branch. Mechanically, she drew the flap of her coat across her bare neck. "I think we're getting close."

"There's the twined oak." Jericho pointed to a massive tree whose gnarled limbs had come together in a strange ballet of twisting bark.

Will angled the car off the road and into the clearing, parking it behind a still-lush thicket and saying, "Hopefully these bushes will obscure our presence long enough."

From the trunk Will retrieved a kerosene camping lantern, which he lit and keyed to a soft glow; a flashlight for Evie; and two shovels, one of which he handed to Jericho. As he did so, Evie was reminded of their grim purpose. Will shouldered his shovel and lifted the lantern toward the imposing wooded mountainside ahead. "This way," he said, leading them up the hill over a faint scar of dirt path. The hazy, dying light lent the woods a deep grayness. Evie tried to picture young John Hobbes living in such isolation, away from the welcoming fires of taverns and the fence-post talk of neighbors, these woods his only companion.

It was straight uphill, and Evie's legs protested the climb. She was glad she'd worn sensible shoes. The air thinned, making each breath more of an effort. She glanced behind them and could no longer see the Ford in its hiding spot.

"How...much...farther?" Evie panted out. Her muscles screamed.

"Almost," Will answered, just as breathless.

Almost magically, the path evened out, flattened. It wound around a jutting face of hillock and the little breath left in Evie's lungs caught.

"Ladies and gentlemen, Old Brethren," Will said in a hushed voice.

They'd come upon the abandoned ruins of the old camp. A handful of moldering log cabins were spread out in the clearing. A splintered door hung open on rusted hinges; its dark, empty windows gave it the appearance of a skull house. Weeds sprang up around the stone carcass of a well. A stone path was still somewhat visible beneath the cover of leaves and clover. It wound through the mist-shrouded trees. To their left, the sound of the river mingled with the chirruping of crickets and birds. Evie's flashlight reflected in the eyes of a fox, making her jump. The fox skittered back to safety; the flashlight shook in her hand.

"The old church," Will said, making quickly for a large square in the center where a raggedy mess of charred timber lay in silent testament like a mausoleum. Carefully, Evie stepped over the splintered threshold, ticklish with tall weeds, and into the remains of the church. In all their late-night philosophical wranglings about the nature of evil, nothing had prepared her for the feel of it, the actual weight of some hungry wickedness pressed against her bare skin. For the old church of Brethren carried within its decay the unmistakable heft and patient persistence of evil. Under the wind, she could nearly make out a child's laugh, a swell of moans, a threat of whispers. She wanted to run. But where was there to run? What place lay beyond the reach of evil?

Piles of crumbling bricks formed a semicircle in one corner, and Evie recognized it as the fire pit she'd seen when she'd held John Hobbes's ring. It was nothing but a blackened trough now, the bricks gone gray and slick with moss. Just behind it in the grass lay a branding iron. Evie picked it up delicately. The Pentacle of the Beast. She dropped it quickly, startling a tiny grass snake slithering out from under a pile of stones. Evie peered into the abandoned pit and saw fresh kindling, half nubs of candles. Someone had used it recently. Her heartbeat quickened at the thought of who or what could be out there in those woods.

"They're still using it as a meetinghouse," Will said, as if reading her thoughts. He pointed to the arrangement of flat rocks placed in a circle around a tin sign. With his shoe, he nudged the sign over. The back was also adorned with the five-pointed star and snake.

Will gazed up at the fading light. "Let's find that grave."

Dusk fell quickly now. The woods were shrouded in dark-blue shadow. A half coin of gauzy moon appeared as they walked beyond the burned church and down the hill. The low stone wall of the graveyard appeared in the light of Will's lantern. Behind it, blackened gravestones tilted like crooked teeth in a rotting mouth. Evie shone the flashlight from stone to stone, trying to read the names there. Jedidiah Blake. Richard Jean. Mary Schultz. Each gravestone bore the inscription HE WILL RISE.

"Look for anything out of the ordinary—animal bones, a pentagram, charms or other offerings. They'd probably want to venerate his grave," Will instructed.

Evie stuck close to Jericho. Her heels sank into the soft ground, and she tried not to think about what was buried beneath that ground. She wished she had on her woolen stockings; it was much colder here than it was in the valley. Their breath came out in small gray puffs, their lungs expelling ghosts of air. The last of the light had slipped from the sky, like a hostess shutting the door on lingering guests. A smattering of early stars twinkled awake. The beam of Evie's flashlight bounced over gravestones made ghoulish in the glare.

"What if we can't find it?" she said.

"We'll have to dig up every grave until we do," Will answered.

The wind whistled over the mountain again. It felt like fingertips brushing her skin, turning her about in some child's game where she was blindfolded.

"Over here," Jericho called. Will came to his side and held the lamp over a spot marked by a simple wooden cross hung with charms. The skull of some small animal had been left at the base of it.

"Do you suppose this is it?" Evie asked.

Will wiped a smudge of dirt from the cross, revealing initials carved into the wood: YHA. "Yohanan Hobbeson Algoode," Will said. "Let's start digging."

Will parked the lantern by the cross. He and Jericho removed their jackets, rolled up their sleeves, and got to work with the shovels. Evie's job was to keep the flashlight trained on them and keep alert for sounds. She jumped at everything, swinging the flashlight wildly.

"Just hold it on us if you would, please," Will advised.

Evie needed something to keep her mind occupied, and so she watched Jericho's forearms working the shovel, paying attention to the pull of muscle, the strength of his grip. She remembered the feel of his hand over hers, like a shield. He was a mystery

486

to her in many ways, and she found that she wanted to know his secrets—not ripped from him via a wallet or favorite pen, but given to her as a gift. She wanted to prove trustworthy. Special. There was something about him that unnerved her. He was slightly dangerous; so was she. It would never work for her to be with a man who didn't understand that about her, the darkness behind the devil-may-care facade, who flirted with it but who would run scared if faced with the storm inside. She watched Jericho's large hands work and imagined those hands caressing her bare skin, imagined the taste of his mouth, the press of his body against hers.

Just as quickly, she tried to rid herself of those images. Jericho was Mabel's fella. Evie thought of her friend's many letters on the subject. But they were romantic schoolgirl fantasies. Jericho and Mabel weren't right for each other. If they had been, it would have happened already, wouldn't it? Evie couldn't take away what Mabel never had, could she?

Silently, Evie scolded herself for even thinking it. Jericho probably needed someone like Mabel. Good, steadfast, sensible Mabel, who would remember to turn off the lamps and bring in the milk. A girl who would take care. Evie had the terrible feeling that she, herself, was the careless sort: Clothing left on the bed unfolded. Books stained with coffee spots. Tabs not paid until the last possible second. Boys kissed and then forgotten in a week's time. She understood this, but understanding it did not bring comfort.

A hollow thump echoed from the grave as Jericho's shovel struck wood. Despite the cold, he and Will were soaked in sweat. Jericho hopped down into the hole. He jimmied the thin edge of the shovel around the edges of the coffin's pine top, loosening the seal. With a grunt, Jericho pried off the lid, exposing the rotted corpse of John Hobbes.

They'd had no body to bury when James died. Nothing to commemorate his passing. There was a grave, which they visited every year on his birthday, but it held no bones, no uniform, no essence of her brother.

The body of John Hobbes lay quietly in his wooden trough in a plain woolen suit, the Pentacle of the Beast pendant shining around his neck. His lips had been stitched together with thread that had sprung free in the corners, revealing long, yellowed teeth. His body was as hollowed of life, as decayed and ruined, as the abandoned cabins of Brethren. He was a thing. Inert. Like a stone. Like a memory. This, then, was what death looked like. Irrefutable. And Evie felt a strange relief that she'd not seen James's body after all, as if in that refusal, she could pretend he had never died.

Jericho reached in and removed the pendant, handing it up to Evie, who held it like she would hold a lizard by the tail. He climbed out and brushed his palms against his pants—a useless gesture, as his pants were as filthy as his hands.

Evie stared at the thing she held. She wanted to throw it out, to burn it right then and there.

"I don't think I should hold this," she said. "Could I have your handkerchief, Unc?"

Carefully, Evie wrapped the pendant in its protective covering. She was just about to hand it over to Will when a high-pitched trill sounded off to the right. Evie swung the flashlight in the direction of the sound. The light trembled over autumnal branches scratching together. Dried leaves scuttled over the ground in the empty space between headstones. Nothing, and then the sound again, from her left. This time she swung the flashlight quickly in that direction. The beam caught a fleeting movement. Evie's hands shook. Another birdcall, straight ahead. Another from behind. To her right, then left. Perched on the edge of the grave, Evie swung the flashlight wildly.

The men from the fairground stepped into the light. Evie counted five of them, plus the boy who'd muddied her coat. They carried rope and hunting knives. The boy held a hunting rifle rigidly at his side. The rifle seemed too big for him, as if he were playing dress-up.

"This be private property. Hallowed ground," the boy said.

Evie concealed the handkerchief-covered pendant in her fist and moved her hand behind her back.

"Yes, yes. Of course," Will said. He sounded frightened, at a loss, and that scared Evie more than the men did.

"What transgression be you about?" the man pressed.

"We heard there was gold buried here," Jericho said suddenly. "It was wrong of us. We see that now. We'll be going. Sorry to have troubled you." Calmly, he bent to retrieve his shovel. A rifle shot punctured the stillness of the graveyard, startling Jericho into dropping the shovel.

Jacob Call came from behind, the rifle still smoking in his hands. "Our enemies deceive us. The Lord said, in the times of tribulation before the Judgment Day, your enemies will be more than the sins of man. They will deceive you," he preached. "This is the word of the Lord's messenger here on earth, the Blessed Pastor Algoode. Amen."

"Amen," the others chorused.

"The faithful have kept his covenant. We be awaiting the Lord's will and purpose. The comet confirms it: 'When the light burns the sky as a dragon's tail.' The Beast will rise."

"He will rise! Hallelujah!" the men exclaimed.

"Judgment Day be comin'. Blessed are we. Hallelujah!"

"Hallelujah," they echoed.

"Please. Listen to me." Will put out a hand to stay them. "John Hobbes is not the Beast his father prophecied. He has no intention of returning to the spiritual plane once he is fully manifest. He is only fulfilling the ritual of the offerings so that he can rule—"

Jacob Call slapped Will hard. "The Beast will slay the wicked. He will bring forth plagues and pestilence upon their Sodom and Gomorrah. The faithful will be anointed." He pulled open the neck of his shirt to show two brands, and Evie could only imagine that there must be more. "We will be known by our marks and spared. Our great army will rise and throw the Beast back into the fires of hell, where the chosen one will be resurrected and glorified! He will rise to the heights of heaven and sit on the heavenly council with Pastor Algoode, and this country will be a Godly country. Hallelujah!"

"Hallelujah!" the faithful echoed.

"How will you send him away once his task is finished? What if the Beast refuses to be vanquished? Have you thought of that? What if, having gained the whole of the earth, he decides he doesn't care to relinquish control?"

"It be ordained. The path be promised in the Book of the Brethren. It is God's will. What God has set in motion, no man may put asunder."

"Hallelujah!"

There was no reasoning with these people. Evie could feel their hatred. Their conviction. They might destroy the pendant and the ghost of John Hobbes, but they couldn't kill what lived on after. The world was a bully.

The boy whispered to Jacob, who trained his narrow eyes on Evie.

"What have you there, Daughter of Eve?"

"Nothing." Evie kept the hand holding the pendant behind her back.

"The harlot lies," the boy said. He brought his gun off his shoulder.

"Don't believe you."

Evie looked to Will, who nodded. Slowly, she brought her hand forward and showed them the pendant.

"Thieves. Idolators. Fornicators. Sinners. What be the punishment for the enemies of God?" Jacob Call thundered.

"They shall burn!" one of the faithful called out. A torch was passed from hand to hand till it reached the tall man, who set it alight. The flame cast ghoulish shadows over the trees' moon-pale trunks.

"You don't want to do this," Will said as a second torch was lit. "It will only bring the police."

One of the men on the edge of the circle began rocking and speaking gibberish, his upturned palms gone stiff. Spittle foamed at the corners of his mouth.

"It will bring attention before the Beast can rise! He will be angry with you!" Will continued desperately. The torches had all been lit. Two of the men approached with the rope. Jericho grabbed his shovel, ready to fight.

"Quiet the deceivers!" Jacob Call ordered. The men came for Jericho, who swung the shovel, keeping them at bay.

"Just let us go and we'll never come back," Will said. But the men kept coming. Jericho swung again and the boy cocked his rifle, ready to take his shot. They were trapped. Helpless. They'd come all this way for nothing. The bullying world would win, just as it had the day her brother was blown apart, leaving nothing to bury and everything to mourn. They were as good as dead.

"The Lord will brook no weakness in his chosen," the boy shouted, and something broke inside Evie. Her fear turned to anger. She glared at the smug, triumphant boy who would burn the whole world in order to be right. She spat in his eye.

"Then that son of a bitch will really like me," she growled. With one quick move, she threw the lantern hard into the grave, where the flame caught on John Hobbes's old woolen suit, setting his corpse ablaze.

"Run!" she yelled and took off into the woods at a clip.

The action and the startling heat of the blaze stunned the new faithful of Brethren into a few necessary seconds of stasis as they tried to decide which was more important: saving the body of their beloved elder or giving chase. It was enough for a head start.

"This way!" Evie shouted, racing down the hill in a direction she hoped was correct, for it had gotten darker, giving the woods a uniformity of color and appearance that made it hard to know where they were.

"Will! Jericho!" she called.

"Here!" Jericho shouted back, and she saw his shirt off to the right.

They ran together as a pack, Evie still clutching the pendant in her fist. The wind picked up, driving into them, the noise of it like a hundred angry voices. She leaned into it, pushing back. The crack of a rifle sounded on the ridge above them. A warning.

"Where's . . . the . . . car?" Evie huffed out.

"This way!" Jericho dragged her after him. She glimpsed the Ford in the trees and ran to it as if it were a lifeboat.

Will ripped open the driver's-side door and slid behind the wheel, fingers seeking out the clutch. "Why won't it start?" he growled.

"The motor's too cold. You'll need the hand crank," Evie said.

"Jericho . . . crank," Will gasped out.

"I'm buying you a new car; I swear I am," Evie vowed.

Jericho raced around to the front of the car and placed one

hand on the hood for balance. With the other, he reached for the crank. Another shot rang out.

"Jericho! Keep your thumb beside your fingers in case the crank snaps back!" Evie called. "You don't want to break your arm!"

Jericho nodded. He pushed the crank forward, *once*, *twice*. The motor belched and coughed and then went silent again. Torches winked in the shadowy trees just above them. The fires on the crest of the hill paused, held their flicker to one space momentarily as if lost, unsure whether they should destroy or illuminate in those woods. Jericho gave one more push. As Evie had warned, the metal bar snapped back quickly, and Jericho barely had time to jump back and avoid injury. The engine shuddered to life—*ta-thacketa, thacketa, thacketa.*

Shouts came from up the hill. The torches, indecisive no longer, zigzagged down the slope, leaving angry tails of flame and smoke. The engine spasmed and threatened to die again.

"No!" Evie shouted, as if her reprimand could get the Tin Lizzie running.

With grim determination, Will worked the clutch, and this time the motor caught, humming into readiness. The torches were close. Evie could make out the full shape of the mob as Jericho came around the side of the old Ford.

The rifle cracked. Jericho recoiled, bumping back into the car in an awful dance.

"Jericho!" Evie shrieked.

Jericho moaned and fell to his knees.

"Will, I think he's been hit!"

"Keep the motor running!" Will said. He ran to Jericho and Evie slid behind the wheel. Her heart thudded in time with the Ford's engine and she cried reflexively, as if she could exorcise her fear through tears and shallow breath. The mob was on the move again.

Will dragged Jericho into the backseat as Evie pumped the accelerator, careful not to flood the engine.

"What are you doing?" Will said.

"I'm driving!" The car lurched forward, the tires spewing up pebbles and leaves as the Ford rattled onto the dirt road. Gunshots followed, but Evie was too fast for the faithful. By the time they reached the road, she had put several car lengths between them.

Jericho moaned as his head lolled against the backseat. Evie's foot pressed down on the accelerator and she took the curve at a dizzying pace, her back wheels sliding out. Uncle Will stared down the cliff at the lights of the valley below. "Dear god," he gasped.

"My father owns a dealership," she shouted. "I've driven everything you can imagine!"

"Just get us there in one piece!"

She hugged the turns, swerving once as she narrowly avoided a car on its way up the hill. The Ford wobbled on two wheels before slamming down onto all four again. In the backseat, Will cursed. At last the lights of the village were visible ahead.

"Where's the hospital in this backwater?" Evie yelled as they rattled onto Main Street.

"Take us back to the inn," Will directed.

"Sweet Mary, he's been shot, Will! He needs a doctor!"

"We can't take him to a hospital."

"Why not?" She turned around.

Will's face was grave. "I'll tell you later. Just trust me for now. We'll tend to him at the inn. Watch the road!"

Evie wanted to scream. She wanted to yell at Will—for the case, for Brethren, for Jericho. It was insanity, and she'd had enough.

"You'd better be right, Unc." She jerked the car away from the center of town and headed back to the inn.

"Whatever I do, follow along," Will said when they arrived, dressing Jericho in his overcoat and buttoning it closed. He disappeared inside and came out with two men, who helped hoist Jericho and haul him into the inn's parlor. The innkeeper's scowling wife looked on with tight-lipped disapproval from behind the desk at this filthy trio dragging a barely conscious young man into her inn.

"I've told you about the wages of sin," Uncle Will said loudly enough for the innkeeper's wife to hear.

"My brother," Evie added, doing her best to look contrite and concerned. She still shook from the ordeal. "Father tries so hard."

"These young people today," the lady clucked.

Once they were inside the room, Uncle Will placed the woozy Jericho on the bed and thanked the men with a tip. Evie shut and locked the door while Will washed the graveyard dirt from his hands and removed Jericho's overcoat. She couldn't see exactly where Jericho had taken the hit. There was no blood to be seen, though his shirt, which was covered in dirt and grass stains, was sopping wet.

"Evie, I need you," Will said. "Open my bag and take out the small zippered leather pouch inside."

Evie found the pouch and handed it to Will. Inside were four small vials filled with a thick blue liquid and a strange syringe. "What is that?"

"No time to explain. Quickly, before his body shuts down. Place the vial in the chamber of the syringe."

Evie did as she was told. There was a sharp sound as Uncle Will ripped open Jericho's shirt. Evie struggled to comprehend what she saw. For a moment, the world slowed as she tried to make sense of it and couldn't. The bullet had left a large hole just below Jericho's heart. Beneath the wound was some sort of machinery, an intricate system of brass tubing and wires.

"Evie!" Will's voice snapped her attention back to the task at hand. Will grabbed the syringe from her, tapping the glass of the vial to clear the bubbles from the blue liquid.

"There's no time to secure him. He's going to become agitated at first. You have to be ready."

"I don't understand. . . ." Evie started, staring in horror as Will plunged the syringe into Jericho's chest and released the lever.

"Another!"

Evie loaded the syringe with a second vial, which Will administered. Jericho didn't move.

"Again!"

"No! We need a doctor!"

"I said, again!"

"Dammit, Will," Evie muttered and loaded a third ampoule.

Will aimed the syringe just as Jericho came off the bed in a fit of thrashing, like a man possessed. His eyes were wild, searching, as if he didn't know where he was or who they were. His left arm swung out, sending the bedside lamp crashing to the floor. His right arm caught Will in the jaw, and he crumpled to the floor, dazed.

"Evie! Push it in. Now!"

Evie dove for the discarded syringe and plunged it into Jericho's leg, scuttling backward into a corner as he whirled around violently.

"Jericho. . ." Evie whispered.

He staggered toward her, wobbled for two seconds, then fell onto the bed and was out.

Evie was still crouched in the corner. "Is he . . . ?"

Will touched his swollen jaw, wincing, and sank onto the other bed, exhausted. "He'll be fine now. Let him sleep."

A loud knock startled them both. Will covered Jericho with a blanket and Evie ran to the door, opening it a crack. The innkeeper's wife tried to see around her but Evie kept the opening narrow. "What the dickens is going on in there?"

"My brother fell and broke a lamp," Evie said, breathless. "My father will pay for the damage, of course."

"This is an establishment for decent folks. I'll have no riffraff here." The woman strained to look over Evie's head.

"Yes. Of course."

Evie shut the door and sat on Will's bed watching as he expertly sutured the ragged skin on Jericho's chest. She watched Jericho sleep. He seemed an angel now.

"What was in that fluid?"

"It's a special serum. I can't tell you much more than that."

Evie's mind reeled out to the breaking point. Her mouth struggled to form words. "What is Jericho?"

"An experiment," Will said with finality, the teacher dismissing the class. He clipped off the thin suture wire and stowed the tools in the kit containing the syringe and vials. "Where is the pendant?"

In the chaos, Evie had forgotten. She went to her coat and retrieved the filthy object, which she handed to her uncle. "What do we do with it?"

"When we get to the museum, we'll form a protective circle. Using what you've gleaned from the missing page, we'll bind his spirit back into the pendant and destroy it."

"Do you think it will work?"

"I have to believe it will," he said.

"I want you to tell me about Jericho," Evie commanded.

Will took out a cigarette. He patted his breast pocket. "Where the devil has my lighter gone to now?"

"You're always losing it." Evie passed him a book of matches. "Jericho?"

Will lit the cigarette and blew out a plume of smoke. "I think it best to let Jericho tell you. It's his story to tell, not mine." He paused. "Evie, that was well done tonight," he said, offering his hand for a shake, which Evie ignored. It if bothered him, he didn't let on. "I think in light of our visitors this evening we should leave early, before dawn," Will said. "You should get some rest."

Evie shook her head. "I'm going to keep watch over Jericho."

"There's no need. He'll be fine."

"I'm going to keep watch."

"There's no need—"

"Will! Someone has to keep watch!" Evie's tone was both angry and pleading, the whole terrible night spilling over into this refusal to be moved from Jericho's side.

Will nodded. "Very well. I'll sleep in your room tonight."

A moment later she could hear him moving about on the other side of the thin wall, probably pacing and smoking. Evie soaked a towel and gently wiped the dirt and serum from Jericho's wound. Then she crawled into Will's empty bed and lay on her side, watching Jericho's chest rise and fall. She kept watch for as long as she could. But she couldn't fight her own exhaustion, and she drifted into restless dreams.

LAMENTATION

Steady rain battered the shuttered stands and stilled rides of Coney Island's boardwalk as Mary White Blodgett woke from her morphine fog with her heart racing and a feeling that the world was spinning too fast on its axis. She started to call for her daughter, then remembered that Eleanor had gone to the casino.

Pain traveled up Mary's arm. Oh, how she wished she could have more morphine. If she was to get through the hours until her ungrateful wretch of a daughter returned, she'd need to occupy her mind. She closed her eyes and remembered her days as a great woman.

Oh, she'd been the belle of the ball before she'd married, with suitors aplenty for a girl of such modest means. But it was Ethan White who'd caught her eye. He was older than she, an imperious, fussy sort, not at all romantic, but with a knack for business that would keep her comfortable, and their wedding had been written up in the Poughkeepsie papers for everyone to see. He'd made money in oil speculation. Some dusty town in Texas had vomited black gold, and the money flowed into the Whites' bank account.

There had been caviar and a house north of the city and box seats at the opera, which Mary didn't really like but which she attended so that everyone could see her there in her fur and jewels, the great lady, Mrs. Ethan White.

She'd known about the girl in Lubbock. It would have been fine if Ethan had chosen to keep her and be discreet. But she was in the family way, and Ethan had suddenly developed romantic notions of chivalry. He meant to leave Mary for the girl. Mary would be scandalized. No more could she sit in the lordly tier at the opera house, peering down at all the little people looking back up at her, envying her life. They'd regard her with pity. Pity, Mary White could not abide. She'd fought with Ethan, pleaded with him even—Mary never pleaded, and even now, in her bed wet with the morphine sweats, she tightened her lips against the distasteful memory—but he was resolute. He would go to the lawyers first thing and draw up the papers. She would be well cared for as long as she kept her mouth shut and didn't make a fuss.

Mary had no intention of becoming the object of gossip.

Ethan always took a glass of sherry in the evening to calm his nerves. Mary had the maid bring the sherry, as always. To this, Mary added the arsenic they kept on hand for the field mice who tried to make a home in the root cellar. In the dark of the bedroom, she'd sat in her rocking chair with a volume of John Donne's poetry while her husband writhed and shook on the bed, one clawed hand reaching toward her as she calmly flipped the pages. At twenty-four, Mary White became a very wealthy widow. She packed her mourning veil along with everything of value and moved to the Plaza Hotel in Manhattan.

A creaking sound roused Mary from her memories and she lay listening, alert, until she was satisfied that it was only the wind and rain lashing the bungalow.

It was on a stormy night that she'd first met Johnny. It was six months after she'd gone to hear the great Theosophist Madame Blavatsky speak at Cooper Union. Mary was captivated by the Russian lady, with her ideas of ever-evolving mankind, of union with the divine and the spirit realm. She met privately with the great woman, offering funding in exchange for esoteric knowledge. "You will meet a man who will offer you a door into another world," Madame Blavatsky told her, and the very next day, during a downpour in which she was without a hansom, an imposing man with mesmerizing blue eyes offered her a ride. His name was John Hobbes, and he shared her fascination with the mystical. He was descendant, he confessed, of a holy tribe called the Brethren, favored by God, and had been chosen among them to fulfill their sacred mission on earth. He showed her wonders she could not explain and shared knowledge she never dreamed possible. He converted her to his faith and promised her a shining path, for she would be his Lady Sun.

It was this sense of destiny, of self-importance, that joined Mary and John. They were above all rules. They existed on a higher plane and for a higher purpose. Before her adventures in the spirit world, Mary had been haunted by occasional doubts about what she'd done to Ethan. But with John's help she saw that it had the sense of rightness about it, a plan preordained: Had she not punished Ethan's wickedness and inherited his money, she would not have been able to help John in his mission. Therefore, it was good and right and meant to be that she'd killed her husband that night in his bed.

A floorboard creaked in the house, but Mary was only vaguely aware of it; she was lost to her reverie. She thought back on John showing her the old book with its eleven offerings, explaining what he meant to do—what he had been chosen to do. At first, she'd admit, she'd had reservations. Fear, even. But he'd kissed her sweetly, then fiercely, overpowering her in the way she liked, the way she craved, and she was utterly his. He was a golden god. And she, Mary White, was his sacred consort. The Beast would rise. The world would burn. A new society would evolve from the ashes. They would rule it as king and queen. She, little Mary White, who came from nothing. And when John saw that he would be taken, a sacrifice like a lesser one two thousand years before, she'd followed his instructions, paying off the guards and a driver, secreting his body through New York's cobblestone streets in the night. She'd had him buried up in the hills behind the ruins of the old village, and, as promised, she'd kept Knowles' End from the wrecking ball or new owners, paying the taxes every month even though she'd had to spend down her fortune and live in a shack to do it. He'd been very specific about that, and when she'd asked why, he'd never answered. It was the one mystery he would not share with her.

The floorboards groaned loudly.

"Who is it? Who's there?" She drew the bedsheets up to her neck. "I'm an old woman! What do you want?"

The creaking came again. It was not the wind playing havoc with a shutter. It was definitely inside, definitely a floorboard. Oh, why had she told Eleanor she could go out tonight?

The creaking sound stopped on the other side of the curtain. Mary's blood pounded against her ears.

"Who...who?" she croaked like an owl.

The curtain opened very slowly and the dark was filled with a golden glow. Mary White let out a small cry of happiness.

"I knew you'd come!"

John Hobbes moved to the foot of the old woman's bed. His shirt was gone, and she gazed at the black ink of the symbols rippling against the glow of his skin. Why was he not rushing to embrace her? Had she grown so old that he was repulsed by her? But her form, her visage, was only a shell; they were joined in spirit. Soon, he'd make her his queen, his Lady Sun! He had come back to her, just as he'd said he would.

"I've been faithful, as I promised. The old house kept."

Silence from him. Nothing but the *tap-tap-tap* of the rain, the banshee wail of the wind. Lightning sparked outside her bedroom window, lighting the side of his face. His eyes. There was something not right about his eyes.

"Johnny. Johnny, my love…" Tears pooled at the corners of her eyes. "It's been so long. Let me look at you."

Still he said nothing. Mary was angry. Hadn't she kept her end of the bargain all these years?

"'Behold and the Beast was made flesh, and when he spake it was as tongues of fire, and the heavens trembled at the sound.'"

Mary White made a small, strangled cry of joy. His voice! After all these years, still so resonant. Still so magnificent.

"Yes, yes, my love…Speak to me, your humble servant.…"

"I need you to write a note, Mary."

"Yes, love. Anything."

The paper appeared as if by magic under her hands. The pen, too. He told her what to write, told her to tuck it into her pocket, where it could be found.

"Found? I don't understand, Johnny.…"

"'At the lamentation of the widow, every tongue was stilled and the heavens opened at her cries.…'"

No. That couldn't be right. Not the tenth offering. He meant the eleventh: the Marriage of the Beast and the Woman Clothed in the Sun. She was his Lady Sun. They would be joined. She would be made immortal, like him. They would be…

"And thus was the tenth offering made."

"John. John!"

"Look upon my new form and be amazed."

All the love she'd felt before turned to a cold fear. In the pulses of lightning, he emerged: A wing. A talon. Tips of teeth sharp as razors. And the eyes, the burning, bottomless eyes, the windows of the soul, but there was no soul in those twin pools of flame. In them, she saw the sham of her life laid out like a book, the foolish belief that she, that anyone, could escape the consequences of this world, could flee from death. That was the deceit. The true serpent in the garden. *And dust you shall eat all the days of your life....*

"Look at me."

Mary White looked and was amazed and could not tear her gaze away from the sight of him, could not stop the dry catch of breath in her throat as her scream died there before it could reach her tongue.

Along the shore, the wind swirled sand into small hills and broke them down again, carrying the grains on. The sideshow workers packed up their cards and dice. A dog barked and was rewarded with hot-dog scraps. The bearded lady sighed at her window; her lover was late. The globe of the world spun and wobbled, set in motion by some invisible finger. A thin cloak of gray clouds passed in the night sky; the moon ducked behind them and hid its face for grief.

SERGEANT LEONARD

Jericho pulled himself to a sitting position and hissed with pain. He was sore and his shirt was off. The faded scar, which snaked down the front of his broad chest, was now partially hidden by a layer of soft down. There was a new wound—a stitched hole above his left pectoral muscle—and Jericho remembered being surrounded in the woods, remembered the gun going off and the impact. He pieced together what must have happened and realized with growing horror that Evie must know everything now. But there she was on the other bed, asleep in her clothes, her shoes still on. She'd stayed with him, he realized. She'd found out and chosen to stay.

Jericho lay back down on his side, watching her breathe just an arm's length from him. She was not beautiful while she slept; her mouth hung open and she snored very lightly, and this, despite everything that had happened, made him smile. Dreaming, she stirred and stretched, and he looked away. The first glimmerings of dawn showed through the window. The tiny tin clock on the bedside table read ten minutes past five. Evie's eyes fluttered open, and Jericho quickly pulled the sheet up to cover his scars.

"Jericho?" Evie asked, her voice still sleep-caked.

"What happened, Evie?"

"You were shot. Unc and I got you back here," she said carefully. "Jericho, what's in those blue vials?"

"How many did it take?"

"Three."

"Did I...did I hurt you or Will?"

"No," she lied. "Jericho, please."

"You won't understand," he said softly.

"Please stop telling me that."

"You won't."

"I won't unless you tell me."

"The infantile paralysis. There was no miracle. It burned through me just like it did my sister. It shut down my legs, then my arms, and finally my lungs. They put me in the metal coffin and told me I'd be in it for the rest of my life. Trapped. I'd never breathe on my own. Never walk or ride a horse again. Never touch anyone." His gaze flicked over the curve of Evie's body. "Never do a thing but stare up at that ceiling till I died. After the war, there were soldiers coming back with their arms and legs missing. Men blown apart. They had a secret innovation they were trying—the Daedalus program—to help the soldiers coming back."

"What sort of innovation?"

Jericho took a deep breath. "A merging of man and machine. A human-automaton hybrid," Jericho said. "They would replace what had been damaged beyond repair in the war or by disease with steel and wires and cogs. We would be the perfect miracle of the industrial age. The robotnik. You're staring."

Evie quickly looked away. "I...I'm sorry. It's so fantastic. I just don't understand...." She looked at him again. "Please."

"We were the test subjects," Jericho continued. "They wouldn't tell us anything except that the machinery would replace our defective parts and, over time, fuse with our very human systems. This was achieved by a new miracle serum—the vials of blue liquid—and vitamin tonic. It was supposed to keep the balance between our two selves. We would change mankind, they promised."

"That's astonishing. But why hasn't it been in the papers? Why isn't this the biggest story since Moses brought down the Ten Commandments?"

"Because it didn't work," Jericho said bitterly.

"But . . . I don't understand."

"I told you there were others." With one finger, Jericho rolled a spent ampoule in his palm. "Their bodies rejected the formula, or the machinery, or both. It might be a few days or a few weeks, but then they'd turn feverish as the infection burned through their ravaged bodies, proving just how human they were after all. But the ones who died were lucky."

"Lucky?" Evie said, incredulous.

Jericho's expression darkened. "Some went mad. They'd see things that weren't there, talk to nothing at all. They'd rage with prophecies. Or they'd go wild until the orderlies would have to come with the restraints, and even then it took an awful lot of men to hold them down. The doctors doped them while they tried to figure out what to do. I watched them shrink back into themselves. Husks sent off to asylums to die."

Jericho placed the ampoule on the bedside table. The glass still had a blue cast to it. "There was this soldier in the bed beside mine. Sergeant Barry Leonard, from Topeka. I remember he told me that if I wanted to know what Topeka looked like, I should just imagine hell with a dry-goods store. And the dry-goods store didn't have anything you wanted, anyway. He was a pretty funny fellow."

Jericho grinned at some private memory, then went serious again.

"He'd come back from the war with both legs and an arm gone. Less than half a man lying in that bed. People walked right past him. They wouldn't even look. It was as if they were afraid that if they looked, they'd catch his bad luck. His pain was more terrifying to them than death."

Evie bent her arm, propped her head up with one hand. Jericho sat up and draped the sheet around him, but not before Evie sneaked a furtive glance at his chest—the soft golden hair, the beautiful muscle, the long older scar alongside the newer one made by Uncle Will. She wanted to touch him, to place a kiss at the center of his chest.

"They took us both for Daedalus, said we were good candidates. They wheeled us in together. Just before I went under the ether, I saw Sergeant Leonard grinning at me. 'Don't take any wooden nickels, kid.' That's what he always used to say." Jericho's smile was wan. "I still remember what it felt like to wiggle my toes for the first time in months. You wouldn't know that a big toe could be so incredible. The first time I walked outside and felt the sun on my face…" He shook his head. "I wanted to reach up and pull the sun down, hold it like a ball you get for a birthday when you're a kid, never let it go. Within a week, I was running. I could run for miles and not tire. Sergeant Leonard ran alongside me, daring me to keep up. When we finished, he patted me on the back like a brother. He said we were a new breed, the future. The way he said it, full of wonder and hope…" Jericho shook away the memory. "We would sit together on the bench in the courtyard, looking out at the sun setting over the hills, marveling at the constancy of it."

Evie felt like she wanted to say something, but she couldn't think of anything that wouldn't sound hollow. Besides, Jericho was talking to her, telling her the story she'd wanted to hear, and she was wary of breaking the spell.

"It started with his hand." Jericho paused, sipped from Evie's glass of water, resumed. "One day, he couldn't make a fist. I remember that moment so clearly. He turned to me and said, 'It's like my doggone hand is drunk. Kid, you didn't take my hand off base for a quick one while I was sleeping, didya?' He said it like it was a joke. But I could tell he was scared. He didn't tell the doctors, though. He just kept telling them he felt fit as a fiddle."

Jericho worried the edge of the sheet between his fingers, pulling it taut, relaxing it again.

"He would get awful moody. Agitated. Once, he threw a plate of potatoes against a wall, and it left a hole there. His eyes were haunted. He asked me to run with him. He ran me into the ground. He couldn't or wouldn't stop. I let him go; I couldn't keep up. Later, I saw him standing in the courtyard in the rain. Just standing there, letting it wash over him. I ran out to tell him to come inside, and he said, 'It's like I've got too much inside me. It just pushes and pushes with nowhere to go.' I got him to come inside and lie down. I could hear him in the dark, whispering, 'Please...please...please.' Anyway, one night he went a little crazy. He stripped off all his clothes and ran through the hospital like an ape, swinging from the pipes, smashing windows. 'I am the future!' he screamed. It took four orderlies to catch him and strap him to the bed. The doctor came in and explained that the process had become unstable. For his own good, they'd need to stop it."

Jericho buried his head in his hands for a minute before continuing.

"He was shouting at them, screaming, 'You can't do this to

me! I'm a man! Look at me—I'm a man!' over and over. They gave him a shot of something to calm him, but he kept struggling, kept screaming that he was a man, he had his rights, they just needed to give him a chance, a stinkin' chance. Then the drug began to take effect; he couldn't struggle much. He was crying, begging, pleading with them and God as they wheeled him out." Jericho shook his head at some memory beyond words. "They reversed the process, I heard. Even worse, they had to take the other arm, too. It had spread throughout his body."

Jericho fell quiet. Outside, someone was trying to start a car in the cold. The motor protested with a shudder.

"He hung himself with his belt in the showers."

"Oh, god," Evie said. "How horrible."

Jericho nodded mechanically. "They couldn't figure out how he'd done it, with no legs and no arms."

The car's motor caught, and they listened to the comfort of its banal purr as it shook, idled, then spurred into action and drove away. Jericho's voice grew even softer, until it was almost a whisper.

"It was late; I'd been sleeping. I woke up to the sound of him crying. The ward was dark, with only the light from the nurses' station bleeding in. 'Kid,' he said to me, and his voice... his voice was like a ghost. Like that part of him had already died and had come back for the rest. 'Kid, this is worse than Topeka.' He told me that once, in the war, he'd come upon a German soldier in the grass with his insides falling out; he was just lying there in agony. The soldier had looked up at Sergeant Leonard, and even though they didn't speak the same language, they understood each other with just a look. The German lying on the ground; the American standing over him. He put a bullet in the soldier's head. He didn't do it with anger, as an enemy, but as a fellow man, one soldier helping another. 'One soldier helping another.' That's how he put it." Again, Jericho fell quiet for a moment. "He told me what he needed me to do. Told me I didn't have to. Told me that if I did, he'd make sure God would forgive me, if that's what I was worried about. One soldier helping another."

Jericho fell quiet. Evie held so still she thought she might break.

"I found his belt in the dresser and helped him into the wheelchair. The hall was quiet on the way to the shower. I remember how clean the floor was, like a mirror. I had to make a new hole in the leather to tighten it around his neck. Even without his arms and legs, he was heavy. But I was strong. Just before, he looked at me, and I'll never forget his face as long as I live—like he'd just realized some great secret, but it was too late to do anything about it. 'Some craps game, this life, kid. Don't let 'em take you without a fight,' he said."

Silence. A dog barking in the distance. A puff of wind against the glass, wanting to be let in.

"After, I took the wheelchair back and parked it in the same spot. Then I slipped under the covers and pretended to sleep until it was morning and they found him. Then I did sleep. For twelve hours straight."

Evie's throat was dry, but she didn't want to reach for her water. She swallowed to soothe her aching throat, trying to make as little sound as possible, and after a moment Jericho continued.

"I don't know if that story about the German soldier was real or something he made up to get me to help him. It doesn't matter. Neither does God's forgiveness. After Sergeant Leonard's death, they shut down the Daedalus program. It was too much of a risk. The doctors and scientists wanted to shut me down, too. They were afraid of what might happen with me. They would've put me right back in that iron coffin to rot, but your uncle stepped in. He said he'd take me home to die with dignity. Then he loaded up a kit with serum. As far as they're concerned, Jericho Jones died ten years ago. If Will hadn't taken me in, I'd be there now, staring at that same ceiling, with no soldier to help me out."

Evie sat up. "But you were cured. You could be the key to some astonishing advance."

"Cured?" Jericho scoffed. "I live every day knowing something could go wrong, and I'll be back in that iron coffin. I'm the only one of my kind. Half man, half machine. A freak."

"You're not a freak."

"I don't even know what I am," Jericho said. He glanced at Evie. "You're different, too."

"So it seems."

"Two of a kind." Jericho reached out and took Evie's hands. He turned her hands palm up and rubbed his thumbs over the insides of her wrists. The softness of her skin was a miracle. Jericho didn't know if he would function like a normal man. He only knew that he had all the feelings of one. He wanted Evie. He wanted her desperately. With his hands on hers, he imagined what it would be like to kiss her, to make love to her. She was a little spoiled and often selfish, a good-time girl with a surprising kind streak. She ran toward life full tilt while Jericho held back, not daring. She made him feel alive, and he wanted more of it.

A loud bang at the door made Evie jump. She was afraid it was the innkeeper come to throw them out, but it was Will who stood outside the door, his hat on and his pocket watch open. The sky was already graying toward daybreak.

"Ah, good. You're up. Almost dawn. Time to go, before the Brethren come looking for us."

SOLOMON'S COMET

Will's filthy car crossed from the South Bronx into Upper Manhattan, and the city appeared under a haze of clouds and smoke like a mirage conjured of dirt and steel. Evie was exhausted from the ordeal in Brethren and from her night watching Jericho and from hearing his heartbreaking confession. She was unsettled, too, by the feelings she had developed for him.

Manhattan's never-ending line of buildings flew past the automobile's windows and she thought how close they had come in Brethren. But they had prevailed. They had the pendant. Tonight they would perform the ritual and banish John Hobbes from this world for good. And after that, she would ask Will to explain what it all meant. She would ask him to tell her exactly what she was and what to do about it. Later. She rested her hand against her own talisman and went to sleep.

Evie walked through the day in a haze of nerves. The museum had never been busier, it seemed, their attendance made doubly large because of Solomon's Comet. The whole city was abuzz. Mayor Walker had asked New Yorkers to dim their lights just before midnight so that the comet could be seen without a haze during its once-in-a-lifetime appearance. Many New Yorkers had already pulled their chairs and cushions—even mattresses—onto the tar beaches of their buildings' rooftops or small terraces. The five-and-dimes sold out of their hats and blowers. Nightclubs advertised special raffles to be held at midnight and offered drinks like the Solomon's Sensation and the Falling Star. There was even a bathing-beauty contest that promised to crown a Miss Comet. It was as if someone was hosting a party and all of Manhattan had been invited. But Evie wasn't feeling celebratory; if they didn't do everything just right, this would be the end. John Hobbes would be here to stay, and hell would come with him.

When the last patron had gone from the museum, Evie locked the doors and she, Sam, and Jericho gathered in the library. It was seven o'clock. The comet was to make its way across New York's skies at one minute before midnight. Jericho rested on the settee, still weak from the previous night's ordeal.

"Are you feeling all right, Jericho?" Evie asked a bit shyly. "Can I get you anything?"

"No, I'm...jake, thanks," he said, trying out the word with a smile.

Sam watched the two of them from the sidelines. Something had happened up in Brethren beyond their finding the pendant and escaping from the new faithful. And Sam didn't like it.

"Gee whiz, I'm a nervous wreck," Evie said. She flipped on the radio. The Paul Whiteman Orchestra was playing a special hour of hot jazz dedicated to "Old King Solomon." The merry songs felt out of place given their purpose tonight.

"There's something I don't get," Sam asked. "How come he

didn't make the tenth offering yet? You think he's going to do the last two offerings together, tonight?"

Evie bit at her fingernail. It *was* odd. "I don't know. All I know is that if we burn the pendant tonight and repeat the incantation, we get rid of John Hobbes forever."

Will burst into the library carrying a bag of supplies. "I've got what we need here."

He handed Evie a piece of chalk and Sam a can of salt. "Evie, draw a wide circle on the floor, and a pentagram inside it. Sam, you go around the perimeter of the room with the salt, please."

There came a knock at the museum's front door, very loud and very insistent.

"What now?" Evie said. "Don't worry—I'll tell them the museum is closed for the evening."

She was stunned to find Detective Malloy at the front door. He was not full of his usual gallows humor. In fact, his expression could only be called grim. Evie felt her stomach drop. Flanked by several officers, he walked right past her on his way to the library. Will paled when he saw them.

"There's been another murder," Malloy said. "Mary White Blodgett was found out at Coney, in the Tunnel of Love. Same markings as all the others. Her tongue had been cut out."

"'At the sight of the Beast, the widow offered lamentations until her tongue was stilled. . . .'" Evie said softly.

"The Lamentation of the Widow. The tenth offering," Sam said.

Will looked pale and sick.

"Mrs. Blodgett's daughter said she'd been visited by you and a young lady two days ago. Said you were asking all sorts of odd questions about John Hobbes," Malloy continued.

"It's true," Will said.

"You didn't think to share that with me, Fitz?" The detective sounded hurt and angry.

"I didn't think…It wasn't relevant. I was playing a hunch."

"I get paid to follow hunches," Malloy said. "And I told you to stay away from the case. And if I ask you whether you have Ruta Badowski's other shoe buckle in your museum, you would say what?"

"I would say that's preposterous," Will answered.

Malloy's face was grim and a bit weary, as if he'd been told of the imminent death of a sick friend. "I'm asking you as a friend, Will."

Will's gaze was steely. "As I said, preposterous."

Malloy nodded slowly. "I hope you're right. Mind if we have a look around, Professor?"

Already, the police were swarming the museum, emptying drawers and opening cabinets. An officer nearly dropped a figurine and Will called out, "Could you be careful with those, please? Those are priceless artifacts."

Another officer reached into Will's desk drawer and pulled out Ruta Badowski's shoe buckle. "It's here. Just like the note said."

"How did that…?" Will stood perfectly still for once, as if he'd been nailed in place. "Wait a moment—what note? What are you talking about?"

"Can you tell me how evidence from a murder victim got into your museum?" Malloy didn't blink.

"I don't know," Will said softly. "I swear I don't, Terrence."

"And I suppose you don't know how your cigarette lighter ended up at a murder scene, either?" Detective Malloy held up Will's missing lighter.

Will's hand went immediately to his empty breast pocket. "I-I lost it recently, and…"

"It was found at Mary White Blodgett's house."

"I took the shoe buckle," Sam blurted out. "Found it out at the seaport and thought I could make a quick buck off it. There are creepy chumps who pay for that stuff."

"Sam, don't," Evie warned.

He gave her a wan smile. "It's okay, doll. Let's call it even on that twenty bucks."

"Nice little crew you've got, Fitz," Malloy said. He took in the room: the pentacle chalked on the floor. The salt, half-poured. The pendant. "What's going on here, Will?"

"If I tell you, you'll think I've gone mad."

"If you don't tell me here, you'll be telling me downtown!" Malloy thundered. "I don't think you understand what sort of trouble you're in here, Fitz!"

"Detective Malloy, please, what note did you find?" Evie pressed.

"It was written by Mrs. Blodgett just before she died and shoved into the pocket of her robe. Her daughter confirms it's her handwriting. It names Will as the murderer."

Will reeled. "What?"

"That's a load of bunk!" Sam shouted.

"She said we'd find the evidence of it at the museum. Said you'd been asking her about the murders for some time, that you did it to drum up interest in the museum." Malloy's beefy shoulders sagged. He seemed to have aged ten years in those few moments spent holding Ruta Badowski's broken shoe buckle. "Mr. Fitzgerald, you're going to need to accompany us downtown and answer some questions. Fellas, bring the little thief, too, for good measure."

"Oh, he's clever. He's very, very clever," Will said, more to himself than to anyone else. "Don't you see? He knew we were close! He knew! He got her to write that note. He laid a trap, and we walked right into it."

"Oh, Unc!" Evie said. "What are we going to do?"

"What are you talking about?" Malloy asked.

"Terrence, this is going to sound like I've gone over the edge, but I assure you I am quite sane. The Pentacle Killer isn't a copycat, and he certainly isn't me. He's John Hobbes."

Malloy's face remained stony. "John Hobbes, who died fifty years ago? You're telling me a dead man committed these murders?"

"Through some sort of sorcery, his spirit manifested on this plane, yes. I know it sounds completely mad—"

"But it's true!" Evie interrupted. "That's why we had to go to Brethren, to his secret grave, and dig up his body. It's why we must destroy his pendant—to release his spirit from this world. And if we don't do it before the comet comes tonight, we're all in for it."

Evie realized how ridiculous they sounded. The other officers snickered. Only Malloy didn't, and he looked very angry, indeed.

"You know, Fitz, I never figured you for believing in that wad of chewing gum you sell here at the museum. I also never figured you for a murderer." He turned to the other officers and said, "Take him."

The officers surrounded Will and Sam, leading them out of the museum.

"Murder. Grave robbing. Destroying property. Thievery. And corruption of the young..." Malloy trailed off, but not before Evie heard the full weariness and disgust in his voice. "I guess you just never really know anybody, do you?"

Evie ran after them, her heels clacking against the marble floor. "Please, you can't take him, Detective Malloy! We have to stop John Hobbes tonight. He's going to strike during Solomon's Comet and become the Beast. It's our last chance!"

"Sweetheart, I don't know what he's been telling you, but there's no such thing as ghost killers. There's no such thing as ghosts, period. There's no bogeyman raising up some Beast bent on bringing the end of the world. That's a fairy tale. That's all. I'm sorry." Malloy's jowly face was filled with sympathy.

"Terrence, please listen to me—you've got to stop him before he makes his last offering tonight," Will pleaded as the officers angled him into the back of a waiting police car.

"If he strikes tonight, you're off the hook, Professor," a nearby officer snarled before closing the door.

Back inside the museum, Evie paced a path around the library. Jericho watched her. "How are we going to stop him? Think, Evie, think."

"They took the pendant with them."

"There has to be another way." Evie opened the Book of the Brethren, carefully examining each page. When she got to the last page, the eleventh offering, she stared at it. The Beast stood over the prone body of the woman, their hands joined. There was a small altar. Above them, the night sky burned with the comet's fire.

"Why would he ask Mary White to keep the house?" Evie mused.

"He needed a place to come home to," Jericho said. "He needed someplace safe."

"But he's left the bodies in very public places. So he could have gone anywhere. Why there? What does he need from it?" Evie was on the move again and traveling the room.

"You're beginning to remind me of your uncle," Jericho said. "And you're making me a bit dizzy."

"Sorry." Evie sat at the long table with its perilous stacks of books, thinking. She took Ida Knowles's diary in hand. "Ida

Knowles's last entry was made just before she went into the cellar, presumably. What was down there?"

"The police never found anything other than a basement full of bones."

"'Anoint thy flesh and prepare ye the walls of your houses. . . .'" Evie recited. She thought back to the day she and Mabel had gone to Knowles' End. She'd noticed a fat chimney from the outside of the house but couldn't seem to find the corresponding fireplace inside. And then later, in the basement, she'd felt a draft.

Evie was suddenly up and scurrying about the library, pocketing matches, gathering flashlights.

"What are you doing?"

"I think there's some sort of secret room, a place that is special to him, and that is where he's hiding whatever it is that's keeping him alive." Evie glanced at the clock. It was ten thirty. "We'll need to hurry if we're to make it in time."

Jericho got to his feet, wincing at the pain from his wound. "Where are we going?"

"We're not going to wait for John Hobbes to take his last victim. We're taking the fight to him. We're going to Knowles' End."

THE BELLY OF THE BEAST

How do you stop a ghost? How do you sever a thread of evil once it has woven itself into the world? Those questions coiled tightly in Evie's mind as she and Jericho drove Will's car through streets crowded with revelers ready to welcome Solomon's Comet. Flappers performed an impromptu cancan as they staggered along to the next party. Just ahead, a stilt-walker wobbled on long, spindly legs, blocking the way. Through the window, a drunken man in a harlequin hat blew a paper horn at Evie rather suddenly, startling a scream from her. "Got ya!" He cackled and reeled away, laughing like a devil. She honked the horn furiously at the stilt-walker until he clambered aside. A path opened and she honked the car's horn as a warning to everyone else.

Farther north, the crowds thinned. Above them, shadows from the great metal cage of the elevated tracks washed over the hood of the Ford, *light, dark, light, dark*. Soon they were driving along the desolate banks of the Hudson, their headlights the only illumination. At last they came to the old Knowles house. It looked down on the street like a forgotten god, the moon fat and white behind it.

Evie slipped around to the broken servants' entrance on the side where she'd gotten in before. The door swung open with a loud creak. The last time she'd been at the house, it had been in the full light of day, bright with sunshine. Now it was very dark, and every shape seemed menacing. Evie turned on her flashlight. The pale beam fell across a broken icebox, a Hoosier cabinet, a sink apron. It illuminated the hunchbacked form of a rat on a counter. The rat swiveled its pointed nose toward the light before skittering away into the comforting dark.

"This way," Evie said.

She led Jericho to the butler's pantry, and tried not to think about John Hobbes waiting inside one of those tall cabinets, ready to leap out as she walked past. She hurried into the hall that connected the kitchen with the rest of the house. "Careful," Evie whispered. "There are traps throughout."

There were many doors, and she couldn't be certain which would lead to the cellar. She certainly didn't want to go down the way she had the last time.

"What could be keeping him alive? What's his conduit into this world?" Jericho asked.

"I don't know, but it must be hidden somewhere in this house. I'll tear down every wall looking for it if I have to," Evie said. "What time is it?"

Jericho put down the cans of kerosene he carried and angled his wristwatch under Evie's flashlight. "Twenty past eleven."

"We don't have long."

The house felt different to her. She struggled to pinpoint what, exactly, had changed. *Alive. Awake. Ready.* Those were the words that came to mind, as if the house were a living organism, a great womb on the verge of some terrible birth. The beam of her light skimmed over the moldy wallpaper. The walls were slick with condensation. Sweat dripped down Evie's back as well. The chill of her last visit had been replaced by an almost stifling heat. She opened a door and found only a shallow closet. The inside of the closet door was damp. They tried other doors and found a bedroom, an office, and a water closet.

"Why can't we find it?" Evie asked. "I don't understand why I can't find the entrance. It was here before. It's almost..." *It's almost as if the house is hiding it from us*, she'd started to say. "Let's keep looking. I'm sure I must be remembering it wrong. There's a parlor to the right."

They came to it, but the parlor's pocket doors were closed. "These were open before."

With effort, they slid them open. Jericho's flashlight moved slowly around the room. But it was different, too. The sheets had been removed from the furniture.

"It wasn't this way before," Evie whispered.

"It's like it was expecting us," Jericho said quietly.

"Why did you say 'it'?" Evie asked. Jericho didn't answer, but they were both feeling it—the house. The house was waiting.

Evie's flashlight beam crawled across the walls. They seemed to bow outward just slightly. *Like lungs, breathing*, she thought, and then chased the thought away. It was hard to see anything in the gloom. Her beam traveled to the broken mirror, blinding her with the reflection. She blinked, and in the afterimage she could swear she'd seen somber, ghostly faces. Gasping, she swung the light around, but there was nothing behind her. The house groaned and creaked.

"I don't like this," Jericho said.

"What choice do we have? If we don't stop him now, tonight, he'll manifest fully. And then we *can't* fight him."

"But we don't have the pendant anymore. How are we..." He

lowered his voice, as if the house might be listening. "How are we going to bind his spirit?"

"We'll find something else," Evie whispered back. "Or we'll burn this place down if we have to."

Jericho moved his hand up and down. "Do you see that light?" He followed the thin beam to a rosette carved into the fireplace. "I think there might be something behind this." He put his face close, trying to see.

"Jericho, don't!" Evie called suddenly.

A gust of dusty air blew into Jericho's face. He coughed and sputtered and waved it away. It had a sickeningly sweet smell, like dying flowers. Jericho blinked and shook his head.

"Are you all right?"

"Yes. Fine," he said, but his voice shook.

The fireplace flared to life, and Evie and Jericho both jumped.

"He knows we're here," Evie whispered.

"How can he know that?"

"I think... I think the house is telling him. We have to hurry. What time is it?"

Jericho checked his watch again. "Eleven twenty."

"You said that last time I asked."

Jericho moved his watch into the beam of Evie's flashlight again. The second hand wasn't moving. "It's not working. It was working fine before we..."

Entered the house. He didn't need to say it.

"I don't like this," Jericho whispered, wiping beads of sweat from his forehead. He was a bit glassy-eyed, and Evie wished that he had his full strength. "You think that whatever is keeping his spirit alive is hidden somewhere inside this house?"

Evie nodded.

"Then I say we waste no time. Let's burn it. Burn it and run."

The wind gusted against the house and it groaned. Will had been very clear that they needed to dispatch the ghost of John Hobbes on his own terms: They should bind him to the pendant and burn it. But the police had the pendant, and Will was in custody. It was up to Evie and Jericho.

"Burn it and run," Evie agreed. She grabbed one can of kerosene. There was an awful lot of house to cover. "We have to destroy it utterly. I'll take the upstairs. You work down here."

Jericho shook his head. "I'm not letting you out of my sight."

"Jericho, be reasonable."

"No. We stay together."

"Let's get to work, then."

They moved quickly from room to room, splashing kerosene over anything that might burn. Evie crept up into the attic room that had once belonged to Ida Knowles. Through a crack in the boards nailed to the window, she could see the city in the distance. People were out there, reveling, dancing, celebrating the comet's return, with no idea what it signified. From downstairs came the faint, dull thrum of music. It sounded vaguely like voices raised in the singing of a hymn. She motioned Jericho to stop sloshing the kerosene and stand still, but she no longer heard it.

"Let's hurry," she said. As they came down the stairs, one gave way, and Jericho nearly plummeted through. Evie had to yank him back to his feet. They returned to the ballroom and Evie gasped. The chairs had been arranged in a circle, as they had been at Brethren.

"Jericho," Evie whispered, backing out of the room.

"*Naughty John, Naughty John does his work with his apron on,*" Jericho sang and laughed.

"Jericho, that isn't funny."

He had the strangest smile. "Do you hear that music?"

Evie cocked her head, listening, but this time she heard nothing but the groans and creaks of the old house. "No."

"It's like a party!" Jericho smiled happily. "Let's dance. You love to dance, don't you, Evie?" He swept her into his arms, turning her around so quickly she felt dizzy.

"Jericho, what's the matter with you?" Evie said, and then she remembered: the puff of dust from the rosette. The powerful plants the Brethren used to make their wine and smoke. Jericho was under its effects now.

"I've always wanted to dance with you," he murmured, nuzzling his face against her neck. "I've watched you, you know. When you didn't think anyone was looking." He brought his mouth to her ear. His breath was warm; it made her skin tingle. "I've thought about you, late at night. So many nights..."

She had to get him out of the house; that was the thing. She'd misjudged this place. It was a coconspirator, every bit as formidable as John Hobbes. It would do anything to protect him. "And dance we will," Evie said, pushing away from Jericho. "But not here."

"Yes. Here," he said, pulling her close again, pressing her against him. The walls sighed, she could swear, and from somewhere came a dreadful cackling.

"I know a better spot! This way," Evie said, dragging Jericho toward the kitchen. She had to get him out the door, out into the fresh air. Then she could toss a lit match into the house and run with Jericho as far away as they could get.

"Where are you taking me?" Jericho asked dreamily.

"Almost there," Evie said, and though she tried to sound offhand, her voice shook. As if it could sense her plan, the door slammed shut.

"No!" Evie pulled on the handle, turning it wildly, but it

wouldn't budge, not even when she threw herself against the door again and again. They were trapped. The house would not let them go.

Jericho held out his hand. "Dance with me," he said hoarsely.

"Jericho, we have to leave. Now. Do you understand?"

"I only understand that I want you."

The smell of kerosene was everywhere. It wouldn't take much to send the whole thing up in a fireball with the two of them inside. Fine. If they couldn't get out this way, she'd try another— pry the shutters off a window, hurl a chair against a lock, whatever it took to get out.

Evie grabbed Jericho's outstretched hand and dragged him along behind her. He was cackling; the sound of it traveled up her spine, made her want to run and leave everything—including him—behind. She'd reached the front door when she heard something from outside. Was someone coming up the street? If she shouted, would they hear her? She raced to the windows beside the front door, ready to pry the wood off with her bare hands if need be.

Whistling. The person coming up the street was whistling that old familiar tune. Goose bumps prickled along her arms.

"He's coming. We have to hide."

Her eyes darting wildly, Evie searched the room, twirling around madly. Where? Where could they hide? What if even now Naughty John was coming home, bringing his last offering with him? Could Evie find it within herself to lie in wait, to strike before he could finish his gruesome task? All she needed was to wait him out and strike before the comet passed. Then it would be over for John Hobbes. She would do it. She had to do it. But where to hide? Evie's flashlight traveled over glistening walls thick with oozing slime.

The whistle was coming closer.

"Can't you hear them?" Jericho murmured. "They're here. They're waiting."

Jericho. She had to shut him up. There was a small room off to the left. Evie pushed him toward it. "In you go," she said. Jericho turned the door handle and the floor gave way beneath him. He disappeared into blackness.

"Jericho! Jericho!" Evie yelled into the dark hole in the floor. There was no response. Did the trap open into the cellar, as the chute had? Could he be there now, on the dirt floor, with a broken leg or a dashed skull? But where was the entrance? She ran into the large foyer again and paused, listening. The whistling had stopped. Her heart beat so hard against the cage of her ribs that she thought they would break from the pressure. Her throat was too dry to allow her to swallow. *Move, Evie*, she told herself, but she was paralyzed with fear. Hopelessness weighted her to the spot. How could she possibly win against such unspeakable evil? Why, if she gave up now, it would be over quickly, and she wouldn't be around to watch the world burn. The house sighed and purred around her, as if murmuring its accord.

And then suddenly she saw it: Under the staircase was a door that hadn't been there before. It was slick with wet, gleaming like bone in the dark.

"Jericho!" she called again. "I'm coming after you. Don't move."

The house took a breath and held it. A shadow passed before the front windows, quick as a bird's wing. He was home. He was coming. With a gasp, Evie rushed for the cellar door. The knob turned easily. The door swung open. There was nowhere to go but down, into the depths of Naughty John's killing ground.

It was pitch-black on the stairs. Evie slid her palms down the walls as she felt for the edge of each step. The plaster was warm to the touch, damp and sticky. Her heartbeat was quick as a bird's; her head thudded with the pulse of her blood. The house had gone quiet again, and she found that more frightening than the whistling. She hoped Jericho wasn't hurt. She willed herself to keep going until she reached the basement floor at last. It was unbearably hot. The dirt floor felt soft, sodden under her feet. It warmed the soles of her shoes, forcing her to move. Evie took small, tentative steps. Which way to go? Where was John Hobbes? Should she turn on her flashlight? Or was she safer cloaked in the gloom? What was out there in the vast, unknowable dark?

The walls were breathing. *Oh, god.* She could hear them! She could stand the dark no longer. Shaking, she clicked on the flashlight.

From somewhere above her, she heard the soft, high whistle of a nursery song. But this song didn't belong in any nursery.

John Hobbes's voice rang out. "'The Lord spake as if with the tongues of a thousand angels. All that remained was the eleventh offering, the Marriage of the Beast and the Woman Clothed in the Sun. . . .' I know you're here, Lady Sun. I can feel you."

Evie's mind struggled to understand. He'd called her Lady Sun. Her. Lady Sun. The Woman Clothed in the Sun. Naughty John was home. He was home and ready to complete his transformation. He was looking for her—for *her*! Evie willed herself to keep going, bouncing the light of her flashlight around the room, looking for Jericho. She wished she were far away from here—at a nightclub or the Bennington or even in the museum's dull library. She had been foolish to think that she could take on a killer, a ghost, the Beast himself.

Above her, the whistling stopped and the song began: "*Naughty John, Naughty John, does his work with his apron on. Cuts your throat and takes your bones. Sells 'em off for a coupla stones. . . .*"

Fear thinned Evie's reason to a useless shaving of itself. She had to get out. Get away. She raced for the rickety steps. She didn't care—she'd take her chances. Run up and out. Get help. Scream her head off till all of New York heard and came. But no—Jericho. She had to find Jericho first. Maybe he'd fallen through and found a way out. She told herself this as she willed her legs forward. Why, even now he was probably running for help, and any moment the door would crash down as the police swarmed this godforsaken lair. Yes, any moment now, she'd hear Jericho's voice shouting her name: "Evie! Evie! You're safe. Come out!" Lost to her fear, Evie started to giggle and clamped a hand over her mouth.

Above her head, the floorboards creaked. Her heart doubled its rhythm. As damp as the room was, her throat was as dry as chalk, and she gagged. The footsteps upstairs thudded with a deliberateness at odds with the chaos raging in her blood. *Thump. Thump. Thump. Thump.* The shadows of two shoes appeared along the thin crack under the door at the top of the stairs.

Sharp, one-word impressions and commands fired in Evie's mind: *Him. Here. Hide. Where? Go. Now. Where? Coming. Coming. Down. Hide. Where?*

She remembered the draft of air she'd felt when she'd come to the house with Mabel, and she sprinted back into the dark cellar and put her hand up, hoping to find it again. A cool draft kissed her palm. She followed it to the far wall, behind the furnace. She might have missed the hidden door entirely if she hadn't put out a hand and felt the crack. She patted around the seam and choked back a sob when she could find no lock or handle, no way in.

The cellar door groaned open. Footsteps on the stairs now.

And then the door in front of her released of its own accord. Light shone from inside. Moonlight, Evie realized. It was a way out. It had to be a way out.

Evie passed through a narrow vestibule, which seemed to open out into a larger chamber. The light, she realized, came from an opening far above, a small window that looked out on the night sky. *The missing chimney,* she thought, and shuddered. The room itself had no windows and no door, except for the passage in. It was oddly shaped, like a star. In one corner sat an old iron brazier. A painted pentacle took up the entire floor. A grand altar carved with a comet had been placed at the very center of the pentacle. She turned slowly, taking in the whole of the room. The walls had been painted with symbols—a symbol for each of the eleven offerings, each of the murders.

A terrible, knowing cold came over her. How could she have been so stupid? How many times had she heard the phrase and thought nothing of it? It was in the Book of the Brethren, and in Ida Knowles's diary. She'd heard Pastor Algoode say it when she was under. The new Brethren disciples had preached it outside the fairgrounds. The rotted houses in the old camp on the hill had been painted with exactly the same symbols.

Prepare ye the walls of your houses. . . .

It wasn't a pendant or a book or any other object keeping John Hobbes alive. It was a place. A room. *This* room.

The Book of the Brethren lay on the altar, opened to the page for the eleventh offering. Evie stared at the drawing of the beautiful girl dressed in a shimmering gown of gold, an all-seeing eye painted on her forehead and outstretched palms. Her chest was open and her heart was in the hands of the Beast.

This was his true lair, then. The reason he'd had Mary White keep the house ready for him. And now she had walked right into it, into the belly of the Beast. She had to get out of there at once. If she had to, she'd throw a match and send Naughty John back to whatever hell would have him.

From deep in the cellar, she heard him singing, "*Naughty John, Naughty John, does his work with his apron on.*"

Evie's fingers fumbled for the matches in her pocket. Yes, she'd throw the match and run. Panic made her thoughts cloudy. Desperate. She sank to her haunches like an animal who knows it's cornered by the wolf.

Don't faint, don't faint, don't faint, whatever you do, don't faint, old girl. . . .

The wolf was at the door. His shadow spilled into the room, taking it over. With shaking fingers, Evie lit a match and tossed it against shadow and air, watching the flame fizzle into smoke. She lit another and another, all reason lost now, the whole book of matches reduced to nubs. And despite her warnings, Evie's mind did not cooperate. Her eyes rolled back in their sockets and she slipped to the ground, unconscious.

THE WOMAN CLOTHED IN THE SUN

Stars. That's what Evie saw first. Above her, the inky sky twinkled with the false hope of stars. Her head ached where she'd hit it on the floor. Her mouth tasted of blood.

"Ah. You're awake," the voice said. "Good."

Her vision blurred for a second, then focused on the sight of John Hobbes. He was a big man with a thick mustache. He'd removed his shirt, and she saw the brands covering his chest, back, and arms, his body a nightmarish tapestry. *Anoint thy flesh. . . .*

The eyes were the same ones she'd seen before: cold and blue.

"Very kind of you to come to me. Saved me the trouble of coming for you." He shimmered before her like candle wax, an unstable thing, but still with the capacity to burn.

"Jericho!" Evie shouted. "Jericho!"

Naughty John smiled. "Your companion is not well at present," he said, and Evie was afraid to ask what that meant.

Evie sat up and was surprised to see that she could do so freely.

"What would be the point in restraints?" he said, as if he could read her thoughts.

Evie was numb with fear. "Why?" she asked. It was all she could manage; the terror had reduced her words.

"Why?" John Hobbes repeated, as if she were an insolent child and he her annoyed but patient teacher. "Why should I let this world go on? It is filled with sin and vice and all manner of corruption. It requires a new god to lead it, Lady Sun."

"I'm n-not your Lady Sun," she whispered.

John Hobbes pulled out the small square of cloth from her gold brocade coat. "The Woman Clothed in the Sun."

He smiled, making Evie's blood throb in her head. Her eyes darted about the room, looking for some means of escape, taking in what might be used to her advantage. Her heart began to race again as she realized that the door was slightly ajar. She darted forward, and as if it sensed her plan, the door shut before she reached it. She beat on it with her fists.

"'And the Lord said, let the Beast be joined with the Woman Clothed in the Sun. Anoint her flesh as your flesh.'"

John Hobbes walked calmly toward the lit brazier. Several branding irons now protruded from it, their symbols growing hot on the coals.

"I . . . I . . ." Fear choked Evie's words in her throat.

Think, Evie, old girl. She had meant to burn down the house, and Naughty John with it, but that plan was gone. She needed a new plan. Will had said they needed to bind his spirit to a holy object like the pendant, then speak the words and destroy that object. But what was at her disposal? Her eyes darted frantically around the room again, searching out something, any object that could be used.

"This room is your strength, isn't it? 'Prepare ye the walls of your houses.' Isn't that what it says? What will happen if I destroy these walls? How will you manifest then?" she asked, stalling.

"Too late for that. The comet's almost overhead. Three minutes more. You will be my bride, and your heart will assure my immortality. And you will live on, like the faithful. It is time, my Brethren."

Beside Evie, the glistening walls breathed. They bowed out like a membrane, and she could see faces and hands pressed against them. Evie stumbled backward toward the altar as bodies pushed through and the room was filled with the hollow dead of Brethren—living corpses with skin weeping red, burned down to bone in places. Skeletal faces without eyes. Mouths torn away. The faithful. The damned. Ready for the final sacrifice, the last offering. They wouldn't stop until her heart was ripped from her chest and the Beast was made whole.

"They are here with me. The chosen of Brethren, sacrificed for the first of the eleven offerings. May it please the Lord!"

It sounded like the wind whipping over Brethren as the faithful replied, "Amen, amen, amen..."

"They demand tribute for their sacrifice. And they shall have it."

The dead of Brethren were coming toward her. Coming *for* her. Evie raced ahead of John Hobbes and grabbed a branding iron from the coals. It burned her hand and she dropped it, crying out in pain. She wrapped the hem of her skirt around the iron handle and picked the iron up again, holding it out in front of her. Her hand shook wildly.

"Into this vessel, I b-bind your spirit. Into the f-fire, I...I..."

She couldn't remember the words.

John Hobbes's laugh bubbled up with all the cruelty of a child delighted by the power of bringing his boot down upon an insect.

"It must be a holy relic! Only a blessed object can contain the spirit."

"Jericho!" Evie screamed again, though she knew it was no use. She flung the branding iron at the walls and it skittered across the floor.

"No matter. I can anoint your flesh when you are dead."

Evie laid a hand across her chest, as if this would be enough to keep the Beast and his faithful from tearing out her heart. Her fingers grazed the edge of her half-dollar pendant and she grabbed it and held fast to it like a frightened child.

Mute no more, the dead of Brethren opened their mouths in a collective din that crawled up Evie's spine. Their jaws unhinged and they vomited out an oily black substance, which fell to the floor like a river of snakes. It crawled up the legs of John Hobbes, where it coalesced with the brands on his skin. It covered him like armor and then was absorbed into him.

"Look upon my form and be amazed!" He stretched out his arms, threw back his head, and cried out in what could have been either agony or ecstasy. His flesh rippled, as if something were trying to break out from within. Evie watched in horror as John Hobbes's face contorted. His mouth curved into a cruel sneer. His teeth grew long and razor-sharp, and his fingertips sprouted claws. From his back, two enormous wings sprouted, white as the down of a lamb. The room was filled with light. He was manifesting into a thing of terrifying beauty right before her. Her eyes hurt to behold him. To be fully complete, he needed only to take her heart.

"The Lord will brook no weakness in his chosen!" The Beast said. His voice was like a thousand voices speaking at once, a demonic symphony.

For a moment, Evie lost all desire to fight. There was no fighting an evil this grand, this perfect. All one could do was submit. Let it happen and be done with it. The night sky seen through the small opening began to brighten: Solomon's Comet on its prophecied return to the skies. The futility of the fight weighed on Evie like stones on a grave.

"The comet is almost overhead," John Hobbes announced.

His hand was a claw, sharp enough to open her. She would be like all the others—Ruta Badowski, in her broken dancing shoes. Tommy Duffy, still with the dirt of his last baseball game under his nails. Gabriel Johnson, taken on the best day of his life. Or even Mary White, holding out for a future that never arrived. She'd be like all those beautiful, shining boys marching off to war, rifles at their hips and promises on their lips to their best girls that they'd be home in time for Christmas, the excitement of the game showing in their bright faces. They'd come home men, heroes with adventures to tell about, how they'd walloped the enemy and put the world right side up again, funneled it into neat lines of yes and no. Black and white. Right and wrong. Here and there. Us and them. Instead, they had died tangled in barbed wire in Flanders, hollowed by influenza along the Western Front, blown apart in no-man's-land, writhing in trenches with those smiles still in place, courtesy of the phosgene, chlorine, or mustard gas. Some had come home shell-shocked and blinking, hands shaking, mumbling to themselves, following orders in some private war still taking place in their minds. Or, like James, they'd simply vanished, relegated to history books no one bothered to read, medals put in cupboards kept closed. Just a bunch of chess pieces moved about by unseen hands in a universe bored with itself.

And now here she was, just another pawn. Evie wanted to cry. From fear. From exhaustion, yes. But mostly from the cruel uselessness, the damned stupid arbitrariness of it all.

"'A great sign appeared in heaven, the sky alight with fire, a woman clothed with the sun and crowned with the stars. And her heart was a gift for the Beast, the heart of the world, which he would devour and become whole and walk upon the earth for a thousand years....'"

The half-dollar rubbed against Evie's hand and she thought of James, and as she did, a horrible, desperate thought took shape. No. She couldn't. There had to be something else.

The dead were coming. They were coming for her.

Shaking, Evie removed the pendant from around her neck and held it in front of her. "Into this vessel, I b-bind your sp-spirit...." She shook so badly she was afraid she wouldn't be able to get the words out.

The dead kept coming. All she could see were hollow eye sockets in shadowed, skeletal faces. Dead white fingers reaching toward her. Blackened mouths oozing black juice down mottled chins.

"Into the fire, I commend your spirit," Evie said louder.

Hands reached for her. Dead fingers splayed over her toes and she kicked them away, screaming, careful not to lose her balance and topple into the unholy throng. The room brightened. How long till the comet? A minute? Thirty seconds?

The hissing howls of the Brethren were deafening. They spoke in a thousand tongues. But beneath the cacophony, she could hear a few moans. Beneath their rage, she could sense their fear. Their urgent, overlapping growls bounced around the room. "Kill her, kill her, kill her. You are the Beast, the Beast, the Beast, The Beast must rise...."

"That coin is no holy relic, Lady Sun," John Hobbes taunted.

Evie gripped the half-dollar tightly, feeling the grooves against her palm, both comfort and punishment. Her only physical tie to her brother.

"It is to me," she croaked. She shouted above the din. "Into the darkness I cast you, Beast, nevermore to rise!"

The souls of the Brethren cried out. Fire licked at the walls. It was like some macabre painting come to life. The Brethren screamed as, once again, they were engulfed in flames. She shut her eyes and hoped. The pendant shook violently in her hand. The hissing was gone. In its place came a skin-crawling symphony of screams and shrieks, guttural growls and barks, sounds she could not and did not want to identify. She smelled smoke. When she opened her eyes, she saw the screeching souls of Brethren being dragged backward as they were sucked into the walls, which were engulfed in the flames of long ago.

Naughty John remained. He'd gotten stronger, thanks to the ten offerings. Perhaps too strong to be contained. And Evie was afraid that whatever she had wouldn't be enough after all.

"I'll break you apart," he growled, lunging at her.

Evie held the half-dollar high. "Into this vessel..." she shouted, stronger this time.

His form flickered, the flesh moving through a series of contortions Evie could only imagine must have been quite painful. Black blood dribbled from the corners of his mouth. His teeth loosened and tumbled out. The mighty claws retracted.

"I-I...bind, I..." Her awe overpowered her memory.

"Destroy me, and you'll never know what happened. Or what is to come," John spat out on broken breath.

He meant to distract her. Trickery. Deceit. "Into this vessel, I bind your spirit...."

John Hobbes cried out. He fell to his knees. His skin crawled as if filled with scrabbling rats. "You'll never know...about your brother," he said.

Evie went cold. "What about my brother?"

A cackle started low in his chest and became a cough. A few droplets of black blood sprayed Evie's face and she fought the urge to scream.

"What about my brother?" she shouted.

"You've no idea . . . what has been . . . unleashed."

"What do you mean?"

John Hobbes grinned. Blood stained his remaining teeth. "Ask . . . James."

He thrashed and his wings nearly upended Evie, who dropped the pendant. With a cry, she dove for it, but so did he; his hand was quicker. They wrestled, the Beast gaining the advantage. He was above her; the comet was so close. A claw peeked through the skin of his right index finger, and then a second poked through his middle finger—enough to cut her open, enough to take her heart.

Evie forced her hand onto the pendant from the other side, her fingers touching his. "Into this vessel, I bind your spirit. Into the fire, I commend your spirit. Into the darkness—"

"You lose. . . ."

"I cast you, Beast, nevermore to rise!" Evie finished.

John Hobbes's blue eyes showed true fear for the first time as Solomon's Comet blazed overhead and his form was sucked into the half-dollar pendant, which shook and glowed red in Evie's hand until she was forced to drop it. A great column of fire shot up from its center and was joined to the comet, the brightness like an explosion. Then, as quickly as it had come, the comet was gone, as was the pendant, which was now nothing more than ash. The night sky darkened and quieted again. A smattering of fresh stars showed in the haze.

Evie heard another hiss and scrambled to her feet. Flames burst from the blackened walls, and this time not from a long-ago memory. This was a real fire. The heat of it made her eyes sting, made it hard to take in a breath without coughing, and again Evie felt a sense of panic. How would she get out? What should she do? For a moment, she stood perfectly still, numbed by her fear and the horror of the evening. She looked up at the sky, as if waiting for it to make a decision for her. Thick black smoke wafted up, blocking the stars. No. She had not come this far, sacrificed what mattered most to her, in order to lie down now. The ceiling buckled, raining down plaster. With an almost animalistic howl, Evie bolted for the door, her hands up to ward off any fiery debris. She ran through the basement and up the stairs on shaking legs, screaming for Jericho.

"Evie? Evie!"

At the sound of Jericho's voice, Evie felt renewed hope. "Jericho! Keep calling!"

She followed Jericho's calls to the room where he had fallen through. She grabbed a flashlight and shone it into the hole. It wasn't so deep—she could see that now. When he'd fallen before, he must've hit his head. She reached an arm down, and it was enough leverage for Jericho to pull himself up.

"We've got to beat it and fast," she grunted out.

"What happened to . . . ?" He rubbed his eyes.

"Gone," she said. "Finished."

Boards splintered. Windows shattered, showering them in slim shards of glass. The house shuddered on its foundation, sinking with the fire as if it meant to take everything and everyone down with it. Evie and Jericho ran toward the kitchen.

"Why did you light the match?" Evie yelled.

"I didn't!" Jericho swore.

The kitchen door wouldn't budge. Evie pulled frantically at the handle. Jericho ran for it, but couldn't release its hold. Evie screamed as the roof sagged and the door was forced open. She didn't wait but grabbed Jericho's hand, pulling him through, and they barreled down the lawn and into the street as the house blew apart.

The fire department turned its hoses on the smoking ruin of Knowles' End as it caved in on itself, a final curtsy. There would be no saving it. The kerosene had seen to that even before Naughty John's last stand.

Evie sat on the curb, a blanket thrown across her shoulders, and watched it burn. Jericho had refused to be seen by a doctor, claiming only a bump on the head. He came and sat beside her, still looking a bit glassy-eyed. A curious crowd looked on from down the street. Several kids tried to inch closer, drawn to the flame and the excitement, and their mothers admonished them to keep a safe distance.

Evie would never believe in safe distances again.

"You're crying," Jericho said.

"Am I?" Evie said faintly. "What a chump."

She put a hand to the empty spot at her neck and wept.

PEOPLE WILL BELIEVE ANYTHING

In the small, dank interrogation room, Will rested his head on his arms. The clock showed five in the afternoon. The door opened and Malloy shifted his bulk into a chair opposite Uncle Will. "We picked up your niece and your assistant at the old Knowles house."

"Is she...?"

"She's fine. The house burned to the ground, but she's fine." Malloy paused for a minute too long. "Swears she struggled with the killer—the spirit of Naughty John Hobbes come back to life."

Will stared at his clasped hands and said nothing.

"It's the damndest thing, but that pendant you dug up? Well, seems when the boys went to take it out of evidence, it was nothing but a pile of ashes. Oddest thing they'd ever seen. Guess you wouldn't know anything about that, would you?"

Will remained silent.

"Heard from the local boys up in Brethren. There was a fire up there last night, too—started around the time the comet came through, the same time as the Knowles' End fire. Hadn't been dry up in those woods—in fact, they'd had a whole day of rain. Wasn't arson, either. No, it seems the old camp in the woods—and just the old camp—burned completely to the ground in a flash. There's nothing left. Not a stone or a stick." Malloy leaned forward. The bags under his eyes were puffier than usual. "Will, what's going on here?"

Will looked up at last. "What do you want me to say?"

Malloy seemed to consider this for a long while, finally letting out an extended soliloquy of a sigh. "Nothing," he said at last. "I don't know, and I don't want to know, Fitz. I'd like to collect my pension in ten years, so *I'm* going to tell *you* what happened. As far as the city's concerned, the Pentacle Killer was shot and killed and burned in the fire, no identity known. He was killed by one of our men in blue. Officer Lyga is due for promotion. He's a good man. Now he's a hero. Heroes are good. Heroes make people sleep better at night. That's the story. You understand?"

"You think people will believe it?"

"People will believe anything if it means they can go on with their lives and not have to think too hard about it." Malloy rose and opened the door. "You're free to go."

At the door, he put a hand on Will's arm. His tone was urgent. "Will, what's happening?"

"Get some rest, Terrence."

"Don't make an enemy of me, Will," Malloy called after him.

Will walked the labyrinthine halls of the police station. He passed a windowed room with half-drawn blinds where two men in dark suits sat waiting to speak with the chief. Both men sat calmly, quietly, as if they had no reason to hurry. As if they were accustomed to getting their way, and this meeting would prove no different.

Will paled and hurried past, pushing through the doors of the station into the gray-wool haze of morning. He tossed two cents at a newspaperman and read the day's late headline about the death of the Pentacle Killer, which featured a posed photograph of Officer Lyga standing beside the American flag above the caption HERO OFFICER KEEPS CITY SAFE. They had worked fast. There was no mention of Will or the museum. Will left the newspaper on a nearby bench and shoved his hands deep into his pants pockets to hide their shaking.

Memphis waited until Octavia was fast asleep, then shut the door to the bedroom where Isaiah slept and crept to his side. He stared at his hands. It had been three years since Memphis had tried to cure his mother and felt the press of spirits amid a great fluttering of wings. Maybe he'd lost the healing gift forever. But he was tired of being too scared to find out.

Memphis kneeled beside the bed. He thought about praying, but what would he pray for? Was he asking for God's help, or his forgiveness? He wasn't sure he believed in either, so he said nothing as he placed his hands on his brother's body and thought about the healing. As Memphis kneeled beside his brother, he felt nothing. No trace of warmth. No smell of flowers before he was transported into the world of spirits and strange sights.

"I'm not giving up, dammit," he said through clenched teeth. "Do you hear me? I will not give up!"

Memphis took a deep breath. It started as a twitch in his fingers. Then the old familiar warmth trickled through his veins like a tap suddenly turned on. And before he had time to think, he was sucked into that shadow realm between worlds. Around him, he felt the press of spirits, their hands placed gently on his shoulders, his arms, a great chain of healing. He heard his mother's voice, soft and low.

"Memphis."

She wore a cloak as iridescent as a moonlit lake. She wasn't sick and gaunt like the last time he'd seen her; she was lovely, if a little somber. It was his mother in this place, and he wanted to run to her.

"Our time is brief, my son."

"Mama? Is it you?"

"I must tell you these things while I can. You will be called to make great choices and great sacrifices," she said a bit sadly. "All will be needed, but only you can decide which is the right path to take. A storm is coming, and you must be ready."

"What about Isaiah?"

His mother didn't answer. "There is something I never told you. Something I should have told you..."

The soft comfort of spirits dissolved. They were standing at the crossroads of his dream. In the distance were the farmhouse and the gnarled tree. The sky roiled with dark clouds mottled with lightning. Memphis's mother looked up at the sky with fear. The wind blew fiercely, kicking up a cloud of dust.

"You can't bring anything back, Memphis. Once it's gone, it's gone. Promise me!"

The dust was nearly upon her.

"Mama, run!"

"Promise me!" she cried as the dust wall swallowed her up.

Memphis stumbled forward on the road, trying to outrun the choking dust. Through the field to his right, he saw the wheat bending into blackened ruin as a thin man in a somber coat and a tall hat cut through. The crow darted across Memphis's path.

The trance was broken. Memphis fell back onto the floor with a hard thud. He was wet with sweat and shaking. He'd been to the healing place. He'd seen his mother in that world.

"Memphis. What you doing on the floor?"

Isaiah was awake and looking at him with sleepy eyes, as if it were any old morning.

"Isaiah?" Memphis choked out. "Isaiah?"

"That's my name. You sure acting funny," Isaiah said, stretching. "I'm thirsty."

His brother was healed. He was healed, and Memphis had done it. His palms still tingled from the touch. He hadn't lost the gift; it was back. Memphis gathered Isaiah up into his arms, crying.

"Whatsa matter?

"Nothing. Nothing, little man. Everything's just fine now."

"I'm still thirsty."

"I'll get you something to drink. Stay right here. Don't go nowhere."

"Anywhere," Isaiah corrected sleepily.

"That, too."

Memphis ran to the kitchen and stuck a glass under the tap, willing it to fill faster. "Thank you," he said, though he didn't know who he was saying it to, or why. He turned off the water and hurried back to Isaiah's side.

Outside the kitchen window, lightning crackled high in the clouds. The crow looked on in silence.

THE COMING STORM

Evie, Theta, and Mabel walked out into the clear, crisp afternoon. It was a bright, cloudless day; the air felt newly born, and Evie had a hankering for a new hat. It had been four days since she'd faced down John Hobbes, the Beast, in that small room. Four days since she'd trapped his soul in her most sacred relic and let it go in order to save them all. Even now, her hand went to her bare neck under her scarf, wishing for the weight of it. She'd not had a single dream since, but she tried not to think about it. She tried not to think about any of it. She and Uncle Will had barely spoken of that night. He seemed even more remote than before, cloistered away with his books and newspaper clippings till he was almost a ghost himself. Later, she would ask him about the Diviners. She would ask him how she would know if there were others like her, and how she could make her power stronger, more within her control. There was so much Evie wanted to know. But that could all wait. For now, she, Mabel, and Theta were on the trolley, headed to a hat shop Theta knew about, where Evie intended to buy a new cloche with a ribbon tied into an elaborate bow to signal that she was single and quite available. This was their city. This was their time. She'd promised Mabel they'd make the most of it, and she intended to fulfill that promise at last.

The trolley idled at a light and just before it moved again Sam hopped on the outside, holding fast to the bars at Evie's shoulder.

"Hiya, ladies," he said.

"Sam! Let go!" Evie scolded.

Sam peered behind him at the rapidly moving street. "Seems like a bad idea."

"I'm still amazed they let you out of the Tombs."

"Chalk it up to my charm, sister. I did manage to make off with some handcuffs, though." His smile suggested something naughty and Evie rolled her eyes.

"Just wanted to let you know I'll be gone for a few days," he told her.

"I'll wear a black veil and cry all night."

Theta and Mabel giggled and looked away.

"You'll miss me. I know you will, sister." He gave her one of those wolfish grins.

"Hey!" the conductor called. "Get down from there!"

"Sam, you're going to get in trouble!"

Sam grinned. "Aw, baby, I thought you loved trouble."

"Will you get down before you kill yourself?"

"Broken up about my well-being?"

"Get. Down."

Sam leaped from the trolley, nearly upending a woman pushing a pram. "Sorry, ma'am." He brushed his hands clean and shouted after them, "One day, Evie O'Neill, you're gonna fall head over heels for me!"

"Don't hold your breath!" Evie shouted back.

Sam mimed an arrow through the heart and fell down. Evie laughed in spite of herself. "Idiot."

Theta's eyebrow inched up. "That boy's got it bad for you, Evil."

Evie rolled her eyes. "Don't kid yourself. It has nothing to do with me. That boy only wants what he can't have."

Theta looked out at the bright lights of Broadway, winking into existence against the dusk. "Don't we all?"

⁂

By the time Evie reached the museum, it was dark and the day's last visitors had gone. Humming a tune she'd heard on the radio, she dropped her scarf, coat, and pocketbook on a chair and made her way to the library. The doors were slightly ajar, and an unfamiliar woman's voice came through the crack.

"The storm's coming, Will. Whether you're ready or not, it's coming."

"What if you're wrong?" Will said. He sounded tense.

"Do you really think this was an isolated occurrence? You read the papers like I do. You've seen the signs."

The conversation grew hushed and Evie edged closer to try to hear.

"I told you then that it would come to no good."

"I tried, Margaret. You know that."

They must have moved; the sound became muffled and Evie could make out only bits and pieces: "Safe haven." "Diviners." "Going to be needed."

Evie leaned closer, straining to hear.

"What about your niece? You know what she is. You have to get her ready. Prepare her."

Evie's heartbeat quickened.

"No. Absolutely not."

"You have to tell her, or I will."

Unable to bear it, Evie burst into the room. "Tell me what?"

"Evie!" Will dropped his cigarettes. "This is a private conversation."

"I heard you talking about me." Evie turned to the tall, imposing woman standing at Will's desk. It was the same woman who'd come calling nearly two weeks ago, the one who'd left her card. The one Will pretended not to know. "What isn't he telling me?"

"Miss Walker was just leaving." Will glanced in warning at the woman, who shook her head slowly—in resignation or disapproval, Evie couldn't be sure.

"I expect I was." The woman secured her hat. "I'll see myself out, thank you. Storm's coming, Will, whether you're ready or not," she said to him again and marched out of the library in her regal way.

Evie waited until she heard the quick snap of the woman's heels on the marble tile outside, then she turned on Will. "Who is that woman?"

"None of your concern."

Will lit one of his cigarettes and Evie snatched it from his fingers, furiously stubbing it out in an ashtray.

"But she was talking about me! I want to know why," Evie demanded. "And you said you didn't know her before!"

For a moment, Will hesitated at the desk, looking utterly lost. Then that scholarly cool washed over him and he was the unimpeachable Will Fitzgerald again. He pretended to adjust the objects on his desk into some phony semblance of order. "Evie, I've been thinking. It might be best if you were to go back to Ohio."

Evie reeled as if she'd been punched. "What? But Unc, you promised me—"

"That you could stay for a while. Evie, I'm an old bachelor, set in my ways. I'm not equipped to look after a girl—"

"I'm seventeen!" she yelled.

"Still."

"You couldn't have solved this case without me."

"I know that. And I'm trying to forgive myself for getting you involved." Will sank into a chair. He wasn't used to sitting still, and he seemed at a loss as to what to do with his hands, resting them at last on the arms of the chair as if he were Lincoln posing for the memorial.

"But . . . why?" Evie said. She stood pathetically before him like a schoolgirl begging the headmaster for another chance. She hated herself for it.

"Because . . ." Will began. "Because it isn't safe here."

Evie could feel that she was on the verge of angry tears. Her voice quavered. "Why won't you tell me what's happening?"

"You have to trust me on this, Evie: The less you know, the better. It's for your own good."

"I'm tired of everyone deciding what's for my own good!"

"There are certain people in this world, Evie. You don't know what they're capable of."

Tears beaded along Evie's mascaraed lashes. "You promised I could stay."

"And I honored that promise. The case is finished. It's time to go home," Will said as gently as he could.

She had helped solve the case. She'd braved the headaches and the bloody battle with John Hobbes and the ghostly congregation of Brethren in that filthy hole. She'd given up the one thing that mattered most to her—the half-dollar talisman and the chance to know what had happened to James—in order to see it through. And this was her reward? It wasn't fair. Not by a long shot.

"I'll hate you forever," she whispered, losing the battle against the tears.

"I know," Will said softly.

Jericho stuck his head in. He spoke with urgency. "Will. You should see this."

The press had gathered on the front steps of the museum, their notepads at the ready. They looked mean and bored and ready for a story with blood in it. The Pentacle Killer had been good for business; it must have been hard to let that slip away. At the front was T. S. Woodhouse himself.

"I'll handle this." Will walked out and the reporters snapped to attention. "Gentlemen. Ladies. To what do I owe this honor? If you're dying for a peek at the museum, we'll open again at ten thirty tomorrow."

"Mr. Fitzgerald! Hey, Fitz—over here!" The reporters tried to outshout one another.

"Have you recovered from your arrest?"

"Yeah, Professor—why'd they take you to the clubhouse? You bump somebody off?"

"What can you tell us about the Pentacle Killer?"

"Any truth to the rumor that there was some element of the supernatural involved? Some old hocus-pocus?" T. S. Woodhouse asked.

Will held out his hands in appeasement. He attempted a smile that came off as a grimace. "I leave the supernatural to the museum."

"Was the killer really a ghost?" T. S. Woodhouse persisted. "That's the rumor floating around, Professor."

"The police have given a statement. You've got your story, ladies and gentlemen. I've nothing more to add to it, I'm afraid. I wish you a good evening."

Woodhouse turned to Evie. "Miss O'Neill? Got a statement for us?"

"Evie. Let's go inside. It's cold," Will said.

Evie stood on the steps, small and pale in the dim lights. She'd left her coat inside and the chilly October wind cut through her dress. Will wanted her to go inside. Then he would send her back to Ohio, where her parents would also tell her to go inside, in effect. She was tired of being told how it was by this generation, who'd botched things so badly. They'd sold their children a pack of lies: God and country. Love your parents. All is fair. And then they'd sent those boys, her brother, off to fight a great monster of a war that maimed and killed and destroyed whatever was inside them. Still they lied, expecting her to mouth the words and play along. Well, she wouldn't. She knew now that the world was a long way from fair. She knew the monsters were real.

"I'll tell you what happened," she said. Her eyes shone with a hard light.

"Evie, don't," Uncle Will warned, but already the press had turned and taken note of her. A man in a black fedora snapped a photograph, and Evie blinked from the white-hot glare of it.

"What's your name, sweetheart?"

"Evangeline O'Neill. But my friends call me Evie. Of course, they usually call me from jail."

The reporters laughed.

"Say, I like this one. She's a real live wire," one said. "And a Sheba to boot."

"Yes, she is," T. S. Woodhouse murmured appreciatively.

"Miss O'Neill! John Linden with the *Gotham Trumpet*. How's about an exclusive for us?"

"Patricia Ready from Hearst, Miss O'Neill. We girls have to stick together, don't you say?"

"Hey, doll—over here! Smile for me. Attagirl!"

They clamored for her story with shouts of "Miss O'Neill! Miss O'Neill!" Her name called in Manhattan, the center of the world.

"Which one of us gets an exclusive?" a reporter shouted.

"That depends—which one of you has the gin?" Evie shot back, and they roared with laughter.

T. S. Woodhouse tipped his hat back and stepped closer to Evie. "Your old pal, T. S. Woodhouse, *Daily News*. No hard feelings still, I hope? You know I've always got a soft spot for you, Sheba. My pencil's nice and sharp—almost as sharp as you are. How's about you giving us the goods, sweetheart?"

Evie glanced back at her uncle and Jericho. Behind them, the museum sat quiet. Above them all, the city glittered with a thousand squares of cold, hard light.

"Miss O'Neill? Evie?" T. S. Woodhouse rested the point of his pencil against his notebook.

"My uncle's not being entirely truthful. Special powers—I guess you could call them supernatural powers—were employed to crack the case. My powers."

The reporters fell into chatter and shouts again.

Evie put up her hands. "Since we're all New Yorkers and not a bunch of chumps, I suppose you'll want a demonstration. You might finally prove useful, Mr. Woodhouse."

The reporters laughed and T.S. bowed to her. "Your wish is my command."

"Swell. Can I have something of yours? A glove, a watch—any sort of object will do, really."

"She wants your wallet," a reporter cracked.

"As long as it isn't your heart, Thomas."

"Haven't you heard? I'm a newsman. I haven't got one of those," Woodhouse shot back.

Evie held out her hand. "Anything at all will do."

He pressed his handkerchief into her hand, allowing his fingers to linger an extra moment on hers. At first, there was nothing, and Evie suppressed a jolt of panic. She closed her eyes and concentrated. At last, her Cupid's bow mouth stretched into a fetching smile. "Mr. Woodhouse, you live in the Bronx, on a street near an Irish bakery called Black Holly's Biscuits. You owe your bookie fifty clams for the Martin-Burns fight. I'd suggest paying that; he doesn't strike me as a patient man."

Woodhouse frowned. "Anybody could know that."

"A seventeen-year-old girl?" another reported yelled.

Evie pressed harder and the handkerchief yielded its deeper secrets. She bent to whisper those intimate secrets in his ear. His expression of surprise yielded to one of bitter understanding.

"New headline," he announced to the crowd. "'Sweetheart Seer Tells All, Breaks Murder Case with Mystery Talent.'"

The reporters pushed closer, demanding. "What happened, Evie?" "Over here, Evie!" "Heya, Miss O'Neill. Smile—that's it!"

T. S. Woodhouse held up his pencil. "My lead's getting cold, sweetheart."

Evie fixed him with a stare. "For some time now, I've had this...gift," she began.

She told them about how her ability to read objects led to them to the killer. She stuck close to the official story—a troubled man killed by the brave men in blue. She didn't tell them that there were things to be afraid of, that the ghosts they imagined on dark nights as a chill on the neck were real. She did not mention the coming storm Miss Walker had warned about. Instead, she thrilled them with another demonstration—just a quick flash of fun facts gleaned from a reporter's notepad. A crowd was gathering. They loved it. They loved *her*. In the greatest city in the world, at its greatest moment, she was there at the center of it all. Will couldn't send her home now. There'd be a protest. She'd organize it herself if she had to.

"Miss O'Neill—hey, beautiful! Over here!" The flash powder exploded into tiny claws of light. There was another flash, and another. They dazzled and bruised Evie's eyes till she was forced to turn her head. She expected to see Will and Jericho, but the steps behind her were empty. Evie turned toward the mob again. Across the street at the edge of the park, Margaret Walker stood perfectly still, watching. The flash popped once more, and when Evie's eyes cleared, she, too, had gone.

PROJECT BUFFALO

Blind Bill Johnson knocked at the door of Aunt Octavia's house and waited until the door creaked open and he heard her asking him inside. They sat in the living room while Octavia brought out cups of coffee and a plate of butter cookies.

"I don't know how to thank you for being there, Mr. Johnson," Octavia said, a catch in her voice.

"Well, ma'am, I'm just glad the Good Lord put me there."

"That sure is a nice new hat and suit you have on, Mr. Johnson."

"Bill. Thank you, Miss. Bought it with my winnings. My number come in big. Won two hundred dollars, just like that." Bill snapped his fingers.

"Must've been a heavenly reward for your good works."

Bill cleared his throat. "And, uh, how is the little man?"

"Oh, haven't you heard?" He could detect the exuberance in the woman's voice. "He's fine. Why, he's better than fine. All healed up like nothing at all happened."

"I see." Bill's hands shook and he clasped them in his lap. "And does he remember what happened?"

"No, no, not a thing. The doctor says it may have been some kind of fever. Guess we'll never know."

"Maybe..." Bill said, then shook his head, as if dismissing the thought out of hand. "It may not be right for me to say."

"What is it?"

"I got to wondering if maybe he just wore himself out guessing cards at Miss Walker's place."

He sipped his coffee and waited. When Octavia finally spoke, her voice was tight with both apprehension and anger. "Miss Walker helps Isaiah with his arithmetic. He has trouble with his sums. I don't know anything about any cards."

"Now I've done it. Said more than I had a right to. Don't pay me no mind, Miss Octavia."

"I would very much appreciate it, Mr. Johnson—"

"Bill."

"Bill, if you would tell me what you know, thank you."

He couldn't see Octavia, but he could hear the rustle of her dress as she poised on the edge of the chair, and he knew he had her.

"Well, Miss, I 'spect I don't rightly know ever'thing. The little man told me he had a gift, and that Miss Walker was teaching him how to use that gift. What my grandmother called the sight." Bill took another cookie, dunked it in his coffee. It was delicious. "But you know how children do. The way I figured it, little man was just telling me stories. You know, trying to puff himself up some."

"I see." She was angry. There wouldn't be any more visits to Miss Walker's house, Bill was fairly certain of that.

"Could I look in on Isaiah, if it wouldn't be too much trouble?"

"Well, he's resting now," Octavia said uncertainly.

"Oh, I see. Well, I wouldn't want to be no trouble. Just felt a might like praying over him."

"Prayers are always welcome."

"Yes, ma'am. I 'spect they are."

Octavia led Bill to a back bedroom and stood him beside Isaiah's bed.

"Oh, Lord," Bill said and bowed his head. "I'm sorry, Miss Octavia, but I'm a might bit shy 'bout prayin' in front of folks."

"Of course," she said, and he heard the door shut.

Bill reached out a hand and touched the boy's head, which was as soft as a lamb. Just a taste. That's all he needed. Just another number. He'd be careful this time. He felt the boy's energy flowing into him, and then, suddenly, he was gagging. He pulled his hands away quickly. His fingers shook. What was that? What had he felt?

In the dimness of the room, Bill could make out the faintest of shapes—the broad bulk of a chifforobe, the weak light of a window. Shapes. Light. He could...see. Just a little, but there it was. And Bill knew somebody had put the healing power on the boy. Somebody had a bigger gift than Isaiah Campbell. Much bigger. Bill's hands itched to try again, but he could hear the boy's aunt calling his name. There would be time. He remembered a story he'd heard back in the fields when he was a kid. Something about a tortoise and a hare. *Slow and steady wins the race.* That was the phrase. Patience. Patience was called for now. Bill would be the tortoise. Yes, there would be time enough.

※

Bill Johnson was long gone by the time Memphis got home, but Aunt Octavia was sitting in the front parlor, her hands working a pair of knitting needles like she meant to kill the sweater instead of knit it.

"What is it? Did something happen with Isaiah?" Memphis asked.

"I know about your trips to Sister Walker, and the cards. I know about it, and it's going to stop," she said in a clipped tone. "It's what you're doing with that Walker woman that brought this on. I believe that."

Memphis looked at the floor. "He's got a gift."

"What has she done to him?"

"Nothing! I told you, he's got a gift."

"Get the Bible. We're gonna pray."

Octavia marched into Isaiah's bedroom. Reluctantly, Memphis followed.

"Memphis John, you need to get beside me. We're gonna pray for your brother now, pray the woman hasn't brought the Devil to this house."

Memphis dropped to his knees next to his aunt at Isaiah's bedside, but he didn't like it. *Why?* he thought. *Why should I pray to God? What has he done for me or my family?* He felt the anger coming up inside, pricking into tears.

"I won't do it."

Octavia's shock faded to a grim determination. "I promised your mama I would look after her boys, and I intend to do that. Now pray with me."

Memphis exploded. "Why don't you ask God why he took my mother? Why don't you ask him when my father's coming home? Why don't you ask him what he has against my little brother?" He wanted to hit something or someone. He wanted to burn up the whole world, heal it, and burn it down again.

He expected Octavia to yell at him for blaspheming the Lord and throw him out of the house. Instead, she said softly, "Go on and get yourself some chicken from the icebox. I'll do the praying, and we'll talk after," and it was almost worse. Octavia bowed her head, "Lord Jesus...please protect this boy. He didn't know what he was doing. He's a good boy, Jesus..."

Isaiah woke up. "Auntie, why you praying? Memphis? Where you going?"

Memphis wasn't hungry, and there was no place for him to be. He hadn't been back to the graveyard since he'd seen Gabe's ghost. He no longer wanted to sit with the dead. It was the living he needed. It was Theta he wanted. He went to the library, and there in its quiet, Memphis offered his own prayer. He opened his notebook and wrote until his fingers were cramped and the light in the restaurant across the street had gone out. He wrote till he felt emptied out. He had a reason to write and someone to write for. At the bottom, he wrote only two words: *For Theta.* His confession complete, he folded it into an envelope and left it for the postman.

❋

At the Globe Theatre, the Ziegfeld revue was in full swing. The audience was a live one tonight. They roared with laughter and applauded enthusiastically. The entire evening had a frenzied, feverish quality to it. Ever since Daisy's murder, interest in the show had been higher than ever; the word backstage was that Hollywood scouts had come looking for the next Louise Brooks or Eddie Cantor. Everyone was giving it their all. Under the lights, Theta glittered in a shiny, low-cut dress as she and Henry traded jokes back and forth.

"That's my brother, Henry," Theta cooed, shaking a hip toward the piano. "At least, that's what I tell my landlord." She winked and the audience roared. They were eating it up, and the press took notice. At the back of the theater, Florenz Ziegfeld smiled. Some poor chumps could work their whole lives and never see their names in lights. But some people just had that special something, and Theta Knight was one of those people. She was about to become a star, whether she liked it or not.

"I'm a baby vamp who loves her daddy, I never wear paste when I can have pearls. So if you've got the Jack then everything's jake, 'cause I'm just one of those girls. . . ." Theta sang.

"Our dear mother taught us that!" Henry yelled, and the audience hooted.

The song was a lie, a shiny bauble meant to distract people from their cares and woes. But they'd all agreed silently to be blinded by it. The stage lights turned Henry and Theta into a pantomime against the painted flat behind them. Henry banged on the keys and Theta sang for all she was worth.

They kept the lie going, and the people loved it.

※

Sam sat at a warped table in the back of a dark gin joint within blocks of the Brooklyn Navy Yard. It was the kind of saloon frequented by roughnecks and old sailors, and it smelled of bad booze and sweat. Sam kept his back to the wall so he could see the whole of the place. He watched the man in the rain-spattered coat shake himself off at the door and walk toward the back. The man slid into the booth beside Sam. They did not speak for a moment. Sam put the postcard down on the table. After a moment, the man lifted the postcard and pocketed the fifty dollars underneath. He turned the postcard over, read it, and passed it back to Sam.

"Project Buffalo. They said they shut it down after the war. But they never did."

"What is it?"

The man shook his head imperceptibly. "A mistake. A dream that went wrong. That old song."

Sam's mouth was tight. "I gave you fifty dollars. Do you know how hard it was for me to get that dough?"

The man rose and squared his hat low over his brow, casting his face in shadow. "She's still alive, if that's what you want to know."

"Where?"

"There are truths in this world people don't really want to know. That's why they hire people like us. So they can go on dancing and working, go home to their little families. Buy radios and toothpaste. Want my advice? Forget this, kid. Get out and enjoy life. Whatever's left of it."

"I'm not like that."

"Then I wish you luck."

"That's it? You really going to blow and leave me with nothing?"

The man chewed the inside of his cheek and took a quick look around to be sure no one was watching. The people surrounding them were oblivious, like most. He took a cheap motel pen from his pocket and wrote a name on the napkin. "You want answers? That's a good place to start."

Sam stared at the name. His jaw tightened. "Is this some kind of joke?"

"I told you to forget it, didn't I?" The man walked to the door and disappeared into the rain and the night.

Sam sat staring at the table. He wanted to punch something. He wanted to get stinking drunk and toss the bottle at the moon. He looked at the name on the napkin and then crumpled it, shoving it into his pocket. He would find his mother and the truth, no matter how long it took or how dangerous it might be. No matter who got hurt along the way.

A man turned slightly toward him. "Don't see me," Sam growled, and the man looked right through him. Sam slipped unnoticed into the crowd, lifting wallets as he went.

A gust of wind howled across the cobblestones of Doyers Street, rattling the paper lanterns of the Tea House. In the back room, the girl with the green eyes came out of her trance with a gasp.

"What is it?" the older man asked. "What did you see?"

"Nothing. I saw nothing."

He frowned. "They told me you had the power to walk in dreams, to talk with the dead."

She shrugged and took his money. "Maybe the dead want nothing to do with you."

"I am an honorable man!" he yelled.

"We'll see."

"You are a liar! A half-breed with no honor!" the man accused. On the way out, he banged the front door so hard it shook the windows.

The young man came out of the kitchen, looking scared. "I thought you said you could keep the ghosts away."

The girl stared out the window. "I was wrong."

Mabel could barely study for the hubbub in the other room. Her parents were having one of their meetings. The conversation had grown more heated in the past twenty minutes, and she could tell this meeting would stretch into the wee hours.

"We do not endorse violence," Mr. Rose said. "We are about reform, not revolution."

"Without revolution, there can be no reform. Look at Russia," a man with a thick accent insisted.

"Yes, look at Russia," another said. "Chaos."

"What about the workers? If we don't stand together, we fall. Unity is strength."

Mabel poked her head out to see what was happening. The room was teeming with smoke and people. Papers and pamphlets were strewn everywhere. Her mother was holding forth about the conditions at a garment factory where the women weren't protected.

"Just like at the Triangle Shirtwaist Factory," she explained.

Mabel was startled to see a handsome young man sitting on the settee. He was looking right at her, and she was sure she recognized him from somewhere. Mabel went back to her room and crawled out onto the fire escape for some fresh, crisp air. A moment later, the handsome man crawled through the window to join her.

"Remember me?"

"From Union Square," Mabel said as the memory came back to her. "You saved me."

He stuck out his hand. "Arthur Brown."

"Mabel Rose," she said, shaking it.

His smile was wry. "I know."

"Shouldn't you be in there with the others?"

"They'll just spend the next hour arguing and getting nowhere," he said, laughing, and Mabel smiled. That was exactly how these evenings tended to go. "In the end, they'll agree to give another speech or write an editorial in the paper. Maybe they'll try to unionize workers on the docks or picket a business or two."

"Isn't that good?" Mabel asked.

"They call themselves radicals, but they're not, really."

"And you are, I suppose?" Mabel felt a little insulted on her parents' behalf. "My parents have sacrificed a great deal for the good of others."

Arthur Brown's gaze was unyielding. "Including their daughter?"

Mabel felt the remark in her marrow. Her cheeks reddened. "That was rude."

"Yes, it was. I'm sorry. They mean well."

Mabel cocked her head. "But . . . ?"

Arthur smiled in an apologetic way. "There are times when change needs a little help. There's a group of us who want to bring about change faster. Our way. If you want to meet up with us sometime, we could use a smart girl like you."

"I'm usually helping my parents," Mabel said.

He nodded. "Of course. Forget I mentioned it. It doesn't have to be a meeting. There's a joint nearby that makes the best egg creams. You like egg creams?"

He had big brown eyes. Mabel felt a small electric thrill when she looked into them. "Doesn't everybody?"

He reached inside his jacket and Mabel saw the outline of a gun. "Here's my card."

Mabel stared at the black lettering. ARTHUR BROWN.

"Is that really your name?" she asked.

He smirked. "It is now."

Mabel shivered in the chilly air. "I should get back to my studying."

"Pleasure, Mabel Rose." He tipped his hat and held the window open for her before returning to the dining room and the arguing, which, Mabel knew, would go on well into the night.

From the safety of her bedroom, she watched Arthur Brown

make his passionate points. He spoke with confidence for someone so young. At one point, he caught her eye and smiled, and Mabel quickly ducked out of sight. She deliberated for a moment, then opened the secret drawer inside her music box and put Arthur Brown's card inside.

*

In the ramshackle apartment in the old Bennington, Miss Addie turned away from the window and fretted about in her room, trying to figure out what to do next. At last she called out to her sister. "Let me change my dress, sister."

She emerged a few moments later in an old nightgown and an apron. "Now."

Miss Lillian brought one of the cats from the kitchen, a tabby named Felix who was a fairly decent mouser, which was a shame. He was limp in her arms after the cream and opium. She laid him on the kitchen table, which had been covered in newspapers. Humming, Miss Addie opened a drawer in the secretary and took out a dagger. The dagger was as sharp as it was old.

"That's a nice tune, sister. What is it?" Lillian asked.

"Something I heard on the radio. It was sung by a soprano, but I didn't like her voice. Too reedy."

"So often that's the case," Miss Lillian clucked. "Are we ready?"

"The time is now," Miss Addie said. Miss Lillian held fast to Felix, whose small heart began to pound. He tried to squirm but was too woozy to do much.

"It'll all be over soon, kitty," Miss Lillian assured him. She closed her eyes and spoke in long tangles of words, old as time, as

Miss Addie plunged the knife into the cat's belly, making the necessary incision. The cat stilled. She reached into the stomach cavity and pulled out its intestines, plopping them into a bowl. Some got on her apron and she was glad she'd changed first. She stared into the bowl, frowning. Miss Lillian left the cat's bloodied corpse and joined her.

"What is it, sister?"

"They're coming," Miss Addie said. "Oh, dear sister, they are coming."

✴

In the quiet museum, Will sat at his desk, the green glow of the banker's lamp the only light. Earlier, he'd noticed the plain sedan parked across the street and the two men in dark suits sitting inside, watching. One of them ate nuts from a paper bag, dropping the shells out the window. Will had locked up and, whistling a carefree tune, strolled to a nearby Automat with a view of the museum for a sandwich and coffee, which he barely touched. Only when he'd seen the sedan drive away did he return to the museum, frowning at the break in the piece of cellophane he'd left across the doorjamb. He took a long, slow walk through the building, examining each room. After a careful inventory, he saw that nothing was missing. It had just been a look-around. For now.

Will craned his neck to gaze at the room's mural, the angels and devils hanging above the hills, plains, and rivers, above the patriots, pioneers, Indians, and immigrants of the new world. Then, in the hushed green glow of the old library, he walked the stacks until he came to a large leather-bound edition of the Declaration of Independence. From inside its pages, he retrieved a worn envelope. The envelope had been stamped on the upper-right-hand corner: U.S. DEPARTMENT OF PARANORMAL, 1917. He opened the file to the first page.

Memorandum. To: William Fitzgerald, Jacob Marlowe, Rotke Wasserman, Margaret Walker

Top Secret.

Project Buffalo.

Will sat at the desk, rereading the file. When he had finished, he sat staring into the shadows.

He sat for a very long time.

THE MAN IN THE STOVEPIPE HAT

The land was a pledge, and the land was an idea of freedom, born from the collective yearning of a restless nation built on dreams. Every rock, every creek, every sunrise and sunset seemed a bargain well-struck, a guarantee of more. The land was robust. Rivers ran swiftly by on currents of desire. Purple mountains crowned sweet-grassed plains. A rejoicing of elms and oaks, mighty redwoods and sheltering pines sang across hillsides that sloped gently toward valleys grateful for their song. Telephone poles jutted up beside roads, their lonely wires stretched across the open fields, thin promises of connection. Ramshackle hickory fences of the kind that made good neighbors bordered rustic farmhouses, curved around red barns and stoic windmills. Corn rustled lightly in warm breezes.

In the towns, there were Main Streets of the sort that lined the halls of hazy, fond memory. A church steeple. Barbershop. Ice-cream parlor. Town square and a public green perfect for picnicking. Butcher. Baker. Candlestick maker. On the far side of the fabled towns, covered bridges made beautiful in the reflected glory of fall foliage hovered atop streams rich with fish fit for a wounded king. In the courthouse under a wheezing ceiling fan, the women's fingers busied themselves with needlepoint—HOME SWEET HOME, GOD BLESS AMERICA—and their husbands fanned themselves with folded newspapers as an argument droned on about whether man had been fashioned in the image of a master craftsman, wound with a key at the back and set into motion to play his part in a mysterious destiny, preordained, or had crawled from the mud and trees of the jungles, cousin to the beasts, an evolutionary experiment of free will let loose in a world of choice and chance. No verdict was reached.

The roads needed room. They stretched. They roamed and conquered. Past the open ranges. The deer and the antelope. The buffalo. Past the tribes pushed to the sides under the watch of the cross, for this nation has its reservations. They kept pace beside the railroad, that great steel spine of progress, backbone of industry. The cicadas' song joined the song of the steam-train whistle, the shrill signal of the redbrick factories as they released the sweat-stained workers at five, then took them in again at seven. The coal miners hacked and hauled their load deep underground, one eye ever on the canary. Out west, oil spewed from hard earth, staining everything in money. In the cotton fields, the weeping left their harps upon the trees.

The roads reached the cities. The gleaming cities frantic with ambition, rich in the commerce of longing, a golden paradise of businessmen prophets, billboards advertising the abundance augured on Wall Street, promised by Madison Avenue: "Physicians say Lucky Strikes—they're toasted for your pleasure!" "Move with the times! Imperial Airways." "Of course you want Colgate's Ribbon Dental Cream!" "Studebaker—the automobile with a reputation behind it!" The people sculpted monuments to great men, men who had built the nation, led the armies, their beliefs safely ensconced in marble and granite. The people made idols and tore them down again, baptizing them in ticker tape parades, blessing them in long tears of profit and loss, throwaway tributes tossed with abandon from tall windows, a celebration of the good times that seem as if they will never stop, the land a fatted calf.

The wheel of sky turned toward dusk; the stars were not yet lit. An anxious wind worried the tops of trees into a fretful sway. From back doors, mothers called children in from games of hide-and-seek and kick-the-can to wash up and say grace before supper. The children complained mightily, but the mothers remained firm and the games were left with promises of tomorrow. Street lamps flickered on. The factories, the schools, the halls of justice, the churches fell quiet. A soft evening fog rolled in like a balm of forgetting.

In the graveyards, the dead lay sleeping with eyes open.

The gray man in the stovepipe hat stepped from the mist and surveyed the land. He had not stood there for some time, and much had changed in his absence. Much always changed. His skin was the mottled gray of a moth's wing. His eyes were narrow and black, his nose sharp, and his lips thin as a new thought. His raggedy coat lay upon him like an undone winding sheet. He shook the dust from its many folds. Crows flew out and up, cawing, into the sky now tinged with the ominous clouds of a coming storm. He spoke to the crows in a whisper. Then he spoke to the trees and the rocks, the rivers and the hills. He spoke in many tongues and in a language beyond words.

In their graves, the dead listened.

The gray man strode into the honey-brown field, letting the stalks tickle the leathery cracks of his palms. The worn shine of his hat reflected a hazy miniature of the land. A rabbit leaped from spot to spot, sniffing for sustenance. Curious, it trundled close to the pointed tip of the gray man's boot, and the man lifted the startled hare by the scruff of its neck. The rabbit twitched and kicked violently. Quick as a magician's sleight of hand, the gray man reached through the rabbit's fur and skin with his long fingers and withdrew its tiny heart, still feverish in its pulsations. The rabbit kicked exactly twice more, a reflex, and then stilled. The man in the stovepipe hat squeezed the heart in his brittle fist. The blood seeped into the fertile ground drop by drop.

The dead heard.

The man in the stovepipe hat closed his eyes and inhaled the sweetness of the air. In his palm, the rabbit's heart beat faintly.

"The time is now," he said in a voice as raggedy as his coat.

The heart slipped from his fingers. He threw back his head and raised his long, bloody fingers to the slate-gray sky. The clouds churned. Wind bent the wheat. He spoke the words, and lightning crackled on the tips of his fingers. It arced up and out. The sky was wild with fierce light. A spear of it struck the side of a lone tree and it caught, a burning signal on the great ochre plain seen by no one but the wind, heard by no one but the waking dead.

The man in the stovepipe hat walked across the broken field, toward the sleeping towns and cities, the factories and cotton fields, the train tracks, roads, telephone poles, and ticker-tape parades. Toward the monuments of heroes, toward the longing and disillusion of the people. Light crackled around him as he walked, and behind him, the ground was black as cinders.

SITTING ON TOP OF
THE WORLD

At the edge of the fog-shrouded forest, James beckoned. Evie could hear the *huh-huh* of her breathing as she followed him through the snow and the trees. The smell of pine was strong, the air was crisp, and even in her dream state, Evie was aware that this was different. Wrong. She had never heard her breath or smelled the pine before. Evie brushed a hand over a tree, and the bark was rough against her palm. As before, she followed James down into the clearing, with its doomed soldiers. She looked to the right. The heavy fog thinned at the top enough to show her a crenulated roofline and what looked to be turrets. *A castle?* Evie wondered.

The sergeant dropped his cigarette and Evie wanted to cry out to him, tell him to run. But she couldn't. She was only a spectator in this dream. The flash, when it came, seemed infinitely brighter, more powerful than it had before. Evie pushed up out of the trench and ran through bloody fields of poppies. James waited. In sleep, her muscles tensed, waiting for the moment when he removed his gas mask and became a hideous apparition.

James's hand went to his mask. When he pulled it away, he was still the golden boy, the favored son.

He opened his mouth and she tensed again, waiting for some new horror.

"Hello, old girl," he said in a voice she had not heard in ten years. "They never should have done it."

Evie woke with a small, strangled gasp, her forehead damp with sweat. Her hands shook. He'd spoken to her! Air. She needed air. She climbed the fire escape and found her spot on the roof. The night air dried the sweat on her arms. She was chilly—it was November now; summer had fled for good—but she couldn't face going back to her little room and her troubled sleep. On the edge of Central Park, a drunk zigzagged from curb to street, howling out a girl's name and crying. Occasionally, he turned his face toward the sky, as if pleading with an unseen court for mercy, then shook his head.

A sound from behind startled Evie. Jericho was there, his coat over his pajamas, book in hand.

"Sorry. I didn't mean to disturb you," Jericho said.

"I'm already disturbed."

"You're shivering."

"I'm fine."

"No, you're not." He took off his coat and put it around her shoulders.

"Now *you'll* be cold."

"I don't feel it so much."

"Oh," Evie said.

"Did you have the dream again?"

She nodded. "But it was different. He spoke to me, Jericho. He looked right at me and said, 'They never should have done it.'"

"Who? Done what?"

"I don't know. But I can't help feeling that this is more than a dream, that he's trying to tell me something very important."

"Or it's just a dream because you miss him. I still dream about my family sometimes."

"Maybe."

Jericho took her hand in his. The thrill of his touch traveled the length of her arm, and this, too, she tried to ignore.

"I didn't think...I didn't dare to hope that you'd understand. I assumed you'd think I was a freak," he said.

"We're all freaks. We could get jobs on the boardwalk. Come see the Misfits of Manhattan! Small children and pregnant ladies not permitted." Evie laughed bitterly, blinking back tears.

"All this time, I thought I was alone. Different. But you're different, too." He was looking at her in a new way. "For the longest time, I wanted to die. I figured that I was dead inside already, that they'd killed me when they turned me into a machine. But I don't feel dead anymore." His face was so close to hers. His hand was on her back. "I know what I want now."

"What's that?" Evie whispered.

There was nothing awkward or tentative about Jericho's kiss. He pressed his mouth against hers with a ferocious insistence. Every part of her felt awake and alive.

Evie pushed him away. "I can't."

"Why not?" His expression hardened. "Is it because of what I am?"

She shook her head. "It's because of Mabel."

He was looking into her eyes. "Well, I don't want Mabel. I want you. Tell me you don't want me to kiss you, and I won't."

Evie said nothing. Jericho pulled her close and kissed her again. Evie kissed him back, happy for the feel of his lips on hers. Happy for his hands knotted in her hair, happy for his shirt gripped in hers. That was how the world worked, wasn't it? You set your sights on something, and life came along with a sucker punch. Mabel wanted Jericho; Jericho wanted Evie. And right now, Evie wanted to forget. Kissing Jericho tonight didn't have to mean anything. Tomorrow, the crank would be turned anew, and the gears of the world would lurch into motion. She could still fix things tomorrow or the day after. But this was right now, and right now she needed this. She needed *him.* Evie nestled against Jericho's broad chest and let him cradle her in his arms. He kissed the top of her head as they looked toward the east, where the sun rose, staining the buildings with a faint watercolor hope.

But something was coming. Something she didn't understand. Something terrible. And she was afraid.

"You all right?" Jericho murmured, his lips against her neck.

"Yeah. Everything's jake," she lied.

Down on the street, the drunk stopped calling for his girl. He sank to his knees, rested his head against the hard cobblestones, and cried. "What we lost, what we lost..."

Somewhere in one of the faceless buildings, a radio played, Al Jolson's cheery voice drowning out the misery of the drunk in the gutter: *"I'm sitting on top of the world ... just rolling along—just rolling along. ..."*

The sun cleared the horizon. The light stung her eyes. "Kiss me," Evie said.

He took her face in his hands and his kiss blotted out the sky.

Author's Note

A lot of research went into creating the world of *The Diviners*. Many hours were logged in various libraries and archives or spent pouring over books, PDFs, primary sources, and photographs. No historians or librarians were harmed in the making of this book, but some were badgered extensively with questions. I am grateful for the aid and expertise of these wonderful, knowledgeable people.

That said, this is a work of fiction, and in order to serve the gods of story, certain liberties must be taken. The author assumes sole responsibility for this willful act of narrative tinkering. (Narrative Tinkering is my new band name. I imagine it's a postmodern hipster band of varying degrees of beardification. But I digress.)

What sorts of tinkering, you might ask? Well, there was an actual Hotsy Totsy Club run by the famous gangster Legs Diamond. It was located near the Theater District of New York City, not Harlem. But that name proved too irresistible to give up, and so I chose to keep it. There is no secret African graveyard in Upper Manhattan, or else it's so secret even I don't know about it; no Museum of the Creepy Crawlies; and no Bennington apartment building occupied by strange, old cat ladies and illuminated by dodgy lighting, except for the one that exists in the imagination.

But much of what you read is straight from the history books, with some of the most disturbing set pieces based on fact: The eugenics movement was quite real, as were those chilling light-up boards at state fairs. Ditto the Fitter Families for Future Firesides, the KKK, the Chinese Exclusion Act (and the Immigration Act of 1924), and the Pillar of Fire Church. Often, the monsters we create in our imagination are not nearly as frightening as the monstrous acts perpetrated by ordinary human beings in the aim of one cause or another.

I've tried to remain as faithful as I can to the time period and actual history while crafting a story that includes mystery, magic, monsters, and the unexplained—or as we call that around my house, just another Tuesday.

There are some dynamite resources out there if you're interested in further research about the time period. A full bibliography can be found on the *Diviners* website: TheDivinersSeries.com. Happy creepy reading.

Acknowledgements

Many people were instrumental in getting *The Diviners* from the initial chaotic impulse of "I've got this crazy idea… " to the finished book, and it would be remiss of me not to acknowledge their invaluable contributions here. Huge thanks are due to the whole gang at Little, Brown Books for Young Readers: Megan Tingley, Andrew Smith, Victoria Stapleton, Zoe Luderitz, Eileen Lawrence, Melanie Chang, Lisa Moraleda, Jessica Bromberg, Faye Bi, Stephanie O'Cain, Renée Gelman, Shawn Foster, Adrian Palacios, and Gail Doobinin.

My editor, the amazing Alvina Ling, works even harder than James Brown (especially now that he's dead), and she guided this manuscript with a sure hand, brilliant insight, and an occasional karaoke interlude. Ditto to editorial assistant Bethany Strout, who has a terrific eye for detail and who sings a mean version of "Baby Got Back."

My agent, Barry Goldblatt, is, as always, a total mensch, and I'd say that even if we weren't married. But, lucky me, we are.

Copy editor JoAnna Kremer is most likely some sort of government agent created in a lab for the purpose of keeping manuscripts free from egregious mistakes. No doubt fact checker Elizabeth Segal came from the same lab. My eternal thanks, ladies.

I could have done none of this without the derring-do of my incredible assistant, the aptly named Tricia Ready, who helped with everything from research to scheduling, manuscript reading to Dr Pepper wrangling.

I am always gobsmacked by the generosity of experts who are willing to help hapless writers with research. To that end, I must thank the incomparable Lisa Gold, research goddess. I want to be selfish and keep her to myself, but she's too awesome for that: www.lisagold.com.

New York City has many wonderful libraries and librarians; quite a few of those librarians came to my aid like superheroes, minus the ostentatious capes. Many thanks and a life-size Ryan Gosling cutout to librarian pals Karyn Silverman, Elisabeth Irwin High School, and Jennifer Hubert Swan, Little Red School House. More thanks and a fruit basket to Eric Robinson at the New-York Historical Society; Richard Wiegel and Mark Ekman at the Paley Center for Media; Virgil Talaid at the New York Transit Museum; Carey Stumm and Brett Dion at the New York Transit Museum Archives; and the staffs of the New York Public Library, the Schomburg Center for Research in Black Culture, and the Brooklyn Public Library.

Historians Tony Robins and Joyce Gold took me on walking "history lesson" tours of Harlem and Chinatown/the Lower East Side, respectively; I can't thank them enough for their time. Dr. Stephen Robertson, University of Sydney, author of *Playing the Numbers: Gambling in Harlem Between the Wars* and the blog Digital Harlem, was kind enough to answer my questions about numbers-running following his lecture at Columbia University. And musician Bill Zeffiro was a font of 1920s musical knowledge.

I owe a debt of gratitude to my Beta readers, Holly Black, Barry Lyga, Robin Wasserman, Nova Ren Suma, and Tricia Ready, for their invaluable insights on early drafts. Much love and thanks to my writing pals who kept me company on parts of this journey, listened to my whining, answered questions, and let me spin out various plot scenarios without once swallowing a cyanide caplet: Holly Black, Coe Booth, Cassandra Clare, Gayle Forman, Maureen Johnson, Jo Knowles, Kara LaReau, Emily Lockhart, Josh Lewis, Barry Lyga, Dan Poblocki, Sara Ryan, Nova Ren Suma, and Robin Wasserman.

Thanks as always to my son, Josh, for his good-natured patience and gentle eye-rolling: "She gets like that on deadline." You're a good egg, kid.

Last but not least, a shout-out to the wonderful baristas at Red Horse Café in Brooklyn — Chris, Derrick, Bianca, Aaron, Jen, Julia, Seth, Brent, Carolina — who kept me supplied with enough coffee for it to qualify as a misdemeanor.

If there's anyone I've missed, please accept my sincerest apologies. Next time you see me, scowl ferociously until I buy you an ice-cream sundae in restitution.